THE RETURN OF THE BLACK WIDOWERS

THE RETURN OF THE BLACK WIDOWERS

ISAAC ASIMOV

FOREWORD BY HARLAN ELLISON®

EDITED BY CHARLES ARDAI

An Otto Penzler Book

CARROLL & GRAF PUBLISHERS
NEW YORK

The Return of the Black Widowers

Carroll & Graf Publishers
An Imprint of Avalon Publishing Group Inc.
245 West 17th Street
New York, NY 10011

First Carroll & Graf edition 2003
Second printing, February 2004

Library of Congress Cataloging-in-Publication Data is available.

ISBN: 0-7867-1248-1

Interior design by Simon Sullivan
Printed in the United States of America
Distributed by Publishers Group West

For Isaac, with love;
for Janet, Janet, and Otto, with thanks;
and for Michael, because I promised.

ACKNOWLEDGMENTS

"Foreword" by Harlan Ellison®, copyright © 2003 by The Kilimanjaro Corporation, published by permission of the author. All rights reserved.

"The Acquisitive Chuckle," copyright © 1972 by Isaac Asimov, "Ph As In Phony," copyright © 1972 by Isaac Asimov, "Early Sunday Morning," copyright © 1973 by Isaac Asimov, "The Obvious Factor," copyright © 1973 by Isaac Asimov, from TALES OF THE BLACK WIDOWERS by Isaac Asimov. Used by permission of Doubleday, a division of Random House, Inc.

"The Iron Gem," copyright © 1974 by Isaac Asimov, from MORE TALES OF THE BLACK WIDOWERS by Isaac Asimov. Used by permission of Doubleday, a division of Random House, Inc.

"To the Barest," copyright © 1979 by Isaac Asimov, from CASEBOOK OF THE BLACK WIDOWERS by Isaac Asimov. Used by permission of Doubleday, a division of Random House, Inc.

"Sixty Million Trillion Combinations," copyright © 1980 by Isaac Asimov, "The Woman In the Bar," copyright © 1980 by Isaac Asimov, "The Redhead," copyright © 1984 by Isaac Asimov, "The Wrong House," copyright © 1984 by Nightfall, Inc., from BANQUETS OF THE BLACK WIDOWERS by Isaac Asimov. Used by permission of Doubleday, a division of Random House, Inc.

"Triple Devil," copyright © 1985 by Isaac Asimov, from PUZZLES OF THE BLACK WIDOWERS by Isaac Asimov. Used by permission of Doubleday, a division of Random House, Inc.

"The Men Who Read Isaac Asimov," copyright © 1978 by William Brittain, reprinted by permission of the author. Originally appeared in Ellery Queen's Mystery Magazine.

"Northwestward" by Isaac Asimov is excerpted from THE FURTHER ADVENTURES OF BATMAN. Published by Bantam Books. Copyright © 1989 by DC Comics. All rights reserved. Used with permission.

"Yes, But Why?", copyright © 1990 by Isaac Asimov, reprinted by permission of the Estate of Isaac Asimov, c/o Ralph M. Vicinanza Ltd. Originally appeared in The Armchair Detective.

"Lost In a Space Warp" and "Police At the Door," copyright © 1990 by Isaac Asimov; "The Haunted Cabin" by Isaac Asimov, copyright © 1990 by Nightfall, Inc.; "The Guest's Guest" by Isaac Asimov, copyright © 1991 by Nightfall, Inc.; all reprinted by permission of the Estate of Isaac Asimov, c/o Ralph M. Vicinanza Ltd. All originally appeared in Ellery Queen's Mystery Magazine.

"The Last Story," copyright © 2002 by Charles Ardai, reprinted by permission of the author. Originally appeared in Ellery Queen's Mystery Magazine.

"Afterword: Birth of the Black Widowers," from I. ASIMOV: A MEMOIR by Isaac Asimov, copyright © 1994 by The Estate of Isaac Asimov. Used by permission of Doubleday, a division of Random House, Inc.

TABLE OF CONTENTS

THE BEST OF THE BLACK WIDOWERS

HOMAGE

THE UNCOLLECTED BLACK WIDOWERS

FOREWORD
HARLAN ELLISON®

Isaac died (Janet abominates "passed away") at 2:30 AM on an otherwise undistinguished Monday in April of 1992. It is close on eleven years, as I sit typing this, since my dear old pal went out through that final door.

Isaac died in '92. I called Isaac today.

I'd dialed the 1 and the New York city-code and the first two numerals of his phone number—still imbedded with the unforgettables—my social security number, my Army dogtag code, the date of my wedding anniversary—before I caught myself and hung up. I call Isaac at least a couple of times a month. And I guarantee you, I probably won't get through this Foreword to the last book of Black Widowers stories without crying.

Now let me clarify something. Do not for an instant think that I manifest the hubris, the nerve, the chutzpah to submit myself as one who misses Isaac more than Robyn or Janet or even Jennifer Brehl, who was his editor at Doubleday for years. Nor even more entitled to mourn than was Isaac's brother, Stan, now himself gone. But I knew him for more than forty years, since I was eighteen, and we were thick as thieves; and at least twice a week for many of those years, when I was mired somewhere in the middle of writing a story, and was stuck for a missing piece of information, rather than do the onerous research to find what I needed, I would punk out and call that number I knew as well as my own.

We played a little game with each other. Because I was

(somewhere in my lazy soul) truly chagrined at interrupting another writer at his creating, knowing it was a pain in the ass, even as such calls cheese me off when *I'm* working, I would try to make "reparations" by either telling him a new joke, or by assuming one of the myriad accents and timbres I use when recording spoken word performances. The more shamefaced I felt, the more complex and well-sculpted the bogus identity:

"Is this Dr. Isaac Emisov?" The voice of a petty functionary. A tax collector. An assistant bank manager. A collection agency goon.

"Asimov. This is Isaac *Asimov.*"

"Ah, yes. Dr. Esimov, this is Walter Cuthbert at Manhattan Central office of the Internal Revenue Service . . . "

A pause. (Had he caught on yet?) Then, a tiny clearing of the throat, and the response in a deeper, more pillar-of-the-community tone. "What may I do for you, sir?"

"Well, to be frank, sir, quite a lot. We've taken under examination your tax returns for the years 1967 through 1990, and we've found sufficient, uh, 'irregularities' that the class auditors have passed it on up to my attention."

Caution. (The man was no fool.) (But with whom did he think he was playing here?) (Without mercy, one *must* be, if one is to pull it off.) "What, precisely, Mr. Cuthbert—" he said, pronouncing my name from perfect memory, as opposed to my relentlessly calling him Emisov, Akisov, Etceterasov, "—do you mean by 'irregularities'?"

"Well, Dr. Uh—"

"Asimov."

"Mm-hmm. For instance, we see in the years 1971, 1972, 1973, 1974, and 1975, you claimed 'entertainment deductions' in an aggregate of $877,463.89; but your total income during that period was only $775,012.44. Don't you find that a bit, well, per*plex*ing, sir?"

"Who is this?"

Shit. He was on to me. "Walter Cuth—"

"None of that," he said, now honked-off at being wired up by some nitwit stealing his time, "who *are* you?"

"Would you believe Ty Cobb?"

"HAAAARRRRLLLAAANNNN!" In exactly the same voice, I'm convinced, was used by Judge Roy Bean when he yelled, "Hang the sonofabitch high enuff so's I can see his boot soles!"

I am not ashamed simply to state that I adored Isaac, before I actually met him, though we famously crossed paths not more than a year or two after I first read him. (And I will not reprise that meeting, which Isaac misremembered at the top of his voice for more than four decades, despite my clearing up the errors an infinite number of times, in person and in print.) Suffice to say, for the *last* time, I did *not* mean to insult him. I was a brash teenager, and I merely misspoke myself as a result of confronting my idol in the, er, rather abundant flesh, for the first time. Snip me some slack, okay?

But as Isaac wrote in a letter to me on 27 August 1973 (which you can find reproduced on page 113 of Stanley's 1995 epistolary compilation, *Yours, Isaac Asimov*):

> *I am constantly asked about my feud with you, and I always answer that you and I are good friends. But it doesn't help. As long as we love each other, however, who cares.*

He meant that, of course, in a real manly guy sort of Iron John bonding love kind of way. Not that there's anything wrong with, oh crap, forget it. Where was I?

With three thousand miles between us most of the time, and with Isaac's refusal to fly, we got together a lot less frequently than either of us would've enjoyed. Conventions through the years, conferences, academic gigs. And when I'd be in Manhattan, we would usually grab lunch. Once in a while, with Janet and my Susan, dinner at the Chinese joint down the block from their apartment. But one lunch Isaac and I shared in the late '70s, before I met and married Susan, is relevant to my being selected from among all the possible candidates to write this Foreword. It was mid-afternoon, in the Spring, if I recall correctly, and Isaac said, "C'mon, let's take a stroll over to The Tavern on the Green." That's Central Park. Nearby.

So we moseyed on over, and we were waiting to order, and he says to me, he says: "How do you justify your existence?"

Oh, yeah? I thought. Gonna run that one on me, are you? As if I hadn't read the first three Black Widowers books. So I responded smartly, "My existence itself justifies my existence."

"Tautology!" he ripostes, trying to sneer, not pulling it off.

"I am unique; a rare jewel existent in the universe in the number of one."

"Hooey," he hoos, trying desperately for a Nero Wolfe moment.

"I am unique, thus justified in my existence, by what I do, that no other can do."

"And what is it that you do?"

"What it is that I *do* . . . is what I do."

He muttered something into his appetizer, but I'm not sure what it was; I think the word "slippery" was in there somewhere with the caramelized onions.

And it was at that lunch tryst that I said to him, "Listen, Toots, you use Lester in those Black Widowers stories, and Sprague and Don Bensen and even Lin Carter, but you've never used me as a character. Howzabout?"

Now, you will, I hope, remember that Isaac appropriated me as the paradigm for the most likeable character in *all* his books, the charming, witty, urbane and insightful Darius Just, 'tec avatar of *Murder at the ABA*. You *do* recall that, am I correct?

So Isaac smiled that lovely son-of-a-Brooklyn-candy-store-owner smile, and he agreed to bring Darius Just in for dinner with the Widowers. The fourth collection, *Banquets of the Black Widowers.* The story is "The Woman in the Bar."

I asked the editor, Mr. Ardai, if he might add that most excellent piece of work to the already-submitted table of contents, but whether the traitorous and untrustworthy Ardai chose to accede to this pathetic, tiny request is something I will not know till I see the finished volume.

(Ardai's own presumptuous story, the penultimate entry in this book, contains veiled references of a most painful nature to your humble essayist. I choose not to make a big Who-Struck-John of it, but as Montresor said to Fortunato in "The Cask of Amontillado": "*Nemo me impune lacessit.*"

(No one harms me with impunity.

(Didn't think I'd notice, eh, Ardai? Thought your heartless little barbs would be politely overlooked, did you? Well, sir, not to make a big Who-Struck-John of it, but be on your watch, Ardai. Gardyloo, I say, sir, gardyloo! The moment of Divine Retribution slithers toward you through the hours, leaving a moist ebon trail of poison and rodomontade! Where was I?)

So that explains why I, the model for Darius Just, having been cast as a guest at one of the Widowers' banquets, was the humble, self-effacing, yet absolutely correct choice to write these words of introduction to the last collection of Black Widowers stories we shall see. Book six, curtain falls.

Isaac loved puzzles. Geezus peezus, that was a dopey thing to say. Of *course* he loved puzzles. Duh. Otherwise, why these six volumes, plus the novels, plus virtually everything he wrote, fiction or nonfiction. It was *all* in aid of solving the puzzles. Of fiction, of life, of the universe around us. And the universe out there.

He wrote sixty-six Black Widowers stories, of which these are the last few. In them, the character of Emmanuel Rubin, who was modeled after one of my earliest mentors, the late Lester del Rey, world-class pain in the ass, is not one scintilla as overbearing and anarchic as the template. Lester could make poison ivy nervous. The magnificent L. Sprague de Camp—Widower Geoffrey Avalon—is not a millionth as arresting and erudite as was the original . . .

(Pardon me yet another digression. This is a true story about Sprague, who was also a friend of mine, though separated from me by even more years than was Isaac. I'd used Sprague as the prototype for the character of the college professor in my story, "No Game For Children" and we'd gotten to know each other pretty well. But I'd met him years earlier, when I was still in high school in Cleveland, and had come to New York under the aegis of Algis Budrys, who took me to a meeting of The Hydra Club, the fabled monthly gathering of the top science fiction professionals, where I met L. Ron Hubbard and Robert Sheckley, as well as, later, Cornell Woolrich; and on and on.

(So there I was, this urchin, and I'm hobbing as well as nobbing with the giants of the field, del Rey, Kornbluth, Pohl, Merril, the lot of them. And right in the middle, tall and lean and elegant as an ebony sword-cane, was Sprague de Camp. And as I had located and read the novels he'd written with Fletcher Pratt, and as he was considered the most sapient humorist in sf at that time, I was especially observant of his actions, hoping AJ or Lester would introduce me. And I watched him as he behaved, well, rather oddly. He would stand at the outer perimeter of a group of people who were heavily into their conversation, and at some point—almost invariably when they broke up with laughter—he would jot notes into a small spiral-top note-pad. Then he'd move to another group of chatters, and the pattern would be repeated. This went on for an hour or so, until Jay Stanton [whose loft it was] grabbed him and, loud enough for everything else to come to a silent standstill, cried out, snatched the note-pad from de Camp's hand, and began leafing through it.

("What the hell is this all about?" Jay demanded.

("What's he been writing?" Lester wanted to know.

("He's been writing down everything we've been saying tonight!"

(Well, an explanation was chivvied out of the great sf-fantasy humorist, and it was this: Sprague had a formidable reputation for writing stories of great wit and humor. But he was, personally, a very proper, almost stiffnecked Late George Apley sort of guy, and apparently he hadn't the smallest clue as to what was actually funny. He hadn't, to be blunt, even the teeniest sense of humor. So he had been trailing around behind people all night, waiting for them to laugh, and then writing down the mots so he could take them back home and, at his leisure, codify, dissect, deconstruct and otherwise unriddle the essence of funnystuff.)

Geoffrey Avalon isn't nearly as idiosyncratic as Sprague. Nor is

Mario Gonzalo AKA Lin Carter, who was—trust me on this—*really* weird.

Well, enough of that. But before I go, before I leave you to the familiar joys of this final Widowers banquet, let me drop in here just *one* of the unsolved puzzles passim these tales. In the story "Triple Devil," a few pages from the end, we find this passage:

> *Halsted said, "The usual image of the devil, with horns, hooves, and a tail, is drawn, actually, from the Greek nature god, Pan. Was it a book about Pan, or with the word 'Pan' in the title?"*
>
> *"Actually," said Manfred, "I can't think of one."*

I am puzzled by this. Isaac, who knew *everything,* who—in this story alone—demonstrates particular familiarity with a congeries of literary referents pursuant to the plot, from Thackeray, Trollope, Sterne, Wordsworth, Browning, H.G. Wells and Sir Walter Scott to Chesterton's Father Brown and Stephen Vincent Benét, has a character who is as literate and fecund as Isaac himself, say "I can't think of one." A novel with the name Pan in it.

Nor do any of the *other* characters, including the all-wise Henry, speak up and say, "Well, what about Arthur Machen's *The Great God Pan*?" A novel Isaac *had* to be as familiar with as he was with the works of Bierce, Blackwood, Charles Williams, and Wm. Seabrook.

I never got around to asking Isaac that. I suppose because I missed the story's magazine appearance in *EQMM.* But when I read it in the page-proofs sent to me by The Beast Ardai (I know where you live, poltroon!), it struck me at once.

A puzzle.

Amid puzzles.

At the terminus of one of the great lives of our time. A final book, a hail and farewell, a kiss from out in the cold by The Good Doctor. For me, for you, for all of us.

When I call him tomorrow, I'll tell him you sent your best.

—Harlan Ellison®

THE BEST OF
THE BLACK WIDOWERS

THE ACQUISITIVE CHUCKLE

Hanley Bartram was the guest, that night, of the Black Widowers, who monthly met in their quiet haunt and vowed death to any female who intruded—for that one night per month, at any rate.

The number of attendees varied: five members were present on this occasion.

Geoffrey Avalon was host for the evening. He was tall, with a neatly trimmed mustache and a smallish beard, more white than black now, but with hair nearly as black as ever.

As host, it was his duty to deliver the ritual toast that marked the beginning of the dinner proper. Loudly, and with gusto, he said, "To Old King Cole of sacred memory. May his pipe be forever lit, his bowl forever full, his fiddlers forever in health, and may we all be as merry as he all our lives long."

Each cried, "Amen," touched his lips to drink, and sat down. Avalon put his drink to the side of his plate. It was his second and was now exactly half full. It would remain there throughout the dinner and was not to be touched again. He was a patent lawyer and he carried over into his social life the minutiae of his work. One and a half drinks was precisely what he allowed himself on these occasions.

Thomas Trumbull came storming up the stairs at the last minute, with the usual cry of "Henry, a scotch and soda for a dying man."

Henry, the waiter at these functions for several years now (and with no last name that any Black Widower had ever heard used), had the scotch and soda in readiness. He was sixtyish but his face was unwrinkled and staid. His voice seemed to recede into the distance even as he spoke. "Right here, Mr. Trumbull."

Trumbull spotted Bartram at once and said to Avalon in an aside, "Your guest?"

"He asked to come," said Avalon, in as near a whisper as he could manage. "Nice fellow. You'll like him."

The dinner itself went as miscellaneously as the Black Widowers' affairs usually did. Emmanuel Rubin, who had the other beard—a thin and scraggly one under a mouth with widely spaced teeth—had broken out of a writer's block and was avidly giving the details of the story he had finished. James Drake, with a rectangular face, a mustache but no beard, was interrupting with memories of other stories, tangentially related. Drake was only an organic chemist but he had an encyclopedic knowledge of pulp fiction.

Trumbull, as a code expert, considered himself to be in the inner councils of government and took it into his head to be outraged at Mario Gonzalo's political pronouncements. "God damn it," he yelled, in one of his less vituperative moods, "why don't you stick to your idiotic collages and your burlap bags and leave world affairs to your betters?"

Trumbull had not recovered from Gonzalo's one-man art show earlier that year, and Gonzalo, understanding this, laughed good-naturedly, and said, "Show me my betters. Name one."

Bartram, short and plump, with hair that curled in ringlets, clung firmly to his role as guest. He listened to everyone, smiled at everyone, and said little.

Eventually the time came when Henry poured the coffee and began to place the desserts before each guest with practiced legerdemain. It was at this moment that the traditional grilling of the guest was supposed to begin.

The initial questioner, almost by tradition (on those occasions when he was present), was Thomas Trumbull. His swarthy face, wrinkled into a perennial discontent, looked angry as he began with the invariable opening question: "Mr. Bartram, how do you justify your existence?"

Bartram smiled. He spoke with precision as he said, "I have never tried. My clients, on those occasions when I give satisfaction, find my existence justified."

"Your clients?" said Rubin. "What is it you do, Mr. Bartram?"

"I am a private investigator."

"Good," said James Drake. "I don't think we've ever had one before. Manny, you can get some of the data correct for a change when you write your tough-guy crap."

"Not from me," said Bartram quickly.

Trumbull scowled. "If you don't mind, gentlemen, as the appointed grillster, please leave this to me. Mr. Bartram, you speak of the occasions upon which you give satisfaction. Do you always give satisfaction?"

"There are times when the matter can be debated," said Bartram. "In fact, I would like to speak to you this evening concerning an occasion that was particularly questionable. It may even be that one of you might be useful in that connection. It was with that in mind that I asked my good friend Jeff Avalon to invite me to a meeting, once I learned the details of the organization. He obliged and I am delighted."

"Are you ready now to discuss this dubious satisfaction you gave or did not give, as the case may be?"

"Yes, if you will allow me."

Trumbull looked at the others for signs of dissent. Gonzalo's prominent eyes were fixed on Bartram as he said, "May we interrupt?" Quickly, and with an admirable economy of strokes, he was doodling a caricature of Bartram on the back of his menu card. It would join the others which memorialized guests and which marched in brave array across the walls.

"Within reason," said Bartram. He paused to sip at his coffee and then said, "The story begins with Anderson, to whom I shall refer only in that fashion. He was an acquisitor."

"An inquisitor?" asked Gonzalo, frowning.

"An *ac*quisitor. He gained things, he earned them, he bought them, he picked them up, he collected them. The world moved in one direction with respect to him; it moved toward him; never away. He had a house into which this flood of material, of varying value, came to rest and never moved again. Through the years, it grew steadily thicker and amazingly heterogeneous. He also had a business partner, whom I shall call only Jackson."

Trumbull interrupted, frowning, not because there was anything to frown about, but because he always frowned. He said, "Is this a true story?"

"I tell only true stories," said Bartram slowly and precisely. "I lack the imagination to lie."

"Is it confidential?"

"I shall not tell the story in such a way as to make it easily recognized, but were it to be recognized, it would be confidential."

"I follow the subjunctive," said Trumbull, "but I wish to assure you that what is said within the walls of this room is never repeated, nor referred to, however tangentially, outside its walls. Henry understands this, too."

Henry, who was refilling two of the coffee cups, smiled a little and bent his head in agreement.

Bartram smiled also and went on, "Jackson had a disease, too. He was honest; unavoidably and deeply honest. The characteristic permeated his soul as though, from an early age, he had been marinated in integrity.

"To a man like Anderson, it was most useful to have honest Jackson as partner, for their business, which I carefully do not describe in detail, required contact with the public. Such contact was not for Anderson, for his acquisitiveness stood in the way. With each object he acquired, another little crease of slyness entered his face, until it seemed a spider's web that frightened all flies at sight. It was Jackson, the pure and the honest, who was the front man, and to whom all widows hastened with their mites, and orphans with their farthings.

"On the other hand, Jackson found Anderson a necessity, too, for Jackson, with all his honesty, perhaps because of it, had no knack for making one dollar become two. Left to himself, he would, entirely without meaning to, lose every cent entrusted to him and would then quickly be forced to kill himself as a dubious form of restitution. Anderson's hands were to money, however, as fertilizer is to roses, and he and Jackson were, together, a winning combination.

"Yet no paradise continues forever, and a besetting characteristic, left to itself, will deepen, widen, and grow more extreme. Jackson's honesty grew to such colossal proportions that Anderson, for all his shrewdness, was occasionally backed to the wall and forced into monetary loss. Similarly, Anderson's acquisitiveness burrowed to such infernal depths that Jackson, for all his morality, found himself occasionally twisted into questionable practices.

"Naturally, as Anderson disliked losing money, and Jackson abhorred losing character, a coolness grew between the two. In such a situation the advantage clearly lay on the side of Anderson, who placed no reasonable limits on his actions, whereas Jackson felt himself bound by a code of ethics.

"Slyly, Anderson worked and maneuvered until, eventually, poor honest Jackson found himself forced to sell out his end of the partnership under the most disadvantageous possible conditions.

"Anderson's acquisitiveness, we might say, had reached a climax, for he acquired sole control of the business. It was his intention to retire now, leaving its everyday running to employees, and concerning himself no further than was required to pocket its profits. Jackson, on the other hand, was left with nothing more than his honesty, and while honesty is an admirable characteristic, it has small direct value in a hockshop.

"It was at this point, gentlemen, that I entered the picture. . . . Ah, Henry, thank you."

The glasses of brandy were being passed about.

"You did not know these people to begin with?" asked Rubin, his sharp eyes blinking.

"Not at all," said Bartram, sniffing delicately at the brandy and just touching it to his upper lip, "though I think one of you in this room did. It was some years ago.

"I first met Anderson when he entered my office in a white heat. 'I want you to find what I've lost,' he said. I have dealt with many cases of theft in my career and so I said, naturally, 'Just what is it you have lost?' And he answered, 'Damn it, man, that's what I've just asked you to find out.'

"The story came out rather raggedly. Anderson and Jackson had quarreled with surprising intensity. Jackson was outraged, as only an honest man can be when he finds that his integrity is no shield against the conniving of others. He swore revenge, and Anderson shrugged that off with a laugh."

"Beware the wrath of a patient man," quoted Avalon, with the air of precision research he brought to even his least portentous statements.

"So I have heard," said Bartram, "though I have never had occasion to test the maxim. Nor, apparently, had Anderson, for he had no fear of Jackson. As he explained, Jackson was so psychotically honest and so insanely law-abiding that there was no chance of his slipping into wrongdoing. Or so Anderson thought. It did not even occur to him to ask Jackson to return the office key; something all the more curious since the office was located in Anderson's house, in among the knickknackery.

"Anderson recalled this omission a few days after the quarrel, for, returning from an early evening appointment, he found Jackson in his house. Jackson carried his old attaché case, which he was just closing as Anderson entered; closing with startled haste, it seemed to Anderson.

"Anderson frowned and said, inevitably, 'What are you doing here?'

" 'Returning some papers which were in my possession and which now belong to you,' said Jackson, 'and returning the key to the office.' With this remark, he handed over the key, indicated papers on the desk, and pushed the combination lock on his battered attaché case with fingers that Anderson could swear trembled a little. Jackson looked about the room with what appeared to Anderson to be a curious, almost a secretively satisfied, smile and said, 'I will now leave.' He proceeded to do so.

"It was not until Anderson heard the motor of Jackson's car whirring into action and then retreating into the distance that he could rouse himself from a kind of stupor that had paralyzed him. He knew he had been robbed, and the next day he came to me."

Drake pursed his lips, twirled his half-empty brandy glass, and said, "Why not to the police?"

"There was a complication," said Bartram. "Anderson did not know what had been taken. When the certainty of theft dawned on him, he naturally rushed to the safe. Its contents were secure. He ransacked his desk. Nothing seemed to be missing. He went from room to room. Everything seemed to be intact as far as he could tell."

"Wasn't he certain?" asked Gonzalo.

"He couldn't be. The house was inordinately crowded with every variety of object and he didn't remember all his possessions. He told me, for instance, that at one time he collected antique watches. He had them in a small drawer in his study; six of them. All six were there, but he was nagged by the faint memory of seven. For the life of him, he could not remember definitely. In fact, it was worse than that, for one of the six present seemed strange to him. Could it be that he had had only six but that a less valuable one had been substituted for a more valuable one? Something of this sort repeated itself a dozen times over in every hideaway and with every sort of oddment. So he came to me—"

"Wait a while," said Trumbull, bringing his hand down hard on the table. "What made him so certain that Jackson had taken anything at all?"

"Ah," said Bartram, "that is the fascinating part of the story. The closing of the attaché case, and Jackson's secretive smile as he looked about the room, served in themselves to rouse Anderson's suspicions, but as the door closed behind him, Jackson chuckled.

It was not an ordinary chuckle. . . . But I'll let Anderson tell it in his own words, as nearly as I remember them.

" 'Bartram,' he said, 'I have heard that chuckle innumerable times in my life. I have chuckled that way myself a thousand times. It is a characteristic chuckle, an unmistakable one, an unmaskable one. It is the acquisitive chuckle; it is the chuckle of a man who has just obtained something he wants very much at the expense of someone else. If any man in all the world knows that chuckle and can recognize it, even behind a closed door, that man is myself. I cannot be mistaken. Jackson had taken something of mine and was glorying in it!'

"There was no arguing with the man on this point. He virtually slavered at the thought of having been victimized and, indeed, I had to believe him. I had to suppose that for all Jackson's pathological honesty, he had been lured, by the once-in-a-lifetime snapping of patience, into theft. Helping lure him must have been his knowledge of Anderson. He must have known Anderson's intent hold on even the least valued of his belongings, and realized that the hurt would extend far deeper and far beyond the value of the object taken, however great that value might have been."

Rubin said, "Maybe it was the attaché case he took."

"No, no, that was Jackson's. He'd owned it for years. So there you have the problem. Anderson wanted me to find out what had been taken, for until he could identify a stolen object and show that the object was, or had been, in the possession of Jackson, he could not prosecute—and he was most intent on prosecution. My task, then, was to look through his house and tell him what was missing."

"How would that be possible, if he himself couldn't tell?" growled Trumbull.

"I pointed that out to him," said Bartram, "but he was wild and unreasoning. He offered me a great deal of money, win or lose; a very handsome fee, indeed, and he put down a sizable portion of it as a retainer. It was clear he resented beyond measure the deliberate insult to his acquisitiveness. The thought that an amateur nonacquisitor like Jackson should dare beard him in this most sacred of his passions had driven him, on this one point, mad, and he was prepared to go to any expense to keep the other's victory from being final.

"I am myself quite human. I accepted the retainer and the fee. After all, I reasoned, I had my methods. I took up the question of insurance lists first. All were outdated, but they served to eliminate the furniture and all the larger items as possible victims of Jackson's thievery, for everything on the lists was still in the house."

Avalon interrupted. "They were eliminated anyway, since the stolen object would have had to fit into the attaché case."

"Provided that it was indeed the attaché case that was used to transport the item out of the house," pointed out Bartram patiently. "It might easily have been a decoy. Prior to Anderson's return, Jackson could have had a moving van at the door and taken out the grand piano had he so chosen, and then snapped the attaché case in Anderson's face to mislead him.

"But never mind that. It wasn't likely. I took him around the house room by room, following a systematic procedure of considering the floor, walls, and ceiling, studying all the shelves, opening every door, considering every piece of furniture, going through every closet. Nor did I neglect the attic and the basement. Never before had Anderson been forced to consider every item of his vast and amorphous collection in order that somewhere, somehow, some item would jog his memory of some companion item that was *not* there.

"It was an enormous house, a heterogeneous one, an endless one. It took us days, and poor Anderson grew more befuddled each day.

"I next tackled it from the other end. It was obvious that Jackson had deliberately taken something unnoticeable, perhaps small; certainly something that Anderson would not easily miss and therefore not something to which he was greatly attached. On the other hand, it made sense to suppose that it was something Jackson would want to take away, and which he would find valuable. Indeed, his deed would give him most satisfaction if Anderson, too, found it valuable—once he realized what it was that was gone. What, then, could it be?"

"A small painting," said Gonzalo eagerly, "which Jackson knew to be an authentic Cézanne, but which Anderson thought was junk."

"A stamp from Anderson's collection," said Rubin, "which Jackson noted had a rare mistake in the engraving." He had once written a story which had hinged on this precise point.

"A book," said Trumbull, "which contained some hidden family secret with which, in due time, Jackson could blackmail Anderson."

"A photograph," said Avalon dramatically, "that Anderson had forgotten but which contained the likeness of an old sweetheart which, eventually, he would give a fortune to buy back."

"I don't know what business they were in," said Drake thoughtfully, "but it might have been the kind where some unvalued gimcrack might actually be of great value to a competitor and drive Anderson to bankruptcy. I remember one case where a formula for a hydrazo-intermediate—"

"Oddly enough," said Bartram, breaking in firmly, "I thought of each of these possibilities, and I went over each with Anderson. It was clear that he had no taste in art and such pieces as he had were really junk, and no mistake. He did not collect stamps, and though he had many books and could not tell for certain whether one was gone, he swore he had no hidden family secrets anywhere that were worth the skipped beat of a blackmailer's heart. Nor had he ever had any old sweethearts, since in his younger days he had confined himself to professional ladies whose photographs he did not prize. As for his business secrets, they were of the sort that would interest the government far more than any competitor, and everything of that sort had been kept far from Jackson's honest eyes in the first place and were still in the safe (or long in the fire) in the second. I thought of other possibilities, but, one by one, they were knocked down.

"Of course, Jackson might betray himself. He might blossom out into sudden wealth, and in ferreting out the source of the wealth, we might learn the identity of the stolen object.

"Anderson suggested that himself and paid lavishly to have a twenty-four-hour watch put on Jackson. It was useless. The man kept a dull way of life and behaved precisely as you would expect someone minus his life savings to behave. He lived parsimoniously, and, eventually, took a menial job, where his honesty and his calm demeanor stood him in good stead.

"Finally, I had but one alternative left—"

"Wait, wait," said Gonzalo, "let me guess, let me guess." He tossed off what was left of his brandy, signaled Henry for another, and said, "You asked Jackson!"

"I was strongly tempted to," said Bartram ruefully, "but that would scarcely have been feasible. It doesn't do in my profession to even hint at an accusation without evidence of any sort. Licenses are too fragile. And in any case, he would simply deny theft, if accused, and be put on his guard against any self-incrimination."

"Well, then . . . ," said Gonzalo blankly, and petered out.

The other four furrowed brows one and all, but only silence followed.

Bartram, having waited politely, said, "You won't guess, gentlemen, for you are not in the profession. You know only what you read in romances and so you think gentlemen like myself have unlimited numbers of alternatives and invariably solve all cases. I, myself, being in the profession, know otherwise. Gentlemen, the one alternative I had left was to confess failure.

"Anderson paid me, however, I'll give him that much credit. By the time I said my goodbyes to him, he had lost some ten pounds. There was a vacant look in his eyes and, as he shook hands with me, they moved round and round the room he was in, still looking, still looking. He muttered, 'I tell you I couldn't possibly mistake that chuckle. He took something from me. He took something from me.'

"I saw him on two or three occasions thereafter. He never stopped looking; he never found the missing object. He went rather downhill. The events I have described took place nearly five years ago, and last month, he died."

There was a short silence. Avalon said, "Without ever finding the missing object?"

"Without ever finding it."

Trumbull said, with disapproval, "Are you coming to us to help you with the problem now?"

"In a way, yes. The occasion is too good to miss. Anderson is dead and whatever is said within these walls will go no farther, we all agree, so that I may now ask what I could not ask before. . . . Henry, may I have a light?"

Henry, who had been listening with a kind of absentminded deference, produced a book of matches and lit Bartram's cigarette.

"Let me introduce you, Henry, to those you so efficiently serve. . . . Gentlemen, may I introduce to you, Henry Jackson."

There was a moment of clear shock and Drake said, "*The* Jackson."

"Exactly," said Bartram. "I knew he was working here and when I heard it was at this club that you met for your monthly meetings, I had to beg, rather shamelessly, for an invitation. It was only here that I could find the gentleman with the acquisitive chuckle, and do so under conditions of both bonhomie and discretion."

Henry smiled and bent his head.

Bartram said, "There were times during the course of the investigation when I could not help but wonder, Henry, whether Anderson might not have been wrong and whether there might possibly have been no theft at all. Always, however, I returned to the matter of the acquisitive chuckle, and I trusted Anderson's judgment."

"You did right to do so," said Jackson softly, "for I *did* steal something from my one-time partner, the gentleman you have referred to as Anderson. I never regretted the act for one moment."

"It was something of value, I presume."

"It was of the greatest value and no day passed without my thinking of the theft and rejoicing in the fact that the wicked man no longer had what I had taken away."

"And you deliberately roused his suspicions in order that you might experience the greater joy."

"Yes, sir."

"And you did not fear being caught?"

"Not for one moment, sir."

"By God," roared Avalon suddenly, his voice soaring to break-neck loudness. "I say it again. Beware the wrath of a patient man. I am a patient man, and I am tired of this endless cross-examination. Beware my wrath, Henry. What was it you carried off in your attaché case?"

"Why, nothing, sir," said Henry. "It was empty."

"Heaven help me! Where did you put whatever it was you took from him?"

"I didn't have to put it anywhere, sir."

"Well, then, what did you take?"

"Only his peace of mind, sir," said Henry gently.

PH AS IN PHONY

The meeting of the Black Widowers was marred, but only slightly, by the restlessness of James Drake.

It was a shame that this had to be so, for the dinner was unusually good, even allowing for the loving care with which the Milano Restaurant took care of its special group every month. And if the veal *cordon bleu* needed anything to add the final bit of luster, it was Henry's meticulous service, which had plates on the table where no plate had been before, yet without any person present able to catch it en route.

It was Thomas Trumbull's turn to host, something he did with a savagery to which no one paid the slightest bit of attention; a savagery made particularly bitter by the fact that, as host, he did not think it fit to come charging in just one second before the pre-dinner drinks had completed their twice-around (three times for Rubin, who never showed the effects).

Trumbull exercised host's privilege and had brought a guest for the grilling. The guest was tall, almost as tall as Geoffrey Avalon, the Black Widowers' patent-attorney member. He was lean, almost as lean as Geoffrey Avalon. He was clean-shaven, though, and lacked the solemnity of Avalon. Indeed, his face was round and his cheeks plump, in a manner so out of keeping with the rest of his body that one might have thought him the product of a head transplant. He was Arnold Stacey, by name.

"Arnold Stacey, Ph.D.," Trumbull had introduced him.

"Ah," said Avalon, with the air of portentousness he automatically brought to his most trivial statement, "Doctor Doctor Stacey."

"Doctor Doctor?" murmured Stacey, his lips parting as though getting ready for a smile at the pleasantry sure to follow.

"It is a rule of the Black Widowers," said Trumbull impatiently, "that all members are doctors by virtue of membership. A doctor for any other reason is—"

"A doctor doctor," finished Stacey. And he smiled.

"You can count honorary doctorates, too," said Rubin, his wide-spaced teeth gleaming over a beard as straggly as Avalon's was crisp, "but then I would have to be called Doctor Doctor Doctor—"

Mario Gonzalo was mounting the stairs just then, bringing with him a faint whiff of turpentine as though he had come straight from his artist's studio. (Trumbull maintained you couldn't draw that conclusion; that Gonzalo placed a drop of turpentine behind each ear before any social engagement.)

Gonzalo was in time to catch Emmanuel Rubin's statement and said, before he had quite reached the top step, "What honorary doctorates did you ever receive, Manny? *Dis*honorary doctorates, I'm ready to believe."

Rubin's face froze as it usually did when he was attacked without warning, but that was merely the short pause necessary to gather his forces. He said, "I can list them for you. In 1938, when I was only fifteen, it so happens I was a revivalist preacher and I received a D.D. from—"

"*No*, for God's sake," said Trumbull, "don't give us the list. We accept it all."

"You're fighting out of your weight, Mario," said Avalon with wooden amiability. "You know Rubin can never be spotted in an inconsistency when he starts talking about his early life."

"Sure," said Gonzalo, "that's why his stories are so lousy. They're all autobiographical. No poetry."

"I have written poetry," began Rubin, and then Drake came in. Usually, he was the first person there; this time, the last.

"Train was late," he said quietly, shucking his coat. Since he had to come in from New Jersey to attend, the only surprise was that it didn't happen oftener.

"Introduce me to the guest," Drake added, as he turned to take the drink Henry held out for him. Henry knew which he preferred, of course.

Avalon said, "Doctor Doctor Arnold Stacey . . . Doctor Doctor James Drake."

"Greetings," said Drake, holding up his glass in salute. 'What's the nature of the lesser doctorate, Doctor Stacey?"

"Ph.D. in chemistry. Doctor Doctor, and call me Arnold."

Drake's small grizzled mustache seemed to bristle. "Ditto," he said. "My Ph.D. is in chemistry, too."

They looked at each other, warily, for a moment. Then Drake said, "Industry? Government? Academic?"

"I teach. Assistant professor at Berry University."

"Where?"

"Berry University. It's not a large school. It's in—"

"I know where it is," said Drake. "I did graduate work there. Considerably before your time, though. Did you get your degree at Berry before you joined the faculty?"

"No, I—"

"Let's sit down, for God's sake," roared Trumbull. "There's more drinking and less eating going on here all the time." He was standing at the host's seat, with his glass raised, glowering at the others as each took his seat. "Sit down! Sit down!" And then he intoned the ritual toast to Old King Cole in singsong while Gonzalo blandly kept time with a hard roll, which he broke and buttered when the last syllable was done.

"What's this?" said Rubin suddenly, staring down at his dish in dismay.

"*Pâte de la maison,* sir," said Henry softly.

"That's what I thought. Chopped liver. Damn it, Henry, I ask you, as a pathologically honest man, is this fit to eat?"

"The matter is quite subjective, sir. It depends on the personal taste of the diner."

Avalon pounded the table. "Point of order! I object to Manny's use of the adjectival phrase 'pathologically honest.' Violation of confidence!"

Rubin colored slightly. "Hold on, Jeff. I don't violate any confidence. That happens to be my opinion of Henry quite independently of what happened last month."

"Ruling from the chair," said Avalon stubbornly.

Trumbull said, "Shut up both of you. It is the ruling of the chair that Henry may be recognized by all Black Widowers as that rare phenomenon, a completely honest man. No reason need be given. It can be taken as a matter of common knowledge."

Henry smiled gently. "Shall I take away the *pâte*, sir?"

"Would *you* eat it, Henry?" asked Rubin.

"With pleasure, sir."

"Then I'll eat it, too." And he did so, with every sign of barely controlled nausea.

Trumbull leaned over to Drake and said in a voice that was low for him, "What the hell's bothering you?"

Drake started slightly and said, "Nothing. What's bothering *you*?"

"You are," said Trumbull. "I've never seen a roll taken apart into so many pieces in my life."

The conversation grew general after that, centering chiefly on Rubin's aggrieved contention that honesty lacked survival value and that all the forces of natural selection combined to eliminate it as a human trait. He did well defending his thesis till Gonzalo asked him if he attributed his own success as a writer ("such as it is," said Gonzalo) to plagiarism. When Rubin met the point head on and tried to prove, by close reasoning, that plagiarism was fundamentally different from other forms of dishonesty and might be treated independently, he was hooted down.

Then, between main course and dessert, Drake left for the men's room and Trumbull followed him.

Trumbull said, "Do you know this guy Stacey, Jim?"

Drake shook his head. "No. Not at all."

"Well, what's wrong, then? I admit you're not an animated phonograph needle like Rubin but you haven't said a word all dinner, damn it. And you keep looking at Stacey."

Drake said, "Do me a favor, Tom. Let me question him after dinner."

Trumbull shrugged. "Sure."

Over the coffee, Trumbull said, "The time has come for the grilling of the guest. Under ordinary circumstances, I, as the possessor of the only logical mind at the table, would begin. On this occasion, I pass to Doctor Doctor Drake since he is of the same professional persuasion as our honored guest."

"Doctor Doctor Stacey," began Drake heavily, "how do you justify your existence?"

"Less and less as time goes on," said Stacey, unperturbed.

"What the hell does that mean?" broke in Trumbull.

"*I'm* asking the questions," said Drake with unaccustomed firmness.

"I don't mind answering," said Stacey. "Since the universities seem to be in deeper trouble each year, and as I do nothing about it, my own function as a university appendage seems continually less defensible, that's all."

Drake ignored that. He said, "You teach at the school where I earned my master's degree. Have you ever heard of me?"

Stacey hesitated. "I'm sorry, Jim. There are a lot of chemists I haven't heard of. No offense intended."

"I'm not sensitive. I never heard of you, either. What I mean is: Have you ever heard of me at Berry U.? As a student there?"

"No, I haven't."

"I'm not surprised. But there was another student at Berry at the same time as myself. He went on for his doctorate at Berry. His name was Faron, F-A-R-O-N; Lance Faron. Did you ever hear of him?"

"Lance Faron?" Stacey frowned.

"Lance may have been short for Lancelot; Lancelot Faron. I don't know. We always called him Lance."

Finally Stacey shook his head. "No, the name isn't familiar."

Drake said, "But you have heard of David St. George?"

"Professor St. George? Certainly. He died the same year I joined the faculty. I can't say I know him, but I've certainly heard of him."

Trumbull said, "Hell and damnation, Jim. What kind of questions are these? Is this old-grad week?"

Drake, who had drifted off into thought, scrambled out of it and said, "Wait, Tom. I'm getting at something, and I don't want to ask questions. I want to tell a story first. My God, this has been bothering me for years and I never thought of putting it up to all of you till now that our guest—"

"I vote the story," shouted Gonzalo.

"On condition," said Avalon, "it not be construed as setting a precedent."

"Chair decides the precedents," said Trumbull at once. "Go ahead, Drake. Only, for God's sake, don't take all night."

"It's simple enough," said Drake, "and it's about Lance Faron, which is his real name, and I'm going to slander him, so you'll have to understand, Arnold, that everything said within these walls is strictly confidential."

"That's been explained to me," said Stacey.

"Go on," shouted Trumbull. "You *will* take all night. I know it."

Drake said, "The thing about Lance is that I don't think he ever intended to be a chemist. His family was rich enough—well, I'll tell you. When he was doing graduate work, he had his lab outfitted with a cork floor at his own expense."

"Why a cork floor?" Gonzalo wanted to know,

"If you'd ever dropped a beaker on a tile floor, you wouldn't ask," said Drake. "He majored in chemistry as an undergraduate because he had to major in something and then he went on to do graduate work in the same field because World War II was on in Europe, the draft was beginning—it was 1940—and graduate work in chemistry would look good to the draft board. And it did; he never got into the Army as far as I know. But that was perfectly legitimate; I never got into uniform, either, and I point no fingers."

Avalon, who had been an army officer, looked austere, but said, "Perfectly legitimate."

Drake said, "He wasn't serious about it—about chemistry, I mean. He had no natural aptitude for it and he never worked, particularly. He was satisfied to get no more than a B minus and it was about all he was good for. Nothing wrong with that, I suppose, and it was good enough to sweat out a master's degree for himself—which doesn't amount to much in chemistry. The grades weren't good enough to qualify him for research toward the doctorate, however.

"That was the whole point. We all—the rest of us who were in graduate chemistry that year—assumed he would only go as far as the master's. Then he'd get some sort of job that would keep his draft exemption going; we figured his father would help out there—"

"Were the rest of you jealous of him?" asked Rubin. "Because that kind of guy—"

"We weren't jealous of *him*," said Drake. "Sure, we envied the situation. Hell, those were the days before government grants fell about us like snowflakes. Every college semester, I lived a suspense story called 'Do I Dig Up the Tuition Or Do I Drop Out?' All of us would have liked to be rich. But Lance was a likable guy. He didn't parade the situation and would lend us a few bucks when we were in a hole and do it unostentatiously. And he was perfectly willing to admit he wasn't a brain.

"We even helped him. Gus Blue tutored him in physical organic—for a fee. Of course, he wasn't always scrupulous. There was one preparation he was supposed to have synthesized in lab, and we knew that he bought a sample at a chemical supply house and turned it in as his own. At least, we were pretty sure he did, but it didn't bother us."

Rubin said, "Why not? That was dishonest, wasn't it?"

"Because it wouldn't do him any good," said Drake in

annoyance. "It just meant another B minus at best. But the reason I bring it up is that we all knew he was capable of cheating."

"You mean the rest of you wouldn't have?" interposed Stacey. There was a touch of cynicism in his voice.

Drake lifted his eyebrows, then dropped them again. "I wouldn't guarantee any of us if we were really pushed. The point is, we weren't. We all had a fighting chance to get through without the risk of cheating, and none of us did. As far as I know. Certainly, I didn't.

"But then there came a time when Lance made up his mind to go on for his Ph.D. It was at a smoker. The war jobs were just beginning to open up and there were a few recruiters on campus. It meant money and complete security from the draft, but Ph.D.'s meant a lot to us and there was some question as to whether we'd come back to school once we got away from class for any reason.

"Someone (not I) said he wished he were in Lance's shoes. Lance had no choice to make. He would take the job.

" 'I don't know,' said Lance, maybe just to be contrary. 'I think I'll stay right here and go on for the Ph.D.'

"He may have been joking. I'm sure he was joking. Anyway, we all thought he was, and we laughed. But we were all a little high and it became one of those laughs without reason, you know. If one of us started to die down, he would catch someone else's eyes and start off again. It wasn't that funny. It wasn't funny at all. But we laughed till we were half suffocated. And Lance turned red, and then white.

"I remember I tried to say, 'Lance, we're not laughing at you,' but I couldn't. I was choking and sputtering. And Lance walked out on us.

"After that, he was going for his Ph.D. He wouldn't talk about it but he signed all the necessary forms and that seemed to satisfy him. After a while, the situation was as before. He was friendly.

"I said to him, 'Listen, Lance, you'll be disappointed. You can't get faculty approval for doctoral research with not a single A on your record. You just can't.'

"He said, 'Why not? I've talked to the committee. I told them I'd take chemical kinetics under St. George, and that I'd make an A in that. I said I'd let them see what I could do.'

"That made less than no sense to me. That was funnier than the remark we laughed at. You'd have to know St. George. You ought to know what I mean, Arnold."

Stacey nodded, "He gave a stiff course in kinetics. One or two of the brightest would get an A minus; Bs and Cs otherwise."

Drake shrugged. "There are some professors who take pride in that. It's a kind of professorial version of Captain Bligh. But he was a good chemist; probably the best Berry has ever had. He was the only member of the faculty to achieve national prominence after the war. If Lance could take his course and get a high mark, that would be bound to be impressive. Even with C's in everything else, the argument would be: 'Well, he hasn't worked much because he hasn't had to, but when he finally decided to buckle down, he showed fire-cracking ability.'

"He and I took chemical kinetics together and I was running and sweating and snorting every day of that course. But Lance sat in the seat next to me and never stopped smiling. He took notes carefully, and I know he studied them, because when I found him in the library it was always chemical kinetics he was working on. It went down to the wire like that. St. George didn't give quizzes. He let everything hang on the discussion periods and on the final examination, which lasted three hours—a *full* three hours.

"In the last week of the course, there were no lectures and the students had their last chance to pull themselves together before finals week. Lance was still smiling. His work in the other courses had been usual Lance quality, but that didn't bother him. We would say, 'How are you doing in kinetics, Lance?' and he would say, 'No sweat!' and sound *cheerful*, damn it.

"Then came the day of the finals—" Drake paused, and his lips tightened.

"Well?" said Trumbull.

Drake said, his voice a little lower, "Lance Faron passed. He did more than pass. He got a 96. No one had ever gotten over 90 before in one of St. George's finals. I doubt somehow that anyone ever did afterward."

"I never heard of anyone getting it in recent times," said Stacey.

"What did you get?" asked Gonzalo.

"I got 82," said Drake. "And except for Lance's, it was the best mark in the class. Except for Lance's."

"What happened to the fellow?" asked Avalon.

"He went on for his Ph.D., of course. The faculty qualified him without trouble and the story was that St. George himself went to bat for him.

"I left after that," Drake went on. "I worked on isotope separation during the war and eventually shifted to Wisconsin for my doctoral research. But I would hear about Lance sometimes from old friends. The last I heard he was down in Maryland somewhere, running a private lab of his own. About ten years ago, I remember I looked up his name in *Chemical Abstracts* and found the record of a few papers he turned out. Run of the mill. Typically Lance."

"He's still independently wealthy?" asked Trumbull.

"I suppose so."

Trumbull leaned back. "If that's your story, Jim, then what the hell is biting you?"

Drake looked about the table, first at one and then at another. Then he brought his fist down so that the coffee cups jumped and clattered. "Because he *cheated*, damn his hide. That was not a legitimate final exam and as long as he has his Ph.D., mine is cheapened by that much—and yours, too," he said to Stacey.

Stacey murmured, "Phony doctor."

"What?" said Drake, a little wildly.

"Nothing," said Stacey, "I was just thinking of a colleague who did a stint at a medical school where the students regarded the M.D. as the only legitimate doctor's degree in the universe. To them, a Ph.D. stood for 'phony doctor.' "

Drake snorted.

"Actually," began Rubin, with the typical air of argumentativeness he could put into even a casual connective, "if you—"

Avalon cut in from his impressive height, "Well, see here, Jim, if he cheated, how did he get through?"

"Because there was nothing to show he cheated."

"Did it ever occur to you," said Gonzalo, "that maybe he didn't cheat? Maybe it was really true that when he buckled down, he had fire-cracking ability."

"No," said Drake, with another coffeecup-rattling fist on the table. "That's impossible. He never showed the ability before and he never showed it afterward. Besides he had that *confidence* all through the course. He had the confidence that could only mean he had worked out a foolproof plan to get his A."

Trumbull said heavily, "All right, say he did. He got his Ph.D. but he didn't do so well. From what you say, he's just off in a corner somewhere, poking along. You know damn well, Jim, that lots of guys get through to all kinds of professional positions, even without cheating, who have all their brains in their elbows, and so what. Why get mad at one particular guy, cheating or not? You know why I think you're off your rocker on the subject, Jim? What gripes you is that you don't know how he did it. If you could figure it out, why you'd forget the whole thing."

Henry interrupted, "More brandy for anyone, gentlemen?"

Five delicate little glasses were raised in the air. Avalon, who measured out his allowance with an eye dropper, kept his down.

Drake said, "Well, then, Tom, you tell me. How did he do it? You're the code expert."

"But there's no code involved. I don't know. Maybe he—he—managed to get someone else to do the test for him and handed in someone else's paper."

"In someone else's handwriting?" said Drake scornfully. "Besides, I thought of it. We all thought of it. You don't suppose I was the only one who thought Lance cheated, do you? We all did. When that 96 went up on that bulletin board, after we got our breath back—and that took a while—we demanded to see his paper. He handed it over without trouble and we all went over it. It was a near-perfect job, but it was in his handwriting and with his turns of phrase. I wasn't impressed by the few errors he made. I thought at the time he threw them in just in order not to have a perfect paper."

"All right," said Gonzalo, "someone else did the test and your friend copied it over in his own words."

"Impossible. There was no one in the class but the students and St. George's assistant. The assistant opened the sealed test papers just before the test started. No one could have written a paper for Lance and another for himself, even if you could imagine no one else seeing it done. Besides, there wasn't anyone in the class capable of turning out a 96-level paper."

Avalon said, "If you were doing it right there, it would be impossible. But suppose someone managed to get a copy of the questions well before the test and then swatted away at the textbooks till he worked out perfect answers. Couldn't Lance have done that somehow?"

"No, he couldn't," said Drake flatly. "You're not suggesting anything we didn't think of then, take my word for it. The university had had a cheating scandal ten years before or so and the whole procedure had been tightened up. St. George followed standard procedure. He worked out the questions and turned it in to his secretary the day before the test. She mimeographed the necessary number of copies in St. George's presence. He proofread them, then destroyed the mimeograph and the original. The question papers were packaged and sealed and placed in the school safe. The safe was opened just before the test and the papers handed to St. George's assistant. There was no chance of Lance seeing the questions."

"Maybe not just then," said Avalon. "But even if the professor had the questions mimeographed the day before the test, how long might he have had the questions in his possession? He might have used a set of questions used on a previous—"

"No," interrupted Drake. "We carefully studied all previous

test papers prepared by St. George as a matter of course before the final exam. Do you think we were fools? There were no duplications."

"All right. But even if he prepared an entirely new test, he might have prepared it at the beginning of the semester for all you know. Lance might somehow have seen the questions early in the semester. It would be a lot easier to work out answers to a fixed number of questions in the course of the semester than to try to learn the entire subject matter."

"I think you've got something there, Jeff," said Gonzalo.

"He's got crud there," said Drake, "because that's not the way St. George worked it. Every question in that final exam turned on some particular point that some particular student goofed up on in class. One of them, and the most subtle, covered a point that I had missed in the last week of lectures. I pointed out what I thought was a mistake in a derivation, and St. George—well, never mind. The point is that the tests had to be prepared after the last lectures."

Arnold Stacey broke in, "Did St. George *always* do that? If he did, he would have been handing a hell of a lot to the kids."

"You mean the students would have been waiting for questions covering errors made in the discussion periods?"

"More than that. The students would have deliberately pulled boners on those parts of the subject they actually knew well in order to lure St. George into placing twenty points' worth on it."

Drake said, "I can't answer that. We weren't in his previous classes, so we don't know whether his previous tests followed the same line."

"Previous classes would have passed on the news, wouldn't they? At least if classes in the forties were anything like classes now."

"They would have," admitted Drake, "and they didn't. He did it that way that year, anyway."

"Say, Jim," said Gonzalo, "how did Lance do in the discussion periods?"

"He kept quiet; played it safe. We all took it for granted he'd do that. We weren't surprised."

Gonzalo said, "What about the department secretary? Couldn't Lance have wheedled her into telling him the questions?"

Drake said grimly, "You don't know the secretary. Besides, he couldn't have. He couldn't have suborned the secretary, or broken into the safe, or pulled any trick at all. From the nature of the questions, we could tell the exam had been constructed in the last week before it had been taken, and during that last week he couldn't have done a thing."

"Are you sure?" asked Trumbull.

"Oh, you bet! It bugged us all that he was so confident. The rest of us were sea green with the fear of flunking and he *smiled.* He kept smiling. On the day of the last lecture, someone said, 'He's going to steal the question sheet.' Actually, *I* said it, but the others agreed and we decided to—to—well, we kept an eye on him."

"You mean you never let him out of your sight?" demanded Avalon. "Did you watch at night in shifts? Did you follow him into the John?"

"Damn near. He was Burroughs' roommate and Burroughs was a light sleeper and swore he knew every time Lance turned over."

"Burroughs might have been drugged one night," said Rubin.

"He might have, but he didn't think so, and no one else thought so. Lance just didn't act suspicious in any way; he didn't even act annoyed at being watched."

"Did he know he was being watched?" said Rubin.

"He probably did. Every time he went somewhere he would grin and say, 'Who's coming along?' "

"Where did he go?"

"Just the normal places. He ate, drank, slept, eliminated. He went to the school library to study, or sat in his room. He went to the post office, the bank, a shoestore. We followed him on every errand all up and down Berry's main street. Besides—"

"Besides, what?" said Trumbull.

"Besides, even if he had gotten hold of the question paper, it could only have been in those few days before the test, maybe only the night before. He would have had to sweat out the answers, being Lance. It would have taken him days of solid work over the books. If he could have answered them just by getting a look at them, he wouldn't have had to cheat; he would have gotten a look at them in the opening minutes of the test period."

Rubin said sardonically, "It seems to me, Jim, that you've painted yourself into a corner. Your man couldn't possibly have cheated."

"That's the whole point," cried Drake. "He *must* have cheated and he did it so cleverly no one could catch him. No one could even figure out how. Tom's right. *That's* what gripes me."

And then Henry coughed and said, "If I may offer a word, gentlemen?"

Every face went up as though some invisible puppeteer had pulled the strings.

"Yes, Henry?" said Trumbull.

"It seems to me, gentlemen, that you are too much at home with petty dishonesty to understand it very well."

"Why, Henry, you hurt me cruelly," said Avalon with a smile, but his dark eyebrows curled down over his eyes.

"I mean no disrespect, gentlemen, but Mr. Rubin maintained that dishonesty has value. Mr. Trumbull thinks that Dr. Drake is only annoyed because the cheating was clever enough to escape detection and not because it existed at all, and perhaps all of you agree to that."

Gonzalo said, "I think you're hinting, Henry, that you're so honest that you're more sensitive to dishonesty than we are and can understand it better."

Henry said, "I would almost think so, sir, in view of the fact that not one of you has commented on a glaring improbability in Dr. Drake's story that seems to me to explain everything."

"What's that?" asked Drake.

"Why, Professor St. George's attitude, sir. Here is a professor who takes pride in flunking many of his students, and who never has anyone get above the 80s on the final examination. And then a student who is thoroughly mediocre—and I gather that everyone in the department, both faculty and students, knew of the mediocrity—gets a 96 and the professor accepts that and even backs him before the qualifying committee. Surely he would have been the first to suspect dishonesty. And most indignantly, too."

There was a silence. Stacey looked thoughtful.

Drake said, "Maybe he couldn't admit that he could be cheated *from*, if you know what I mean."

Henry said, "You find excuses, sir. In any situation in which a professor asks questions and a student answers them, one always feels somehow that if there is dishonesty, it is always the student's dishonesty. *Why?* What if it were the professor who were dishonest?"

Drake said, "What would he get out of that?"

"What does one usually get? Money, I suspect, sir. The situation as you described it is that of a student who was quite well off financially, and a professor who had the kind of salary a professor had in those days before the government grants began to come. Suppose the student had offered a few thousand dollars—"

"For what? To hand in a fake mark? We saw Lance's answer paper, and it was legitimate. To let Lance see the questions before having them mimeographed? It wouldn't have done Lance any good."

"Look at it in reverse, sir. Suppose the student had offered those few thousand dollars to let him, the student, show the professor the questions."

Again the invisible puppeteer worked and there was a chorus of "What?"s in various degrees of intonation.

"Suppose, sir," Henry went on patiently, "that it was Mr. Lance Faron who wrote the questions, one by one in the course of the semester, polishing them as he went along. He polished them as the semester proceeded, working hard. As Mr. Avalon said, it is easier to get a few specific points straight than to learn the entire subject matter of a course. He included one question from the last week's lectures, inadvertently making you all sure the test had been created entirely in the last week. It also meant that he turned out a test that was quite different from St. George's usual variety. Previous tests in the course had not turned on students' difficulties. Nor did later ones, if I may judge from Dr. Stacey's surprise. Then at the end of the course, with the test paper completed, he would have mailed it to the professor."

"Mailed it?" said Gonzalo.

"I believe Dr. Drake said the young man visited the post office. He might have mailed it. Professor St. George would have received the questions with, perhaps, part of the payment in reasonably small bills. He would then have written it over in his own handwriting, or typed it, and passed it on to his secretary. From then on all would be normal. And, of course, the professor would have had to back the student thereafter all the way."

"Why not?" said Gonzalo enthusiastically. "Good God, it makes sense."

Drake said slowly, "I've got to admit that's a possibility that never occurred to any of us. . . . But, of course, we'll never know."

Stacey broke in loudly. "I've hardly said a word all evening, though I was told I'd be grilled."

"Sorry about that," said Trumbull. "This meathead, Drake, had a story to tell because you came from Berry."

"Well, then, because I come from Berry, let me add something. Professor St. George died the year I came, as I said, and I didn't know him. But I know many people who did know him and I've heard many stories about him."

"You mean he was known to be dishonest?" asked Drake.

"No one said that. But he was known to be unscrupulous and I've heard some unsavory hints about how he maneuvered government grants into yielding him an income. When I heard your story about Lance, Jim, I must admit I didn't think St. George would be involved in quite that way. But now that Henry has taken the trouble to think the unthinkable from the mountain height of his own honesty—why, I believe he's right."

Trumbull said, "Then that's that. Jim, after thirty years, you can forget the whole thing."

"Except—except"—a half smile came over Drake's face and then he broke into a laugh—"I *am* dishonest because I can't help thinking that if Lance had the questions all along, the bastard might have passed on a hint or two to the rest of us."

"After you had all laughed at him, sir?" asked Henry quietly, as he began to clear the table.

EARLY SUNDAY MORNING

Geoffrey Avalon swirled his second drink as he sat down to the table. It had not yet diminished to the halfway mark and he would take one more sip before abandoning it. He looked unhappy.

He said, "This is the first time within my memory that the Black Widowers have met without a guest." His bushy eyebrows, still black (although his mustache and trim beard had become respectably gray with the years), seemed to twitch.

"Oh, well," said Roger Halsted, flicking his napkin with an audible slap before placing it over his knees. "As host this session, it's my decision. No appeal. Besides, I have my reasons." He placed the palm of his hand on his high forehead and made a motion as though to brush back hair that had disappeared from the forepart of his pate years before.

"Actually," said Emmanuel Rubin, "there's nothing in the bylaws that says we *must* have a guest. The only thing we *must* have present at the dinner is no women."

"The *members* can't be women," said Thomas Trumbull, glowering out of his perpetually tanned face. "Where does it say that a guest can't be a woman?"

"No," said Rubin sharply, his sparse beard quivering. "Any guest is a member *ex officio* for the meal and must abide by all the rules, including not being a woman."

"What does *ex officio* mean, anyway?" asked Mario Gonzalo. "I always wondered."

But Henry was already presenting the first course, which

seemed to be a long roll of pasta, stuffed with spiced cheese, broiled, and sauce-covered.

At last Rubin, looking pained, said, "As near as I can make out this seems to be a roll of pasta, stuffed—"

But by that time, the conversation had grown general and Halsted seized a break to announce that he had his limerick for the third book of the *Iliad.*

Trumbull said, "Damn it to hell, Roger, are you going to inflict one of those on us at every meeting?"

"Yes," said Halsted thoughtfully. "I was planning just that. It keeps me working at it. Besides, you have to have some item of intellectual worth at the dinner. . . . Say, Henry, don't forget that if it's steak tonight, I want mine rare."

"Trout tonight, Mr. Halsted," said Henry, refilling the water glasses.

"Good," said Halsted. "Now here it is:

"Menelaus, though not very mighty,
Was stronger than Paris, the flighty.
Menelaus did well in
The duel over Helen,
But was foiled by divine Aphrodite."

Gonzalo said, "But what does it mean?"

Avalon interposed, "Oh, well, in the third book, the Greeks and Trojans decide to settle the matter by means of a duel between Menelaus and Paris. The latter had eloped with the former's wife, Helen, and that was what caused the war. Menelaus won, but Aphrodite snatched Paris away just in time to save his life. . . . I'm glad you didn't use Venus in place of Aphrodite, Roger. There's too much of the use of Roman analogues."

Halsted, through a full mouth, said, "I wanted to avoid the temptation of obvious rhyming."

"Didn't you ever read the *Iliad*, Mario?" asked James Drake.

"Listen," said Gonzalo, "I'm an artist. I have to save my eyes."

It was with dessert on the table that Halsted said, "Okay, let me explain what I have in mind. The last four times we met, there's been some sort of crime that's come up every discussion, and in the course of that discussion, it's been solved."

"By Henry," interrupted Drake, stubbing out his cigarette.

"All right, by Henry. But what kind of crimes? Rotten crimes. The first time I wasn't here, but I gather the crime was a robbery, and not much of one either, from what I understand. The second time, it was worse. It was a case of cheating on an examination, for heaven's sake."

"That's not such a minor thing," muttered Drake.

"Well, it's not exactly a major thing. The third time—and I was here then—it was theft again, but a better one. And the fourth time it was a case of espionage of some sort."

"Believe me," said Trumbull, "that wasn't minor."

"Yes," said Halsted in his mild voice, "but there was no violence anywhere. Murder, gentlemen, murder!"

"What do you mean, murder?" asked Rubin.

"I mean that every time we bring a guest, something minor turns up because we take it as it comes. We don't deliberately invite guests who can offer us interesting crimes. In fact, they're not even supposed to offer us crimes at all. They're just guests."

"So?"

"So there are now six of us present, no guests, and there must be one of us who knows of some killing that's a mystery and—"

"Hell!" said Rubin in disgust. "You've been reading Agatha Christie. We'll each tell a puzzling mystery in turn and Miss Marple will solve it for us. . . . Or Henry will."

Halsted looked abashed. "You mean they do things like that—"

"Oh, God," said Rubin emotionally.

"Well, you're the writer," said Halsted. "I don't read murder mysteries."

"That's your loss," said Rubin, "and it shows what an idiot you are. You call yourself a mathematician. A proper mystery is as mathematical a puzzle as anything you can prepare and it has to be constructed out of much more intractable material."

"Now wait a while," said Trumbull. "As long as we're here, why don't we see if we can dig up a murder?"

"Can you present one?" said Halsted hopefully. "You're with the government, working on codes or whatever. You must have been involved with murder, and you don't have to name names. You know that nothing gets repeated outside these walls."

"I know that better than you," said Trumbull, "but I don't know about any murders. I can give you some interesting code items but that's not what you're after. . . . How about you, Roger? Since you bring this up, I suppose you have something up your sleeve. Some mathematical murder?"

"No," said Halsted thoughtfully, "I don't think I can recall being involved in a single murder."

"You don't think? You mean there's a doubt in your mind?" asked Avalon.

"I guess I'm certain. How about you, Jeff? You're a lawyer."

"Not the kind that gets murderers for clients," Avalon said, with an apparently regretful shake of his head. "Patent complications are my thing. You might ask Henry. He's more at home with crimes than we are, or he sounds it."

"I'm sorry, sir," said Henry softly as he poured the coffee with practiced skill. "In my case, it is merely theory. I have been fortunate enough never to be involved with violent death."

"You mean," said Halsted, "that with six of us here—seven, counting Henry—we can't scare up a single murder?"

Drake shrugged. "In my game, there's always a good chance of death. I haven't witnessed one in the chem lab personally, but there've been poisonings, explosions, even electrocutions. At worst, though, it's murder through negligence. I can't tell you anything about any of them."

Trumbull said, "How come you're so quiet, Manny? In all your colorful career, you mean you've never had occasion to kill a man?"

"It would be a pleasure sometimes," said Rubin, "like now. But I don't really have to. I can handle them perfectly well at any size without having to lay a hand on them. Listen, I remember—"

But Mario Gonzalo, who had been sitting there with his lips clamped tightly together, suddenly said, "I've been involved in a murder."

"Oh? What kind?" asked Halsted.

"My sister," he said broodingly, "about three years ago. That was before I joined the Black Widowers."

"I'm sorry," said Halsted. "I guess you don't want to talk about it."

"I wouldn't mind talking about it," said Mario, shrugging, his large and prominent eyes looking them all in the face, one by one, "but there's nothing to talk about. No mystery. It's just another one of those things that make this city the fun place it is. They broke into the apartment, tried to loot it, and killed her."

"Who did?" asked Rubin.

"Who knows? Addicts! It happens all the time in that neighborhood. In the apartment house she and her husband lived in, there'd been four burglaries since New Year's and it was only the end of April when it happened."

"Were they all murders?"

"They don't have to be. The smart looter picks a time when the apartment is empty. Or if someone's there, they just scare them or tie them up. Marge was stupid enough to try to resist, to fight back. There were plenty of signs of a struggle." Gonzalo shook his head.

Halsted said, after a painful pause, "Did they ever get the ones who did it?"

Gonzalo's eyes lifted and stared into Halsted's without any attempt at masking the contempt they held. "Do you think they even looked? That sort of thing goes on all day long. Nobody can do anything. Nobody even cares. And if they got them, so what? Would it bring back Marge?"

"It might keep them from doing it to others."

"There'd be plenty of other miserable creeps to do it." Gonzalo drew a deep breath, then said, "Well, maybe I'd *better* talk about it and get it out of my system. It's all my fault, you see, because I wake up too early. If it weren't for that, maybe Marge would be alive and Alex wouldn't be the wreck he is now."

"Who's Alex?" asked Avalon.

"My brother-in-law. He was married to Marge, and I liked him. I think I liked him better than I ever did her, to be truthful. She never approved of me. She thought being an artist was just my way of goofing off. Of course, once I started making a decent living—no, she never really approved of me even then and most of the time she was, meaning no disrespect to the dead, one big pain. She liked Alex, though."

"He wasn't an artist?" Avalon was carrying the burden of the questioning and the others seemed willing to leave it to him.

"No. He wasn't much of anything when they married, just a drifter, but afterward he became exactly what she wanted. She was what he needed to get a little push into him. They needed each other. She had something to care for—"

"No children?"

"No. None. Unless you want to count one miscarriage. Poor Marge. Something biological, so she couldn't have kids. But it didn't matter. Alex was her kid, and he flourished. He got a job the month he was married, got promoted, did well. They were getting to the point where they were planning to move out of that damned death trap, and then it happened. Poor Alex. He was as much to blame as I was. More, in fact. Of all days, he had to leave the house on that one."

"He wasn't in the apartment, then?"

"Of course not. If he was, he might have scared them off."

"Or he might have gotten killed himself."

"In which case they would probably have run off and left Marge alive. Believe me, I've listened to him list the possibilities. No matter how he slices it, she'd still be alive if he hadn't left that day, and it bothers him. And let me tell you, he's gone to pot since it happened. He's just a drifter again now. I give him money when I can and he gets odd jobs now and then. Poor Alex. He had that five years of marriage when he was really making it. He was a go-getter. Now it's all for nothing. Nothing to show for it."

Gonzalo shook his head. "What gets me is that the victim isn't the one who gets the worst of it. It's a senseless murder—hell, everything they got in the apartment amounted to no more than about ten, fifteen dollars in small bills—but at least Marge died quickly. The knife was right in the heart. But Alex suffers every day of his life now, and my mother took it hard. And it bothers me, too."

"Listen," said Halsted, "if you don't want to talk about it—"

"It's all right. . . . I think of it nights sometimes. If I didn't wake up early that day—"

"That's the second time you said that," said Trumbull. "What's your waking up early got to do with it?"

"Because people who know me count on it. Look, I always wake up at eight A.M. sharp. It doesn't vary by as much as five minutes one way or the other. I don't even bother keeping the clock by my bed; it stays in the kitchen. It's got something to do with rhythms in the body."

"The biological clock," muttered Drake. "I wish it worked that way with me. I *hate* getting up in the morning."

"It works with me all the time," said Gonzalo, and even under the circumstances, there was a hint of complacence in his voice as he said so. "Even if I go to sleep late—three in the morning, four—I always wake up at exactly eight. I go back to sleep later in the day if I'm knocked out, but at eight I wake up. Even on Sunday. You'd think I'd have the right to sleep late on Sunday, but even then, damn it, I wake up."

"You mean it happened on a Sunday?" asked Rubin.

Gonzalo nodded. "That's right. I should have been asleep. I should have been the kind of person people would know better than to wake early Sunday morning—but they don't hesitate. They know I'll be awake, even on Sunday."

"Nuts," said Drake, apparently still brooding over his difficulties in the morning. "You're an artist and make your own hours. Why do you have to get up in the morning?"

"Well, I work best then. Besides, I'm time-conscious, too. I don't have to live by the clock, but I like to know what time it is at all times. That clock I have. It's trained, you know. After it happened, after Marge was killed, I wasn't home for three days and it just happened to stop either eight P.M. Sunday or eight A.M. Monday. I don't know. Anyway, when I came back there it was with the hands pointing to eight as though rubbing it in that that was wake-up time."

Gonzalo brooded for a while and no one spoke. Henry passed around the small brandy glasses with no expression on his face, unless you counted the merest tightening of his lips.

Gonzalo finally said, "It's a funny thing but I had a rotten night, that night before, and there was no reason for it. That time of year, end of April, cherry-blossom time, is my favorite. I'm not exactly a landscape artist, but that's the one time I do like to get into the park and make some sketches. And the weather was good. I remember it was a nice mild Saturday, the first really beautiful weekend of the year, and my work was doing pretty well, too.

"I had no reason to feel bad that day, but I got more and more restless. I remember I turned off my little television set just before the eleven-o'clock news. It was as though I felt that I didn't want to hear the news. It was as though I felt there would be bad news. I *remember* that. I didn't make it up afterward, and I'm not a mystic. But I had a premonition. I just did."

Rubin said, "More likely you had a touch of indigestion."

"All right," said Gonzalo, moving his hands as though to take in and welcome the suggestion. "Call it indigestion. All I know is that it was before eleven P.M. and I went into the kitchen and wound the clock—I always wind it at night—and said to myself, 'I can't go to bed *this* early,' but I did.

"Maybe it *was* too early, because I couldn't sleep. I kept tossing and worrying—I don't remember about what. What I should have done was get up, do some work, read a book, watch some late movie—but I just didn't. I just made up my mind to stay in bed."

"Why?" asked Avalon.

"Don't know. It seemed important at the time. God, how I remember that night, because I kept thinking, maybe I'll sleep late because I'm not sleeping now and I knew I wouldn't. I must have dropped off at about four A.M., but at eight I was up and crawled out of bed to get myself breakfast.

"It was another sunny day. Pleasant and cool, but you knew it was going to have all the warmth of spring with none of the heat of summer. Another nice day! You know it hurts me, now and then, that I didn't like Marge better than I did. I mean, we got along all right, but we weren't close. I swear I visited them more to be with Alex than to be with her. And then I got a call."

Halsted said, "You mean a telephone call?"

"Yes. Eight o'clock of a Sunday morning. Who would make a call at that time to anyone unless they knew the jerk always got up at eight. If I had been asleep and had been awakened, and growled into the mouthpiece, the whole thing would have been different."

"Who was it?" asked Drake.

"Alex. He asked if he woke me. He knew he didn't, but he felt guilty calling that early, I suppose. He asked what time it was. I looked at the clock and said, 'It's eight-oh-nine A.M. Of course I'm awake.' I was sort of proud of it, you see.

"And then he asked if he could come over, because he had had an argument with Marge and had stamped out of the house and didn't want to go back till she had cooled down. . . . I tell you, I'm glad I never married.

"Anyway, if I'd only said no. If I'd only told him I'd had a bad night and I needed my sleep and I didn't want company, he'd have gone back to his apartment. He had no place else to go. And then it all wouldn't have happened. But no, big-hearted Mario was so proud of being an early riser that he said, 'Come on over and I'll fix you coffee and eggs,' because I knew Marge wasn't one for early Sunday breakfasts, and I knew Alex hadn't eaten.

"So he was over in ten minutes and by eight-thirty I had the scrambled eggs and bacon in front of him, and Marge was alone in the apartment, waiting for murderers."

Trumbull said, "Did your brother-in-law tell his wife where he was going?"

Gonzalo said, "I don't think so. I assumed he didn't. I figure what happened was he stamped out in a fit of rage without even knowing where he was going himself. Then he thought of me. Even if he knew he was going to visit me, he might not have told her. He would figure: Let her worry."

"All right," said Trumbull, "and then when the junkies came to the door and maybe tried the lock, she figured it was Alex coming back and she opened the door to them. I'll bet the lock wasn't broken."

"No, it wasn't," said Gonzalo.

"Isn't Sunday morning a queer time for junkies to make the rounds?" asked Drake.

"Listen," said Rubin, "they'll do it any time. The craving for drugs knows no season."

"What was the fight about?" asked Avalon suddenly. "I mean, between Alex and Marge?"

"Oh, I don't know. A little thing. Alex had done something at work that must have looked bad and that was one thing that Marge couldn't stand. I don't even know what it was, but whatever it was, it must have been a blow at her pride in him and she was sore.

" 'The trouble was that Alex never learned to just let her run down. When we were kids, I always did that. I would say, 'Yes, Marge; yes, Marge,' and then she'd run down. But Alex would always try to defend himself and then things would just get worse. That time, most of the night was filled with argument. . . . Of course, he says now that if he only hadn't made a federal case out of it, he wouldn't have left, and then none of it would have happened."

" 'The moving finger writes,' " said Avalon. "Brooding on these ifs does no good."

"Sure, but how do you stop, Jeff? Anyway, they had a bad night and I had a bad night. It was as though there were some kind of telepathic communication."

"Oh, bull," said Rubin.

"We were twins," said Gonzalo defensively.

"Only fraternal twins," said Rubin, "unless you're a girl underneath all those clothes."

"So what?"

"So it's only identical twins that are supposed to have this telepathic sympathy, but that's bull, too."

"Anyway," said Gonzalo, "Alex was with me and I ate and he didn't eat much, and he cried on my shoulder about how hard Marge was on him sometimes, and I sympathized and said, 'Listen, why do you pay so much attention to her? She's a good kid if you'll only not take her seriously.' You know all the consoling things people say. I figured in a couple of hours he'd be talked out and he'd go home and make it up and I'd go out to the park or maybe back to bed. Only in a couple of hours the telephone rang again, and it was the police."

"How'd they know where to find Alex?" asked Halsted.

"They didn't. They called *me*. I'm her brother. Alex and I went over and identified her. For a while there, he looked like a dead man. It wasn't just that she was dead. After all, he'd had a fight with her and the neighbors must have heard. Now she was dead, and they always suspect the husband. Of course, they questioned him and he admitted the fight and leaving the apartment and coming to my place—the whole thing."

"It must have sounded phony as hell," said Rubin.

"I corroborated the fact that he was at my place. I said he'd arrived at my place at eight-twenty, maybe eight twenty-five, and had been there since. And the murder had taken place at nine."

"You mean there were witnesses?" asked Drake.

"Hell, no. But there'd been noise. The people underneath heard. The people across the hall heard. Furniture being overturned; a scream. Of course, no one saw anyone; no one saw anything. They sat behind their locked doors. But they heard the noise and it was around nine o'clock. They all agreed to that.

"That settled it as far as the police were concerned. In that neighborhood, if it isn't the spouse, it's some petty thief, probably an addict. Alex and I went out and he got drunk and I stayed with him a couple of days because he was in no condition to be left alone and that's all there is to the story."

Trumbull said, "Do you ever see Alex these days?"

"Once in a while. I lend him a few bucks now and then. Not that I expect to get paid back. He quit his job the week after Marge was killed. I don't think he ever went back to work. He was just a broken man—because he blamed himself, you know. Why did he have to argue with her? Why did he have to leave the house? Why did he have to come over to my place? Anyway, there it is. It's a murder but no mystery."

There was silence for a time, and then Halsted said, "Do you mind, Mario, if we speculate about it, just—just—"

"Just for fun?" said Mario. "Sure, go ahead, have fun. If you have questions, I'll answer as best I can but as far as the murder is concerned, there's nothing to say."

"You see," said Halsted awkwardly, "no one *saw* anybody. It's only an assumption that some nameless addicts came in and killed her. Someone might have killed her with a better reason, knowing that it would be blamed on addicts and he'd be safe. Or she, maybe."

"Who's the someone?" said Mario skeptically.

"Didn't she have any enemies? Did she have money that somebody wanted?" said Halsted.

"Money? What there was was in the bank. It all went to Alex, of course. It was his to begin with; everything was joint."

"How about jealousy?" said Avalon. "Maybe she was having an affair. Or he was. Maybe that's what the argument was about."

"And he killed her?" said Gonzalo. "The fact is he was in my apartment at the time she was killed."

"Not necessarily he. Suppose it was her boyfriend, or his girl friend. The boyfriend, because she was threatening to break off the affair. The girlfriend, because she wanted to marry your brother-in-law."

Mario shook his head. "Marge was no femme fatale. I was always surprised she made it with Alex. For that matter, maybe she didn't."

"Did Alex complain about that?" asked Trumbull with sudden interest.

"No, but then he's no great lover, either. Listen, he's been a widower for three years now and I'm willing to swear he has no girl of any kind. No boy, either, before you start talking about that."

Rubin said, "Hold it, you still don't know what the argument was really about. You said it was something that happened at work. Did he actually tell you what it was and you've just forgotten; or did he never tell you?"

"He didn't go into detail, and I didn't ask. It wasn't my business."

"All right," said Rubin, "how about this? It was an argument about something big at work. Maybe Alex had stolen fifty thousand dollars and Marge was sore about it, and that was the argument. Or Marge had made him steal it and he was getting cold feet about it and that was the argument. And maybe the fifty thousand was in the house and someone knew about it and that someone killed her and took it and Alex doesn't dare mention it."

"What someone?" demanded Gonzalo. "What theft? Alex wasn't that kind of guy."

"Famous last words," intoned Drake.

"Well, he wasn't. And if he had done it, the firm he worked for wouldn't have kept quiet. No chance."

Trumbull said, "How about the kind of in-fighting that goes on in apartment houses? You know, feuds between tenants. Was there someone who hated her and finally let her have it?"

"Hell, if there were anything that serious, I'd know about it. Marge never kept things like that quiet."

Drake said, "Could it be suicide? After all, her husband had just walked out on her. Maybe he said he was never coming back and she was in despair. In a fit of irrational depression, she killed herself."

"It was a knife from the kitchen," said Gonzalo. "There's that. But Marge isn't the suicidal type. She might kill someone else, but not herself. Besides, why would there be that struggle and the scream if she had killed herself?"

Drake said, "In the first place, things might have been knocked about during the argument with her husband. In the second place, she might have faked a murder to get her husband into trouble. Vengeance is mine, saith the aggrieved wife."

"Oh, come on," said Gonzalo contemptuously. "Marge wouldn't do something like that in a million years."

"You know," said Drake, "you don't really know all that much about another person—even if she's a twin."

"Well, you won't get me to believe it."

Trumbull said, "I don't know why we're wasting our time. Why don't we ask the expert? . . . Henry?"

Henry, whose face mirrored only polite interest, said, "Yes, Mr. Trumbull?"

"How about telling us all about it? Who killed Mr. Gonzalo's sister?"

Henry's eyebrows lifted slightly. "I do not represent myself to be an expert, Mr. Trumbull, but I must say that all the suggestions made by the gentlemen at the table, including yours, are unlikely in the extreme. I myself think that the police are perfectly correct and that if, in this case, the husband did not do it, then housebreakers did. And these days, one must assume that those housebreakers were drug addicts desperate for money or for something they can convert into money."

"You disappoint me, Henry," said Trumbull.

Henry smiled gently.

"Well, then," said Halsted, "I guess we'd better adjourn after we settle who hosts next time, and I suppose we'd better go back to having guests. This scheme of mine didn't work out so well."

"Sorry I couldn't make it better, folks," said Gonzalo.

"I didn't mean it that way, Mario," said Halsted hastily.

"I know. Well, let's forget it."

They were leaving, with Mario Gonzalo bringing up the rear. A light tap at his shoulder caused Gonzalo to turn.

Henry said, "Mr. Gonzalo, could I see you privately, without the others knowing? It's quite important."

Gonzalo stared a moment and said, "Okay, I'll go out, say my good-byes, take a taxi, and have it bring me back." He was back in ten minutes.

"Is this something about my sister, Henry?"

"I'm afraid so, sir. I thought I had better talk to you, privately."

"All right. Let's go back into the chamber. It's empty now."

"Better not, sir. Anything said in that room can't be repeated outside and I do not wish to talk in confidence. I don't mind finding myself hushed up about average run-of-the-mill misdeeds, but murder is another thing altogether. There's a corner here that we can use."

They went together to the indicated place. It was late and the restaurant was virtually empty.

Henry said, in a low voice, "I listened to the account and I would like your permission to repeat some of it just to make sure I have it right."

"Sure, go ahead."

"As I understand it, on a Saturday toward the end of April, you felt uneasy and went to bed before the eleven-o'clock news."

"Yes, just before eleven o'clock."

"And you didn't hear the news."

"Not even the opening headlines."

"And that night, even though you didn't sleep, you didn't get out of bed. You didn't go to the bathroom or the kitchen."

"No, I didn't."

"And then you woke up at exactly the same time you always do."

"That's right."

"Well, now, Mr. Gonzalo, that is what disturbs me. A person who wakes up every morning at exactly the same time, thanks to some sort of biological clock inside him, wakes up at the wrong time twice a year."

"What?"

"Twice a year, sir, in this state, ordinary clocks are shifted, once when Daylight Saving Time starts, and once when it ends, but biological time doesn't change suddenly. Mr. Gonzalo, on the last Sunday in April, Daylight Saving Time starts. At one A.M. Sunday morning the clocks are shifted to two A.M. If you had listened to the eleven-o'clock news you would have been reminded to do that. But you wound your clock before eleven P.M. and you said nothing about adjusting it. Then you went to bed and never touched it during the night. When you woke at eight A.M., the clock should have said *nine* A.M. Am I right?"

"Good Lord," said Gonzalo.

"You left after the police called and you didn't come back for days. When you came back the clock was stopped, of course. You had no way of knowing that it was an hour slow when it had stopped. You set it to the correct time and never knew the difference."

"I never thought of that, but you're perfectly right."

"The police should have thought of that, but it's so easy these days to dismiss run-of-the-mill crimes of violence as the work of addicts. You gave your brother-in-law his alibi and they followed the line of least resistance."

"You mean he—"

"It's possible, sir. They fought, and he killed her at nine A.M. as the statements of the neighbors indicated. I doubt that it was premeditated. Then, in desperation, he thought of you—and rather clever of him it was. He called you and asked you what time it was. You said eight-oh-nine and he knew you hadn't altered the clock and rushed over to your place. If you had said nine-oh-nine, he would have tried to get out of town."

"But, Henry, why should he have done it?"

"It's hard to tell with married couples, sir. Your sister may have had too high standards. You said she disapproved of your way of life, for instance, and probably made that very plain, plain enough to cause you not to like her very well. Now she must have disapproved of her husband's way of life, as it was before she had married him. He was a drifter, you said. She made of him a respectable, hard-working employee and he may not have liked it. After he finally exploded and killed her, he became a drifter again. You think this is so out of despair; he may have nothing more than the feeling of relief."

"Well . . . What do we do?"

"I don't know, sir. It would be a hard thing to prove. Could you really remember, after three years, that you didn't adjust the clock? A cross-examining attorney would tear you apart. On the other hand, your brother-in-law might break down if faced with it. You'll have to consider whether you wish to go to the police, sir."

"I?" said Gonzalo hesitantly.

"It was your sister, sir," said Henry softly.

THE OBVIOUS FACTOR

Thomas Trumbull looked about the table and said, with some satisfaction, "Well, at least you won't get yourself pen-and-inked into oblivion, Voss. Our resident artist isn't here. . . . *Henry!*"

Henry was at Trumbull's elbow before the echo of the bellow had died, with no sign of perturbation on his bright-eyed and unlined face. Trumbull took the scotch and soda the waiter had on his tray and said, "Has Mario called, Henry?"

"No, sir," said Henry calmly.

Geoffrey Avalon had reduced his second drink to the halfway point and swirled it absently. "After last month's tale about his murdered sister, it could be that he didn't—"

He did not complete the sentence, but put down his glass carefully at the seat he intended to take. The monthly banquet of the Black Widowers was about to begin.

Trumbull, who was host, took the armchair at the head of the table and said, "Have you got them all straight, Voss? At my left is James Drake. He's a chemist and knows more about pulp fiction than about chemistry, and that probably isn't much. Then Geoffrey Avalon, a lawyer who never sees the inside of a courtroom; Emmanuel Rubin, who writes in between talking, which is practically never; and Roger Halsted. . . . Roger, you're not inflicting another limerick on us this session, are you?"

"A limerick?" said Trumbull's guest, speaking for the first time. It was a pleasant voice, light and yet rich, with all consonants carefully pronounced. He had a white beard, evenly cut from temple to temple, and white hair, too. His youthful face shone pinkly within its fence of white. "A poet, then?"

"A poet?" snorted Trumbull. "Not even a mathematician, which is what he claims to be. He insists on writing a limerick for every book of the *Iliad*."

"And *Odyssey*," said Halsted, in his soft, hurried voice. "But, yes, I have my limerick."

"Good! It's out of order," said Trumbull. "You are not to read it. Host's privilege."

"Oh, for heaven's sake," said Avalon, the flat lines of his well-preserved face set in disappointment. "Let him recite the poor thing. It takes thirty seconds and I find it fun."

Trumbull pretended not to hear. "You've all got it straight about my guest now? He's Dr. Voss Eldridge. He's a Ph.D. So is Drake, Voss. We're all doctors, though, by virtue of membership in the Black Widowers." He then raised his glass, gave the monthly invocation to Old King Cole, and the meal was officially begun.

Halsted, who had been whispering to Drake, passed a paper to him. Drake rose and declaimed:

"Next a Lycian attempted a ruse
With an arrow—permitted by Zeus.
Who will trust Trojan candor, as
This sly deed of Pandarus
Puts an end to the scarce-proclaimed truce?"

"Damn it," said Trumbull. "I ruled against reading it."

"Against *my* reading it," said Halsted. "Drake read it."

"It's disappointing not to have Mario here," said Avalon. "He would ask what it means."

"Go ahead, Jeff," said Rubin. "I'll pretend I don't understand it and you explain."

But Avalon maintained a dignified silence while Henry presented the appetizer and Rubin fixed it with his usual suspicious stare.

"I hate stuff," he said, "that's so chopped up and drowned in goop that you can't see what the ingredients are."

Henry said, "I think you'll find it quite wholesome."

"Try it; you'll like it," said Avalon.

Rubin tried it, but his face showed no signs of liking it. It was noted later, however, that he had finished it.

Dr. Eldridge said, "Is there a necessity of explaining these limericks, Dr. Avalon? Are there tricks to them?"

"No, not at all, and don't bother with the doctorate. That's only for formal occasions, though it's good of you to humor the club idiosyncrasy. It's just that Mario has never read the *Iliad*; few have, these days."

"Pandarus, as I recall, was a go-between and gives us the word 'pander.' That, I take it, was the sly deed mentioned in the limerick."

"Oh, no, no," said Avalon, unsuccessfully hiding his delight. "You're thinking now of the medieval Troilus tale, which Shakespeare drew on for his *Troilus and Cressida.* Pandarus was the go-between there. In the *Iliad* he was merely a Lycian archer who shot at Menelaus during a truce. That was the sly deed. He is killed in the next book by the Greek warrior Diomedes."

"Ah," said Eldridge, smiling faintly, "it's easy to be fooled, isn't it?"

"If you want to be," said Rubin, but he smiled as the London broil arrived. There was no mistaking the nature of the components there. He buttered a roll and ate it as though to give himself time to contemplate the beauty of the meat.

"As a matter of fact," said Halsted, "we've solved quite a few puzzles in recent meetings. We did well."

"We did lousy," said Trumbull. "Henry is the one who did well."

"I *include* Henry when I say 'we,' " said Halsted, his fair face flushing.

"Henry?" asked Eldridge.

"Our esteemed waiter," said Trumbull, "and honorary member of the Black Widowers."

Henry, who was filling the water glasses, said, "You honor me, sir."

"Honor, hell. I wouldn't come to any meeting if you weren't taking care of the table, Henry."

"Its good of you to say so, sir."

Eldridge remained thoughtfully quiet thereafter, as he followed the tide of conversation that, as was usual, grew steadily in intensity. Drake was making some obscure distinction between Secret Agent X and Operator 5, and Rubin, for some reason known only to himself, was disputing the point.

Drake, whose slightly hoarse voice never rose, said, "Operator 5 may have used disguises. I won't deny that. It was Secret Agent X, however, who was 'the man of a thousand faces.' I can send you a photocopy of a contents page of a magazine from my library to prove it." He made a note to himself in his memo book.

Rubin, scenting defeat, shifted ground at once. "There's no such thing as a disguise, anyway. There are a million things no one can disguise, idiosyncrasies of stance, walk, voice; a million habits you can't change because you don't even know you have them. A disguise works only because no one *looks*."

"People fool themselves, in other words," said Eldridge, breaking in.

"Absolutely," said Rubin. "People *want* to be fooled."

The ice-cream parfait was brought in, and not long after that, Trumbull struck his water glass with his spoon.

"Inquisition time," he said. "As Grand Inquisitor I pass, since I'm the host. Manny, will you do the honors?"

Rubin said, at once, "Dr. Eldridge, how do you justify the fact of your existence?"

"By the fact that I labor to distinguish truth from folly."

"Do you consider that you succeed in doing so?"

"Not as often as I wish, perhaps. And yet as often as most. To distinguish truth from folly is a common desire; we all try our hands at it. My interpretation of Pandarus' deed in Halsted's limerick was folly and Avalon corrected me. The common notion of disguise you claimed to be folly and you corrected it. When I find folly, I try to correct it, if I can. It's not always easy."

"What is your form of folly correction, Eldridge? How would you describe your profession?"

"I am," said Eldridge, "Associate Professor of Abnormal Psychology."

"Where do you? . . . " began Rubin.

Avalon interrupted, his deep voice dominating, "Sorry, Manny, but I smell an evasion. You asked Dr. Eldridge's profession and he gave you a title . . . What do you do Dr. Eldridge, to occupy your time most significantly?"

"I investigate parapsychological phenomena," said Eldridge.

"Oh, God," muttered Drake, and stubbed out his cigarette.

Eldridge said, "You disapprove of that, sir?" There was no sign of annoyance on his face. He turned to Henry and said, "No, thank you, Henry, I've had enough coffee," with perfect calmness.

Henry passed on to Rubin, who was holding his cup in the air as a signal of its emptiness.

"It's not a question of approval or disapproval," said Drake. "I think you're wasting your time."

"In what way?"

"You investigate telepathy, precognition, things like that?"

"Yes. And ghosts and spiritual phenomena, too."

"All right. Have you ever come across something you couldn't explain?"

"Explain in what way? I could explain a ghost by saying, 'Yes, that's a ghost.' I take it that's not what you mean."

Rubin broke in. "I hate to be on Drake's side right now, but he means to ask, as you well know, whether you have ever come across any phenomenon you could not explain by the accepted and prosaic laws of science."

"I have come across many such phenomena."

"That you could not explain?" asked Halsted.

"That I could not explain. There's not a month that passes but that something crosses my desk that I cannot explain," said Eldridge, nodding his head gently.

There was a short silence of palpable disapproval and then Avalon said, "Does that mean that you are a believer in these psychic phenomena?"

"If you mean: Do I think that events take place that violate the laws of physics? No! Do I think, however, that I know all there is to know about the laws of physics? Also, no. Do I think anyone knows all there is to know about the laws of physics? No, a third time."

"That's evasion," said Drake. "Do you have any evidence that telepathy exists, for instance, and that the laws of physics, as presently accepted, will have to be modified accordingly?"

"I am not ready to commit myself that far. I well know that in even the most circumstantial stories, there are honest mistakes, exaggerations, misinterpretations, outright hoaxes. And yet, even allowing for all that, I come across incidents I cannot quite bring myself to dismiss."

Eldridge shook his head and continued, "It's not easy, this job of mine. There are some incidents for which no conceivable run-of-the-mill explanation seems possible; where the evidence for something quite apart from the known rules by which the universe seems to run appears irrefutable. It would seem I *must* accept—and yet I hesitate. Can I labor under a hoax so cleverly manipulated, or an error so cleverly hidden, that I take for the gold of fact what is only the brass of nonsense? I can be fooled, as Rubin would point out."

Trumbull said, "Manny would say that you *want* to be fooled."

"Maybe I do. We all want dramatic things to be true. We want to be able to wish on a star, to have strange powers, to be irresistible to women—and would inwardly conspire to believe such things no matter how much we might lay claim to complete rationality."

"Not me," said Rubin flatly. "I've never kidded myself in my life."

"No?" Eldridge looked at him thoughtfully. "I take it then that you will refuse to believe in the actual existence of parapsychological phenomena under all circumstances?"

"I wouldn't say that," said Rubin, "but I'd need damned good evidence—better evidence than I've ever seen advanced."

"And how about the rest of you gentlemen?"

Drake said, "We're all rationalists. At least I don't know about Mario Gonzalo, but he's not here this session."

"You, too, Tom?"

Trumbull's lined face broke into a grim smile. "You've never convinced me with any of your tales before this, Voss. I don't think you can convince me now."

"I never told you tales that convinced *me*, Tom. . . . But I have one now; something I've never told you and that no one really knows about outside my department. I can tell it to you all and if you can come up with an explanation that would require no change in the fundamental scientific view of the universe, I would be greatly relieved."

"A ghost story?" said Halsted.

"No, not a ghost story," said Eldridge. "It is merely a story that defies the principle of cause and effect, the very foundation stone on which all science is built. To put it another way, it defies the concept of the irreversible forward flow of time."

"Actually," said Rubin, at once, "it's quite possible, on the subatomic level, to consider time as flowing either—"

"Shut up, Manny," said Trumbull, "and let Voss talk."

Quietly, Henry had placed the brandy before each of the diners. Eldridge lifted his small glass absently and sniffed at it, then nodded to Henry, who returned a small, urbane smile.

"It's an odd thing," said Eldridge, "but so many of those who claim to have strange powers, or have it claimed for them, are young women of no particular education, no particular presence, no particular intelligence. It is as though the existence of a special talent has consumed what would otherwise be spread out among the more usual facets of the personality. Maybe it's just more noticeable in women.

"At any rate, I am speaking of someone I'll just call Mary for now. You understand I'm not using her real name. The woman is still under investigation and it would be fatal, from my point of view, to get any kind of pubicity hounds on the track. You understand?"

Trumbull frowned severely. "Come on, Voss, you know I told you that nothing said here is ever repeated outside the confines of these walls. You needn't feel constrained."

"Accidents happen," said Eldridge equably. "At any rate, I'll return to Mary. Mary never completed grade school and has earned what money she could earn by serving behind a counter at the five-and-ten. She is not attractive and no one will sweep her away from the counter, which may be good, for she is useful there and serves well. You might not think so, since she cannot add correctly and is given to incapacitating headaches, during which she will sit in a back room and upset the other employees by muttering gibberish to herself in a baleful sort of way. Nevertheless, the store wouldn't dream of letting her go."

"Why not?" asked Rubin, clearly steeling himself to skepticism at every point.

"Because she spots shoplifters, who, as you know, can these days bleed a store to death through a thousand small cuts. It isn't that Mary is in any way shrewd or keen-eyed or unrelenting in pursuit. She just knows a shoplifter when he or she enters the store, even if she has never seen the person before, and even if she doesn't actually see the person come in.

"She followed them herself at first for brief intervals; then grew hysterical and began her muttering. The manager eventually tied the two things together—Mary's characteristic behavior and the shoplifting. He started to watch for one, then the other, and it didn't take long for him to find out that she never missed.

"Losses quickly dropped to virtually nothing in that particular five-and-ten despite the fact that the store is in a bad neighborhood. The manager, of course, received the credit. Probably, he deliberately kept the truth from being known lest anyone try to steal Mary from him.

"But then I think he grew afraid of it. Mary fingered a shoplifter who wasn't a shoplifter but who later was mixed up in a shooting incident. The manager had read about some of the work my department does, and he came to us. Eventually, he brought Mary to us.

"We got her to come to the college regularly. We paid her, of course. Not much, but then she didn't ask for much. She was an unpleasant not-bright girl of about twenty, who was reluctant to talk and describe what went on in her mind. I suppose she had spent a childhood having her queer notions beaten out of her and she had learned to be cautious, you see."

Drake said, "You're telling us she had a gift for precognition?"

Eldridge said, "Since precognition is just Latin for seeing-things-before-they-happen, and since she sees things before they happen, how else can I describe it? She sees unpleasant things only, things that upset or frighten her, which, I imagine, makes her life a hell. It is the quality of becoming upset or frightened that breaks down the time barrier."

Halsted said, "Let's set our boundary conditions. What does she sense? How far ahead in time does she see things? How far away in space?"

"We could never get her to do much for us," said Eldridge. "Her talent wasn't on tap at will and with us she could never relax. From what the manager told us and from what we could pick up, it seemed she could never detect anything more than a few minutes ahead in time. Half an hour to an hour at the most."

Rubin snorted.

"A few minutes," said Eldridge mildly, "is as good as a century. The principle stands. Cause and effect is violated and the flow of time is reversed.

"And in space, there seemed no limits. As she described it, when I could get her to say anything at all, and as I interpreted her rather clumsy and incoherent words, the background of her mind is a constant flickering of frightening shapes. Every once in a while, this is lit up, as though by a momentary lightning flash, and she sees, or becomes aware. She sees most clearly what is close by or what she is most concerned about—the shoplifting, for instance. Occasionally, though, she sees what must be taking place farther away. The greater the disaster, the farther she can sense things. I suspect she could detect a nuclear bomb getting ready to explode anywhere in the world."

Rubin said, "I imagine she speaks incoherently and you fill in the rest. History is full of ecstatic prophets whose mumbles are interpreted into wisdom."

"I agree," said Eldridge, "and I pay no attention—or at least not much—to anything that isn't clear. I don't even attach much importance to her feats with shoplifters. She might be sensitive enough to detect some characteristic way in which shoplifters look and stand, some aura, some *smell*—the sort of thing you talked about, Rubin, as matters no one can disguise. But then—"

"Then?" prompted Halsted.

"Just a minute," said Eldridge. "Uh—Henry, could I have a refill in the coffee cup after all?"

"Certainly," said Henry.

Eldridge watched the coffee level rise. "What's *your* attitude on psychic phenomena, Henry?"

Henry said, "I have no general attitude, sir. I accept whatever it seems to me I must accept."

"Good!" said Eldridge. "I'll rely on you and not on these prejudiced and preconcepted rationalists here."

"Go on, then," said Drake. "You paused at the dramatic moment to throw us off."

"Never," said Eldridge. "I was saying that I did not take Mary seriously, until one day she suddenly began to squirm and pant and mumble under her breath. She does that now and then, but this time she muttered 'Eldridge. Eldridge.' And the word grew shriller and shriller.

"I assumed she was calling me, but she wasn't. When I responded, she ignored me. Over and over again, it was 'Eldridge! Eldridge!' Then she began to scream, 'Fire! Oh, Lord! It's burning! Help! Eldridge! Eldridge!' Over and over again, with all kinds of variations. She kept it up for half an hour.

"We tried to make sense out of it. We spoke quietly, of course, because we didn't want to intrude more than we had to, but we kept saying, 'Where? Where?' Incoherently enough, and in scraps, she told us enough to make us guess it was San Francisco, which, I need not tell you, is nearly three thousand miles away. There's only one Golden Gate Bridge after all, and in one spasm, she gasped out, 'Golden Gate,' over and over. Afterward it turned out she had never heard of the Golden Gate Bridge and was quite shaky as to San Francisco.

"When we put it all together, we decided that there was an old apartment house somewhere in San Francisco, possibly within eyeshot of the Bridge, that had gone up in fire. A total of twenty-three people were in it at the time it burst into fire, and of these, five did not escape. The five deaths included that of a child."

Halsted said, "And then you checked and found there *was* a fire in San Francicso and that five people had died, including a child."

"That's right," said Eldridge. "But here's what got me. One of the five deaths was that of a woman, Sophronia Latimer. She had gotten out safely and then discovered that her eight-year-old boy had not come out with her. She ran wildly back into the house, screaming for the boy, and never came out again. The boy's name was Eldridge, so you can see what she was shouting in the minutes before her death.

"Eldridge is a very uncommon first name, as I need not tell you, and my feeling is that Mary captured that particular event, for all that it was so far away, entirely because she had been sensitized to the name, by way of myself, and because it was surrounded by such agony."

Rubin said, "You want an explanation, is that it?"

"Of course," said Eldridge. "How did this ignorant girl see a fire in full detail, get all the facts correct—and believe me, we checked it out—at three thousand miles."

Rubin said, "What makes the three-thousand-mile distance so

impressive? These days it means nothing; it's one sixtieth of a second at the speed of light. I suggest that she heard the tale of the fire on radio or on television—more likely the latter—and passed it on to you. That's why she chose that story; because of the name Eldridge. She figured it would have the greatest possible effect on you."

"Why?" asked Eldridge. "Why should she put through such a hoax?"

"Why?" Rubin's voice faded out momentarily, as though with astonishment, then came back in a shout. "Good God, you've been working with these people for years and don't realize how much they *want* to hoax you. Don't you suppose there's a feeling of power that comes with perpetrating a good hoax; and money, too, don't forget."

Eldridge thought about it, then shook his head. "She doesn't have the brains to put something like this across. It takes brains to be a faker—a good one, anyway."

Trumbull broke in. "Well, now, Voss. There's no reason to suppose she's in it on her own. A confederate is possible. She supplies the hysteria, he supplies the brains."

"Who might the confederate be?" asked Eldridge softly.

Trumbull shrugged. "I don't know."

Avalon cleared his throat and said, "I go along with Tom here, and my guess is that the confederate is the manager of the five-and-ten. He had noted her ability to guess at shoplifters, and thought he could put this to use in something more splashy. I'll bet that's it. He heard about the fire on television, caught the name Eldridge, and coached her."

"How long would it take to coach her?" asked Eldridge. "I keep telling you that she's not very bright."

"The coaching wouldn't be difficult," said Rubin quickly. "You say she was incoherent. He would just tell her a few key words: Eldridge, fire, Golden Gate, and so on. She then keeps repeating them in random arrangements and you intelligent parapsychologists fill it in."

Eldridge nodded, then said, "That's interesting, except that there was no time at all to coach the girl. That's what precognition is all about. We know exactly what time she had her fit and we know exactly what time the fire broke out in San Francisco. It so happens the fire broke out at just about the minute that Mary's fit died down. It was as though once the fire was actual, it was no longer a matter of precognition, and Mary lost contact. So you see, there could be no coaching. The news didn't hit the network TV news programs till that evening. That's when *we* found out and began our investigation in depth."

"But wait," said Halsted. "What about the time difference? There's a three-hour time difference between New York and San Francisco, and a confederate in San Francisco—"

"A confederate in San Francisco?" said Eldridge, opening his eyes wide, and staring. "Are you imagining a continental conspiracy? Besides, believe me, I know about the time difference also. When I say that the fire started just as Mary finished, I mean allowing for the time difference. Mary's fit started at just about one-fifteen P.M. Eastern Standard Time, and the fire in San Francisco started at just about ten forty-five A.M. Pacific Standard Time."

Drake said, "I have a suggestion."

"Go on," said Eldridge.

"This is an uneducated and unintelligent girl—you keep saying that over and over—and she's throwing a fit, an epileptic fit, for all I know."

"No," said Eldridge firmly.

"All right, a prophetic fit, if you wish. She's muttering and mumbling and screaming and doing everything in the world but speaking clearly. She makes sound which *you* interpret, and which you make fit together. If it had occurred to you to hear her say something like 'atom bomb,' then the word you interpreted as 'Eldridge' would have become 'Oak Ridge,' for instance."

"And Golden Gate?"

"You might have heard that as 'couldn't get' and fitted it in somehow."

"Not bad," said Eldridge. "Except that we know that it is hard to understand some of these ecstatics and we are bright enough to make use of modern technology. We routinely tape-record our sessions and we tape-recorded this one. We've listened to it over and over and there is no question but that she said 'Eldridge' and not 'Oak Ridge,' 'Golden Gate' and not 'couldn't get.' We've had different people listen and there is no disagreement on any of this. Besides, from what we heard, we worked out all the details of the fire before we got the facts. We had to make no modifications afterward. It all fit exactly."

There was a long silence at the table.

Finally Eldridge said, "Well, there it is. Mary foresaw the fire three thousand miles away by a full half-hour and got all the facts correct."

Drake said uneasily, "Do *you* accept it? Do *you* think it was precognition?"

"I'm trying not to," said Eldridge. "But for what reason can I disbelieve it? I don't want to fool myself into believing it, but what choice have I? At what point am I fooling myself? If it wasn't precognition, what was it? I had hoped that perhaps one of you gentlemen could tell me."

Again a silence.

Eldridge went on. "I'm left in a position where I must refer to Sherlock Holmes's great precept: 'When the impossible has been eliminated, then whatever remains, however improbable, is the truth.' In this case, if fakery of any kind is impossible, the precognition must be the truth. Don't you all agree?"

The silence was thicker than before, until Trumbull cried out, "Damn it all, Henry is grinning. No one's asked *him* yet to explain this. Well, Henry?"

Henry coughed. "I should not have smiled, gentlemen, but I couldn't help it when Professor Eldridge used that quotation. It seems the final bit of evidence that you gentlemen *want* to believe."

"The hell we do," said Rubin, frowning.

"Surely, then, a quotation from President Thomas Jefferson would have sprung to mind."

"What quotation?" asked Halsted.

"I imagine Mr. Rubin knows," said Henry.

"I probably do, Henry, but at the moment I can't think of an appropriate one. Is it in the Declaration of Independence?"

"No, sir," began Henry, when Trumbull interrupted with a snarl.

"Let's not play Twenty Questions, Manny. Go on, Henry, what are you getting at?"

"Well, sir, to say that when the impossible has been eliminated, whatever remains, however improbable, is the truth, is to make the assumption, usually unjustified, that everything that is to be considered has indeed been considered. Let us suppose we have considered ten factors. Nine are clearly impossible. Is the tenth, however improbable, therefore true? What if there were an eleventh factor, and a twelfth, and a thirteenth . . ."

Avalon said severely, "You mean there's a factor we haven't considered?"

"I'm afraid so, sir," said Henry, nodding.

Avalon shook his head. "I can't think what it can be."

"And yet it is an obvious factor, sir; the *most* obvious one."

"What is it, then?" demanded Halsted, clearly annoyed. "Get to the point!"

"To begin with," said Henry, "it is clear that to explain the ability of the young lady to foretell, as described, the details of a fire three thousand miles away except by precognition is impossible. But suppose precognition is also to be considered impossible. In that case—"

Rubin got to his feet, straggly beard bristling, eyes magnified through thick-lensed glasses, staring. "Of course! The fire was *set*. The woman could have been coached for weeks. The accomplice goes to San Francicso and they coordinate. She predicts something she *knows* is going to happen. He causes something he *knows* she will predict."

Henry said, "Are you suggesting, sir, that a confederate would deliberately plan to kill five victims, including an eight-year-old boy?"

"Don't start trusting in the virtue of mankind, Henry," said Rubin. "You're the one who is sensitive to wrongdoing."

"The minor wrongdoings, sir, the kind most people overlook. I find it difficult to believe that anyone, in order to establish a fancied case of precognition, would deliberately arrange a horrible multimurder. Besides, to arrange a fire in which eighteen of twenty-three people escape and five specific people die requires a bit of precognition in itself."

Rubin turned stubborn. "I can see ways in which five people can be trapped; like forcing a card in conjuring—"

"Gentlemen!" said Eldridge peremptorily, and all turned to look at him. "I have not told you the cause of the fire."

He went on, after looking about the table to make sure he had the attention of all, "It was a stroke of lightning. I don't see how a stroke of lightning could be arranged at a specified time." He spread out his hands helplessly. "I tell you. I've been struggling with this for weeks. I don't want to accept precognition, but . . . I suppose this spoils your theory, Henry?"

"On the contrary, Professor Eldridge, it confirms it and makes it certain. Ever since you began to tell us this tale of Mary and the fire, your every word has made it more and more certain that fakery is impossible and that precognition has taken place. If, however, precognition is impossible, then it follows of necessity, Professor, that you have been lying."

Not a Black Widower but exclaimed at that, with Avalon's shocked "Henry!" loudest of all.

But Eldridge was leaning back in his chair, chuckling. "Of course I was lying. From beginning to end. I wanted to see if all you so-called rationalists would be so eager to accept parapsychological phenomena that you would overlook the obvious rather than spoil your own thrill. When did you catch me out, Henry?"

"It was a possibility from the start, sir, which grew stronger each time you eliminated a solution by inventing more information. I was certain when you mentioned the lightning. That was dramatic enough to have been brought in at the beginning. To be mentioned only at the very end made it clear that you created it on the spot to block the final hope."

"But why was it a possibility from the start, Henry?" demanded Eldridge. "Do I *look* like a liar? Can you detect liars the way I had Mary detect shoplifters?"

"Because this is *always* a possibility and something to be kept in mind and watched for. That is where the remark by President Jefferson comes in."

"What was that?"

"In 1807, Professor Benjamin Silliman of Yale reported seeing the fall of a meteorite at a time when the existence of meteorites was not accepted by scientists. Thomas Jefferson, a rationalist of enormous talent and intelligence, on hearing the report, said, 'I would sooner believe that a Yankee professor would lie than that a stone would fall from heaven.' "

"Yes," said Avalon at once, "but Jefferson was wrong. Silliman did *not* lie and stones *did* fall from heaven."

"Quite so, Mr. Avalon," said Henry, unruffled. "That is why the quotation is remembered. But considering the great number of times that impossibilities have been reported, and the small number of times they have been proven possible after all, I felt the odds were with me."

Afterword

This story first appeared in the May 1973 issue of *Ellery Queen's Mystery Magazine*, under the title I gave it.

I hope that no reader thinks the solution in this tale "isn't fair." In real life, a great many reports of unconventional phenomena are the results of deviations from the truth, either deliberate or unconscious. And I am sick and tired of mysteries that end up with some indication that perhaps, after all, something supernatural really did happen.

As far as I am concerned, if, when everything impossible has been eliminated and what remains is supernatural, then someone is lying. If that be treason, make the most of it.

THE IRON GEM

Geoffrey Avalon stirred his drink and smiled wolfishly. His hairy, still dark eyebrows slanted upward and his neat graying beard seemed to twitch. He looked like Satan in an amiable mood.

He said to the Black Widowers, assembled at their monthly dinner, "Let me present my guest to you—Latimer Reed, jeweler. And let me say at once that he brings us no crime to solve, no mystery to unravel. Nothing has been stolen from him; he has witnessed no murder; involved himself in no spy ring. He is here, purely and simply, to tell us about jewelry, answer our questions, and help us have a good, sociable time."

And, indeed, under Avalon's firm eye, the atmosphere at dinner was quiet and relaxed and even Emmanuel Rubin, the ever quarrelsome polymath of the club, managed to avoid raising his voice. Quite satisfied, Avalon said, over the brandy, "Gentlemen, the postprandial grilling is upon us, and with no problem over which to rack our brains.—Henry, you may relax."

Henry, who was clearing the table with the usual quiet efficiency that would have made him the nonpareil of waiters even if he had not proved himself, over and over again, to be peerlessly aware of the obvious, said, "Thank you, Mr. Avalon. I trust I will not be excluded from the proceedings, however."

Rubin fixed Henry with an owlish stare through his thick glasses and said loudly, "Henry, this blatantly false modesty does not become you. You know you're a member of our little band, with all the privileges thereto appertaining."

"If that is so," said Roger Halsted, the soft-voiced math teacher, sipping at his brandy and openly inviting a quarrel, "why is he waiting on table?"

"Personal choice, sir," said Henry quickly, and Rubin's opening mouth shut again.

Avalon said, "Let's get on with it. Tom Trumbull isn't with us this time so, as host, I appoint you, Mario, as griller in chief."

Mario Gonzalo, a not inconsiderable artist, was placing the final touches on the caricature he was making of Reed, one that was intended to be added to the already long line that decorated the private room of the Fifth Avenue restaurant at which the dinners of the Black Widowers were held.

Gonzalo had, perhaps, overdrawn the bald dome of Reed's head and the solemn length of his bare upper lip, and made over-apparent the slight tendency to jowl. There was indeed something more than a trace of the bloodhound about the caricature, but Reed smiled when he saw the result, and did not seem offended.

Gonzalo smoothed the perfect Windsor knot of his pink and white tie and let his blue jacket fall open with careful negligence as he leaned back and said, "How do you justify your existence, Mr. Reed?"

"Sir?" said Reed in a slightly metallic voice.

Gonzalo said, without varying pitch or stress, "How do you justify your existence, Mr. Reed?"

Reed looked about the table at the five grave faces and smiled—a smile that did not, somehow, seriously diminish the essential sadness of his own expression.

"Jeff warned me," he said, "that I would be questioned after the dinner, but he did not tell me I would be challenged to justify myself."

"Always best," said Avalon sententiously, "to catch a man by surprise."

Reed said, "What can serve to justify any of us? But if I must say something, I would say that I help bring beauty into lives."

"What kind of beauty?" asked Gonzalo. "Artistic beauty?" And he held up the caricature.

Reed laughed. "Less controversial forms of beauty, I should hope." He pulled a handkerchief out of his inner jacket pocket and, carefully unfolding it on the table, exposed a dozen or so gleaming, deeply colored bits of mineral.

"All men agree on the beauty of gems," he said. "That is independent of subjective taste." He held up a small deep red stone and the lights glanced off it.

James Drake cleared his throat and said with his usual mild hoarseness just the same, "Do you always carry those things around with you?"

"No, of course not," said Reed. "Only when I wish to entertain or demonstrate."

"In a handkerchief?" said Drake.

Rubin burst in at once. "Sure, what's the difference? If he's held up, keeping them in a locked casket won't do him any good. He'd just be out the price of a casket as well."

"Have you ever been held up?" asked Gonzalo.

"No," said Reed. "My best defense is that I am known never to carry much of value with me. I strive to make that as widely known as possible, and to live up to it, too."

"That doesn't look it," said Drake.

"I am demonstrating beauty, not value," said Reed. "Would you care to pass these around among yourselves, gentlemen?"

There was no immediate move and then Drake said, "Henry, would you be in a position to lock the door?"

"Certainly, sir," said Henry, and did so.

Reed looked surprised. "Why lock the door?"

Drake cleared his throat again and stubbed out the pitiful remnant of his cigarette with a stained thumb and forefinger. "I'm afraid that, with the kind of record we now have at our monthly dinners, those things will be passed around and one will disappear."

"That's a tasteless remark, Jim," said Avalon, frowning.

Reed said, "Gentlemen, there is no need to worry. These stones may all disappear with little loss to me or gain to anyone else. I said I was demonstrating beauty and not value. This one I am holding is a ruby—quite so—but synthetic. There are a few other synthetics and here we have an irreparably cracked opal. Others are riddled with flaws. These will do no one any good and I'm sure Henry can open the door."

Halsted said, stuttering very slightly in controlled excitement, "No, I'm with Jim. Something is just fated to come up. I'll bet that Mr. Reed has included one very valuable item—quite by accident, perhaps—and that one will turn up missing. I just don't believe we can go through an evening without some puzzle facing us."

Reed said, "Not that one. I know every one of these stones and, if you like, I'll look at each again." He did so and then pushed them out into the center of the table. "Merely trinkets that serve to satisfy the innate craving of human beings for beauty."

Rubin grumbled, "Which, however, only the rich can afford."

"Quite wrong, Mr. Rubin. Quite wrong. These stones are not terribly expensive. And even jewelry that is costly is often on display for all eyes—and even the owner can do no more than look at what he owns, though more frequently than others. Primitive tribes might make ornaments as satisfying to themselves as jewelry is to us out of shark's teeth, walrus tusks, sea shells, or birch bark. Beauty is independent of material, or of fixed rules of aesthetics, and in my way I am its servant."

Gonzalo said, "But you would rather sell the most expensive forms of beauty, wouldn't you?"

"Quite true," said Reed. "I am subject to economic law, but that bends my appreciation of beauty as little as I can manage."

Rubin shook his head. His sparse beard bristled and his voice, surprisingly full-bodied for one with so small a frame, rose in passion. "No, Mr. Reed, if you consider yourself a purveyor of beauty only, you are being hypocritical. It's rarity you're selling. A synthetic ruby is as beautiful as a natural one and indistinguishable chemically. But the natural ruby is rarer, more difficult to get, and therefore more expensive and more eagerly bought by those who can afford it. Beauty it may be, but it is beauty meant to serve personal vanity.

"A copy of the 'Mona Lisa,' correct to every crack in the paint, is just a copy, worth no more than any daub, and if there were a thousand copies, the real one would still remain priceless because it alone would be the unique original and would reflect uniqueness on its possessor. But that, you see, has nothing to do with beauty."

Reed said, "It is easy to rail against humanity. Rareness does enhance value in the eyes of the vain, and I suppose that something that is sufficiently rare and, at the same time, notable would fetch a huge price even if there were no beauty about it—"

"A rare autograph," muttered Halsted.

"Yet," said Reed firmly, "beauty is always an enhancing factor, and I sell only beauty. Some of my wares are rare as well, but nothing I sell, or would care to sell, is rare without being beautiful."

Drake said, "What else do you sell besides beauty and rarity?"

"Utility, sir," said Reed at once. "Jewels are a way of storing wealth compactly and permanently in a way independent of the fluctuations of the market place."

"But they can be stolen," said Gonzalo accusingly.

"Certainly," said Reed. "Their very values—beauty, compactness, permanence—make them more useful to a thief than anything else can be. The equivalent in gold would be much heavier; the equivalent in anything else far more bulky."

Avalon said, with a clear sense of reflected glory in his guest's profession, "Latimer deals in eternal value."

"Not always," said Rubin rather wrathfully. "Some of the jeweler's wares are of only temporary value, for rarity may vanish. There was a time when gold goblets might be used on moderately important occasions but, for the real top of vanity, the Venetian cut glass was trotted out—until glass-manufacturing processes were improved to the point where such things were brought down to the five-and-ten level.

"In the 1880s, the Washington Monument was capped with nothing less good than aluminum and, in a few years, the Hall process made aluminum cheap and the monument cap completely ordinary. Then, too, value can change with changing legend. As long as the alicorn—the horn of a unicorn—was thought to have aphrodisiac properties, the horns of narwhals and rhinoceroses were valuable. A handerchief of a stiffish weave which could be cleaned by being thrown into the fire would be priceless for its magical refusal to burn—till the properties of asbestos became well known.

"Anything that becomes rare through accident—the first edition of a completely worthless book, rare because it *was* worthless—becomes priceless to collectors. And synthetic jewelry of all sorts may yet make your wares valueless, Mr. Reed."

Reed said, "Perhaps individual items of beauty might lose some of their value, but jewelry is only the raw material of what I sell. There is still the beauty of combination, of setting, the individual and creative work of the craftsman. As for those things which are valuable for rarity alone, I do not deal with them; I will not deal with them; I have no sympathy with them, no interest in them. I myself own some things that are both rare and beautiful—own them, I mean, with no intention of ever selling them—and nothing, I hope, that is ugly and is valued by me only because it is rare. Or almost nothing, anyway."

He seemed to notice for the first time that the gems he had earlier distributed were lying before him. "Ah, you're all through with them, gentlemen?" He scooped them toward himself with his left hand. "All here," he said, "each one. No omissions. No substitutions. All accounted for." He looked at each individually. "I have showed you these, gentlemen, because there is an interesting point to be made about each of them—"

Halsted said, "Wait. What did you mean by saying 'almost nothing'?"

"Almost nothing?" said Reed, puzzled.

"You said you owned nothing ugly just because it was rare. Then you said 'almost nothing.' "

Reed's face cleared. "Ah, my lucky piece. I have it here somewhere." He rummaged in his pocket, "Here it is. —You are welcome to look at it, gentlemen. It is ugly enough, but actually I would be more distressed at losing it than any of the gems I brought with me." He passed his lucky piece to Drake, who sat on his left.

Drake turned it over in his hands. It was about an inch wide, ovoid in shape, black and finely pitted. He said, "It's metal. Looks like meteoric iron."

"That's exactly what it is as far as I know," said Reed.

The object passed from hand to hand and came back to him. "It's my iron gem," said Reed. "I've turned down five hundred dollars for it."

"Who the devil would offer five hundred dollars for it?" asked Gonzalo, visibly astonished.

Avalon cleared his throat. "A collector of meteorites might, I suppose, if for any reason this one had special scientific value. The question really is, Latimer, why on Earth you turned it down."

"Oh," and Reed looked thoughtful for a while. "I don't really know. To be nasty, perhaps. I didn't like the fellow."

"The guy who offered the money?" asked Gonzalo.

"Yes."

Drake reached out for the bit of black metal and, when Reed gave it to him a second time, studied it more closely, turning it over and over. "Does this have scientific value as far as you know?"

"Only by virtue of its being meteoric," said Reed. "I've brought it to the Museum of Natural History and they were interested in having it for their collection if I were interested in donating it without charge. I wasn't. —And I don't know the profession of the man who wanted to buy it. I don't recall the incident very well—it was ten years ago—but I'm certain he didn't impress me as a scientist of any type."

"You've never seen him since?" asked Drake.

"No, though at the time I was sure I would. In fact, for a time I had the most dramatic imaginings. But I never saw him again. It was after that, though, that I began to carry it about as a luck charm." He put it in his pocket again. "After all, there aren't many objects this unprepossessing I would refuse five hundred for."

Rubin, frowning, said, "I scent a mystery here—"

Avalon exploded. "Good God, let's have no mystery! This is a social evening. Latimer, you *assured* me that there was no puzzle you were planning to bring up."

Reed looked honestly confused. "I'm not bringing up any puzzle. As far as I'm concerned, there's nothing to the story. I was offered five hundred dollars; I refused; and there's an end to it."

Rubin's voice rose in indignation. "The mystery consists in the reason for the offer of the five hundred. It is a legitimate outgrowth of the grilling and I demand the right to prove the matter."

Reed said, "But what's the use of probing? I don't know why he offered five hundred dollars unless he believed the ridiculous story my great-grandfather told."

"There's the value of probing. We now know there is a ridiculous story attached to the object. Go on, then. What was the ridiculous story your great-grandfather told?"

"It's the story of how the meteorite—assuming that's what it is—came into the possession of my family—"

"You mean it's an heirloom?" asked Halsted.

"If something totally without value can be an heirloom, this is one. In any case, my great-grandfather sent it home from the Far East in 1856 with a letter explaining the circumstances. I've seen the letter myself. I can't quote it to you, word for word, but I can give you the sense of it."

"Go ahead," said Rubin.

"Well—to begin with, the 1850s were the age of the clipper ship, the *Yankee Clipper*, you know, and the American seamen roamed the world till first the Civil War and then the continuing development of the steamship put an end to sailing vessels. However, I'm not planning to spin a sea yarn. I couldn't. I know nothing about ships and couldn't tell a bowsprit from a binnacle, if either exists at all. However, I mention it all by way of explaining that my great-grandfather—who bore my name; or rather, I bear his—managed to see the world. To that extent his story is conceivable. Between that and the fact that his name, too, was Latimer Reed, I had a tendency, when young, to want to believe him.

"In those days, you see, the Moslem world was still largely closed to the men of the Christian West. The Ottoman Empire still had large territories in the Balkans and the dim memory of the days when it threatened all Europe still lent it an echo of far-off might. And the Arabian Peninsula itself was, to the West, a mystic mixture of desert sheiks and camels.

"Of course, the old city of Mecca was closed to non-Moslems and one of the daring feats a European or American might perform would be to learn Arabic, dress like an Arab, develop a knowledge of Moslem culture and religion, and somehow participate in the ritual of the pilgrimage to Mecca and return to tell the story. —My great-grandfather claimed to have accomplished this."

Drake interrupted. "Claimed? Was he lying?"

"I don't know," said Reed. "I have no evidence beyond this letter he sent from Hong Kong. There was no apparent reason to lie since he had nothing to gain from it. Of course, he may merely have wanted to amuse my great-grandmother and shine in her eyes. He had been away from home for three years and had only been married three years prior to his sailing, and family legend has it that it was a great love match."

Gonzalo began, "But after he returned—"

"He never returned," said Reed. "About a month after he wrote the letter he died under unknown circumstances and was buried somewhere overseas. The family didn't learn of that till considerably later of course. My grandfather was only about four at the time of his father's death and was brought up by my great-grandmother. My grandfather had five sons and three daughters and I'm the second son of his fourth son and there's my family history in brief."

"Died under unknown circumstances," said Halsted. "There are all sorts of possibilities there."

"As a matter of fact," said Reed, "family legend has it that his impersonation of an Arab was detected, that he had been tracked to Hong Kong and beyond, and had been murdered. But you know there is no evidence for that whatever. The only information we have about his death was from seamen who brought a letter from someone who announced the death."

"Does that letter exist?" asked Avalon, interested despite himself.

"No. But where and how he died doesn't matter—or even *if* he died, for that matter. The fact is he never returned home. Of course," Reed went on, "the family has always tended to believe the story, because it is dramatic and glamorous and it has been distorted out of all recognition. I have an aunt who once told me that he was torn to pieces by a howling mob of dervishes who detected his imposture in a mosque. She said it was because he had blue eyes. All made up, of course; probably out of a novel."

Rubin said, "Did he have blue eyes?"

"I doubt it," said Reed. "We all have brown eyes in my family. But I don't really know."

Halsted said, "But what about your iron gem, your lucky piece?"

"Oh, that came with the letter," said Reed. "It was a small package actually. And my lucky piece was the whole point of the letter. He was sending it as a memento of his feat. Perhaps you know that the central ceremony involved in the pilgrimage to Mecca is the rites at the Kaaba, the most holy object in the Moslem world."

Rubin said, "It's actually a relic of the pre-Moslem world. Mohammed was a shrewd and practical politician, though, and he took it over. If you can't lick them, join them."

"I dare say," said Reed coolly. "The Kaaba is a large, irregular cube—the word 'cube' comes from 'Kaaba' in fact—and in its southeast corner about five feet from the ground is what is called the Black Stone, which is broken and held together in metal bands. Most people seem to think the Black Stone is a meteorite."

"Probably," said Rubin. "A stone from heaven, sent by the gods. Naturally it would be worshiped. The same can be said of the original statue of Artemis at Ephesus—the so-called Diana of the Ephesians—"

Avalon said, "Since Tom Trumbull is absent, I suppose it's my job to shut you up, Manny. *Shut up*, Manny. Let our guest speak."

Reed said, "Anyway, that's about it. My iron gem arrived in the package with the letter, and my great-grandfather said in his letter that it was a piece of the Black Stone which he had managed to chip off."

"Good Lord," muttered Avalon. "If he did that, I wouldn't blame the Arabs for killing him."

Drake said, "If it's a piece of the Black Stone, I dare say it would be worth quite a bit to a collector."

"Priceless to a pious Moslem, I should imagine," said Halsted.

"Yes, yes," said Reed impatiently, "*if* it is a piece of the Black Stone. But how are you going to demonstrate such a thing? Can we take it back to Mecca and see if it will fit into some chipped place, or make a very sophisticated chemical comparison of my lucky piece and the rest of the Black Stone?"

"Neither of which, I'm sure," said Avalon, "the government of Saudi Arabia would allow."

"Nor am I interested in asking," said Reed. "Of course, it's an article of faith in my family that the object *is* a chip of the Black Stone and the story was occasionally told to visitors and the package was produced complete with letter and stone. It always made a sensation.

"Then sometime before World War I there was some sort of scare. My father was a boy then and he told me the story when I was a boy, so it's all pretty garbled. I was impressed with it when I was young, but when I considered it after reaching man's estate, I realized that it lacked substance."

"What was the story?" asked Gonzalo.

"A matter of turbaned strangers slinking about the house, mysterious shadows by day and strange sounds by night," said Reed. "It was the sort of thing people would imagine after reading sensational fiction."

Rubin, who, as a writer, would ordinarily have resented the last adjective, was too hot on the spoor on this occasion to do so. He said, "The implication is that they were Arabs who were after the chip of the Black Stone. Did anything happen?"

Avalon broke in. "If you tell us about mysterious deaths, Latimer, I'll know you're making up the whole thing."

Reed said, "I'm speaking nothing but the truth. There were no mysterious deaths. Everyone in my family since Great-grandfather died of old age, disease, or unimpeachable accident. No breath of foul play has ever risen. And in connection with the tale of the turbaned strangers, nothing at all happened. Nothing! Which is one reason I dismiss the whole thing."

Gonzalo said, "Did anyone ever attempt to steal the chip?"

"Never. The original package with the chip and the letter stayed in an unlocked drawer for half a century. No one paid any particular heed to it and it remained perfectly safe. I still have the chip as you saw," and he slapped his pocket.

"Actually," he went on, "the thing would have been forgotten altogether but for me. About 1950, I felt a stirring of interest. I don't have a clear memory why. The nation of Israel had just been established and the Middle East was much in the news. Perhaps that was the reason. In any case, I got to thinking of the old family story and I dredged the thing out of its drawer."

Reed took out his iron gem absently and held it in the palm of his hand. "It did look meteoritic to me but, of course, in my great-grandfather's time meteorites weren't as well known to the general public as they are now. So, as I said earlier, I took it to the Museum of Natural History. Someone said it *was* meteoritic and would I care to donate it. I said it was a family heirloom and I couldn't do that, but—and this was the key point for me—I asked him if there were any signs that it had been chipped off a larger meteorite.

"He looked at it carefully, first by eye, then with a magnifying glass, and finally said he could see no sign of it. He said it must have been found in exactly the condition I had it. He said meteoritic iron is particularly hard and tough because it has nickel in it. It's more like alloy steel than iron and it couldn't be chipped off, he said, without clear signs of manhandling.

"Well, that settled it, didn't it? I went back and got the letter and read it through. I even studied the original package. There was some blurred Chinese scrawl on it and my grandmother's name and address in a faded angular English. There was nothing to be made of it. I couldn't make out the postmark but there was no reason to suppose it wasn't from Hong Kong. Anyway, I decided the whole thing was an amiable fraud. Great-grandfather Latimer had picked up the meteorite somewhere, and probably had been spending time in the Arab world, and couldn't resist spinning a yarn."

Halsted said, "And then a month later he was dead under mysterious circumstances."

"Just dead," said Reed. "No reason to think the death was mysterious. In the 1850s, life was relatively brief. Any of a number of infectious diseases could kill. —Anyway, that's the end of the story. No glamour. No mystery."

Gonzalo objected vociferously at once. "That's not the end of the story. It's not even the beginning. What's the bit about the offer of five hundred dollars?"

"Oh, *that*!" said Reed. "That happened in 1962 or 1963. It was a dinner party and there were some hot arguments on the Middle East and I was taking up a pro-Arab stance as a kind of devil's advocate—it was well before the Six-Day War, of course—and that put me in mind of the meteorite. It was still moldering away in the drawer and I brought it out.

"I remember we were all sitting about the table and I passed the package around and they all looked at it. Some tried to read the letter, but that wasn't so easy because the handwriting is rather old-fashioned and crabbed. Some asked me what the Chinese writing was on the package and of course I didn't know. Just to be dramatic, I told them about the mysterious turbaned strangers in my father's time and stressed Great-granddad's mysterious death, and didn't mention my reasons for being certain it was all a hoax. It was just entertainment.

"Only one person seemed to take it seriously. He was a stranger, a friend of a friend. We had invited a friend, you see, and when he said he had an engagement, we said, well, bring your friend along. That sort of thing, you know. I don't remember his name any more. All I do remember about him personally is that he had thinning red hair and didn't contribute much to the conversation.

"When everybody was getting ready to go, he came to me hesitantly and asked if he could see the thing once more. There was no reason not to allow it, of course. He took the meteorite out of the package—it was the only thing that seemed to interest him—and walked to the light with it. He studied it for a long time; I remember growing a little impatient; and then he said, 'See here, I collect odd objects. I wonder if you'd let me have this thing. I'd pay you, of course. What would you say it was worth?'

"I laughed and said I didn't think I'd sell it and he stammered out an offer of five dollars. I found that rather offensive. I mean, if I were going to sell a family heirloom it surely wouldn't be for five dollars. I gave him a decidedly brusque negative and held out my band for the object. I took such a dislike to him that I remember feeling he might steal it.

"He handed it back reluctantly enough and I remember looking at the object again to see what might make it attractive to him, but it still seemed what it was, an ugly lump of iron. You see, even though I knew its point of interest lay in its possible history and not in its appearance, I was simply unable to attach value to anything but beauty.

"When I looked up, he was reading the letter again. I held out my hand and he gave me that too. He said, 'Ten dollars?' and I just said, 'No!' "

Reed took a sip of the coffee that Henry had just served him. He said, "Everyone else had left. This man's friend was waiting for him, the man who was *my* friend originally, Jansen. He and his wife were killed in an auto accident the next year, driving the very car at whose door he stood then, waiting for the man he had brought to my house. What a frightening thing the future is if you stop to think of it. Luckily, we rarely do.

"Anyway, the man who wanted the object stopped at the door and said to me hurriedly, 'Listen, I'd really like that little piece of metal. It's no good to you and I'll give you five hundred dollars for it. How's that? Five hundred dollars. Don't be hoggish about this.'

"I can make allowances for his apparent anxiety, but he was damned offensive. He did say 'hoggish'; I remember the word. After that, I wouldn't have let him have it for a million. Very coldly I told him it wasn't for sale at any price, and I put the meteorite, which was still in my hand, into my pocket with ostentatious finality.

"His face darkened and he growled that I would regret that and there would be those who wouldn't be so kind as to offer money, and then off he went— The meteorite has stayed in my pocket ever since. It is my ugly luck piece that I have refused five hundred dollars for." He chuckled in a muted way and said, "And that's the whole story."

Drake said, "And you never found out why he offered you five hundred dollars for that thing?"

"Unless he believed it was a piece of the Black Stone, I can't see any reason why he should," said Reed.

"He never renewed his offer?"

"Never. It was over ten years ago and I have never heard from him at all. And now that Jansen and his wife are dead, I don't even know where he is or how he could be located if I decided I wanted to sell."

Gonzalo said, "What did he mean by his threat about others who wouldn't be so kind as to offer money?"

"I don't know," said Reed. "I suppose he meant mysterious turbaned strangers of the kind I had told him about. I think he was just trying to frighten me into selling."

Avalon said, "Since a mystery has developed despite everything, I suppose we ought to consider the possibilities here. The obvious motive for his offer is, as you say, that he believed the object to be a piece of the Black Stone."

"If so," said Reed, "he was the only one there who did. I don't think anyone else took the story seriously for a moment. Besides, even if it were a chip of the Black Stone and the guy were a collector, what good would it be to him without definite proof? He could take any piece of scrap iron and label it 'piece of the Black Stone' and it would do him no less good than mine."

Avalon said, "Do you suppose he might have been an Arab who knew that a chip the size of your object had been stolen from the Black Stone a century before and wanted it out of piety?"

"He didn't seem Arab to me," said Reed. "And if he were, why was the offer not renewed? Or why wasn't there an attempt at taking it from me by violence?"

Drake said, "He studied the object carefully. Do you suppose he saw something there that convinced him of its value—whatever that value might be?"

Reed said, "How can I dispute that? Except that, whatever he might have seen, I certainly never have. Have you?"

"No," admitted Drake.

Rubin said, "This doesn't sound like anything we can possibly work out. We just don't have enough information.—What do you say, Henry?"

Henry, who had been listening with his usual quiet attention, said, "I was wondering about a few points."

"Well then, go on, Henry," said Avalon. "Why not continue the grilling of the guest?"

Henry said, "Mr. Reed, when you showed the object to your guests on that occasion in 1962 or 1963, you say you passed the package around. You mean the original package in which the letter and the meteorite had come, with its contents as they had always been?"

"Yes. Oh yes. It was a family treasure."

"But since 1963, sir, you have carried the meteorite in your pocket?"

"Yes, always," said Reed.

"Does that mean, sir, that you no longer have the letter?"

"Of course it doesn't mean that," said Reed indignantly. "We certainly do have the letter. I'll admit that after that fellow's threat I was a little concerned so I put it in a safer place. It's a glamorous document from the family standpoint, hoax or not."

"Where do you keep it now?" asked Henry.

"In a small wall safe I use for documents and occasional jewels."

"Have you seen it recently, sir?"

Reed smiled broadly. "I use the wall safe frequently, and I see it every time. Take my word for it, Henry, the letter is safe; as safe as the luck piece in my pocket."

Henry said, "Then you don't keep the letter in the original package anymore."

"No," said Reed. "The package was more useful as a container for the meteorite. Now that I carry that object in my pocket, there was no point in keeping the letter alone in the package."

Henry nodded. "And what did you do with the package, then, sir?"

Reed looked puzzled. "Why, nothing."

"You didn't throw it out?"

"No, of course not."

"Do you know where it is?"

Slowly, Reed frowned. He said at last, "No, I don't think so."

"When did you last see it?"

The pause was just as long this time. "I don't know that either."

Henry seemed lost in thought.

Avalon said, "Well, Henry, what do you have in mind?"

Henry said, "I'm just wondering"—quietly he circled the table removing the brandy glasses—"whether that man wanted the meteorite at all."

"He certainly offered me money for it," said Reed.

"Yes," said Henry, "but first such small sums as would offer you no temptation to release it, and which he could well afford to pay if you called his bluff. Then a larger sum couched in such offensive language as to make it certain you would refuse. And after that, a mysterious threat which was never implemented."

"But why should he do all that," said Reed, "unless he wanted my iron gem?"

Henry said, "To achieve, perhaps, precisely what he did, in fact, achieve—to convince you he wanted the meteorite and to keep your attention firmly fixed on that. He gave you back the meteorite when you held out your hand for it; he gave you back the letter—but did he give you back the original package?"

Reed said, "I don't remember him taking it."

Henry said, "It was ten years ago. He kept your attention fixed on the meteorite. You even spent some time examining it yourself and during that time you didn't look at him, I'm sure. —Can you say you've seen the package since that time, sir?"

Slowly, Reed shook his head. "I can't say I have. You mean he fastened my attention so tightly on the meteorite that he could walk off with the package and I wouldn't notice?"

"I'm afraid you didn't. You put the meteorite in your pocket, the letter in your safe, and apparently never gave another thought to the package. This man, whose name you don't know and whom you can no longer identify thanks to your friends' death, has had the package for ten years with no interference. And by now you could not possibly identify what it was he took."

"I certainly could," said Reed stoutly, "if I could see it. It has my great-grandmother's name and address on it."

"He might not have saved the package itself," said Henry.

"I've got it," cried out Gonzalo suddenly. "It was that Chinese writing. He could make it out somehow and he took it to get it deciphered with certainty. The message was important."

Henry's smile was the barest flicker. "That is a romantic notion that had not occurred to me, Mr. Gonzalo, and I don't know that it is very probable. I was thinking of something else. —Mr. Reed, you had a package from Hong Kong in 1856 and at that time Hong Kong was already a British possession."

"Taken over in 1848," said Rubin briefly.

"And I think the British had already instituted the modern system of distributing mail."

"Rowland Hill," said Rubin at once, "in 1840."

"Well then," said Henry, "could there have been a stamp on the original package?"

Reed looked startled. "Now that you mention it, there was something that looked like a black stamp, I seem to recall. A woman's profile?"

"The young Victoria," said Rubin.

Henry said, "And might it possibly have been a rare stamp?"

Gonzalo threw up his arms. "Bingo!"

Reed sat with his mouth distinctly open. Then he said, "Of course, you must be right. —I wonder how much I lost."

"Nothing but money, sir," murmured Henry. "The early British stamps were not beautiful."

TO THE BAREST

Emmanuel Rubin said in a scandalized whisper, "He offered to *pay* for the dinner." He glanced with owlish ferocity at the guest who was attending that month's Black Widowers' banquet.

"Yes, he did," said Mario Gonzalo casually.

"And I suppose you accepted," said Rubin.

"No, I didn't, though I don't see why he shouldn't if he wants to. If someone is anxious to pay for the privilege of dining with us, why not let him?"

"Because we would be selling our freedom of choice, you idiot, and that is without price to the rest of us. Do you think I'm willing to eat with anyone who'll pick up my check? I *choose* my companions. Damn it, Mario, if he offered to buy us that should in itself instantly disqualify him as a guest."

"Well, it doesn't, so why not calm down, Manny, and listen? I've told the others already and saved you for last because I knew you'd rant away. He got in touch with me. . . ."

"Do you know him?"

"No, but he introduced himself. He's Matthew Parris, and he's a lawyer. He knew of the Black Widowers. He knew I was to be the next host and he wanted to see us professionally, *all* of us. He asked to join us at our banquet and offered to pay if that would help. He seemed like an interesting guy, so why not?"

Rubin said discontentedly, "Why should professional matters intrude on the banquet? What does he want to do, serve us with summonses?"

"No," said Gonzalo with an affectation of eye-rolling impatience. "He represents Ralph Ottur. We still send Ralph invitations, and that's how this guy, Parris, knew I was the next host. He got in touch with me at Ralph's instructions. I suppose you remember Ralph."

Rubin's eyes flashed behind his thick-lensed glasses. "Of course I remember him. I'm surprised you do. I didn't know you had become a member before he left."

"Memory decays with age, Manny."

Rubin ignored that. "That was twelve, fifteen years ago when he left us, when the Black Widowers were just beginning. That was before we met at the Milano—before Henry's time." He looked in Henry's direction with a smile and said, "It doesn't seem possible we could have had meetings of the Black Widowers without Henry. But then, in those days we wouldn't have believed it possible to have dinners without Ralph. It was in '65 he went to California, wasn't it? We were kids then."

"I believe," said Geoffrey Avalon, who had drifted toward them, his neatly bearded face solemn, "that you and I, Manny, were fortyish even then. Scarcely kids."

"Oh well," Rubin said. "What does Ralph want with us, Mario?"

"I don't know," said Gonzalo. "Parris wouldn't say. Have you heard from him lately?"

"Not a word in years. He doesn't even send in a refusal card to the invitations. Have you heard from him, Geoff?"

"No," said Avalon. "Tom Trumbull says Ralph is teaching navigation at CIT but has had no personal communication."

"Well, then, Geoff, what do we do about this lawyer Mario has dragged in?"

"Treat him as any other guest. What else can we do?"

Henry approached, his smooth and unwrinkled face radiating the efficiency that was characteristic of this best of waiters. He said, "Mr. Gonzalo, we are ready to begin dinner if you will be so kind as to call the meeting to order."

• • •

The dinner was quieter than usual as Matthew Parris somehow absorbed the attention of the others. He seemed oblivious to that, however, his smooth-shaven face shining pinkly, his graying hair slicked smoothly back, his smile wide and unaffected, his speech precise and with a flat midwestern accent.

At no time did he refer to the business at hand, but confined himself to discussing the Middle Eastern situation. The trouble, he said, was that both sides were playing for time. The Arabs felt that as oil supplies dwindled, world hunger for energy would bring victory. Israel felt that as oil supplies dwindled, Arab influence would dwindle with it.

To which James Drake said somberly that as oil supplies dwindled, civilization might break down and the whole matter of victory (quote, unquote, he said) in the Middle East or anywhere else would be irrelevant.

"Ah," said Parris, "but your fiery ideolog doesn't care about trivial things such as survival. He would rather win in hell than lose in heaven."

Mario Gonzalo, who had put aside his rather blinding pea-green jacket and was eating veal cordon bleu in his striped shirt-sleeves, leaned toward Thomas Trumbull and whispered, "This whole thing may be a practical joke, Tom. I only met Ralph two or three times before he left. He was a peculiar fellow as I recall."

Trumbull's bronzed forehead furrowed under his white thatch of hair. "So are we all, I hope. Ralph Ottur founded this club. We used to eat at his house during the first two or three years. He was a widower, a gourmet cook, an astronomer, and a word buff."

"That's what I remember. The word-buff bit."

"Yes," said Trumbull. "He's written books on acrostics and on novelty verse of all kinds. Conundrums involving word play and puns were a specialty of his. He's the one who got Roger Halsted interested in limericks."

Gonzalo laughed. "How did you stand it, Tom?"

Trumbull shrugged. "It wasn't the sole topic of conversation, and I was younger then. However, Ralph remarried, as you probably remember, went to the West Coast, and we never heard from him again. Then Jim Drake and I found the Milano, and the Black Widowers has been here ever since, better than ever."

Henry refilled the coffee cups, and Gonzalo played a melodious tattoo on his water glass with his spoon.

"Jim," he said, "as the oldest member and the one who best knew Ralph Ottur in the old days when even Manny claims to have been a kid, would you do the grilling honors?"

James Drake lit a fresh cigarette and said, "Mr. Parris, how do you justify your existence?"

"At the moment," said Parris, "by attempting to make you somewhat richer than you have been hitherto. Or if not you, Dr. Drake, then another one of you."

"Don't you know which?"

"I'm afraid not, gentlemen. In order to know, I must complete the reading of the will."

"Will? What will?" Drake took the cigarette from his mouth, placed it in an ashtray, and looked uneasy.

A heavy silence descended on the rest of the table. Henry, who had been serving brandy, desisted.

Parris said seriously, "I was instructed to say nothing concerning the matter till I was a guest at a Black Widowers' banquet and till I was being grilled. Not till this moment."

Drake said, "It *is* this moment. Go on."

Parris said, "I'm sorry to have to tell you that Mr. Ralph Ottur died last month. He had been pretty much of a recluse since his second wife died three years ago and, at his request, no announcement of his death was made. Though he had made a clean break with his life in New York after he left for California, he did not, apparently, forget his old friends of the Black Widowers. He asked that I hand out one of these to each of you, provided all six were present, and you all are."

Envelopes were passed out to each of the stunned Black

Widowers. Each bore the name of a Black Widower in careful India ink lettering.

Drake muttered, "There's his monogram." Each envelope bore a stylized sketch of what was unmistakably an otter with a fish in its mouth.

Trumbull said, "Did we each get the same?"

Gonzalo said, "Read it and we'll see."

Trumbull hesitated, then read in a low monotone, " 'Well, don't sit there like idiots. There's no reason to get into a mood. Remember, "mood" spelled backward is "doom." I've been with you in spirit every month since I left, even if you haven't heard from me, and I'm with you again now, ready for our last game.' "

"That's what mine says," said Gonzalo.

There was a murmur of agreement from the rest.

"Well, then," said Parris briskly, "I'll now read the will—not the entire will, you understand, but only that portion that applies to the club. If you're ready . . ."

There was silence and Parris read, "It is my further wish and desire to make a bequest to the Black Widowers, a club I helped found and for the members of which I have always had a profound affection. Therefore, I wish to leave a sum of money, which, after taxes are paid, is to come to ten thousand dollars. This sum is to go to one of the following gentlemen, all of whom were members of the club at the last meeting I attended and all of whom, I believe, are still alive. They are: Thomas Trumbull, James Drake, Emmanuel Rubin, Geoffrey Avalon, Roger Halsted, and Mario Gonzalo."

Parris looked up and said, "For the record, there are six of you at the table and I believe you are the six whose names I have read off. Are there any discrepancies?"

Gonzalo said, "There is a seventh member. Henry, our waiter, is the best Black Widower of them all."

Halsted said, "He wasn't a member in Ralph's day. Hell, I can't believe he's dead. Do you remember that time he asked us to find a common English word that contained the letters 'ufa' in that order? It kept us quiet all that evening."

"Yes," said Drake, "and it was you who got it. That's why you remember."

Rubin said, *"Quiet!"* His straggly beard bristled. "I demand silence. The will hasn't been read yet. What does Ralph mean that *one* of us will get the money? Why only one and which one?"

Parris cleared his throat. "I don't know. It is at this point I have been instructed to open a small envelope labeled, 'One.' Here it is."

"Well, don't open it just yet," said Rubin violently. "Mario, you're the host, but listen to me. If any bequest were left to the club or to the six of us in equal division, that would be all right. To leave it to only one of us would, however, create hard feelings. Let's agree, then, that whoever gets the money sets up a fund for the use of the Black Widowers as an entity."

Gonzalo said, "I'm willing. Any arguments?"

There was none, and Gonzalo said, "Open the envelope, Mr. Parris."

Parris opened it, withdrew a three-by-five card, glanced at it, looked surprised, and said, "It says, 'To the barest.' "

"What?" said Trumbull indignantly.

Parris looked on the other side, shook his head, and said, "That's all it says. See for yourselves." The card was passed around.

Avalon chuckled and said, "Don't you get it? He said in his note there would be a last game and this is it."

"What kind of game?" said Gonzalo.

Rubin snorted and said, "Not one of his good ones. Go ahead and explain, Geoff."

Avalon looked solemn and said, "In the Greek myths, the sea nymph Thetis married the mortal Peleus, and to the wedding all the gods and goddesses were invited. The goddess of discord, Eris, was overlooked. Furious, she appeared unbidden and, into the happy throng, tossed a golden apple, then left. Hermes picked it up and noticed a small message attached. What it said was, 'To the fairest.' Three goddesses at once reached for it—Hera, the queen of heaven; Athena, the goddess of wisdom; and Aphrodite, the goddess of love and beauty. The quarrel that resulted ended in the Trojan War."

"Exactly," said Rubin, "and I suggest we not play Ralph's game. I don't know what the hell he means by the barest, but if we start arguing about which one of us qualifies for ten thousand dollars we will end with everyone of us aggrieved, winner and losers alike, even if we put the money into a fund. Earlier, Mr. Parris said that ideologs valued victory above survival, but I don't. I don't want to see the Black Widowers come to an end over the question of who wins ten thousand dollars."

"Hear, hear," said Gonzalo. "Even you say something sensible now and then, Manny. Let's agree that each one of us is in a six-way tie for barest, take the money, and put it into the fund."

"Excellent," said Avalon. "I don't see that there would be any objection to that."

Again, there was a silence, but Parris said, "I'm afraid my instructions were to allow discussion and then to open another small envelope marked 'Two.' " Gonzalo looked surprised and said, "Well, open it."

Parris opened the second envelope, removed a folded piece of paper, and unfolded it to find a single-spaced typewritten message. He glanced over it and chuckled.

He said, "Here is what it says: 'I have no doubt that Geoff Avalon, in his endearingly pedantic way, will have by now explained the connection of the message with the apple of discord at the wedding of Thetis and Peleus. . . .' "

Avalon, having flushed to his hairline, said stiffly, "I have never denied that I have a touch of pedantry about me. I trust that I have never been offensively so, or if I have, that I may count on my outspoken comrades of the Black Widowers to tell me so."

"Don't get defensive, Geoff," said Trumbull. "We're all pedants. Go on, Mr. Parris."

Parris nodded and said, " '. . . of Thetis and Peleus. It may also be that someone, possibly Manny Rubin, will suggest that the game be refused and that the money be shared. Not so! Sorry to insist, but only one person gets the money, and that person will be he who can demonstrate himself to be the barest to the satisfaction of the executor of the will. Failing that, no one of them will get the money. I dare say Geoff can explain the appropriateness of this, if he has not already done so."

Avalon cleared his throat and looked harassed. "I don't think it's necessary I do so."

Rubin said, "It's all right, Geoff. I'll take over. Everyone knows *I'm* no pedant."

"Not bright enough," muttered Gonzalo.

Rubin, glaring briefly at Gonzalo, said, "As Geoff said, three goddesses claimed that apple. Hermes, who had picked it up, could see at once that this was no place for an innocent god, and he absolutely declined to make a decision. One by one, the other gods also declined. After considerable discussion, someone suggested that some poor mortal be stuck with the task. The one selected was a shepherd boy on the slopes of Mount Ida near Troy.

"The three goddesses appeared to him in all their magnificence, and each, fearing she might not win in a fair contest, attempted to bribe the judge. Hera offered him world conquest; Athena offered him the crown of wisdom; and Aphrodite offered him the most beautiful girl in the world as his wife.

"The shepherd boy was young enough to find the third bribe the most attractive, and chose Aphrodite. Undoubtedly, she would have won in a fair contest of fairness, but it was a disastrous choice just the same. The most beautiful girl in the world was Helen, queen of Sparta, and the shepherd boy some years later carried her off with Aphrodite's help, and that started the Trojan War.

"The shepherd boy's name was Paris, and he was one of the fifty sons of Priam, king of Troy. The decision among the goddesses is a favorite scene among artists and is commonly referred to as 'The Judgment of Paris.' Clearly, Ralph couldn't resist playing on words and setting up 'The Judgment of Parris'—two r's."

Parris smiled and said, "I seem to have the worst of it. Instead of choosing among three glorious goddesses, I am faced with deciding among six not particularly attractive men."

Rubin said, "You're not faced with any decision at all, actually. Ralph can't make us play the game. If the only way we can get the ten thousand dollars is to compete for it, then I suggest we let the whole thing go. Ten thousand dollars is something we can live without—we have lived without it all these years. What we can't live without is our mutual friendship."

Halsted looked regretful, "Well, now, we can use the money. It could defray part of the costs of the banquets. What with inflation, I, for one, am finding it difficult to cover the expenses. Since I'm the most nearly bald member of the group, can't we say I'm obviously the barest and let it go at that?"

Gonzalo said, "We could decide that 'barest' means 'the most nearly nude.' Then I can strip to my underwear, collect, and we'll set up the fund."

"Oh God," said Rubin. "Look, I'd pay you ten thousand dollars, if I had it to spare, *not* to strip."

Drake said dreamily, "If we were ecdysiasts, it would all be simple. A nice six-way tie."

Parris said, "Now, gentlemen, wait. This is serious. I disapprove of wills such as this one, but I am the executor and I must treat it seriously. I don't know what Mr. Ottur means by the 'barest,' but it is undoubtedly something that is first, not obvious, and second, compelling. If one of you can demonstrate what is meant by 'barest' and then show compellingly that one or another of you is 'barest,' I will release the money. Otherwise I can't. Baldness and, for that matter, nudity, do not strike me as clever explanations of the meaning of the phrase. Try again."

"No, we won't," said Rubin. "You ought to be ashamed of yourself, Roger, for that baldness suggestion. If you need money that badly, I'll contribute to the payment when it's your turn to host."

Halsted turned red and he pointed an angry finger at Rubin, "I don't need money that badly; and I wouldn't come to you for help if I were starving."

Avalon said, "Well, the apple of discord is beginning to do its work, obviously. Manny is right. Let's let it go, while we're still on speaking terms."

Halsted frowned as he passed the palm of his hand over his high forehead, but he kept quiet.

Rubin muttered, "Sorry, Rog. I meant no offense."

Halsted waved a briefly forgiving hand.

Parris said, with considerably more than a trace of apology, "My instructions are that after you have had time for discussion, I am to open the small envelope marked, 'Three.' "

Drake said softly, "How many envelopes do you have, Mr. Parris? This can go on all night."

"This is the last envelope," said Parris.

"Don't open it," roared Rubin. "There's nothing he can say that will change our minds."

Parris said, "I am compelled to open and read this third message by the ethics of my profession. I can't compel you to listen, of course, so if any of you wish to leave the room, you may."

No one did, however; not even Rubin.

Parris opened the third envelope and this time he looked grim as he scanned the message.

"I think you had better listen," he said. "The message reads, 'I think it possible that the group may decide to turn down the bequest rather than play the game. If they do so, or if they play but do not solve the riddle, I do will and bequeath the money, unconditionally, to the American Nazi Party."

There was a unanimous wordless rumble from the Black Widowers.

Parris nodded. "That's what it says. See for yourselves."

"You can't do that," said Halsted.

"I am legally compelled to do so," said Parris, "if you refuse to play the game. I am just a sluice through which the money passes. I cannot take independent action. Of course, any or all of you may contest the will, but I don't see what grounds you can possibly have—what legal grounds, that is. A man can do as he wishes with his property within certain clearly defined legal limits, and those limits don't seem to be transgressed here."

"Then let's play the game," said Halsted. "I say I'm the barest because I'm the baldest. I don't say that to win the money, Manny; I say it to keep it out of the hands of the Nazis. Now if you'll agree to that, Mr. Parris, you can hand over the money, and we'll put it into the fund, and that's that."

Parris hesitated. "I'd like to. I would really like to. The trouble is I can't."

"Why not? Do you want the money to go to the Nazis?"

"Of course not," said Parris, with some indignation, "but my only duty here is to respect the will of my client, and he wants one of you to demonstrate that he is the barest in so clever and unmistakable a way that I will be compelled to accept it and to select one of the six of you as the winner. After that, the money is the property of the winner and he is free to do with it as he wishes—keep it, divide it equally among the six of you, set up a trust fund for whatever legal purpose, or anything else."

"Are you sure?" said Trumbull. "No more clever little notes?"

"No more," said Parris. "The reading is complete. I must remind you now that it's a case of 'The Judgment of Parris.' You have to convince me of the validity of the solution or I have to give the money to—to— I have no choice."

Gonzalo said, "According to Manny, Paris—the original Paris—was bribed into giving his judgment. Does that mean . . ."

Parris said seriously, "Please don't finish that remark, Mr. Gonzalo. It will not be funny."

Rubin said, "Then we have no choice. We have to play the game. Who's the barest?"

Halsted says, "We can't answer that until we find out what the old b— Well, *nil nisi bonum* and all that. What does Ralph mean by 'barest,' if he doesn't mean baldest?"

"He may mean 'poorest,' the person who is barest of money," said Gonzalo. "I think I'm in the running for that."

"Or shortest," said Avalon, "the one who most nearly barely exists, so to speak. That's you, Manny."

"You may have eight inches on me, Geoff," said Rubin, "but that could be eight inches of solid bone. How about the one with the smallest wardrobe, which eliminates Mario, or else the lowest IQ, which puts him right back in the running again?"

"Gentlemen, gentlemen," interposed Parris, "none of this sounds in the least convincing. Please be serious."

"You're right," said Rubin, "this is too serious a matter for fooling, but I hate this thing too much to be able to think clearly about it. I say we get Henry into the thing right now."

Henry, who had been standing at the sideboard, listening attentively, now shook his head. "I'm sorry, gentlemen, but that would not be fitting. The deceased did not know of me, did not consider me a member of the club, and I do not qualify to play the game."

"You're a member now," said Trumbull gruffly. "You may not qualify to inherit the money, but you qualify to advise us as to who may. Go on and tell us, Henry."

Henry said, "I don't think I can, Mr. Trumbull. If I am a member of the Black Widowers, I am the only member who has never met Mr. Ottur. I do not know the cast of his thought."

Trumbull said, "There's no mystery there. You've heard us discussing him. He was a word nut. Come on, Henry, if you didn't know Ralph, neither did he know you. He didn't know your faculty for seeing the simple things."

Henry sighed. "I will do my best, sir. May I ask some questions? For instance, am I correct in taking it for granted that the deceased was not a Nazi sympathizer?"

"Hell, no," said Rubin with a snort. "Quite the reverse. During the 1950s he was in trouble because some people thought his views were too leftist."

"Then he doesn't want the money to be left to the Nazis?"

"Of course not."

"So he expects you to win."

Avalon said, "He expects us to do so, but he may overestimate our abilities."

Henry said, "Do you suppose his eagerness to have you win would extend to his giving you a hint?"

Gonzalo said, "What kind of a hint?"

"I'm not sure, Mr. Gonzalo, but let us see. Is Mr. Ottur's name spelled in the usual way?"

"You mean like the animal?" said Trumbull. "O-t-t-e-r? No. It's spelled O-t-t-u-r. With a 'u.' "

Henry said, "I believe that when the preliminary envelopes were handed out, Dr. Drake said something about Mr. Ottur's monogram."

Drake said, "I meant this sketch on the envelope."

"Yes. I had thought that might possibly be so. Has he always used that monogram, Dr. Drake?"

"As long as I've known him, and that goes back a long time."

Henry said, "I can understand the otter, which is a clear reference to Mr. Ottur's name, in a punning sort of way. May I ask if it is known whether the fish in the otter's mouth is a trout?"

There was no reply at first, but finally Avalon said, "I don't know that I gave that any thought. It could be a trout, I suppose. Why do you ask?"

"Only because trout, t-r-o-u-t, is an anagram of Ottur, o-t-t-u-r. The two words consist of the same letters in different arrangements. An otter holding a trout is double reference to his last name by way of a pun and an anagram. Does that fit his character?"

"Absolutely," said Rubin. "The otter was obvious to all of us but I never thought of the trout. He never explained that, as far as I can recall, but then he never explained anything. He wanted everything worked out. But what does all this have to do with the problem facing us, Henry?"

"It seemed to me, gentlemen, that the preliminary message was not really a neccessary prelude to the will and might well have been omitted. Furthermore, I saw no point in giving each one of you an identical message. A single message read out would have done as well, as in the case of the three messages in the three envelopes that were part of the will.

"Looking at it in that fashion," Henry went on, "it occurs to me that he was really handing out his monogram and making sure that each one of you got a good look at it, and will therefore perhaps think of using it as a clue to the nature of the game. The monogram is a pun and anagram on Mr. Ottur's last name. The solution to the problem facing us may rest in just that—puns and anagrams on last names."

The six Black Widowers looked thoughtful at that, each in his own way, and finally Drake stirred.

He said, "You know, that sounds like Ralph, and if so, let me point out that d-r-a-k-e can be rearranged into r-a-k-e-d, and a piece of ground that has been raked is bare, to say nothing of the fact that it is only one letter removed from n-a-k-e-d, which is certainly barest."

Parris said, " 'Raked' doesn't sound compelling to me, and 'naked' is completely impermissible. I don't think we would be allowed to substitute letters."

Rubin said, "Let me offer a pun, then. We don't have to rearrange the letters r-u-b-i-n. Just change it into two words, r-u-b i-n, 'rub in.' Cold cream, which is rubbed into the skin, appears to vanish and leave the skin bare. How about that?"

"Even more farfetched than 'raked,' " said Parris.

Gonzalo said, "g-o-n-z-a-l-o can be rearranged to a-z-o-l-o-n-g, which is 'a so long' in a German accent. A good-bye, in other words, and when everyone says good-bye, you're left bare of company."

"Good God!" said Rubin.

"I can't think of anything else," said Gonzalo defensively.

"If we're going to misspell," said Halsted, "my name can be rearranged into s-t-e-a-l-d-h, which is a misspelling of 'stealth,' and if people steal away, the place is left bare."

"Worse and worse," said Rubin.

"I'm worst of all," said Trumbull, scowling. "The only vowels in my name are two u's, and I can't do anything with that."

Parris said impatiently, "You are still not serious, gentlemen. None of this is worth anything at all. Please! If you want to keep the money from falling into vile hands, you *must* do better."

Avalon, who had had a tight smile on his face for the preceding few minutes, now hunched his magnificent eyebrows down over his eyes and let out a satanic cackle. "But I have it, gentlemen, and I'm delighted to be able to say that Henry, our unexcelled waiter, has overlooked the key clue. No matter, Henry. Even Homer nods."

"Far less often than I do, Mr. Avalon. What clue did I overlook, sir?"

"Why, in the preliminary message, there is not only the monogram, as you correctly pointed out, Henry, but also a reference to the fact that m-o-o-d, spelled backward, is d-o-o-m. That statement is rather a *non sequitur*, and we have a right to wonder why it's brought in at all."

"Because that's the way Ralph thinks—or thought," said Drake.

"Undoubtedly, but if you will take the trouble to spell Avalon backward, you have n-o l-a-v-a. No puns, no rearrangements, just do as Ralph did in the message."

Parris clenched both hands in excitement. "Now, that's the most interesting thing I've heard yet. But why 'no lava'?"

Avalon said, "A piece of ground over which lava has not flowed is bare."

Parris considered this and shook his head. "We might just as easily consider that ground over which lava has not flowed is rich in vegetation and is *not* bare. In that sense, it would be land which lava *has* flowed that would be bare."

Avalon said, "Very well, then, we can rearrange the letters slightly and we have o-n l-a-v-a. By Councilor Parris's argument there would be no vegetation on lava, and that anagram represents bareness."

"What about the reversed lettering?" said Gonzalo. "Mood to doom and all that."

"Well," said Avalon, "we'll have to eliminate that."

Parris said, "I liked 'no lava,' but it was not convincing. The reason I liked it, though, was that the backward spelling did seem to be a reasonable solution. 'On lava' without the backward spelling has nothing to recommend it."

There was a moment of silence and Rubin said, "You know, this is getting less funny all the time. Are we going to end up giving the money to the Nazis, even with Henry's help?"

Gonzalo said, "Well, let's ask him. What are we doing wrong, Henry?"

Henry said, "I'm not sure, Mr. Gonzalo. It does occur to me, though, that so far we have been punning and anagramming our last names—that is, the potential answers. Ought we to be working the question as well?"

"I don't see what you mean, Henry," said Avalon.

"It strikes me, Mr. Avalon, that the phrase 'to the barest' might just possibly be punned into 'to the bearest'; that is, b-e-a-r-e-s-t, the Black Widower most like a bear."

Trumbull said, "Terrible! It's a terrible pun and it's a terrible suggestion. I don't see how we can get any one of us to be clearly most like a bear anymore than we can get any one of us most bare."

Gonzalo said, "I don't know, Tom. You've got a terrible temper. You're the most bearish."

"Not while Manny is alive," said Trumbull hotly.

"I've never lost my temper in my life, damn it," shouted Rubin, just as hotly.

"Yes, like now," said Halsted.

Parris said, "Gentlemen, this is getting us nowhere either. Unless someone can think of something, we'll have to give up."

Henry said, "But we now have our solution, to my way of thinking, Mr. Parris. If we take the challenge to be that of finding the Black Widower most like a bear, may I point out that if we change the position of but one letter in r-u-b-i-n, we get b-r-u-i-n, the common name for the bear in the medieval animal epics, and still used today. I believe there is a hockey team known as the 'Bruins.' "

Parris said energetically, "I'll buy that. It is a clear solution that fits and is unique."

The Black Widowers broke into applause, and Henry turned pink.

Rubin said, "Since the money is mine, then, I will set up the trust fund with directions that the earned interest be turned over to Henry as an honorarium for his services to the club."

There was applause again.

Henry said, "Gentlemen, please don't. I will be overpaid."

"Come, come, Henry," said Rubin, "Are you refusing?"

Henry considered, sighed, and said, "I accept, sir, with thanks."

SIXTY MILLION TRILLION COMBINATIONS

Since it was Thomas Trumbull who was going to act as host for the Black Widowers that month, he did not, as was his wont, arrive at the last minute, gasping for his preprandial drink.

There he was, having arrived in early dignity, conferring with Henry, that peerless waiter, on the details of the menu for the evening, and greeting each of the others as he arrived.

Mario Gonzalo, who arrived last, took off his light overcoat with care, shook it gently, as though to remove the dust of the taxicab, and hung it up in the cloakroom. He came back, rubbing his hands, and said, "There's an autumn chill in the air. I think summer's over."

"Good riddance," called out Emmanuel Rubin, from where he stood conversing with Geoffrey Avalon and James Drake.

"I'm not complaining," called back Gonzalo. Then, to Trumbull, "Hasn't your guest arrived yet?"

Trumbull said distinctly, as though tired of explaining, "I have not brought a guest."

"Oh?" said Gonzalo, blankly. There was nothing absolutely irregular about that. The rules of the Black Widowers did not require a guest, although not to have one was most unusual. "Well, I guess that's all right."

"It's more than all right," said Geoffrey Avalon, who had just drifted in their direction, gazing down from his straight-backed height of seventy-four inches. His thick graying eyebrows hunched over his eyes and he said, "At least that guarantees us one meeting in which we can talk aimlessly and relax."

Gonzalo said, "I don't know about that. I'm used to the problems that come up. I don't think any of us will feel comfortable without one. Besides, what about Henry?"

He looked at Henry as he spoke and Henry allowed a discreet smile to cross his unlined, sixtyish face. "Please don't be concerned, Mr. Gonzalo. It will be my pleasure to serve the meal and attend the conversation even if there is nothing of moment to puzzle us."

"Well," said Trumbull, scowling, his crisply waved hair startlingly white over his tanned face, "you won't have that pleasure, Henry. I'm the one with the problem and I hope someone can solve it: *you* at least, Henry."

Avalon's lips tightened, "Now by Beelzebub's brazen bottom, Tom, you might have given us *one* old-fashioned—"

Trumbell shrugged and turned away, and Roger Halsted said to Avalon in his soft voice, "What's that Beelzebub bit? Where'd you pick that up?"

Avalon looked pleased. "Oh, well, Manny is writing some sort of adventure yarn set in Elizabeth's England—Elizabeth I of course—and it seems—"

Rubin, having heard the magic sound of his name, approached and said, "It's a sea story."

Halsted said, "Are you tired of mysteries?"

"It's a mystery also," said Rubin, his eyes flashing behind the thick lenses of his glasses. "What makes you think you can't have a mystery angle to *any* kind of story?"

"In any case," said Avalon, "Manny has one character forever swearing alliteratively and never the same twice and he needs a few more resounding oaths. Beelzebub's brazen bottom is good, I think."

"Or Mammon's munificent mammaries," said Halsted.

Trumbull said, violently, "There you are! If you don't come up with some problem that will occupy us in worthwhile fashion and engage our Henry's superlative mind, the whole evening would degenerate into stupid triplets—by Tutankhamen's tin trumpet."

"It gets you after a while," grinned Rubin, unabashed.

"Well, get off it," said Trumbull. "Is dinner ready, Henry?"

"Yes it is, Mr. Trumbull."

"All right, then. If you idiots keep this alliteration up for more than two minutes, I'm walking out, host or no host."

The table seemed empty with only six about it, and conversation seemed a bit subdued with no guest to sparkle before.

Gonzalo, who sat next to Trumbull, said, "I ought to draw a cartoon of you for our collection since you're your own guest, so to speak." He looked up complacently at the long list of guest-caricatures that lined the wall in rank and file. "We're going to run out of space in a couple of years."

"Then don't bother with me," said Trumbull, sourly, "and we can always make space by burning those foolish scrawls."

"Scrawls!" Gonzalo seemed to debate within himself briefly concerning the possibility of taking offense. Then he compromised by saying, "You seem to be in a foul mood, Tom."

"I seem so because I am. I'm in the situation of the Chaldean wise men facing Nebuchadnezzar."

Avalon leaned over from across the table. "Are you talking about the Book of Daniel, Tom?"

"That's where it is, isn't it?"

Gonzalo said, "Pardon me, but I didn't have my Bible lesson yesterday. What are these wise men?"

"Tell him, Jeff," said Trumbull. "Pontificating is your job."

Avalon said, "It's not pontificating to tell a simple tale. If you would rather—"

Gonzalo said, "I'd rather you did, Jeff. You do it much more authoritatively."

"Well," said Avalon, "it's Rubin, not I, who was once a boy preacher, but I'll do my poor best.—The second chapter of the Book of Daniel tells that Nebuchadnezzar was once troubled by a bad dream and he sent for his Chaldean wise men for an interpretation. The wise men offered to do so at once as soon as they heard the dream but Nebuchadnezzar couldn't remember the dream, only that he had been disturbed by it. He reasoned, however, that if wise men could interpret a dream, they could work out the dream, too, so he ordered them to tell him both the dream *and* the interpretation. When they couldn't do this, he very reasonably—by the standards of Oriental potentates—ordered them all killed. Fortunately for them Daniel, a captive Jew in Babylon, could do the job."

Gonzalo said, "And that's your situation, too, Tom?"

"In a way. I have a problem that involves a cryptogram—but I don't have the cryptogram. I have to work out the cryptogram."

"Or you'll be killed?" asked Rubin.

"No. If I fail, I won't be killed, but it won't do me any good, either."

Gonzalo said, "No wonder you didn't feel it necessary to bring a guest. Tell us about it."

"Before the brandy?" said Avalon, scandalized.

"Tom's host," said Gonzalo, defensively. "If he wants to tell us now—"

"I don't," said Trumbull. "We'll wait for the brandy as we always do, and I'll be my own griller, if you don't mind."

When Henry was pouring the brandy, Trumbull rang his spoon against his water glass and said, "Gentlemen, I will dispense with the opening question by admitting openly that I cannot justify my existence. Without pretending to go on by question-and-answer, I will simply state the problem. You are free to ask questions, but for God's sake, don't get me off on any wild-goose chases. This is serious."

Avalon said, "Go ahead, Tom. We will do our best to listen."

Trumbull said, with a certain weariness, "It involves a fellow named Pochik. I've got to tell you a little about him in order to let you understand the problem but, as is usual in these cases, I hope you don't mind if I tell you nothing that isn't relevant.

"In the first place he's from Eastern Europe, from someplace in

Slovenia, I think, and he came here at about fourteen. He taught himself English, went to night school and to University Extension, working every step of the way. He worked as a waiter for ten years, while he was taking his various courses, and you know what that means.—Sorry, Henry."

Henry said, tranquilly, "It is not necessarily a pleasant occupation. Not everyone waits on the Black Widowers, Mr. Trumbull."

"Thank you, Henry. That's very diplomatic of you.—However, he wouldn't have made it, if it weren't plain from the start that he was a mathematical wizard. He was the kind of young man that no mathematics professor in his right mind wouldn't have moved heaven and earth to keep in school. He was their claim to a mark in the history books—that they had taught Pochik. Do you understand?"

Avalon said, "We understand, Tom."

Trumbull said, "At least, that's what they tell me. He's working for the government now, which is where I come in. They tell me he's something else. They tell me he's in a class by himself. They tell me he can do things no one else can. They tell me they've got to have him. I don't even know what he's working on, but they've got to have him."

Rubin said, "Well, they've got him, haven't they? He hasn't been kidnapped and hijacked back across the Iron Curtain, has he?"

"No, no," said Trumbull, "nothing like that. It's a lot more irritating. Look, apparently a great mathematician can be an idiot in every other respect."

"Literally an idiot?" asked Avalon. "Usually idiots savants have remarkable memories and can play remarkable tricks in computation, but that is far from being any kind of mathematician, let alone a great one."

"No, nothing like that, either." Trumbull was perspiring and paused to mop at his forehead. "I mean he's childish. He's not really learned in anything but mathematics and that's all right. Mathematics is what we want out of him. The trouble is that he feels backward; he feels stupid. Damn it, he feels inferior, and when he feels *too* inferior, he stops working and hides in his room."

Gonzalo said, "So what's the problem? Everyone just has to keep telling him how great he is all the time."

"He's dealing with other mathematicians and they're almost as crazy as he is. One of them, Sandino, hates being second best and every once in a while he gets Pochik into a screaming fit. He's got a sense of humor, this Sandino, and he likes to call out to Pochik, 'Hey, waiter, bring the check.' Pochik can't ever learn to take it."

Drake said, "Read this Sandino the riot act. Tell him you'll dismember him if he tries anything like that again."

"They did," said Trumbull, "or at least as far as they quite dared to. They don't want to lose Sandino either. In any case, the horseplay stopped but something much worse happened.—You see there's something called, if I've got it right, 'Goldbach's conjecture.' "

Roger Halsted galvanized into a position of sharp interest at once. "Sure," he said. "Very famous."

"You know about it?" said Trumbull.

Halsted stiffened. "I may just teach algebra to junior high school students, but yes, I know about Goldbach's conjecture. Teaching a junior high school student doesn't *make* me a junior—"

"All right. I apologize. It was stupid of me," said Trumbull. "And since you're a mathematician, you can be temperamental too. Anyway, can you explain Goldbach's conjecture?—Because I'm not sure I can."

"Actually," said Halsted, "it's very simple. Back in 1742, I think, a Russian mathematician, Christian Goldbach, stated that he believed every even number greater than 2 could be written as the sum of two primes, where a prime is any number that can't be divided evenly by any other number but itself and 1. For instance, $4 = 2 + 2$; $6 = 3 + 3$; $8 = 3 + 5$; $10 = 3 + 7$; $12 = 5 + 7$; and so on, as far as you want to go."

Gonzalo said, "So what's the big deal?"

"Goldbach wasn't able to prove it. And in the two hundred and something years since his time, neither has anyone else. The greatest mathematicians haven't been able to show that it's true."

Gonzalo said, "So?"

Halsted said patiently, "Every even number that has ever been checked always works out to be the sum of two primes. They've gone awfully high and mathematicians are convinced the conjecture is true—but no one can *prove* it."

Gonzalo said, "If they can't find any exceptions, doesn't *that* prove it?"

"No, because there are always numbers higher than the highest we've checked, and besides we don't know all the prime numbers and can't, and the higher we go, then the harder it is to tell whether a particular number is prime or not. What is needed is a *general* proof that tells us we don't have to look for exceptions because there just aren't any. It bothers mathematicians that a problem can be stated so simply and seems to work out, too, and yet that it can't be proved."

Trumbull had been nodding his head. "All right, Roger, all right. We get it. But tell me, does it *matter*? Does it really matter to anyone who isn't a mathematician whether Goldbach's conjecture is true or not; whether there are any exceptions or not?"

"No," said Halsted. "Not to anyone who isn't a mathematician; but to anyone who is and who manages either to prove or disprove Goldbach's conjecture, there is an immediate and permanent niche in the mathematical hall of fame."

Trumbull shrugged. "There you are. What Pochik's really doing is of great importance. I'm not sure whether it's for the Department of Defense, the Department of Energy, NASA, or what, but it's vital. What *he's* interested in, however, is Goldbach's conjecture, and for that he's been using a computer."

"To try higher numbers?" asked Gonzalo.

Halsted said promptly, "No, that would do no good. These days, though, you can use computers on some pretty recalcitrant problems. It doesn't yield an elegant solution, but it is a solution. If you can reduce a problem to a finite number of possible situations—say, a million—you can program a computer to try every one of them. If every one of them checks out as it's supposed to, then you have your proof. They recently solved the four-color mapping problem that way; a problem as well known and as recalcitrant as Goldbach's conjecture."

"Good," said Trumbull, "then that's what Pochik's been doing. Apparently, he had worked out the solution to a particular lemma. Now what's a lemma?"

Halsted said, "It's a partway solution. If you're climbing a mountain peak and you set up stations at various levels, the lemmas are analogous to those stations and the solution to the mountain peak."

"If he solves the lemma, will he solve the conjecture?"

"Not necessarily," said Halsted, "any more than you'll climb the mountain if you reach a particular station on the slopes. But if you *don't* solve the lemma, you're not likely to solve the problem, at least not from that direction."

"All right, then," said Trumbull, sitting back. "Well, Sandino came up with the lemma first and sent it in for publication."

Drake was bent over the table, listening closely. He said, "Tough luck for Pochik."

Trumbull said, "Except that Pochik says it wasn't luck. He claims Sandino doesn't have the brains for it and couldn't have taken the steps he did independently; that it is asking too much of coincidence."

Drake said, "That's a serious charge. Has Pochik got any evidence?"

"No, of course not. The only way that Sandino could have stolen it from Pochik would have been to tap the computer for Pochik's data and Pochik himself says Sandino couldn't have done that."

"Why not?" said Avalon.

"Because," said Trumbull, "Pochik used a code word. The code word has to be used to alert the computer to a particular person's questioning. Without that code word, everything that went in *with* the code is safely locked away."

Avalon said, "It could be that Sandino learned the code word."

"Pochik says that is impossible," said Trumbull. "He was afraid of theft, particularly with respect to Sandino, and he never wrote down the code word, never used it except when he was alone in the room. What's more, he used one that was fourteen letters long, he says. Millions of trillions of possibilities, he says. No one could have guessed it, he says."

Rubin said, "What does Sandino say?"

"He says he worked it out himself. He rejects the claim of theft as the ravings of a madman. Frankly, one could argue that he's right."

Drake said, "Well, let's consider. Sandino is a good mathematician and he's innocent till proven guilty. Pochik has nothing to support his claim and Pochik actually denies that Sandino could possibly have gotten the code word, which is the only way the theft could possibly have taken place. I think Pochik has to be wrong and Sandino right."

Trumbull said, "I *said* one could argue that Sandino's right, but the point is that Pochik won't work. He's sulking in his room and reading poetry and he says he will never work again. He says Sandino has robbed him of his immortality and life means nothing to him without it."

Gonzalo said, "If you need this guy so badly can you talk Sandino into letting him have his lemma?"

"Sandino won't make the sacrifice and we can't make him unless we have reason to think that fraud was involved. If we get any evidence to that effect we can lean on him hard enough to squash him flat.—But now listen, I think it's possible Sandino *did* steal it."

Avalon said, "How?"

"By getting the code word. If I knew what the code word was, I'm sure I could figure out a logical way in which Sandino could have found it out or guessed it. Pochik, however simply won't let me have the code word. He shrieked at me when I asked. I explained why, but he said it was impossible. He said Sandino did it some other way—but there is no other way."

Avalon said, "Pochik wants an interpretation but he won't tell you the dream, and you have to figure out the dream first and then get the interpretation."

"Exactly! Like the Chaldean wise men."

"What are you going to do?"

"I'm going to try to do what Sandino must have done. I'm going to try to figure out what the fourteen-letter code word was and present it to Pochik. If I'm right, then it will be clear that what I could do, Sandino could do, and that the lemma was very likely stolen."

There was a silence around the table and then Gonzalo said, "Do you think you can do it, Tom?"

"I don't think so. That's why I've brought the problem here. I want us all to try. I told Pochik I would call him before 10:30 P.M. tonight"—Trumbull looked at his watch—"with the code word just to show him it *could* be broken. I presume he's waiting at the phone."

Avalon said, "And if we don't get it?"

"Then we have no reasonable way of supposing the lemma was stolen and no really ethical way of trying to force it away from Sandino. But at least we'll be no worse off."

Avalon said, "Then you go first. You've clearly been thinking about it longer than we have, and it's your line of work."

Trumbull cleared his throat. "All right. My reasoning is that if Pochik doesn't write the thing down, then he's got to remember it. There are some people with trick memories and such a talent is fairly common among mathematicians. However, even great mathematicians don't always have the ability to remember long strings of disjointed symbols and, upon questioning of his coworkers, it would seem quite certain that Pochik's memory is an ordinary one. He can't rely on being able to remember the code unless it's easy to remember.

"That would limit it to some common phrase or some regular progression that you couldn't possibly forget. Suppose it were ALBERT EINSTEIN, for instance. That's fourteen letters and there would be no fear of forgetting it. Or SIR ISAAC NEWTON, or ABCDEFGHIJKLMN, or, for that matter, NMLKJIHGFEDCBA. If Pochik tried something like this, it could be that Sandino tried various obvious combinations and one of them worked."

Drake said, "If that's true, then we haven't a prayer of solving the problem. Sandino might have tried any number of different possibilities over a period of months. One of them finally worked. If he got it by hit-and-miss over a long time, we have no chance in getting the right one in an hour and a half, without even trying any of them on the computer."

"There's that, of course," said Trumbull, "and it may well be that Sandino had been working on the problem for months. Sandino pulled the waiter routine on Pochik last June, and Pochik, out of his mind, screamed at him that he would show him when his proof was ready. Sandino may have put this together with Pochik's frequent use of the computer and gotten to work. He may have had months, at that."

"Did Pochik say something on that occasion that gave the code word away?" asked Avalon.

"Pochik swears all he said was 'I'll show you when the proof is ready,' but who knows? Would Pochik remember his own exact words when he was beside himself?"

Halsted said, "I'm surprised that Pochik didn't try to beat up this Sandino."

Trumbull said, "You wouldn't be surprised if you knew them. Sandino is built like a football player and Pochik weighs 110 pounds with his clothes on."

Gonzalo said, suddenly, "What's this guy's first name?"

Trumbull said, "Vladimir."

Gonzalo paused a while, with all eyes upon him, and then he said, "I knew it. VLADIMIR POCHIK has fourteen letters. He used his own name."

Rubin said, "Ridiculous. It would be the first combination anyone would try."

"Sure, the purloined letter bit. It would be so obvious that no one would think to use it. Ask him."

Trumbull shook his head. "No, I can't believe he'd use that."

Rubin said, thoughtfully, "Did you say he was sitting in his room reading poetry?"

"Yes."

"Is that a passion of his? Poetry? I thought you said that outside mathematics he was not particularly educated."

Trumbull said, sarcastically, "You don't have to be a Ph.D. to read poetry."

Avalon said, mournfully, "You would have to be an idiot to read modern poetry."

"That's a point," said Rubin. "Does Pochik read contemporary poetry?"

Trumbull said, "It never occurred to me to ask. When I visited him, he was reading from a book of Wordsworth's poetry, but that's all I can say."

"That's enough," said Rubin. "If he likes Wordsworth then he doesn't like contemporary poetry. No one can read that fuddy-duddy for fun and like the stuff they turn out these days."

"So? What difference does it make?" asked Trumbull.

"The older poetry with its rhyme and rhythm is easy to remember and it could make for code words. The code word could be a fourteen-letter passage from one of Wordsworth's poems, possibly a common one: LONELY AS A CLOUD has fourteen letters. Or any fourteen-letter combinations from such lines as 'The child is father of the man' or 'trailing clouds of glory' or 'Milton! thou shouldst be living at this hour.'—Or maybe from some other poet of the type."

Avalon said, "Even if we restrict ourselves to passages from the classic and romantic poets, that's a huge field to guess from."

Drake said, "I repeat. It's an impossible task. We don't have the time to try them all. And we can't tell one from another without trying."

Halsted said, "It's even more impossible than you think, Jim. I don't think the code word was in English words."

Trumbull said, frowning, "You mean he used his native language?"

"No, I mean he used a random collection of letters. You say that Pochik said the code word was unbreakable because there were millions of trillions of possibilities in a fourteen-letter combination. Well, suppose that the first letter could be any of the twenty-six, and the second letter could be any of the twenty-six, and the third letter, and so on. In that case the total number of combinations would be 26 x 26 x 26, and so on. You would have to get the product of fourteen 26's multiplied together and the result would be"—he took out his pocket calculator and manipulated it for a while—"about 64 million trillion different possibilities.

"Now, if you used an English phrase or a phrase in any reasonable European language, most of the letter combinations simply don't occur. You're not going to have an HGF or a QXZ or an LLLLC. If we include only *possible* letter combinations in words then we might have trillions of possibilities, probably less, but certainly not millions of trillions. Pochik, being a mathematician, wouldn't say millions of trillions unless he meant exactly that, so I expect the code word is a random set of letters."

Trumbull said, "He doesn't have the kind of memory—"

Halsted said, "Even a normal memory will handle fourteen random letters if you stick to it long enough."

Gonzalo said, "Wait awhile. If there are only so many combinations, you could use a computer. The computer could try every possible combination and stop at the one that unlocks it."

Halsted said, "You don't realize how big a number like 64 million trillion really is, Mario. Suppose you arranged to have the computer test a billion different combinations every second. It would take two thousand solid years of work, day and night, to test all the possible combinations."

Gonzalo said, "But you wouldn't have to test them all. The right one might come up in the first two hours. Maybe the code was AAAAAAAAAAAAAA and it happened to be the first one the computer tried."

"Very unlikely," said Halsted. "He wouldn't use a solid-A code any more than he would use his own name. Besides Sandino is enough of a mathematician not to start a computer attempt he would know could take a hundred lifetimes."

Rubin said, thoughtfully, "If he did use a random code I bet it wasn't truly random."

Avalon said, "How do you mean, Manny?"

"I mean if he doesn't have a superlative memory and he didn't write it down, how could he go over and over it in his mind in order to memorize it? Just repeat fourteen random letters to yourself and see if you can be confident of repeating them again in the exact order immediately afterward. And even if he *had* worked out a random collection of letters and managed to memorize it, it's clear he had very little self-confidence in anything except mathematical reasoning. Could he face the possibility of not being able to retrieve his own information because he had forgotten the code?"

"He could start all over," said Trumbull.

"With a new random code? And forget that, too?" said Rubin. "No. Even if the code word seems random, I'll bet Pochik has some foolproof way of remembering it, and if we can figure out the foolproof way, we'd have the answer. In fact, if Pochik would give us the code word, we'd see how he memorized it and see how Sandino broke the code."

Trumbull said, "And if Nebuchadnezzar would only have remembered the dream, the wise men could have interpreted it. Pochik won't give us the code word, and if we work it with hindsight, we'll never be sufficiently sure Sandino cracked it without hindsight.—All right, we'll have to give it up."

"It may not be necessary to give it up," said Henry, suddenly. "I think—"

All turned to Henry, expectantly. "Yes, Henry," said Avalon.

"I have a wild guess. It may be all wrong. Perhaps it might be possible to call up Mr. Pochik, Mr. Trumbull, and ask him if the code word is WEALTMDITEBIAT," said Henry.

Trumbull said, *"What?"*

Halsted said, his eyebrows high, "That's some wild guess, all right. Why that?"

Gonzalo said, "It makes no sense."

No one could recall ever having seen Henry blush, but he was distinctly red now. He said, "If I may be excused. I don't wish to explain my reasoning until the combination is tried. If I am wrong, I would appear too foolish.—And, on second thought, I don't urge it be tried."

Trumbull said, "No, we have nothing to lose. Could you write down that letter combination, Henry?"

"I have already done so, sir."

Trumbull looked at it, walked over to the phone in the corner of the room, and dialed. He waited for four rings, which could be clearly heard in the breath-holding silence of the room. There was then a click, and a sharp, high-pitched "Hello?"

Trumbull said, "Dr. Pochik? Listen. I'm going to read some letters to you—No, Dr. Pochik, I'm not saying I've worked out the code. This is an exper— It's an experiment sir. We may be wrong—No, I can't say how—Listen, W, E, A, L— Oh, good God." He placed his hand over the mouthpiece. "The man is having a fit."

"Because it's right or because it's wrong?" asked Rubin.

"I don't know." Trumbull put the phone back to his ear. "Dr. Pochik, are you there?—Dr. Pochik?—The rest is"—he consulted the paper—"T, M, D, I, T, E, B, I, A, T." He listened. "Yes, sir, I think Sandino cracked it, too, the same way we did. We'll have a meeting with you and Dr. Sandino, and we'll settle everything. Yes—please, Dr. Pochik, we will do our best."

Trumbull hung up, heaved an enormous sigh, then said, "Sandino is going to think Jupiter fell on him.—All right, Henry, but if you don't tell us how you got that, you won't have to wait for Jupiter. I will kill you personally."

"No need, Mr. Trumbull," said Henry. "I will tell you at once. I merely listened to all of you. Mr. Halsted pointed out it would have to be some random collection of letters. Mr. Rubin said, backing my own feeling in the matter, that there had to be some system of remembering in that case. Mr. Avalon, early in the evening, was playing the game of alliterative oaths, which pointed up the importance of initial letters. You yourself mentioned Mr. Pochik's liking for old-fashioned poetry like that of Wordsworth.

"It occurred to me then that fourteen was the number of lines in a sonnet, and if we took the initial letters of each line of some sonnet we would have an apparently random collection of fourteen letters that could not be forgotten as long as the sonnet was memorized or could, at worst, be looked up.

"The question was: which sonnet? It was very likely to be a well-known one, and Wordsworth had written some that were. In fact, Mr. Rubin mentioned the first line of one of them: 'Milton! thou shouldst be living at this hour.' That made me think of Milton, and it came to me that it *had* to be his sonnet 'On His Blindness' which as it happens, *I* know by heart. Please note the first letters of the successive lines. It goes:

"When I consider how my light is spent
Ere half my days, in this dark world and wide,
And that one talent which is death to hide,
Lodged with me useless, though my soul more bent
To serve therewith my Maker, and present
My true account, lest he returning chide;
'Doth God exact day-labor, light denied?'
I fondly ask; But Patience, to prevent
That murmur, soon replies, 'God doth not need
Either man's work or his own gifts; who best

Bear his mild yoke, they serve him best. His state
Is kingly. Thousands at his bidding speed
And post o'er land and ocean without rest: . . . . ' "

Henry paused and said softly, "I think it is the most beautiful sonnet in the language, Shakespeare's not excepted, but that was not the reason I felt it must hold the answer. It was that Dr. Pochik had been a waiter and was conscious of it, and I am one, which is why I have memorized the sonnet. A foolish fancy, no doubt, but the last line, which I have not quoted, and which is perhaps among the most famous lines Milton ever constructed—"

"Go ahead, Henry," said Rubin. "Say it!"

"Thank you, sir," said Henry, and then he said, solemnly,

" *'They also serve who only stand and wait.'* "

THE REDHEAD

Mario Gonzalo, host of that evening's meeting of the Black Widowers, had evidently decided to introduce his guest with éclat. At least he rattled his glass with a spoon and, when all had broken off their preprandial conversations and looked up from their cocktails, Mario made his introduction. He had even waited for Thomas Trumbull's as-usual late arrival before doing so.

"Gentlemen," he said, "this is my guest, John Anderssen—that's an *s-s-e-n* at the end. You can discover anything you want about him in this evening's grilling. One thing, however, I must tell you now because I know that this bunch of asexual loudmouths will never discover it on their own. John has a wife who is, absolutely, the most gorgeous specimen of femininity the world has ever seen. And I say this as an artist with an artist's eye."

Anderssen reddened and looked uncomfortable. He was a blond young man, perhaps thirty, with a small mustache and a fair complexion. He was about five-ten in height and had rather chiseled features that came together to form a handsome face.

Geoffrey Avalon, looking down from his stiff-backed seventy-four inches, said, "I must congratulate you, Mr. Anderssen, although you need not take seriously Mario's characterization of ourselves as asexual. I'm sure that each of us is quite capable of appreciating a beautiful woman. I, myself, although I might be considered to be past the first flush of hot-blooded youth, can—"

Trumbull said, "Spare us, Jeff, spare us. If you are going to give an embarrassing account of your prowess, you are better off being interrupted. From my point of view, the next best thing to having the young woman in our midst—if our customs allowed it—would be to see her photograph. I imagine, Mr. Anderssen, you carry a photo of your fair wife in your wallet. Would you consent to let us look at it?"

"No," said Anderssen, emphatically. Then, blushing furiously, he said, "I don't mean you can't look at it. I mean I don't have a photograph of her with me. I'm sorry." But he said it challengingly, and was clearly not sorry.

Gonzalo, unabashed, said, "Well, that's your loss, my friends. You should see her hair. It's gloriously red, a live red that just about glows in the dark. And natural, totally natural—and no freckles."

"Well," said Anderssen in half a mutter, "she stays out of the sun.—Her hair *is* her best feature."

Emmanuel Rubin, who had been standing on the outskirts, looking rather dour, said in a low voice, "And temper to match, I suppose."

Anderssen turned to him, and said, with an edge of bitterness, "She has a temper." He did not elaborate.

Rubin said, "I don't suppose there's a more durable myth than the one that redheads are hot-tempered. The redness of the hair is that of fire, and the principles of sympathetic magic lead people to suppose that the personality should match the hair."

James Drake, who shared, with Avalon, the dubious privilege of being the oldest of the Widowers, sighed reminiscently, and said, "I've known some very hot-blooded redheads."

"Sure you have," said Rubin. "So has everyone. It's a self-fulfilling assumption. Redheaded children, especially girls, are forgiven for being nasty and ill-behaved. Parents sigh fatuously and mutter that it goes with the hair, and the one with red hair in the family explains how Great-Uncle Joe would mop up the floor with anyone in the barroom who said anything that was less than a grovelling compliment. Boys usually grow up and have the stuffing knocked out of them by nonredheaded peers and that teaches them manners, but girls don't. And, if they're beautiful besides, they grow up knowing they can indulge their impoliteness to the hilt. An occasional judicious kick in the fanny would do them worlds of good."

Rubin carefully did not look at Anderssen in the course of his comment and Anderssen said nothing at all.

Henry, the indispensable waiter at all the Black Widower functions, said quietly, "Gentlemen, you may be seated."

The chef at the Milano had clearly decided to be Russian for the evening, and an excellent hot borscht was followed by an even more delightful beef Stroganoff on a bed of rice. Rubin, who usually endured the food with an expression of stoic disapproval, on principle, allowed a smile to play over his sparsely bearded face on this occasion, and helped himself lavishly to the dark pumpernickel.

As for Roger Halsted, whose affection for a good meal was legendary, he quietly negotiated a second helping with Henry.

The guest, John Anderssen, ate heartily, and participated eagerly in the conversation which, through a logical association, perhaps, dealt largely with the shooting down of the Korean jetliner by the Soviets. Anderssen pointed out that the ship had been widely referred to as "Flight 007," which was the number on the fuselage, during the first couple of weeks. Then someone must have remembered that 007 was the code number of James Bond, so when the Soviets insisted the liner had been a spy plane, it became "Flight 7" in the news media, and the "00" disappeared as though it had never been.

He also maintained vigorously that the jetliner, having gone off course almost immediately after leaving Alaska, should not have been left uninformed of the fact. He was shouting, red-faced, that failure to do so, when the Soviet Union was known to be on the hair trigger with respect to American reconnaissance planes and to Reagan's "evil empire" rhetoric, was indefensible.

He paid no attention, in fact, to his dessert, a honey-drenched baklava; left his coffee half-finished; and totally ignored Henry's soft request that he make his wishes known with respect to the brandy.

He was actually pounding the table when Gonzalo rattled his spoon against his water glass. Avalon was forced to raise his baritone voice to a commanding, "Mr. Anderssen, *if* you please—"

Anderssen subsided, looking vaguely confused, as though he were, with difficulty, remembering where he was.

Gonzalo said, "It's time for the grilling, and Jeff, since you seem to have the commanding presence needed in case John, here, gets excited, suppose you do the honors."

Avalon cleared his throat, gazed at Anderssen solemnly for a few moments, then said, "Mr. Anderssen, how do you justify your existence?"

Anderssen said, "What?"

"You exist, sir. Why?"

"Oh," said Anderssen, still collecting himself. Then, in a low harsh voice, he said, "To expiate my sins in an earlier existence, I should think."

Drake, who was at the moment accepting a refresher from Henry, muttered, "So are we all.—Don't you think so, Henry?"

And Henry's sixtyish unlined face remained expressionless as he said, very softly, "A Black Widowers banquet is surely a reward for virtue rather than an expiation for sins."

Drake lifted his glass. "A palpable hit, Henry."

Trumbull growled, "Let's cut out the private conversations."

Avalon raised his hand. "Gentlemen! As you all know, I do not entirely approve of our custom of grilling a guest in the hope of searching out problems that might interest us. Nevertheless, I wish to call your attention to a peculiar phenomenon. We have here a young man—young, certainly, by the standards of old mustaches such as ourselves—well-proportioned, of excellent appearance, seeming to exude good health and an air of success in life, though we have not yet ascertained what the nature of his work is—"

"He's in good health and is doing well at his work," put in Gonzalo.

"I am glad to hear it," said Avalon, gravely. "In addition, he is married to a young and beautiful woman, so that one can't help but wonder why he should feel life to be such a burden as to lead him to believe that he exists only in order to expiate past sins. Consider, too, that during the meal just concluded, Mr. Anderssen was animated and vivacious, not in the least abashed by our older and wiser heads. I believe he shouted down even Manny, who is not one to be shouted down with impunity—"

"Anderssen was making a good point," said Rubin, indignantly.

"I think he was, too," said Avalon, "but what I wish to stress is that he is voluble, articulate, and not backward at expressing his views. Yet during the cocktail period, when the conversation dealt with his wife, he seemed to speak most reluctantly. From this, I infer that the source of Mr. Anderssen's unhappiness may be Mrs. Anderssen.—Is that so, Mr. Anderssen?"

Anderssen seemed stricken and remained silent.

Gonzalo said, "John, I explained the terms. You must answer."

Anderssen said, "I'm not sure how to answer."

Avalon said, "Let me be indirect. After all, sir, there is no intention to humiliate you. And please be aware that nothing said in this room is ever repeated by any of us elsewhere. That includes our esteemed waiter, Henry. Please feel that you can speak freely.—Mr. Anderssen, how long have you been married?"

"Two years. Actually, closer to two and a half."

"Any children, sir?"

"Not yet. We hope to have some one day."

"For that hope to exist, the marriage must not be foundering. I take it you are not contemplating divorce."

"Certainly not."

"I take it then that you love your wife?"

"Yes. And before you ask, I am quite satisfied she loves me."

"There is, of course, a certain problem in being married to a beautiful woman," said Avalon. "Men *will* flock about beauty. Are you plagued by jealousy, sir?"

"No," said Anderssen. "I've no cause for it. Helen—that's my wife—has no great interest in men—"

"Ah," said Halsted, as though a great light had dawned.

"Except for myself," said Anderssen, indignantly. "She's not in the least bit asexual. Besides," he went on, "Mario exaggerates. She does have this luxuriant head of remarkable red hair, but aside from that she is not really spectacular. Her looks, I would say, are average—though I must rely now on your assurance that all said here is confidential. I would not want *that* assessment to be repeated. Her figure is good, and *I* find her beautiful, but there are no men caught helplessly in her toils, and I am not plagued by jealousy."

"What about her temper?" put in Drake, suddenly. "That's been mentioned and you've admitted she had one. I presume there's lots of fighting and dish throwing?"

"Some fights, sure," said Anderssen, "but no more than is par for the course. And no dish throwing. As Mr. Avalon has pointed out, I'm articulate, and so is she, and we're both pretty good at shouting, but after we work off our steam, we can be just as good at kissing and hugging."

"Then am I to take it, sir, that your wife is *not* the source of your troubles?" said Avalon. Anderssen fell silent again.

"I must ask you to answer, Mr. Anderssen," said Avalon.

Anderssen said, "She *is* the problem. Just now, anyway. But it's too silly to talk about."

Rubin sat up at that and said, "On the contrary. Till now, I felt that Jeff was just wasting our time over the kind of domestic irritations that we attend these dinners, in part, to escape. But if there's something *silly* involved, then we want to hear it."

"If you must know," said Anderssen. "Helen says she's a witch."

"Oh?" said Rubin. "Has she always claimed this, or just recently?"

"Always. We joke about it. She would say she put me under enchantment to get me to marry her, and that she would cast spells and get me a promotion or a raise. Sometimes, when she is furious, she'll say, 'Well, don't blame me if you blotch out in pimples just because you're going to be that stupid and mean.' That sort of thing."

Rubin said, "It sounds harmless to me. She probably *did* put you under enchantment. You fell in love with her and any woman of reasonable intelligence and looks can make a young man fall in love with her if she works hard enough being charming. You can call that enchantment if you wish."

"But I *do* get the promotions and raises."

"Surely that could be because you deserve them. Do you get the pimples, too?"

Anderssen smiled. "Well, I managed to trip and sprain an ankle and, of course, she said she had changed the spell because she didn't want to spoil my pretty face."

Halsted laughed and said, "You don't really act disturbed at this, Mr. Anderssen. After all, this sort of playacting by a young and vivacious woman isn't unusual. Personally, I find it charming. Why don't you?"

Anderssen said, "Because she pulled it on me once too often. She did something that I can't understand." He threw himself back in his chair and stared somberly at the table in front of him.

Trumbull bent to one side as though to look into Anderssen's eyes and said, "You mean you think she really is a witch?"

"I don't know what to think. I just can't explain what she did."

Avalon said, forcibly, "Mr. Anderssen, I must ask you to explain just what it was that Mrs. Anderssen did. Would you do that, sir?"

"Well," said Anderssen, "maybe I should. If I talk about it, maybe I can forget it.—But I don't think so."

He brooded a bit and the Widowers waited patiently.

Finally, he said, "It was just about a month ago—the sixteenth. We were going out for dinner, just the two of us. We do that once in a while, and we like to try new places. We were trying a new place this time, the door to which was reached by passing through the lobby of a small midtown hotel. It was an unpretentious restaurant, but we had had good reports of it.—The trouble started in the lobby.

"I don't remember exactly what set it off. In fact, I don't even remember what it was all about, really. What happened afterward pushed it out of my mind. What it amounted to was that we had a—a disagreement. In less than a minute, we would have been inside the restaurant and studying the menu, and instead, we were standing to one side of the lobby, under a plastic potted plant of some sort. I can remember the sharply pointed leaves touching my hand disagreeably when I waved it to make a point. The registration desk was across the way, between the door to the restaurant and the door to the street. The scene is still painted in my mind.

"Helen was saying, 'If that's your attitude, we don't have to have dinner together.'

"I swear to all of you, I don't remember what my attitude was, but we're both of us highly vocal, and we were both of us furious, I admit. The whole thing was highly embarrassing. It was one of those times when you and someone else—usually your wife or girlfriend, I suppose—are shouting at each other in whispers. The words are being squeezed out between clenched teeth, and every once in a while one of you says, 'For Heaven's sake, people are staring,' and the other says, 'Then shut up and listen to reason,' and the first one says, 'You're the one who isn't listening,' and it just keeps on and on."

Anderssen shook his head at the memory. "It was the most intense argument we had ever had up to that time, or since, and yet I can't remember what it was about. Unbelievable!

"Then she suddenly said, 'Well, then, I'm going home. Good-bye.' I said, 'Don't you dare humiliate me by leaving me in public.' And she said, 'You can't stop me.' And I said, 'Don't tempt me, or I *will* stop you.' And she said, 'Just try,' and dashed into the restaurant.

"That caught me by surprise. I had thought she would try to get past me to the door to the street—and I was ready to seize her wrist and hang on. It would have been better to let her go than to make a scene, I suppose, but I was past reason. In any case, she fooled me, and made a dash for the restaurant.

"I was stunned for a moment—two moments—and then I hurried in after her. I may have been twenty seconds behind her.—Let me describe the restaurant. It was not a large one, and it had the deliberate decor of a living room. In fact, the restaurant is called The Living Room.—Are any of you acquainted with it?"

There was a blank murmur about the table, but Henry, who had cleared the dishes with his usual unobtrusive efficiency and was standing by the sideboard, said, "Yes, sir. It is, as you say, a small but well-run restaurant."

"It had about a dozen tables," Anderssen proceeded, "the largest of which would hold six. There were windows with drapes, but not real windows. They had city views painted on them. There was a fireplace in the wall opposite the entrance door with artificial logs in it, and a couch facing it. The couch was real and, I suppose, could be used by people who were waiting for the rest of their party to arrive. At least, there was one man sitting on the left end of the couch. He had his back to me, and was reading a magazine that he held rather high and close to his head as though he were nearsighted. I judged from its typography that it was *Time*—"

Avalon put in suddenly, "You seem to be a good observer and you are going into minutiae. Is this important that you've just told us?"

"No," said Anderssen, "I suppose not, but I am trying to impress on you that I was not hysterical and that I was entirely myself and saw everything there was to see quite clearly. When I came in, about half the tables were taken, with two to four people at each. There may have been fifteen to twenty people present. There were no waitresses on the scene at the moment and the cashier was stationed just outside the restaurant, to one side of the door in a rather unobtrusive recess, so it really did look like a living room."

Drake stubbed out his cigarette. "It sounds like an idyllic place. What was present there that disturbed you?"

"Nothing was present that disturbed me. That's the point. It was what was absent there. Helen wasn't there.—Look, she had gone in. I saw her go in. I am *not* mistaken. There was no other door on that side of the lobby. There was no crowd within which she might have been lost to view for a moment. My vision was entirely unobstructed and she went in and did not come out. I followed in her tracks and entered, at the most, twenty seconds after her—maybe less, but not more. And she was not there. I could tell that at a glance."

Trumbull growled. "You can't tell anything at a glance. A glance will fool you."

"Not in this case," said Anderssen. "Mario mentioned Helen's hair. There's just nothing like it. At least I've seen nothing like it. There may have been, at most, ten women there and not one had red hair. Even if one of them had been a redhead, I doubt she would have been a redhead in quite the fluorescent and lavishly spectacular way that Helen was. Take my word for it. I looked right—left, and there was no Helen. She had disappeared."

"Gone out to the street by another entrance, I suppose," said Halsted.

Anderssen shook his head. "There was no entrance to the street. I checked with the cashier afterward, and with the fellow at the registration desk. I've gone back there since to order lunch and managed to look over the place. There isn't any entrance to the outside. What's more, the windows are fakes and they're solid something-or-other. They don't open. There are ventilation ducts, of course, but they're not big enough for a rabbit to crawl through."

Avalon said, "Even though the windows are fake, you mentioned drapes. She might have been standing behind one of them."

"No," said Anderssen, "the drapes hug the wall. There would have been an obvious bump if she were behind one. What's more, they only came down to the bottom of the window and there are two feet of bare wall beneath them. She would have been visible to midthigh if she were standing behind one."

"What about the ladies' room?" inquired Rubin. "You know, so strong is the taboo against violating the one-sex nature of these things, we tend to forget the one we don't use is even there."

"Well, I didn't," said Anderssen, with clear exasperation. "I looked around for it, didn't see any indication, and when I asked later, it turned out that both restrooms were in the lobby. A waitress did show up while I was looking around and I said to her in, I suppose, a rather distracted voice, 'Did a redheaded woman just come in here?'

"The waitress looked at me in a rather alarmed way, and mumbled, 'I didn't see anyone,' and hastened to deliver her tray load to one of the tables.

"I hesitated because I was conscious of my embarrassing position, but I saw no way out. I raised my voice and said, 'Has anyone here seen a redheaded woman come in just a moment ago?' There was dead silence. Everyone looked up at me, staring stupidly. Even the man on the couch turned his head to look at me and he shook his head at me in a clear negative. The others didn't even do that much, but their vacant stares were clear enough indication that they hadn't seen her.

"Then it occurred to me that the waitress must have emerged from the kitchen. For a minute, I was sure that Helen was hiding there and I felt triumphant. Regardless of the fact that my actions might induce some of the staff to call hotel security, or the police, even, I marched firmly through a pair of swinging doors into the kitchen. There was the chef there, a couple of assistants, and another waitress. No Helen. There was one small further door which might have been a private lavatory for the kitchen staff, and I had gone too far to back down. I walked over and flung the door open. It *was* a lavatory, and it was empty. By then the chef and his assistants were shouting at me, and I said, 'Sorry,' and left quickly. I didn't see any closets there large enough to hold a human being.

"I stepped back into the restaurant. Everyone was still looking at me, and I could do nothing but return to the lobby. It was as though the instant Helen had passed through the doorway into the restaurant, she had vanished."

Anderssen sat back, spread his hands in blank despair. "Just vanished."

Drake said, "What did you do?"

Anderssen said, "I went out and talked to the cashier. She had been away from her station for a few moments and she hadn't even seen me go in, let alone Helen. She told me about the rest-rooms and that there was no exit to the street.

"Then I went to talk to the room clerk, which demoralized me further. He was busy and I had to wait. I wanted to yell, 'This is a matter of life and death,' but I was beginning to think I would be carried off to an asylum if I didn't behave in a totally proper way. And when I spoke to him, the room clerk turned out to be a total zero, though what could I really have expected from him?"

"And then what did you do?" asked Drake.

"I waited in the lobby for about half an hour. I thought Helen might show up again; that she had been playing some practical joke and that she would return. Well, no Helen. I could only spend my time fantasizing, as I waited, of calling the police, of hiring a private detective, of personally scouring the city, but you know—What do I tell the police? That my wife has been missing for an hour? That my wife vanished under my eyes? And I don't know any private detectives. For that matter, I don't know how to scour a city. So, after the most miserable half hour of my whole life, I did the only thing there was to do. I hailed a taxi and went home."

Avalon said, solemnly, "I trust, Mr. Anderssen, that you are not going to tell us your wife has been missing ever since."

Gonzalo said, "She can't be, Jeff. I saw her two days ago."

Anderssen said, "She was waiting for me when I got home. For a minute, a wave of intense thankfulness swept over me. It had been a terrible taxi ride. All I could think of was that she would have to be missing twenty-four hours before I could call the police and how would I live through the twenty-four hours? And what would the police be able to do?

"So I just grabbed her and held on to her. I was on the point of weeping, I was so glad to see her. And then, of course, I pushed her away and said, 'Where the hell have you been?'

"She said, coolly, 'I told you I was going home.'

"I said, 'But you ran into the restaurant.'

"She said, 'And then I went home. You don't suppose I needed a broomstick, do you? That's quite old-fashioned. I just—*pfft*—and I was home.' She made a sweeping motion of her right hand.

"I was furious. I had gotten completely over my relief. I said, 'Do you know what you've put me through? Can you imagine how I felt? I rushed in like a damn fool and tried to find you and then I just stood around.—I almost went to the police.'

"She grew calmer and icier and said, 'Well, it serves you right for what you did. Besides, I *told* you I was going home. There was no need for you to do anything at all but go home, too. Here I am. Just because you refuse to believe I have the power is no reason for you to begin scolding me, when I did exactly what I told you I would do.'

"I said, 'Come on, now. You didn't *pfft* here. Where were you in the restaurant? How did you get here?'

"I could get no answer from her on that. Nor have I been able to since. It's ruining my life. I *resent* her having put me through an hour of hell. I *resent* her making a fool of me."

Avalon said, "Is the marriage breaking up as a result? Surely, you need not allow one incident—"

"No, it's not breaking up. In fact, she's been sweet as apple pie ever since that evening. She hasn't pulled a single witch trick, but it bothers the dickens out of me. I brood about it. I *dream* about it. It's given her a kind of—superiority—"

Rubin said, "She's got the upper hand now, you mean."

"Yes," said Anderssen, violently. "She's made a fool of me and gotten away with it. I *know* she's not a witch. I *know* there are no such things as witches. But I don't know how she did it, and I've got this sneaking suspicion she's liable to do it again, and it keeps me—it keeps me—*under*."

Anderssen then shook his head and said, in a more composed way, "It's such a silly thing, but it's poisoning my life."

Again there was silence about the table, and then Avalon said, "Mr. Anderssen, we of the Black Widowers are firm disbelievers in the supernatural. Are you telling us the truth about the incident?"

Anderssen said, fiercely, "I assure you I have told you the truth. If you have a Bible here, I'll swear on it. Or, which is better as far as I am concerned, I'll give you my word as an honest man that everything I've told you is as completely true as my memory and my human fallibility will allow."

Avalon nodded. "I accept your word without reservation."

Gonzalo said, in an aggrieved way, "You might have told me, John. As I said, I saw Helen two days ago, and nothing seemed wrong to me. I had no idea—Maybe it's not too late for us to help."

"How?" said Anderssen. "How could you help?"

Gonzalo said, "We might discuss the matter. Some of us may have some ideas."

Rubin said, "I have one, and, I think, a very logical one. I begin by agreeing with Anderssen and everyone else here that there is no witchcraft and that, therefore, Mrs. Anderssen is no witch. I think she went into the restaurant and somehow managed to evade her husband's eyes. Then when he was busy in the kitchen or at the registration desk, she left the restaurant and the hotel quickly, took a taxi, went home, and then waited for him. Now she won't admit what it is she has done in order to stay one-up in this needless marriage combat. My own feeling is that a marriage is useless if—"

"Never mind the homilies," said Anderssen, the shortness of his temper fuse showing. "Of *course* that's what happened. I don't need you to explain it to me. But you skip over the hard part. You say she went into the restaurant and 'somehow managed to evade her husband's eyes.' Would you please tell me just how she managed that trick?"

"Very well," said Rubin. "I will. You came in, looked right and left, and were at once certain she wasn't there. Why? Because you were looking for an unmistakable redhead.—Have you ever heard of a wig; Mr. Anderssen?"

"A *wig*? You mean she put on a *wig*?"

"Why not? If she appeared to have brown hair, your eyes would pass right over her. In fact, I suspect that her red hair is so much the most important thing you see in her that if she were wearing a brown wig and had taken a seat at one of the tables, you could have been staring right at her face without recognizing it."

Anderssen said, "I insist I would have recognized her even so, but that point is of no importance. The important thing is that Helen has never owned a wig. For her to use one is unthinkable. She is as aware of her red hair as everyone else is, and she is vain about it, and wouldn't dream of hiding it. Such vanity is natural. I'm sure everyone here is vain about his intelligence."

Rubin said, "I grant you. Intelligence is something to be vain about. Yet, if it served some purpose that seemed important to me, I would pretend to be an idiot for a few minutes, or even considerably longer. I think your wife would have been willing to slip on a brown wig just long enough to escape your eye. Vanity is never an absolute in anyone who isn't an outright fool."

Anderssen said, "I know her better than you do, and I say she wouldn't wear a wig. Besides, I told you this was a month ago. It was the height of summer and it was a hot evening. All Helen was wearing was a summer dress with only summer underwear beneath, and she had a light shawl to put on against the air conditioning. She was holding a small pocketbook, just large enough to contain some money and her makeup. There was nowhere she could have hidden a wig. She had no wig with her. Why should she have brought one with her, anyway? I can't and won't believe that she was deliberately planning to have a fight, and to trick me in this way in order to achieve a long-term upper hand. She's a creature of impulse, I tell you, and is incapable of making plans of that kind. I *know* her."

Trumbull said, "Conceding her vanity and impulsiveness, what about her dignity? Would she have been willing to duck under one of the tables and let the tablecloth hide her?"

"The tablecloths did not come down to the ground. I would have seen her.—I tell you I've gone back to the restaurant and studied it in cold blood. There is *nowhere* she could have hidden. I was even desperate enough to wonder if she could have worked her way up the chimney, but the fireplace isn't real and isn't attached to one."

Drake said, "Anyone have any other ideas? I don't."

There was silence.

Drake turned half about in his chair. "Do you have anything to volunteer, Henry?"

Henry said, with a small smile, "Well, Dr. Drake, I have a certain reluctance to spoil Mrs. Anderssen's fun."

"Spoil her fun?" said Anderssen in astonishment. "Are you telling me, waiter, that you know what happened?"

Henry said, "I know what might easily have happened, sir, that would account for the disappearance without the need for any sort of witchcraft and I assume, therefore, that that was, indeed, what happened."

"What was it, then?"

"Let me be certain I understand one point. When you asked the people in the restaurant if they had seen a redheaded woman enter, the man on the couch turned around and shook his head in the negative. Is that right?"

"Yes, he did. I remember it well. He was the only one who really responded."

"But you said the fireplace was at the wall opposite the door into the restaurant and that the couch faced it, so that the man had his back to you. He had to turn around to look at you. That means his back was also to the door, and he was reading a magazine. Of all the people there, he was least likely to see someone enter the door, yet he was the one person to take the trouble to indicate he had seen no one. Why should he have?"

"What has all that got to do with it, waiter?" said Anderssen.

"Call him Henry," muttered Gonzalo.

Henry said, "I would suggest that Mrs. Anderssen hurried in and took her seat on the couch, an ordinary and perfectly natural action that would have attracted no attention from a group of people engaged in dining and in conversation, even despite her red hair."

"But I would have seen her as soon as I came in," said Anderssen. "The back of the couch only reaches a person's shoulders and Helen is a tall woman. Her hair would have blazed out at me."

"On a chair," said Henry, "it is difficult to do anything but sit. On a couch, however, one can lie down."

Anderssen said, "There was a man already sitting on the couch."

"Even so," said Henry. "Your wife, acting on impulse, as you say she is apt to do, reclined. Suppose you were on a couch, and an attractive redhead, with a fine figure, dressed in a skimpy summer costume, suddenly stretched out and placed her head in your lap; and that, as she did so, she raised her finger imploringly to her mouth, pleading for silence. It seems to me there would be very few men who wouldn't oblige a lady under those circumstances."

Anderssen's lips tightened. "Well—"

"You said the man was holding his magazine high, as though he were nearsighted, but might that not be because he was holding it high enough to avoid the woman's head in his lap? And then, in his eagerness to oblige a lady, would he not turn his head and unnecessarily emphasize that he hadn't seen her?"

Anderssen rose. "Right! I'll go home right now and have it out with her."

"If I may suggest, sir," said Henry. "I would not do that."

"I sure will. Why not?"

"In the interest of family harmony, it might be well if you would let her have her victory. I imagine she rather regrets it and is not likely to repeat it. You said she has been very well behaved this last month. Isn't it enough that you know in your heart how it was done so that you needn't feel defeated yourself? It would be her victory without your defeat and you would have the best of both worlds."

Slowly, Anderssen sat down and, amid a light patter of applause from the Black Widowers, said, "You may be right, Henry."

"I think I am," said Henry.

THE WRONG HOUSE

The guest at the monthly banquet of the Black Widowers frowned at the routine question asked him by that best of all waiters, Henry.

"No," he said, vehemently. "Nothing! Nothing!—No, not even ginger ale. I'll just have a glass of water, if you don't mind."

He turned away, disturbed. He had been introduced as Christopher Levan. He was a bit below average height, slim, and well-dressed. His skull was mostly bald but was so well-shaped that the condition seemed attractive rather than otherwise.

He was talking to Mario Gonzalo and returned to the thread of his conversation with an apparent effort, saying, "The art of cartooning seems simple. I have seen books that show you how to draw familiar shapes and forms, starting with an oval, let us say, then modifying it in successive stages till it becomes Popeye or Snoopy or Dick Tracy. And yet how does one decide what oval to make and what modifications to add in the first place? Besides, it is not easy to copy. No matter how simple the steps seem to be, when I try to follow them, the end result is distorted and amateurish."

Gonzalo looked, with a certain complacency, at the cartoon he had just drawn of the guest, and said, "You have to allow for a kind of inborn talent and for years of experience, Mr. Levan."

"I suppose so, and yet you didn't draw any oval with modifications. You simply drew that head freehand as quickly as you could and without any effort as far as I could tell.—Except that somehow my head looks shiny. Is it?"

"Not particularly. That's just cartoonist's license."

"Except that," said Emmanuel Rubin, drawing near with a

drink in his hand, "if licenses were required for cartooning, Mario would never qualify. Some may have talent, but Mario gets by with effrontery."

Gonzalo grinned. "He means chutzpah. Manny knows about that. He writes stories which he actually submits to editors."

"And sells," said Rubin.

"An indication of occasional editorial desperation."

Levan smiled. "When I hear two people spar like that, I am certain that there is actually a profound affection between them."

"Oh, God," said Rubin, visibly revolted. His sparse beard bristled and his eyes, magnified through the thick lenses of his glasses, glared.

"You've hit it, Mr. Levan," said Gonzalo. "Manny would give me the shirt off his back if no one were looking. The only thing he wouldn't give me is a kind word."

Geoffrey Avalon, the host of this banquet, called out, "Are you getting tangled up in some nonsense between Manny and Mario, Chris?"

"Voluntarily, Jeff," said Levan. "I like these bouts with pillows and padded bats."

"It gets wearisome," said Avalon, staring down from his seventy-four-inch height, "past the fifty-seven thousandth time.—But come and sit down, Chris. We are having nothing less good than lobster tonight."

It is not to be denied that an elaborate lobster dinner tends to inhibit conversation a bit. The cracking of shells takes considerable concentration and the dipping into drawn butter is not a matter to be carried through casually. The period between the Portuguese fish chowder and the *coupe aux marrons* was largely silent, therefore, as far as the human voice was concerned, though the nutcracking play kept the table at a low growl.

"I despise lobster salad," said Roger Halsted over the coffee. "It's like eating seedless watermelon cut into cubes. The worth of the prize is directly proportional to the pains taken to win it."

Levan said, "I suppose, then, you would be very much against interest-free loans," and he chuckled with a sated air.

"Well," said James Drake, in his hoarsely muted voice, "I imagine even Roger would consider that as carrying a principle too far."

Thomas Trumbull fixed Levan with a glowering eye. "That's a banker's joke. Are you a banker?"

"One moment, Tom," said Avalon. "You're beginning to grill and the grilling session has not yet been opened."

"Well, then, open it, Jeff. We're on our coffee, and Henry is going to come around with the brandy in a millisecond." Trumbull looked at his watch. "And the lobster has delayed us, so let's go."

"I was about to begin," said Avalon, with dignity. He tapped his glass three or four times. "Tom, since you are so anxious, won't you begin the grilling."

"Certainly," said Trumbull. "Mr. Levan, are you a banker?"

"That is not the traditional opener," said Gonzalo.

Trumbull said, "Who asked you? What you're thinking of is traditional; it's not mandatory.—Mr. Levan, are you a banker?"

"Yes, I am. At least, I'm the vice president of a bank."

"Hah," said Trumbull. "*Now* I'll ask you the traditional opener. Mr. Levan, how do you justify your existence?"

Levan's smile became a beam. "Easiest thing in the world. The human body is completely dependent on blood circulation, which is driven by the heart. The world economy is completely dependent on money circulation, which is driven by the banks. I do my bit."

"Are the banks motivated in this by a desire for the good of the world or for the profits of their owners?"

Levan said, "Socialist claptrap, if you don't mind my saying so. You imply that the two motives are mutually exclusive, and that is not so. The heart drives the blood into the aorta and the first arteries to branch off are the coronaries, which feed what? The heart! In short, the heart's first care is for the heart, and that is as it should be, for without the heart all else fails. Let the coronaries get choked up and you'll find yourself agreeing with the heart, and wishing it were anything else that was on short rations."

"Not the brain," said Drake. "Sooner the heart. Better die of a heart attack than live on in senility."

Levan thought a bit. "That's hard to disagree with, but we may treat and reverse senility a lot sooner than we are likely to be able to treat and reverse death."

Gonzalo, frowning, said, "Come on, what's this subject we've latched on to? And on a full stomach, too. Hey, Tom, may I ask a question?"

Trumbull said, "All right. Subject changed. Ask a question, Mario, but don't make it a dumb one."

Gonzalo said, "Mr. Levan, are you a member of Alcoholics Anonymous?"

There was a sudden silence about the table and then Trumbull, face twisted in anger, growled, "I *said*, don't make it—"

"It's a legitimate question," insisted Gonzalo, raising his voice, "and the rules of the game are that the guest must answer."

Levan, not smiling, and looking grim rather than embarrassed, said, "I'll answer the question. I am *not* a member of Alcoholics Anonymous, and I am not an alcoholic."

"Are you a teetotaler, then?"

For some reason, Levan seemed to find more difficulty answering that. "Well, no. I drink on occasion—a bit. Not much."

Gonzalo leaned back in his chair and frowned.

Avalon said, "May we change the subject once again and try to find something more civilized to discuss?"

"No, wait a while," said Gonzalo. "There's something funny here and I'm not through. Mr. Levan, you refused a drink. I was talking to you at the time. I watched you."

"Yes, I did," said Levan. "What's wrong with that?"

"Nothing," said Gonzalo, "but you refused it angrily.—Henry!"

"Yes, Mr. Gonzalo," said Henry at once, momentarily suspending his brandy-pouring operation.

"Wasn't there something funny about Mr. Levan's refusal?"

"Mr. Levan was a bit forceful, I believe. I would not undertake to say that it was 'funny.' "

"Why was it forceful, do you think?"

"There could be—"

Drake interrupted. "This is the damndest grilling session I can remember. Bad taste all around. Whom are we grilling, anyway? Mr. Levan or Henry?"

"I agree," said Rubin, nodding his head vigorously. "Come on, Jeff, you're the host. Make a ruling and get us on track."

Avalon stared at his water glass, then said, "Gentlemen, Christopher Levan is a vice president of the largest bank in Merion. In fact, he is my personal banker, and I know him socially. I have seen him drink in moderation but I have never seen him drunk. I did not hear him refuse a drink, but somehow I'm curious. Chris, *did* you refuse a drink forcefully? If so, why?"

Levan frowned, and said, "I'm on the edge of resenting this."

"Please don't, Chris," said Avalon. "I explained the rules when you accepted my invitation, and I gave you a chance to back out. Nothing said here goes beyond the walls. Even if you were to tell us you were absconding with bank funds, we would be unable to tell anyone that—though I'm sure we would all urge you quite forcibly to abandon your intention."

"I am not an absconder, and I resent being forced to make that statement. I don't take this kindly of you, Jeff."

"This *has* gone far enough," said Halsted. "Let's end the session."

"Wait," said Gonzalo, stubbornly, "I want an answer to my question."

"I *told* you," said Levan. "I merely refused—"

"Not my question to you, Mr. Levan. My question to Henry. Henry, *why* did Mr. Levan refuse the drink so vehemently? If you don't answer, this session might end prematurely, and that would be the first time it did so, at least during *my* membership in the club."

Henry said, "I can only guess, sir, from what little knowledge of human nature I have. It may be that Mr. Levan, although ordinarily a moderate drinker, refused a drink this time, because in the near past he had suffered keen embarrassment or humiliation through drink, and, for a time at least, would rather not drink again."

Levan had whitened distinctly. *"How did you know that, waiter?"*

Gonzalo grinned with proprietary pride. "His name is Henry, Mr. Levan. He's an artist, too. The rest of us draw the ovals, and he adds the modifications and produces the final picture."

The mood of the table had changed subtly. Even Trumbull seemed to soften, and there was an almost wheedling quality to his voice. "Mr. Levan, if something has happened that has left a lasting effect, it might help you to talk about it."

Levan looked about the table. Every eye was fixed on him. He said in half a mutter, "The waiter—Henry—is quite right. I made a total fool of myself and, right now, I firmly intend never to drink again. Jeff told you he's never seen me drunk. Well, he never has, but he's not always around. Once in a long while I do manage to get high. Nothing in particular ever came of it until two weeks ago, and then—it hardly bears thinking of."

He frowned in thought, and said, "It might help if I *did* tell you. You might be able to suggest something I can do. So far, the only one I've told is my wife."

"I imagine she's furious," said Halsted.

"No, she's not. My first wife would have been. She *was* a teetotaler, but she's dead now, rest her soul. My children would have been sardonically amused, I think, but they're in college, both of them. My present wife, my second, is a worldly woman, though, who is not easily shaken by such things. She has a career of her own; in real estate, I believe. She has grown children, too. We married for companionship—and out of affection—but not in order to impose on each other. The world doesn't crash about her ears if I get drunk. She just gives me good practical advice and that ends it."

"But what happened?" asked Avalon.

"Well—I live on a rather exclusive street—four houses. They're very nice houses, not extraordinarily large, but well-designed and comfortable: three bedrooms, a television room, three baths, finished cellar, finished attic, all-electric (which is expensive), backyards stretching to the creek, ample space between the houses, too. All four were put up by one contractor at one time about a dozen years ago. They're all identical in appearance and plan, and they were sold on ironclad condition that they be kept identical. We can't paint our house another color, or put on aluminum siding, or add a sun porch unless all four house owners agree to do the same. Well, you can't get agreement ever, as you can well imagine, so there have been no changes."

"Is that legal?" asked Halsted.

"I don't know," said Levan, "but we all agreed."

"Can you make changes inside?" asked Gonzalo.

"Of course. We don't have standardized furniture or wallpaper or anything like that. The agreement concerns only the appearance from the outside. The houses are called the Four Sisters. Right, Jeff?"

Avalon nodded.

Levan went on. "Anyway, I was out for the evening. I had warned Emma—my wife—that I might not be back till three in the morning. I didn't seriously intend to stay out that late, but I felt I might, because—well, it was one of those college reunions and at fifty-five, there's this wild urge for *one* evening to be twenty-two again. It never really works, I suppose.

"I even thought I could carry my liquor, but by midnight I was pretty well smashed. I didn't think I was, but I must have been, because I can't carry my liquor well, and because several of the others tried to persuade me to go home. I didn't want to and I seem to remember offering to knock one of them down." He rubbed his eyes fiercely, as though trying to wipe out the mental image.

Drake said, dryly, "Not the thing for a bank vice president?"

"We're human, too," said Levan, wearily, "but it doesn't help the image.—Anyway, in the end, two or three of them helped me out to a car and drove me out to Merion. When they found the street in question, I insisted they let me out on the corner. You see I didn't want to wake the neighbors. It was a noisy car, or I thought it was.

"They did let me out on the corner; they were glad to get rid of me, I imagine. I realized I wasn't going to get anywhere much trying to fumble my key into the lock. Besides I knew a better trick. There's a side door that I was pretty sure would be open. There's no crime in our section to speak of—no burglaries—and the side door is never closed during the day. Half the time, it's not closed at night, either.

"So I made my way to it. I felt my way along the side of the house and found the door. It was open, as I thought it would be. I tiptoed in as quietly as I could, considering my condition, and closed it behind me just as quietly. I was in a small anteroom mostly used for hanging up clothes, keeping umbrellas and rubbers, and so on. I just made my way around the umbrella stand and sank into a chair.

"By that time, I was feeling rather dizzy and very tired. The dark was soothing, and I liked the feel of the soft old padding under me. I think I would have gone to sleep right then, and might not have been found by Emma until morning, except that I became woozily aware of a dim light under the door that led to the kitchen.

"Was Emma awake? Was she having a midnight snack? I was too far gone to try to reason anything out, but it seemed to me that my only chance of not embarrassing her, and myself, was to walk in casually and pretend I was sober. I was drunk enough to think I could do that.

"I got up very carefully, made my way to the door with some difficulty, flung it open, and said, in a loud, cheery voice, 'I'm home, dear, I'm home.'

"I must have filled the air with an alcoholic fragrance that explained my condition exactly, even if my behavior had been perfectly sober, which I'm sure it wasn't.

"However, it was all for nothing, because Emma wasn't there. There were two *men* there. Somehow I knew at once they weren't burglars. They *belonged* there. Drunk as I was, I could tell that. And I knew—my God, I *knew* that I was in the wrong house. I had been too drunk to get to the right one.

"And there on the table was a large suitcase, open, and stuffed with hundred-dollar bills. Some of the stacks were on the table, and I stared at them with a vague astonishment.

"I don't know how I could tell, gentlemen. Modern techniques can produce some damned good imitations, but I've been a banker for thirty years. I don't have to look at bills to know they're counterfeit. I can smell counterfeit, feel it, just know it by the radiations. I might be too drunk to tell my house from another house, but as long as I am conscious at all, I am not too drunk to tell a real hundred-dollar bill from a fake one.

"I had interrupted two crooks, that's what it amounted to. They had neglected to lock the side door or just didn't know it was open, and I knew that I was in a dangerous situation."

Levan shook his head, then went on. "They might have killed me, if I had been sober, even though they would then have had all the trouble of having to get rid of the body and of perhaps rousing police activity in an undesirable way. But I was drunk, and clearly on the point of collapse. I even think I heard someone say in a kind of hoarse whisper, "He's dead drunk. Just put him outside." It might even have been a woman's voice, but I was too far gone to tell. In fact, I don't remember anything else for a while. I *did* collapse.

"The next thing I knew I was feeling a lamppost and trying to get up. Then I realized I *wasn't* trying to get up. Someone was trying to lift me. *Then* I realized it was Emma, in a bathrobe. She had found me.

"She got me into the house somehow. Fortunately, there was no one else about. There was no indication before or since that anyone had seen me lying in the gutter, or seen Emma having to drag me home.—Remember your promise of confidentiality, gentlemen. And I hope that includes the waiter."

Avalon said, emphatically, "It does, Chris."

"She managed to get me undressed," said Levan, "and washed, and put me to bed without asking me any questions, at least as far as I can remember. She's a terrific woman. I woke in the morning with, as you might suspect, a king-sized headache, and a sense of relief that it was Sunday morning and that I was not expected to be at work.

"After breakfast, which was just a soft-boiled egg for me, and several quarts of orange juice, it seemed, Emma finally asked me what had happened. 'Nothing much,' I said. 'I must have had a little too much to drink, and they brought me home and left me at the corner and I didn't quite make it to the house.' I smiled weakly, hoping she would find the understatement amusing, and let it go at that.

"But Emma just looked at me thoughtfully—she's a very practical woman, you know, and wasn't going to act tragic over my being drunk for the first and only time in her acquaintanceship with me—and said, 'A funny thing happened.'

" 'What?' I asked.

" 'Someone called me,' she said. 'It was after midnight. Someone called and said, "Your husband is outside drunk or hurt. You'd better go and get him." I thought it was some practical joke, or a ruse to get me to open the door. Still I thought if it was true and you were in trouble, I would have to risk it. I took your banker-of-the-year award with me, just in case I had to use it to hit somebody, went out in the street, and found you.—Now who could have called me? They didn't say who they were.'

"She stared at me, frowning, puzzled, and my memory stirred. My face must have given me away at once, because Emma—who's a penetrating woman—said at once, 'What happened last night? What are you remembering?'

"So I told her and when I had finished she looked at me with a troubled expression, and said, 'That's impossible. There can't be any counterfeiting in this block.'

" 'Yes,' I said, 'I'm sure there is. Or at least someone in one of the other three houses is involved in it, even if the counterfeiting isn't actually taking place on the premises.'

" 'Well, which house were you in?' she wanted to know. But how could I tell? I didn't know.

" 'Which house did you find me outside?' I asked.

" '*Our* house,' she said.

" 'Well, then, they just took me outside and put me in front of our house. That means they knew which house I belonged to. It's one of our neighbors.'

" 'It can't be,' she kept repeating.

"But that's the way it is, just the same. I haven't the faintest idea which wrong house I'd gotten into, and I don't know who is involved in counterfeiting. And I can't report it."

"Why not?" asked Gonzalo.

"Because I would have to explain that I was falling-down drunk. How else could I account for the fuzziness of the information?" said Levan. "I don't want to do that. I don't want to look like a fool or a drunken idiot and, frankly, I don't want to lose my job. The story would be bound to get out and it wouldn't look good at the bank.

"Besides, what would the police do? Search all three houses? They would find nothing, and three householders, two of whom would be completely innocent, would be outraged. We would have to sell our house and leave. Life would become unbearable, otherwise.

"Emma pointed all this out carefully. In fact, she said, there would be a strong presumption that I had fantasied it all; that I was having d.t.'s. I'd be ruined. Emma's a bright woman, and persuasive.

"Yet it eats at me. Counterfeiting! That's the banker's nightmare; it's *the* crime. I had stumbled onto something that might be big and I could do nothing about it.—I haven't touched a drink since, and

I don't intend ever to, and that's why I was a bit vehement when Henry asked me, for the second time, if I would have one."

There was a silence about the table for a time, and then Avalon, drumming his fingers lightly on the tablecloth, said, "I know where you live, Chris, but I don't know your neighbors. Who are they? What do they do?"

Levan shrugged. "All well on in years. All in their fifties and beyond. Not a small child on the street. And all beyond suspicion, damn them.—Let's see, if you're facing the front of the four houses, the one on the left holds the Nash couple. He's an insurance agent, and she's arthritic; a nice lady, but a terrible bore. She's the kind you say hello to when you pass her, but keep on walking. The merest hesitation would be fatal.

"The second house holds the Johnstones. He's in his seventies and she's perhaps two or three years younger. He's retired and they're supposed to be quite wealthy, but they don't bank in our bank and I have no personal knowledge of the matter. They sort of shuttle between Maine in the summer and Florida in the winter, but they have a bachelor son, about forty, who stays in the house year-round and is not employed.

"The third house is ours, and the fourth belongs to two sisters, one a Mrs. Widner and the other a Mrs. Chambers. Both are widows and they seem to cling to each other for warmth. They're in their fifties and very wide awake. I'm astonished they weren't aware of my being picked up at the lamppost. They're light sleepers and have a sixth sense for local catastrophe.

"Across the street, there are no houses but only a large lawn and a stand of trees belonging to the Presbyterian Church which is a distance off.—That's it."

He looked about helplessly, and Rubin cleared his throat. "If we go by probabilities, the obvious choice is the bachelor son. He has the house to himself for a couple of months at a time and has nothing to do but work at his counterfeiting, with or without the knowledge of his parents. If the Johnstones are mysteriously wealthy, that may be why. I'm astonished you overlook this."

"You wouldn't be if you knew the boy," said Levan. "Even though he's middle-aged, it's hard to think of him as a man. He's boyish in appearance and attitude, and without being actually retarded in any way, is clearly unequipped to make his way in the world."

"He's capable enough," said Rubin, "to take care of the house for a couple of months at a time."

"He's not retarded," repeated Levan, impatiently. "He's emotionally immature, that's all. Naive. And good-hearted in the extreme. It's impossible to think of him being involved in crime."

Rubin said, "It might be that he's acting. Perhaps he's clever enough to appear incredibly naive so as to hide the fact that, actually, he is a criminal."

Levan pondered. "I just can't believe that. No one could be *that* good an actor."

"If he *were* innocent and childlike," said Rubin, "it might make it all the easier for him to be used by criminals. He might be an unwitting pawn."

"That doesn't make sense to me. They couldn't trust him; he'd give it away."

"Well," said Rubin, "however much you doubt it, that seems to me to be the most reasonable possibility, and if you want to do a little investigating on your own, you had better take a closer look at young Johnstone." He sat back and folded his arms.

Halsted said, "What about the two men with the suitcase? Had you ever seen them before?"

Levan said, "I wasn't at my best, of course, but at the time it seemed to me they were strangers. They were certainly not members of any of the households.

Halsted said, "If they were outside associates of the counterfeiting ring, we might be reasonably sure that the two widows weren't involved. They'd be reluctant to have men in the house, it seems to me."

"I'm not sure about that," said Levan. "They're feisty ladies and they're not old maids. Men are no new experience to them. Still, I agree; I don't see them as gun molls, so to speak."

"And yet," said Drake, thoughtfully, "there may have been at least one woman present. Didn't you say, Mr. Levan, that someone said, 'He's dead drunk. Just put him outside,' and that it was a woman?"

Levan said, "It was a whisper, and I couldn't tell for sure. It might have been a woman, but it might have been a man, too. And even if it were a woman, it might have been another outsider."

Drake said, "I should think someone who belonged there would have to be on the spot. The house wouldn't be abandoned to outsiders, and there's at least one woman in each house."

"Not really," said Halsted. "Not in the Johnstone house, since the old folks should be away in Maine now. If we eliminate the widows, then that leaves the house on the left corner, the Nash house. Then, if Mr. Levan were let off on the corner, and was so under the weather he had difficulty walking, it would be likely that he would go into the first house he came to and that would be the Nashes', wouldn't it?"

Levan nodded. "Yes, it would, but I can't remember that that's what I did.—So what's the use? However much we argue and reason, I have nothing with which to go to the police. It's just guesswork."

Trumbull said, "Surely these people don't live in their houses by themselves. Don't they have servants?"

Levan said, "The widows have a live-in woman-of-all-work."

"Ah," said Trumbull.

"But that doesn't strike me as significant. It just means three women in the house instead of two; a third widow, as a matter of fact, and quite downtrodden by the sisters. She has no more brains than is necessary to do the housework, from what little I know of her. She's impossible as a criminal conspirator."

"I think you're entirely too ready to dismiss people as impossible," said Trumbull. "Any other servants?"

Levan said, "The Nashes have a cook, who comes in for the day. The Johnstones have a handyman who works mainly in the yards, and helps the rest of us when he has time. Emma and I don't have any servants in the house. Emma is strong and efficient and she dragoons me into helping her—which is only right, I suppose. She doesn't believe in servants. She says they destroy privacy and never do things right anyway, and I agree with her. Still, I do wish we could have someone to do the vacuuming besides myself."

Trumbull said, with a trace of impatience, "Well, the vacuuming is not an issue. What about the Nash cook and the Johnstone handyman?"

"The cook has five children at home, with the oldest in charge, according to the Nashes, and if she has spare time for criminality I think she should get a medal. The handyman is so deeply religious that it is ludicrous to think of him as breaking the commandment against theft."

"Sanctimoniousness can easily be assumed as a cloak," said Trumbull.

"I see no signs of it in this case."

"You don't suspect him?"

Levan shook his head.

"Do you suspect anyone?"

Levan shook his head.

Gonzalo said, suddenly, "What about whoever it was who called your wife to tell her you were outside in the gutter? Did she recognize the voice?"

Levan shook his head emphatically. "She couldn't have. It was just a whisper."

"Is that just your judgment, or does she say so?"

"She would have told me at once if she had recognized it."

"Was it the same whisper you heard in the house?"

Levan said, impatiently, "She heard one and I heard the other. How can we compare?"

"Was the voice your wife heard that of a woman?"

"Emma never said. I doubt that she could tell. She said she thought it might be a way of getting her to open the door, so maybe it seemed to her to be a man. I don't know."

Gonzalo seemed annoyed, and said rather sharply, "Maybe

there's no one to suspect. You may think you can sense counterfeit money, but how do you know you can do so when you're totally sozzled? It could be you saw real money and there's no counterfeiting going on at all."

"No," said Levan, emphatically, "and even if that were so, what would two strangers be doing with a suitcase of hundred-dollar bills? New ones. I could smell the ink. Even if it weren't counterfeiting, there would have to be some sort of crime."

Gonzalo said, "Maybe the whole thing—"

He let it trail off, and Levan said, flushing a little, "—is a pink elephant? You think I imagined it all?"

"Isn't that possible? If there's no one to suspect, if no one could be involved, maybe nothing really happened."

"No," said Levan. "I know what I saw."

"Well, what did you see?" said Drake suddenly, peering at Levan through the smoke of his cigarette. "You were in the kitchen. You saw the wallpaper, if any, the color scheme, the fixtures. The kitchen details aren't identical, are they? You can walk into each house and then identify which kitchen you were in, can't you?"

Levan flushed, "I wish I could. The truth is, I saw nothing. There were just the two men, the suitcase on the table, and the money. It occupied all my attention, and I can't even really describe the suitcase." He added, defensively, "I was not myself. I was—was— And besides, after fifteen or thirty seconds, I had passed out. I just don't know where I was."

Avalon, looking troubled, said, "What are you doing about it, Chris? Are you doing any investigating on your own? That might be dangerous, you know."

"I know," said Levan, "and I'm not an investigator. Emma, who has more common sense in her left thumb than I have in my whole body, said that if I tried to do any questioning or poking about for clues, I would not only make a fool of myself, but I might get into trouble with the police. She said I had better just alert the bank to be on the lookout for bogus hundred-dollar bills and investigate those, when they came in, by the usual methods. Of course, no hundred-dollar bills are coming in. I don't suppose the counterfeiters will pass them in this area."

Gonzalo said, discontentedly, "Then we haven't gotten anywhere and that's frustrating.—Henry, can you add anything to all this?"

Henry, who was standing at the sideboard, said, "There is a question I might ask, if permitted."

"Go ahead," said Levan at once.

"Mr. Levan, you said, earlier, that your wife has a career of her own in real estate, but you said, 'I believe.' Aren't you sure?"

Levan looked startled, then laughed. "Well, we married five years ago, when we had each been single for quite a while, and were each used to independence. We try to interfere with each other as little as possible. Actually, I'm sure she *is* engaged in real estate, but I don't ask questions and she doesn't. It's one of these modern marriages; worlds different from my first."

Henry nodded and was silent.

"Well," said Gonzalo, impatiently. "What do you have in mind, Henry? Don't hang back."

Henry looked disturbed. "Mr. Levan," he said, softly, "when you entered the house by the side door and closed it behind you, you were then in the dark, I believe."

"I certainly was, Henry."

"You circled an umbrella stand. How did you know it was an umbrella stand?"

"After I sat down, I happened to feel it. If it wasn't an umbrella stand, it was something just like it."

Henry nodded. "But you circled it before you felt it, and you dropped into a chair in the dark with relief, and enjoyed feeling the soft padding, you said."

"Yes."

"Mr. Levan," said Henry. "The houses were alike in every particular on the outside, but were free to vary on the inside, you said, and presumably they all did so vary. Yet in your not-quite-sober state, you managed to dodge the umbrella stand and drop into a chair. You did not bump into one or miss the other. You did not have the slightest idea you were in the wrong house at the time, did you?"

"No, I didn't," said Levan, looking alarmed. "It was only when I opened the kitchen door and saw the men—"

"Exactly, sir: You expected to find the arrangement of objects as it was in your own house, and you found that to be so. When you sat in the chair, which you must have thought was your own, you felt nothing to disabuse yourself of the notion."

"Oh, my God," said Levan.

"Mr. Levan," said Henry, "I think you must have been in your own house after all. Drunk as you were, you found your way home."

"Oh, my God," said Levan, again.

"You were not expected till much later, so you caught your wife by surprise. In your modern marriage, you clearly didn't know enough about her. Yet she did show affection for you. She did not allow you to be harmed. She had you carried out, and then came to get you with an invented story about a phone call. By then the men and the suitcase had gone and since then she has worked very hard to keep you from telling the story to the police or doing anything about it.—I'm afraid that's the only explanation that fits what you have told us."

For a moment, there was an absolute silence over the horrified group.

Levan said, in a small voice, "But what do I do?"

And Henry said, sorrowfully, "I don't know, Mr. Levan.—But I wish you had not refused that drink."

TRIPLE DEVIL

It was not surprising that at this particular banquet of the Black Widowers, the conversation turned on the subject of self-made men.

After all, Mario Gonzalo, host of the evening, was bringing as his guest the well-known retired owner of a chain of bookstores, Benjamin Manfred. It was also well known that Manfred had delivered newspapers as a young lad, more than half a century before, and was the son of poor but honest parents—very honest, and very, very poor.

And now here he was, not exactly a Getty or an Onassis, but very comfortably situated. And with four children and a number of grandchildren all engaged in dealing with one portion or another of the chain, he was even the founder of a dynasty.

Since Manfred had phoned to say, with many regrets, that he would be a little delayed, but would certainly be there before the actual banquet was begun, it meant that the cocktail hour was taking place in his absence and the conversation could continue freely without the inhibition produced by the very presence of one of those who was the subject of discussion.

Nor was it surprising that the loudest of the pontificators was Emmanuel Rubin.

"There is no such thing as a self-made man—or woman, for that matter—anymore," said Rubin with passion, and when he spoke with passion, there was no choice but to listen. If his sixty-four inches made him the shortest of the Black Widowers, his voice was undoubtedly the loudest. Add to that the bristling of his sparse gray beard, and the flashing of his eyes through the thick lenses that served to magnify them almost frighteningly, and he was not to be ignored.

"Ben Manfred is a self-made man," said Gonzalo defensively.

"Maybe he is," said Rubin, reluctant to make any exceptions to any generalization he had launched, "but he self-made himself in the 1920s and 1930s. I'm talking about *now*—post-World War Two America, which is prosperous and welfare-minded. You can always find help making your way through school, tiding yourself over unemployment, getting grants of some sort to help you get started. Sure you can make it, but not by yourself, never by yourself. There's a whole set of government apparatuses helping you."

"Perhaps there is something in what you say, Manny," said Geoffrey Avalon, looking down with a somewhat distant amusement. His seventy-four inches made him the tallest of the Black Widowers. "Nevertheless, wouldn't you consider yourself a self-made man? I never heard that you inherited or married wealth, and I don't see you, somehow, accepting government handouts."

"Well, I haven't gotten anything the easy way," said Rubin, "but you can't be a self-made man until you're *made.* If I didn't have a rich father, and don't have a rich wife, neither am I exactly rich myself. I can afford some of the niceties of life, but I'm not *rich.* What we have to do is define the self-made man. It's not enough that he's not starving. It's not enough that he's better off than he used to be. A self-made man is someone who starts off poor, without any money above the subsistence level. Then, without getting large slabs of money from the outside, he manages, through hard work and shrewd business acumen, or through enormous talent, to become a millionaire."

"How about luck?" growled Thomas Trumbull. "Suppose someone enters a sweepstakes and wins a million dollars, or suppose he consistently backs winners at a racetrack."

Rubin said, "You *know* that doesn't count. You're just a luck-made man then. That goes if you pull an old man from under a hackney coach and he calls down heaven's blessing on you and gives you a million dollars. And I'm not counting those people who get rich by illegal activity. Al Capone, from a standing start, was making sixty million dollars a year before he was thirty, at a time when the dollar was worth a dollar and not twenty-two cents. He paid no taxes on it, either. You can call him self-made, but not by my definition."

"The trouble with you, Manny," said Roger Halsted, "is that you want to restrict the term to people you approve of morally. Andrew Carnegie was a self-made man and he was a great philanthropist after he had made his millions, and, as far as I know, he was never put in jail. Still, on his way up, I'll bet he engaged in questionable business activities and that he managed to grind the faces of the poor when that was necessary."

Rubin said, "Within the law is all I ask for. I don't expect people to be saints."

Gonzalo said, with a totally unconvincing air of innocence, "What about your friend, Isaac Asimov, Manny—"

And, of course, Rubin rose to the bait at once. "My *friend?* Just because I lend him a few bucks now and then to help him pay the rent, money that I don't ever expect to see again, he goes around telling everyone he's my friend."

"Come on, Manny. No one's going to believe that libel. He's well-heeled. And according to his autobiography, he started with nothing. He worked in his father's candy store, and he delivered newspapers, too. He's a self-made man."

"Is that so?" said Rubin. "Well, if he's a self-made man, all I can say is that he certainly worships his creator."

There was no telling how long Rubin would have gone on to improvise variations on this theme, but it was at this moment that Benjamin Manfred arrived, and conversation stopped at once while Gonzalo made the introductions.

Manfred was of average height, quite thin, with a lined but good-natured face. His hair was sparse and white, his clothing neat and old-fashioned. He wore a vest, for instance, and one was surprised that the chain of a pocket watch was not looped from one side to the other. He wore a wristwatch instead, but it was so old-fashioned that it had a stem-winder.

He acknowledged the introductions with a pleasant smile, and when he shook hands with Rubin, said, "I'm so pleased to meet you, Mr. Rubin. I read your mysteries with such pleasure."

"Thank you, sir," said Rubin, trying manfully to be modest.

"In my stores, I can always count on good sales for your books. You almost match Asimov."

And he turned away to greet James Drake, while Rubin slowly turned a furious magenta, and the five other Black Widowers suffered substantial internal pain in their desperate efforts not to laugh.

Henry, the perennial waiter of the Black Widowers, having seen to it that the old man was supplied with a generous dry martini, announced that dinner was served.

Drake stubbed out his cigarette and looked at the small mound of caviar on his plate with pleasure. He helped himself to the condiments being passed around by Henry, hesitating at the chopped onion and then firmly taking two helpings.

He whispered to Gonzalo, "How come you can afford caviar, Mario?"

Mario whispered back, "Old man Manfred is paying me very nicely for a portrait he's sitting for. That's how I know him, and I might as well show him a bit of a good time with his money."

"It's nice to know people still want their portraits painted."

"Some people still have good taste," said Gonzalo.

Drake grinned. "Would you care to repeat that loudly enough for Manny to hear it?"

"No, thanks," said Gonzalo. "I'm host and I'm responsible for the decorum of the table."

The table, as it happened, was perfectly decorous. Rubin seemed subdued and let pass a dozen opportunities to tell Manfred what was wrong with the bookselling business and how it contributed to the impoverishment of worthy young authors.

If the Black Widowers were quieter for Rubin's withdrawal from the fray, they were happy enough, and loud in their praise of the courses as they passed—the turtle soup, the roast goose with the potato pancakes and red cabbage, the baked Alaska—and perhaps just a trifle less than tactful in their clear surprise that a dinner hosted by Gonzalo should have such Lucullan overtones.

Gonzalo bore it with good humor and, when it was time to tinkle the water glass melodiously with his spoon, he even made a noble attempt to mollify Rubin.

He said, "Manny, you're the book person here and, as we all agree, the best in your class, bar none. Would you please do the honors in grilling Mr. Manfred?"

Rubin snorted loudly, and said with only his normal supply of grumpiness, "I might as well. I doubt that any of the rest of you are literate enough."

He turned to Manfred and said, "Mr. Manfred, how do you justify your existence?"

Manfred did not seem surprised at the question. He said, "If there's one person who shouldn't have trouble justifying his existence, it is someone whose business it is to purvey books. Books, gentlemen, hold within them the gathered wisdom of humanity, the collected knowledge of the world's thinkers, the amusement and excitement built up by the imaginations of brilliant people. Books contain humor, beauty, wit, emotion, thought, and, indeed, all of life. Life without books is empty."

Halsted muttered, "These days there's movies and TV."

Manfred heard. He said, with a smile, "I watch television also. Sometimes I will see a movie. Just because I appreciate a meal such as the one we have just had doesn't mean that I may not eat a hot dog now and then. But I don't confuse the two. No matter how splendid movies and television may seem, they are junk food for the mind, amusement for the illiterate, a bit of diversion for those who are momentarily in the mood for nothing more."

"Unfortunately," said Avalon, looking solemn, "Hollywood is where the money is."

"Of course," said Manfred, "but what does that mean? Undoubtedly, a chain of hamburger joints will make more money than a four-star restaurant, but that doesn't convert hamburger to Peking duck."

"Still," said Rubin, "since we are discussing money, may I ask if you consider yourself a self-made man?"

Manfred's eyebrows lifted. "That is rather an old-fashioned phrase, is it not?"

"Right," said Rubin, with a stir of enthusiasm. "I maintained exactly that over the cocktails. It is my opinion that nowadays it is impossible for anyone to be a truly self-made man. There is too much routine government help."

Manfred shook with silent laughter. "Before the New Deal, that was not so. The government in those days was a highly moral and neutral referee. If a large corporation had an argument with a small employee, the government's job was to see that both sides had only the help they could afford. What could be fairer than that? Of course the rich always won, but that was just a coincidence, and if the poor man didn't see that, the government sent in the National Guard to explain things to him. Those were great days."

"Nevertheless, the point is that you were poor when you were young, were you not?"

"Very poor. My parents arrived in the United States from Germany in 1907 and brought me with them. I was three at the time. My father was employed at a tailor shop and made five dollars a week to begin with. I was the only child then, but you can imagine how it improved his economic position when he later had three daughters one after the other. He was a Socialist, and a vocal one, and as soon as he became a citizen he voted for Eugene V. Debs. This made some people, whose views on freedom of speech were strictly limited to freedom of *their* speech, feel he ought to be deported.

"My mother helped out by part-time work in between babies. From the age of nine, I delivered papers in the morning before school and had odd jobs after school. Somehow my father managed to accumulate enough money to make a down payment on a small tailor shop of his own, and I worked with him after school. Once I turned sixteen, I didn't have to stay in school anymore, so I quit at once to work in the shop full-time. I never finished high school."

Rubin said, "You don't sound like an uneducated man."

"It depends on how you define education. If you are willing to allow the kind of education you pick up for yourself in books, then I'm educated, thanks to old Mr. Lineweaver."

"This Mr. Lineweaver gave you books?"

"Only one, actually. But he got me interested in books. In fact, I owe nearly everything to him. I couldn't have gotten my start without him, so that maybe I'm *not* a self-made man. And yet, he didn't *give* me anything. I had to work it out for myself, so maybe I *am* a self-made man. You know, I'm honestly not sure."

Drake said, "You've got me confused, Mr. Manfred. What was it you had to work out for yourself? A puzzle of some sort?"

"In a way."

"Is it a well-known episode in your life?"

Manfred said, "There was some mention in newspapers at the time, but it was a long time ago and it has been forgotten. Sometimes, though, I wonder how fair the whole thing was. Did I take advantage? I was accused of undue influence and who knows what, but I won out."

Rubin said, "I'm afraid, Mr. Manfred, I must ask you to tell us the story in detail. Whatever you say will be held completely confidential."

Manfred said, "So Mr. Gonzalo told me, sir, and I accept that." But, for a moment, Manfred's eyes rested on Henry, who stood, with his usual air of respectful attention, at the sideboard.

Trumbull caught the glance and said, "Our waiter, whose name is Henry, is a member of the club."

"In that case," said Manfred, "I will tell you the story. And if you find it dull, you have only yourselves to blame."

"But wait," interjected Gonzalo eagerly, "if there's some kind of puzzle or mystery involved, I figure you solved it. Right?"

"Oh, yes. There is no mystery waiting to be solved." He waved his hands, as though in erasure. "No puzzle."

"In that case," said Gonzalo, "when you tell the story about Mr. Lineweaver, don't tell us the answer to the puzzle. Let us guess."

Manfred chuckled. "You won't guess. Not correctly."

"Good," said Rubin, "please continue with the story, and we will try not to interrupt."

Manfred said, "The story starts when I was not quite fifteen, just after the end of the war—the first one, World War I. It was Saturday, no school, but I still had papers to deliver, and the last stop on the route was an old mansion. I left the paper in a little hook on the side of the door, and once a week, I rang the bell and a servant came out and gave me the money for the papers and would hand me a quarter as a tip. The general payment was a dime, so I was always grateful to this particular place.

"Saturday was collection day, so I rang the bell, and this time, for the first time I could remember, out came old Mr. Lineweaver himself. Maybe he just happened to be near the door when I rang the bell. He was about seventy and I thought he was just another servant—I had never seen him before.

"It was a bitterly cold day in January—1919, it was—and I was inadequately dressed. I wore the only coat I had and it was rather thin. My hands and face were blue and I was shivering. I wasn't particularly sorry for myself, because I had delivered papers on many cold days and that was the way it was, that's all. What could I do about it?

"Mr. Lineweaver was perturbed, however. He said, 'Come inside, boy. I'll pay you where it's warm.' His air of authority made me realize he was the owner of the house, and that scared me.

"Then, when he paid me, he gave me a dollar as a tip. I had never heard of a dollar tip. Next he brought me into his library—a large room, with bookshelves from floor to ceiling on every wall, and a balcony with additional books. He had a servant bring me hot cocoa, and he kept me there for almost an hour, asking me questions.

"I tried to be very polite, but I finally told him I had to go home or my parents would think I was run over. I couldn't call to reassure them, for, in 1919, very few people had telephones.

"When I came home, my parents were very impressed, especially with the dollar tip, which my father took and put away. It wasn't cruelty on his part; it was merely that there was a common coffer for the earnings of the entire family, and none of us could hold out any of it for themselves. My allowance for the week was exactly zero.

"The next Saturday, old Mr. Lineweaver was waiting for me. It wasn't nearly as cold as the week before, but he invited me in for hot cocoa again. When he offered me another dollar, I followed my father's instructions and told him that it was too much, and that a quarter would be enough. My father, I'm afraid, had learned from life to distrust unexplained generosity. Mr. Lineweaver laughed and said he had nothing smaller and that I must take it.

"I suspect he noticed the curious looks I was giving the books, for he asked if I had any books at home. I said my father had a couple, but they were in German. He asked if I went to school and, of course, I said yes, but that as soon as I was sixteen I would have to quit. He asked if I went to the public library, and I said that I did sometimes, but what with the newspaper delivery and the tailor shop, I didn't really have much chance to do so.

" 'Would you like to look at these books?' he asked, waving his hands toward the walls.

" 'I might get them dirty, Mr. Lineweaver,' I said diffidently, looking at my hands, which were black with newspaper ink, of course.

"He said, 'I tell you what. On Sundays, when you have no school and the tailor shop is closed, you come here after you've delivered your papers and you can wash your hands and stay in the library as long as you want and read some of those books. Would you like that?'

" 'Oh, yes,' I said.

" 'Good,' he said. 'Then you tell your parents you'll be spending the time here.'

"I did and, for ten years, I was there faithfully every Sunday except when I was sick or he was away. Eventually, when I grew older, I came by on Saturday afternoons, and even on a few weekday evenings.

"He had a wonderfully wide variety of books for me to choose from, and was strong on British fiction. I read Thackeray and Trollope and puzzled over *Tristram Shandy.* I remember being fascinated by Warren's *Ten Thousand a Year.* It was a mixture of humor and incredibly reactionary politics. The antihero was Tittlebat Titmouse and there was a very effective villain named Oily Gammon. I eventually learned, from my reading, that 'gammon' was a slang term equivalent to our present slang term of 'boloney.'

"I read Pope, Byron, Shelley, Keats, Tennyson, Coleridge—didn't like Wordsworth or Browning, for some reason. There was lots of Shakespeare, naturally. I wasn't strong on nonfiction, but I remember trying to read Darwin's *Origin of Species* and not getting very far. There was a new book, *Outline of History* by H. G. Wells, that fascinated me. I read some American writers, too. Mark Twain and Hawthorne, but I couldn't stay with *Moby Dick.* I read some of Walter Scott. All this was spread out over years, to be sure."

Trumbull, at this point, stirred in his seat and said, "Mr. Manfred, I take it this Lineweaver was a wealthy man."

"Quite well-to-do, yes."

"Did he have children?"

"Two grown sons. A grown daughter."

"Grandchildren?"

"Several."

"Why did he make a surrogate son of you, then?"

Manfred considered. "I don't know. The house was empty except for servants. He was a widower. His children and grandchildren rarely came to visit. He was lonely, I suppose, and liked having a youngster in the house, now and then. I'm under the impression he thought I was bright and he certainly enjoyed my pleasure in the books. He would occasionally sit and talk to me about them, ask me what I thought of this book or that, and suggest new ones I might read."

"Did he ever give you any money?" asked Trumbull.

"Only that dollar a week, which he handed me without fail each Saturday. Eventually, I dropped the paper route, but he didn't know that. I kept on delivering his paper every day. I'd buy it myself and deliver it."

"Did he feed you?"

"The hot cocoa. When I stayed through lunch, a servant would bring me a ham sandwich and milk, or the equivalent."

"Did he give you books?"

Manfred shook his head slowly, "Not while he was alive. Never. He wouldn't give me one, or let me borrow one. I could read whatever I liked, but only as long as I sat in the library. I had to wash my hands before I walked into the library and I had to put each book back on the shelf in the place where I had got it before taking another."

Avalon said, "I should think Mr. Lineweaver's children would resent you."

"I think they did," said Manfred, "but I never saw them while the old man was alive. Once he said to me, with a little chuckle, 'One of my sons said I must keep an eye on you, or you'll take some of my books.' I must have looked horrified at the insult to my parents. Would that be the kind of son they would bring up? He laughed and tousled my hair and said, 'I told him he didn't know what he was talking about.' "

Rubin said, "Were his books valuable?"

"At the time, it never occurred to me that they might be. I had no idea what books cost, or that some might be worth more than others. I found out, eventually, though. He was proud of them, you see. He told me he had bought every one of them himself. I said that some of them looked so old he must have bought them when he was a little boy.

"He laughed, and said, 'No, I bought many of them in second-hand bookstores. They were old when I got them, you see. If you do that, sometimes you can pick up some very valuable books for almost nothing. Triple devil,' he said. 'Triple devil.'

"I thought he was referring to himself and how clever he was to find these valuable books. Of course, I didn't know which ones might be the valuable ones.

"As the years passed, I developed an ambition. What I wanted was to own a bookstore someday. I wanted to be surrounded by books and sell them till I had made enough money to build a library of my own, a collection of books I wouldn't have to sell and that I could read to my heart's content.

"I told this to Mr. Lineweaver once, when he questioned me. I said I was going to work in the tailor shop and save every cent till I had enough to buy a bookstore—or maybe an empty store and then buy the books.

"Lineweaver shook his head. 'That will take a long time, Bennie. The trouble is I've got children of my own to take care of, even though they're a selfish lot. Still, there's no reason I can't help you out in some sneaky way that they won't be able to do anything about. Just remember I own a very valuable book."

"I said, 'I hope it's hidden away, Mr. Lineweaver.'

" 'In the best place in the world,' he said. 'Do you remember your Chesterton? What's the best place to hide a pebble?'

"I grinned. The Father Brown stories were new then, and I loved them. 'On the beach,' I said, 'and the best place to hide a leaf is in a forest.'

" 'Exactly right,' said Mr. Lineweaver, 'and my book is hidden in my library.'

"I looked about curiously. 'Which one?' I asked, and was instantly sorry, for he might have thought I would want to take it.

"He shook his head. 'I won't tell you. Triple devil! Triple devil!' Again, I felt he was referring to his own slyness in not revealing his secret.

"In early 1929, ten years almost to the day after I had first met him, he died, and I received a call from the lawyers to attend a reading of the will. That astonished me, but my mother was in seventh heaven. She felt I would inherit a great deal of money. My father frowned and worried that the money belonged to the family, and that I would be a thief to take it from them. He was that kind of person.

"I attended, dressed in my best clothes, and felt incredibly ill at ease and out of place. I was surrounded by the family, the children and grandchildren I had never before seen, and their looks at me were the reverse of loving. I think they, too, thought I would get a great deal of money.

"But they didn't have to worry. I was left one book—*one*—from his library. Any book I wished. It was to be my free choice. I knew he wanted me to have the valuable one, but he had never told me which one that was.

"The bequest did not satisfy the family. You would think they could spare one book out of perhaps ten thousand, but they apparently resented my even being mentioned in the will. The lawyer told me I could make my choice as soon as the will was probated.

"I asked if I might go into the library and study the books in order to make that choice. The lawyer seemed to think that was reasonable, but this was objected to at once by the family, who pointed out that the will said nothing about my going into the library.

" 'You have been in the library often enough and long enough,' said the older son. 'Just make your choice and you can have it when the will is probated.'

"The lawyer wasn't exactly pleased by that and he said that he would seal the library till probation, and no one could go in. That made me feel better, because I thought that perhaps the family knew which book was valuable and would remove it themselves.

"It took time for the will to be probated, so I refused to make the choice immediately. The family grumbled at that, but the lawyer held his ground there. I spent the time thinking. Had old Mr. Lineweaver ever said anything to me that was puzzling and that might have been intended as a hint? I could think of nothing but the 'triple devil' he used to call himself when he wanted to praise his own slyness.—But he only said that when he discussed the valuable book. Could the phrase refer to the book, and not to himself?

"I was twenty-four now, and far from the innocent child I had been ten years before. I had a vast miscellany of information at my fingertips, thanks to my reading, and when the time came for me to make my choice, I did not have to walk into the library. I named the book I wanted and explained exactly where it would be on the shelves, for I had read it, of course, though I had never dreamed it was valuable.

"The lawyer himself went in and got it for me, and it was the right book. As a book dealer, I now know why it was valuable, but never mind that. The point is that I had the lawyer—a good man—arrange to have it appraised, and then to have it sold at a public auction. It brought in seventy thousand dollars, a true fortune in those days. If it were offered for sale now it would bring in a quarter of a million, but I needed the money *then.*

"The family was furious, of course, but there was nothing they could do. They brought suit, but the fact they had not let me enter the library and study the books lost them a great deal of sympathy. In any case, after the legal hassle was over, I bought a bookstore, made it pay through the Depression, when books were one form of relatively cheap amusement, and built things up to where they now are.—So am I a self-made man?"

Rubin said, "In my opinion, this doesn't come under the heading of luck. You had to pick one book out of ten thousand on the basis of a small and obscure hint, and you did. That's ingenuity, and, therefore, you earned the money. Just out of curiosity, what was the book?"

"Hey," said Gonzalo angrily.

Manfred said, "Mr. Gonzalo asked me not to give you the solution. He said you might want to work on it yourselves."

The smoke from Drake's cigarette curled up toward the ceiling. He said, in his softly hoarse voice, "One out of ten thousand on the basis of 'triple devil.' We never saw the library and you did. You knew what books were present and we don't. It's scarcely a fair test."

"I admit that," said Manfred, "so I'll tell you if you wish."

"No," said Gonzalo. "We've got to have a chance. The book must have had 'devil' in the title. It might have been 'The Devil and Daniel Webster,' for instance."

"That's a short story by Stephen Vincent Benét," said Manfred, "and wasn't published till 1937."

Halsted said, "The usual image of the devil, with horns, hooves and a tail, is drawn, actually, from the Greek nature god, Pan. Was it a book about Pan, or with the word 'Pan' in the title?"

"Actually," said Manfred, "I can't think of one."

Avalon said, "The witch goddess, Hecate, is often thought of as triple—maid, matron, and crone—because she was a Moon goddess, too, and those were the phases—first quarter, full, and last quarter. As a witch goddess, she might be looked at as a triple devil. *Memoirs of Hecate County* was published too late to be the solution, but is there something earlier with Hecate in the title?"

"Not that I know of," said Manfred. There was a silence about the table, and Rubin said, "We just don't have enough information. I think the story was interesting in itself, and that Mr. Manfred can now tell us the solution."

Gonzalo said, "Henry hasn't had his chance. Henry—have you any idea what the book might be?"

Henry smiled. "I have a small notion."

Manfred smiled, too. "I don't think you will be correct."

Henry said, "Perhaps not. In any case, people are often afraid to mention the devil by name, lest they call him up in the process, so they use numerous nicknames or euphemisms for him. Very frequently, they use the diminutive of some common masculine name as a kind of friendly gesture that might serve to placate him. 'Old Nick' springs to mind."

Manfred half rose from his seat, but Henry paid no attention.

"Once one thinks of that, it is simple to go on to think of *Nicholas Nickleby* which, so to speak, is old Nick twice, and is therefore 'double devil.' "

"But we want 'triple devil,' Henry," said Gonzalo.

"The diminutive of Richard gives us 'dickens,' a very well known euphemism for 'devil,' as in 'What the dickens?' and the author of *Nicholas Nickleby* is, of course, Charles Dickens, and there is the 'triple devil.' Am I right, Mr. Manfred?"

Manfred said, "You're completely right, Henry. I'm afraid I wasn't as ingenious as I've thought these past fifty-five years. You did it in far less time than I did, and without even seeing the library."

Henry said, "No, Mr. Manfred. I deserve far less credit than you. You see, you gave the solution away in your account of events."

"When?" said Manfred, frowning. "I was careful not to say anything at all that would give you a hint."

"Exactly, sir. You mentioned so many authors and never once mentioned the outstanding English novelist of the nineteenth century, or probably any other century, or even, perhaps, any other language. Your failure to mention him made me think at once there was particular significance to the name Charles Dickens, and 'triple devil' then had no mystery to me."

HOMAGE

THE MEN WHO READ ISAAC ASIMOV

WILLIAM BRITTAIN

"I called you here today to see if we could agree among ourselves on a sequence of five numbers."

Paul Haskill, the local history teacher, got to his feet, his chair scraping against the bare floorboards of The Merry Tinker tavern. "But before formally presenting our guest, I think I should explain to him that the sole purpose of our little group is to emulate as far as possible an assemblage of men who exist only in the imagination and writings of Dr. Isaac Asimov."

Edgar Varsey, who'd come to Holcomb Mills to write a story for his newspaper, *The Times-Herald*, looked up quizzically at Haskill. His pencil was poised over the notebook in which he had been jotting impressions of the tavern and its occupants.

"Who?" the reporter asked.

"Asimov. That scientist fella who does all the writing." The voice of Jasper Zimmerman, a linesman for the Holcomb Mills Telephone Company, reminded Varsey of the chattering of a squirrel. There was nothing squirrel-like, however, about the other two men at the table. Gabriel Doone, the blacksmith, was huge, with muscles that bunched and rippled under his sweat-stained work shirt. And portly Sidney Warwick was the image of small-town respectability as befitted his position as president of the Holcomb Mills National Bank.

"A lot of Asimov's material is about science," said Haskill. "Several of his books are standard references over at our school."

"He's written about history too," Zimmerman put in.

"And mathematics." Numbers, especially as they related to money, were never far from the thoughts of banker Warwick.

"He writes good stories," rumbled Doone. "With rockets and robots and all kinds of exciting things. Better'n television."

Poetry, mythology, the Bible . . . the men tossed subjects at the astounded Varsey like verbal baseballs being peppered about a conversational infield until the reporter shook his head in dismay. "You mean one man has turned out all that?"

Haskill nodded. "Asimov's output is incredible."

"Not so." Zimmerman grinned. "All anyone would need is the ability to use both hands and both feet to keep four typewriters goin' at the same time."

"The Black Widowers, however, are of special interest to us." Haskill indicated Doone, Warwick, Zimmerman, and himself.

"The Black . . . what?" asked Varsey.

"In addition to his other works," Haskill explained, "Dr. Asimov has written a series of detective short stories. They concern a club called the Black Widowers—a group of men, most of whom have out-of-the-ordinary occupations, who meet monthly. At each meeting an invited guest is asked to pose a problem. The Black Widowers then attempt to solve it through a discussion which is carried on while postprandial drinks are served."

He turned toward the bar at the far end of the room. "And speaking of drinks, the sun's over the yardarm, and I could use one now. Anyone else?"

There was a chorus of assent from around the table.

"Findlay!" Haskill shouted. "A round for us here. Bourbon is traditional, Mr. Varsey. Okay with you?"

The reporter nodded. "Tell me more about the Black Widowers and you four," he said.

"It's five, including Findlay," said Haskill. "At any rate, while talking here one day we found we all shared an interest in the Black Widower stories. So we decided to meet from time to time, to solve problems just as they do."

"And how many problems have you solved?" asked Varsey.

The table was enveloped in sudden silence. Finally Doone cleared his throat. "You're the first, Mr. Varsey."

"Not that much happens in a small village like Holcomb Mills," added Warwick.

"We daydream a lot," Zimmerman mumbled.

The drinks arrived, carried by an astonishingly agile old man dressed in black, who put Varsey in mind of a cricket. "This is Findlay," said Warwick, "the proprietor of The Merry Tinker, and a charter member of our little group. He seldom offers an opinion, but when he does, he makes incredibly good sense."

"Verra fine o' ye tae say that, Mr. Warwick," said the elfin Findlay in accents reminiscent of plaid kilts, bagpipes, and heather. He passed out the drinks with spasmodic jerks of his hands, then returned to his place behind the bar.

Paul Haskill sipped from his glass and then rubbed his hands together expectantly. "Now then, Mr. Varsey. The problem. Pose it for us, if you please."

Varsey pocketed his notebook and got to his feet. "I guess you already know most of the background material," he began.

"Go over it anyway," urged Zimmerman. "From the beginning. If we're going to be like the Black Widowers, we've got to do things right."

Varsey shrugged good-naturedly. "Okay, here goes. Just up the street here in Holcomb Mills one of the biggest revolutions in retail selling in the country is now going on. The Value Today department store. That's the story I want to get for my newspaper."

"If Value Today gets any bigger," grumbled Doone, "there won't be a parking space in town during business hours."

"Davey Lotus—formerly David Lotocetto—owns the store," the reporter went on. "He was born and brought up right here in Holcomb Mills. As a kid he raised more hell than most, and everybody predicted he'd come to a bad end. But then, at the age of twenty-two, he got into a high-stake poker game."

"I remember it well," sighed Warwick. "He walked away with nearly three thousand dollars—a good part of it my money."

"Yes, but much to the surprise of the townspeople Lotus didn't fritter away his winnings. Instead, he rented an old building that had once been the Grange Hall. Within a month he'd painted VALUE TODAY across the front of it, installed a couple of display windows, and stocked it with merchandise, most of it obtained on credit. He sold items usually not found in a small town—the latest fashions, quality sporting goods, exotic perfumes, and such. Essentially, Lotus had created a huge department store, much too large for a village this size.

"People laughed at him, expecting him to go bankrupt within a year. But Lotus had the last laugh. Soon customers were coming from all over the county, then the state, because of a sales gimmick he'd developed."

"He let folks dicker with the clerks over prices," chirped Zimmerman. "It was fun. And for a while we figured we was puttin' one over on ol' Davey. But he was too smart for that."

"Yes, he was," agreed Varsey. "Every item in the store had its price clearly marked. But after the price came a series of letters—for example, $7.00, VUY. Most people just thought it was a shipping code or something. Then, after several months, a clerk let the cat out of the bag what those letters meant. But by that time Lotus was well on his way to becoming a millionaire."

"The letters was really numbers," said Doone.

"Exactly. Davey Lotus used the letters of his own name and assigned to each of them a number. D was 1, A was 2, V was 3, and so on, right up to the final letter S, which was zero. $7.00—VUY meant that the article cost Lotus $3.95, and between $3.95 and $7.00 the clerk was entitled to do a little bargaining. Lotus never claimed the idea was original, but he turned it into a bundle of money.

"Eventually, of course, people caught on. The resulting national publicity didn't do Value Today any harm either, and by then Lotus was into his next selling gimmick—a rare gold coin placed in plain sight somewhere inside the store. For weeks people hunted, until at last it was found—glued to a display bottle of perfume, where it looked like part of the fancy label. Meanwhile, with all those people coming into the store, the cash registers were ringing merrily.

"Senior-citizen beauty contests, games, raffles—Lotus constantly promoted Value Today, and the store continued to thrive. But now he's come up with the greatest sales campaign of all."

"The safe," nodded Haskill.

"Yes," said Varsey. "An old safe which Lotus discovered in the basement of the building. The thing has a combination dial with one hundred numbers on it. Lotus set the combination and placed the safe in one of his display windows. Then he invited one and all to try and dial the correct five-number combination. The person who opens the safe door gets the thousand-dollar bill that Lotus has placed inside."

"Huh," grunted Warwick. "With a hundred numbers on the dial the possible variations are almost endless."

"Apparently the people lined up to try their luck don't agree with you," said Varsey. "They come in to open the safe, of course. But they're buying, gentlemen. They're also buying."

"That's the problem, then?" asked Zimmerman. "You want us to see if we can figure out what the correct combination is?"

"I do. My paper sent me down here to do a feature story on Lotus. One of the first people I contacted was Mr. Haskill here. As a history teacher, as well as the village's unofficial historian, I knew he'd have all the background information."

"I also suggested that if our group could figure out the safe's combination it would add reader interest," said Haskill.

"A moment, please," interrupted Warwick, the banker. "We're getting into difficulties here. When the Black Widowers confront a problem, there are clues, hints, inferences that can be made. But here we're presented with nothing but a dial with a hundred numbers on it, from which we're to pick five. Unfair, Mr. Varsey."

"Not as unfair as you think," replied Varsey. "I ran into Lotus out in front of his store and mentioned that very problem."

"What did he say?" asked Doone, the blacksmith.

"He insists the numbers aren't random at all. There are clues."

"Clues?" Zimmerman sat up straighter in his chair. "Where?"

The reporter made an expansive wave of his hand. "Lotus pointed at those display windows of his. 'Right there,' he told me. I took pictures of both of them. Here, look at these."

From his pocket the reporter produced two color photographs. "Here's the left window," he said, holding up one photo. "You can see the safe—the name Mapes etched in the door is apparently the name of the manufacturer—and the line of people. Down in front of the safe are some fake bills and coins to stress the money angle."

He held up the second photograph. "And here's the other window. You'll note the huge telephone dial with the five silk scarves draped vertically through its holes. Above it is a sign that reads: 'From White to Bright, It's a Call to Fashion.' "

"What's that over on the other side of the window?" asked Warwick.

"A series of posters on sale in the stationery department. Great moments in American history. The Revolutionary War is represented by that painting of the three marching men. Then there's Woodrow Wilson, a prospector panning for gold, Charles Lindbergh, and finally, Babe Ruth."

Varsey placed both photographs on the table. "Well, there you have it, gentlemen. What is there in one or both of these pictures that would indicate the correct combination?"

Doone and Warwick took the picture of the safe and examined it closely. Zimmerman and Haskill showed equal interest in the scarves and posters.

Findlay was almost ignored as he brought a second round of drinks. At length Varsey broke the silence.

"Any ideas?"

There was a murmur of assent. The four men sat back in their chairs, each smiling confidently.

"You first, Gabriel," suggested Haskill.

The blacksmith rose ponderously. "A fine piece of metalwork, that safe." He looked about as if daring someone to contradict him.

"We all yield to your knowledge of the subject, Gabriel," said Warwick. "But get on with your theory."

"The people who made that old safe were proud of their work," Doone continued. "Carved the company name right into the steel of the door. Not just painted on or a paper label like today's products. Mapes—a good name. An honest name."

"We agree, we agree," nodded Zimmerman, the phone-company linesman. "But what's the point you're havin' such trouble makin'?"

"Davey Lotus has the safe in his window. Why wouldn't he have the clue to the combination right on the safe itself? Right there on the door? The combination has five numbers. The name Mapes has five letters."

"But how—" Warwick began.

"Let him go on, Sidney," interrupted Haskill. "I see what he's driving at."

"If we find where each of the five letters comes in the alphabet, we'll have five numbers." Doone consulted a greasy bit of paper on which he'd scribbled some notes. "Like M is the thirteenth letter. A is the first. See what I mean?"

Varsey took out his notebook and looked up expectantly at Doone. "So your idea of the combination is—"

He quickly wrote down the blacksmith's answer:

13–1–16–5–19

"Who's next?" the reporter asked.

"I'll go, if I may," said Warwick. "Like Gabriel, I too was interested in the window containing the safe. But unlike him, I wasn't taken by the safe itself as much as the display of money."

"I'll bet you talk banking in your sleep, Sidney," said Zimmerman.

Warwick ignored the gibe. "The display of money includes

both bills and coins. But why coins, since the money inside is said to be a thousand-dollar bill? Could there be some hidden meaning to the coins? Certainly not in the way they're displayed, just dumped in a pile." He paused dramatically.

Zimmerman groaned. "Sidney, you can say fewer things using more words than anybody else I know."

"Scoff if you will, Jasper. But when I saw the coins, it immediately struck me that America has exactly five coins which make up fractions of a dollar—the penny, the nickel, the dime, the quarter, and the half dollar. Five coins, gentlemen—one for each number of the combination. And each with a specific numerical value. It's quite obvious that my solution is the correct one."

Edgar Varsey put Warwick's solution directly under Doone's:

1–5–10–25–50

then, after a moment's hesitation,

or 50–25–10–5–1

"Mr. Zimmerman?" he said when he'd finished. "Do you agree with either Mr. Doone or Mr. Warwick?"

"It ain't just their ideas I don't agree with," said Zimmerman. "I don't even think they were lookin' at the right window. There's only one place in either window where numbers actually appear. And that's on the big telephone dial with the scarves hangin' from it."

"And you accused me of always thinking about my work," chided Warwick. "I'll just bet you were itching to string a wire from that huge dial."

"You'll be sorry you said that when my numbers open the safe," Zimmerman commented.

"What numbers, Jasper?" asked Haskill.

"Look, the scarves are stuck through the five holes at the top of the dial—numbers 1 through 5. And they hang vertically, so each scarf covers a second numbered hole below. The 1 connects with the zero, the 2 with the 9, and so on. Furthermore, the right-hand scarf is white. The further left, the more colorful the scarf, until the last one—which covers the 5 and 6—is red."

"Yeah, we see that in the picture. But so what, Jasper?" queried Doone.

"The sign, Gabriel. The sign. 'From White to Bright.' That's how the numbers go. The white scarf covers the 1 and zero, making 10. That's the first number of the combination, and—"

Varsey made the next entry in his notebook:

10–29–38–47–56

"I guess now it's your turn, Paul." Varsey nodded in Haskill's direction.

"Like the rest of you, I may have let my work get in the way of my detecting," said the teacher. "I chose the same window Jasper did. But I was interested in those five posters on American history. And you know, it wasn't hard to assign a specific number to each of them."

"Oh?" Warwick asked. "How?"

"Take the first one—the painting. It's called 'The Spirit of '76.' Next, Woodrow Wilson. His Fourteen Points—his war aims—are known to any high-school student. Or at least they should be."

Varsey chuckled at the teacher's sternness. "Continue," he urged him.

"The prospector mining for gold?" Haskill went on. "A 'Forty-niner,' of course—the year of the California gold rush." He hummed a few bars of "Clementine," and his listeners nodded their agreement.

"And then Lindbergh. The Lone Eagle, the first man to fly solo across the Atlantic Ocean. What could he represent except the number 1?

"Finally, Babe Ruth. And even though it was finally broken, who can ever forget his record number of home runs?"

"Sixty!" chimed in Warwick and Zimmerman together.

"So there you have it, Edgar. Put my numbers in that book of yours with the rest of 'em."

Varsey did just that:

76–14–49–1–60

"Come on," said the reporter, draining his glass and getting to his feet. "Let's go down and get on that line to try the safe. We'll soon know which one of you has the right answer."

Two hours later the little group was back at their table in the taproom of The Merry Tinker. Full glasses mirrored despondent faces.

None of the suggested combinations had coaxed the safe's door to open.

"And we wanted to be like the Black Widowers," moaned Zimmerman. "I'm glad that Asimov fella ain't here at this meeting. I'd have to hide my face."

"A failure," said Warwick. "A complete fiasco."

"A bunch of dunderheads trying to be detectives," Doone murmured. "That's us."

"Hey, let's not be too hard on ourselves." Paul Haskill managed a weak smile. "At least we tried. That should get us a mention in your newspaper, huh, Edgar?"

Varsey shook his head. "The public wants to read about winners," he said. "Not losers."

The reporter pushed back his chair. "Well, it's been fun. But I've got to be getting back to—"

"Wait a bit. Wait a bit," came a reedy voice from beside him. Varsey turned and found himself looking at the seamed face of Findlay, the barman and proprietor of The Merry Tinker.

"I could nae let ye go till ye've heard from all of us," said Findlay. "Could I now, Mr. Varsey?"

"But everybody had a turn."

"I didn't. Ye see, trouble with these fellers is, they've nae read the Black Widower yarns thorough enough."

"Come again, Findlay?" said the reporter.

"They clean forgot, sir, that while most of the Black Widowers sit at table for the meal, there's one who's up and about the entire time."

"Henry the waiter," breathed Haskill. "Of course."

"Aye," said Findlay. "Henry. And while the others blather on at great length—just as you gentlemen have done—it's Henry as gets down to findin' the solutions. That waiter has an odd and refreshingly original way of lookin' at problems. Something I've been accused of meself."

"Wait a minute." Varsey eyed Findlay closely. "Are you saying you saw something in one of those windows that none of the rest of us saw?"

"Nae, not a bit of it." Findlay shook his head firmly. "Ye see, them windows ye've been examinin' with such care have naught tae do with the clue Davey Lotus was givin' out about the combination."

"But they have to! Lotus told me—" the reporter began.

"Sit down, Henry—ah—Findlay," interrupted Haskill, dragging up a chair from the next table. "Are you telling us you've got the right solution? What are the numbers? How did you get them? What do you mean—"

"Easy, Mr. Haskill. Now first, I'll remind ye all of one set of numbers ye've apparently overlooked. I'm speakin', of course, of the ones Davey Lotus assigned tae his name when he first opened his Value Today store. That story's still well known."

"Yeah, yeah," said Zimmerman impatiently. "D is 1, A is 2, right up to S is zero. And even if we paired 'em—12, 34, 56, and *so* forth—that idea was tried the first day Lotus put the safe in the window."

"And Lotus said the clue was in the windows." Varsey pounded the table positively. "When we talked in front of the store."

"Did he now?" replied Findlay. "Did he say that in so many words? I didn't get that impression when you first spoke of the conversation."

Varsey wrinkled his brow thoughtfully. "No," he replied slowly. "When I asked him where the clues were, he just said, 'Right there.' But he pointed to the windows."

"Are ye certain sure?" asked Findlay. "Or did he just wave, like?" The little barman made a vague gesture with his hand toward the corner of the room. "Ez ye did yerself, when ye spoke of it earlier."

"Well—yes, that was about the way he did it," admitted the reporter. "But except for the windows, there's nothing special about that old building he could have been pointing to."

"With deepest respect," countered Findlay, "I submit there is something, Mr. Varsey. Ye could hardly uv missed it, standin' where the two o' ye was."

"Look, Findlay," said Warwick, "are you saying we've been studying those damned windows when Lotus was actually pointing to something else? What was it?"

"It was letters—ten uv 'em, tae be exact. At least a foot high. And they spell out the name of Davey Lotus' store—Value Today."

"You—you mean the store sign was the clue, Findlay? But how?"

"Don't it strike ye odd, sir, that every one o' them ten letters in Value Today is found somewhere in Davey Lotus' own name. Quite a coincidence, ain't it? Only I don't really think it is one. I think Davey had this little scheme in mind from the time he found the safe and opened the store. He named the place accordingly."

"Value Today," mused Haskill while the others buzzed excitedly. "Ten letters. Now if we break them down into two-letter groups—"

"Exactly, Mr. Haskill," grinned Findlay. "Take VA, for example. Now we assign numbers tae them letters, based on the way Davey first used his name to code prices. VA, therefore, becomes 32."

"And LU is 69, because L is the sixth letter in Davey's name, and U the ninth," added Varsey.

"Now ye have it, sirs." Findlay reached across the table and pulled a piece of paper from Varsey's notebook. "Unless I'm far off the mark, these numbers'll open that safe."

He began to write with a stub of pencil:

32–69–48–71–25

Warwick leaped to his feet. "Come on. Let's go down there and give it a whirl."

The words were scarcely out of his mouth when there was the sound of a door opening, then slamming shut. A thin lively woman darted into the room, looking about sharply. She spotted Findlay and hurried over to him. "I got it, Findlay! I got it!" she cried excitedly. "See?"

She reached into the depths of her ample purse and withdrew a rectangle of green paper. It bore a portrait of President Grover Cleveland, as well as the figure 1000 in all four corners.

"Gentlemen," said Findlay, "I'd like ye tae meet Dorrie, my wife. I sent her on ahead tae test me theory."

He peered slyly at the little group at the table. "I did nae think ye'd mind, since yer own interest was purely in the problem itself, not the money involved."

The others looked at one another ruefully, shaking their heads.

"There is one thing ye could do fer me though, Mr. Haskill."

"Anything, Findlay," said the teacher.

"Could ye find me the address uv the gude Dr. Asimov? I'd like tae write him a letter an' ask him tae extend tae each an' every one o' the Black Widowers me personal thanks."

THE UNCOLLECTED BLACK WIDOWERS

NORTHWESTWARD

Thomas Trumbull said to Emmanuel Rubin in a low voice, "Where the devil have you been? I've been trying to reach you for a week."

Rubin's eyes flashed behind the thick lenses of his spectacles, and his sparse beard bristled. "I was away at the Berkshires for a week. I was *not* aware I had to apply for permission to you for that."

"I wanted to speak to you."

"Then speak to me now. Here I am. That is, supposing you can think of something intelligent to say."

Trumbull looked about hastily. The Black Widowers had gathered for the monthly banquet at the Milano, and Trumbull had managed to arrive on time because he was the host.

He said, "Keep your voice down, for God's sake, Manny. I can't speak freely now. It's about," his voice dropped to a mere mouthing, "my guest."

"Well, what about him?" Rubin glanced in the direction of the tall, distinguished-looking elderly man who was conversing with Geoffrey Avalon in the far corner. The guest was a good two inches taller than Avalon, who was usually the tallest person at the gathering. Rubin, who was ten inches shorter than Avalon, grinned.

"I think it does Jeff good to have to look up now and then," he said.

"Listen to me, will you?" said Trumbull. "I've talked to the others, and you were the only one I was really worried about and the only one I couldn't reach."

"But what are you worried about? Get to the point."

"It's my guest. He's peculiar."

"If he's your guest—"

"Sh! He's an interesting guy, and he's not nuts, but you may consider him peculiar and I don't want you to mock him. You just let him be peculiar and accept it."

"How is he peculiar?"

"He has an *idée fixe,* if you know what that means."

Rubin looked revolted. "Can you tell me why it's so necessary for an American with a stumbling knowledge of English to say *idée fixe* when the English phrase 'fixed idea' does just as well?"

"He has a fixed idea, then. It will come out because he can't keep it in. Please don't make fun of it, or of him. *Please* accept him on his own terms."

"This violates the whole principle of the grilling, Tom."

"It just bends it a little. I'm asking you to be polite, that's all. Everyone else has agreed."

Rubin's eyes narrowed. "I'll try, but so help me, Tom, if this is some sort of gag—if I'm being set up for something—I'll stand on a stool if I have to, and I'll punch you right in the eye."

"There's no gag involved."

Rubin wandered over to where Mario Gonzalo was putting the finishing touches on his caricature of the guest. Not much of a caricature at that. He was turning out a Gibson man, a collar ad.

Rubin looked at it, then turned to look at the guest. He said, "You're leaving out the lines, Mario."

"Caricature," said Gonzalo, "is the art of truthful exaggeration, Manny. When a guy looks that good at his age, you don't spoil the effect by sticking in lines."

"What's his name?"

"I don't know. Tom didn't give it. He says we ought to wait for the grilling to ask."

Roger Halsted ambled over, drink in hand, and said in a low voice, "Tom was looking for you all week, Manny."

"He told me. And he found me right here."

"Did he explain what he wanted?"

"He didn't explain it. He just asked me to be nice."

"Are you going to?"

"I will, until I get the idea that this is a joke at my expense. After which—"

"No, he's serious."

Henry, that quiet bit of waiter-perfection, said in his soft, carrying voice, "Gentlemen, dinner is served."

And they all sat down to their crableg cocktails.

James Drake had stubbed out his cigarette since, by general vote, there was to be no smoking during the actual meal, and handed the ashtray to Henry.

He said, "Henry's announcement just now interrupted our guest in some comments he was making about Superman, which I'd like him to repeat, if he doesn't mind."

The guest nodded his head in a stately gesture of gratitude and, having finished an appreciative mouthful of veal marengo, said, "What I was saying was that Superman was a travesty of an ancient and honorable tradition. There has always been a branch of literature concerning itself with heroes; human beings of superior strength and courage. Heroes, however, should be supernormal but not supernatural."

"As a matter of fact," said Avalon, in his startling baritone, "I agree. There have always been characters like Hercules, Achilles, Gilgamesh, Rustum—"

"We get the idea, Jeff," said Rubin, balefully.

Avalon went on, smoothly, "Even half a century ago, we had the development of Conan by Robert Howard, as a modern legend. These were all far stronger than we puny fellows are, but they were not godlike. They could be hurt, wounded, even killed. They usually were, in the end."

"In the *Iliad,*" said Rubin, perfectly willing, as always, to start an argument, "the gods could be wounded. Ares and Aphrodite were each wounded by Diomedes."

"Homer can be allowed liberties," put in the guest. "But compare, say, Hercules with Superman. Superman has X-ray eyes, he can fly through space without protection, he can move faster than light. None of this would be true of Hercules. But with Superman's abilities, where is the excitement, where's the suspense? Then, too, where's the fairness? He fights off human crooks who are less to him than a ladybug would be to me. How much pride can I take in flipping a ladybug off my wrist?"

Drake said, "One trouble with these heroes, though, is that they're musclebound at the temples. Take Siegfried. If he had an atom of intelligence, he took care never to show it. For that matter, Hercules was not remarkable for the ability to think, either."

"On the other hand," said Halsted, "Prince Valiant had brains, and so, especially, did Odysseus."

"Rare exceptions," said Drake.

Rubin turned to the guest and said, "You seem very interested in storybook heroes."

"Yes, I am," said the guest, quietly. "It's almost an *idée fixe* with me." He smiled with obvious self-deprecation. "I keep talking about them all the time, it seems."

It was soon after that that Henry brought on the baked Alaska.

Trumbull tapped his water glass with his spoon at about the time that Henry was carefully supplying the brandy. Trumbull had waited well past the coffee, as though reluctant to start the grilling, and even now the tinkle of metal against glass seemed less authoritative than customary.

Trumbull said, "It is time we begin the grilling of our guest, and I would like to suggest that Manny Rubin do the honors."

Rubin favored Trumbull with a hard stare, then said to the guest, "Sir, it is usual to ask our guest to begin by justifying his existence, but against all custom, Tom has not introduced you by name. May I, therefore, ask you what your name is?"

"Certainly," said the guest. "My name is Bruce Wayne."

Rubin turned immediately toward Trumbull, who made an unobtrusive, but clear, quieting gesture with his hands.

Rubin took a deep breath and managed a smile. "Well, Mr. Wayne, since we were speaking of heroes, I can't resist asking you if you are ever kidded about being the comic-strip hero, Batman. Bruce Wayne is Batman's real name, as you probably know."

"I do know," said Wayne, "because I *am* Batman."

There was a general stir at the table at this, and even the ordinarily imperturbable Henry raised his eyebrows. Wayne was apparently accustomed to this reaction, for he sipped at his brandy without reacting.

Rubin cast another quick glance at Trumbull, then said carefully, "I suppose that, in saying this, you imply that you are, in one way or another, to be identified with the comic-strip character, and not with something else named Batman, as, for instance, an officer's orderly in the British army."

"You're right," said Wayne. "I'm referring to the comic-strip character. Of course," and he smiled gently, "I'm not trying to convince you I am literally the comic-strip Batman, cape, bat symbol, and all. As you see, I am a three-dimensional living human being, and I assure you I am aware of that. However, I *inspired* the existence of the comic-strip character Batman."

"And how did that come about?" asked Rubin.

"In the past, when I was considerably younger than I am now—"

"How old are you now?" asked Halsted, suddenly.

Wayne smiled. "Tom has told me I must answer all questions truthfully, so I will tell you, though I'd prefer not to. I am seventy-three years old."

Halsted said, "You don't look it, Mr. Wayne. You could pass for fifty."

"Thank you. I try to keep fit."

Rubin said, with a trace of impatience, "Would you get back to my question, Mr. Wayne? Do you want it repeated?"

"No, my memory manages to limp along satisfactorily. When I

was considerably younger than I am now, I was of some help to various law enforcement agencies. At that time, there was money to be had in these comic strips about heroes, and a friend of mine suggested that I serve as a model for one. Batman was invented with a great many of my characteristics and much of my history.

"It was, of course, distinctly romanticized. I do not go about with a cape and never have done so, or had a helicopter of my own, but I did insist that Batman be given no supernatural powers but be restricted to entirely human abilities. I admit they do stretch it a bit sometimes. Even the villains Batman faces, although they are invariably grotesque, are exaggerations of people with whom I had problems in the past and whom I helped put out of circulation."

Avalon said, "I see why Superman annoys you, then. There was a television Batman for two seasons. What about that?"

"I remember it well. Especially Julie Newmar playing Catwoman. I would have liked to have met her as an opponent in real life. The program was played for laughs, you know, and good-natured fun."

"Well," said Drake, looking about the table and carefully lighting a cigarette now that the meal was over (and cupping it in his hand in the obvious belief that that would trap the smoke), "you seem to have had an amusing life. Are you the multimillionaire that the comic-strip Batman is?"

"As a matter of fact," said Wayne, "I'm very well off. My house in the suburbs is elaborate, and I even have an adjoining museum, but you know, we're all human. I have my problems."

"Married? Children?" asked Avalon.

"No, there I also resemble my alter ego—or he resembles me. I have never been married and have no children. Those are not my problems. I have a butler who tends to my household needs, along with some other servants who are of comparatively trivial importance."

"In the comic strip," said Gonzalo, "your butler is your friend and confidant. Right?"

"Well—yes." And he sighed.

Rubin looked thoughtful, and said, "Tell us about the museum, Mr. Wayne. What kind of museum is it? A headquarters for science and criminology?"

"Oh, no. The comic strip continues successfully, but my own day as an active upholder of the law is over. My museum consists of curios. There have been a great many objects made that have been based on the Batman cartoon and his paraphernalia. I have, I believe, at least one of every single piece ever made in that fashion, Batman notepaper, large-scale models of the Batmobile, figurines of every important character in the strip, copies of every magazine issue featuring the character, cassettes of all the television shows, and so on.

"It pleases me to have all this. After all, I am sure the strip will survive me, and it will be the part of me that will be best remembered after my death. I don't have children to revere my memory and I have done nothing very much in my real life to make me part of history. These evidences of my fictional life are the best I can do to bring myself a little nearer to immortality."

Rubin said, "I see. Now I'm going to ask a question that may cause you to feel a little uncomfortable, but you must answer. You said—Oh, for God's sake, Tom, this is a legitimate question. Why don't you let me ask it before you start jumping."

Trumbull, looking both abashed and troubled, sank back in his chair.

Rubin said, "A little while ago, Mr. Wayne, you said that you too have your problems and, almost immediately afterward, when you mentioned your butler, you looked distinctly uncomfortable. Are you having trouble with your butler?—What are you laughing at, Tom?"

"Nothing," said Trumbull, chuckling.

Wayne said, "He's laughing because he bet me five dollars that if I just answered any questions about me, and did so naturally and truthfully, the Black Widowers would have this out of me within twenty minutes, and he's won."

"I take it, then, that Tom Trumbull knows about this."

"Yes, I do," said Trumbull, "but I'm dealing myself out of this one for that reason. The rest of you handle it."

"I would suggest," interposed Avalon, "that Tom and Manny both quiet down and that we ask Mr. Wayne to tell us his troubles with his butler."

"My butler's name," began Wayne, "is Cecil Pennyworth—"

"Don't you mean Alfred Pennyworth?" put in Halsted.

"No interruptions," said Trumbull, clinking his water glass.

Wayne said, "That's all right, Tom. I don't mind being interrupted. Alfred Pennyworth was indeed my butler originally, and with his permission, his name was used in the strip. However, he was older than I, and in the course of time, he died. Characters do not necessarily age and die in comic strips, but real life is rather different, you know. My present butler is Alfred's nephew."

"Is he a worthy substitute?" asked Drake softly.

"No one could ever replace Alfred, of course, but Cecil has given satisfaction—" here Wayne frowned "—in all but one respect, and there my problem rests.

"You must understand that I sometimes attend conventions that are devoted to comic-strip heroes. I don't make a big issue of my being Batman, and I don't put on a cape or anything like that, although the publishers sometimes hire actors to do so.

"What I do is set up an exhibition of my Batman memorabilia. Sometimes my publishers set up the more conventional items for sale, not so much for the money that is taken in as for the publicity, since it keeps the thought of Batman alive in the minds of people. I have nothing to do with the commercial aspect. What I do is exhibit a selection of some of the more unusual curios that are *not* for sale. I allow them to be seen and studied, while I give a little lecture on the subject. That has its publicity value, too.

"Needless to say, it is necessary to keep a sharp eye on all the exhibits. Most of them have no intrinsic value to speak of, but they are enormously valuable to me and sometimes, I'm afraid, to the fans. While the vast majority of them wouldn't think of appropriating any of the items, there are bound to be occasional individuals who, out of a natural dishonesty or, more likely, an irresistible desire, would try to make off with one or more items. We have to watch for that.

"I am even the target for more desperate felons. On two different occasions there have been attempts to break into my museum; attempts that, I am glad to say, were foiled by our rather sophisticated security system. I see you are smiling, Mr. Avalon, but actually my memorabilia, however trivial they might seem, could be disposed of quietly for a considerable sum of money.

"One item I have *does,* in fact, have a sizable intrinsic value. It is a Batman ring in which the bat symbol is cut out of an emerald. I was given it under circumstances that, if I may say so, reflected well on the real Batman—myself—and it has always been much dearer to me for that reason than because of the value of the emerald itself. It is the *pièce de résistance* of my collection and I put it on display only very occasionally.

"A year or so ago, though, I had promised to appear at a convention in Minneapolis, and I did not quite feel up to going. As you see, I am getting on in age, and for all my fitness program, my health and my sense of well-being are not what they once were.

"I therefore asked Cecil Pennyworth to attend the convention as my substitute. On occasion I have asked him to fill in for me, though, till then, not at a major convention. I had promised an interesting display, but I had to cut that to Cecil's measure. I chose small items that could all be packed systematically—so they could be quickly checked to make sure the display was intact—in a single good-sized suitcase. I sent Cecil off with the usual unnecessary admonition to keep a close watch on everything.

"He called me from Minneapolis to assure me of his safe arrival and, again, a few hours later, to apprise me of the fact that an attempt had been made to switch suitcases.

" 'And failed, I hope,' I said.

"He assured me that he had the right suitcase and that the display was safe and intact, but he asked me if I really felt he should display the ring. You see, since I was sending only small items, I felt that I was, in a way, cheating my public, and I therefore included my ring so that at least they could see this rarest and most valuable of all my curios. I told Cecil, therefore, that he should certainly display the ring, but keep the sharpest of eyes upon it.

"I heard from him again two mornings later, when the convention was drawing to a close. He was breathless and sounded strained.

" 'Everything is safe, Mr. Wayne,' he said, 'but I think I am being followed. I can duck them, though. I'm going northwest, and I'll see you soon.'

"I said, rather alarmed, 'Are you in danger?'

"He only said, 'I must go now,' and hung up.

"I was galvanized into activity—it's the Batman in me, I suppose. I threw off all trace of my indisposition and made ready for action. It seemed to me that I knew what was happening. Cecil was being tracked by someone intent on that suitcase, and he was not himself a strong person of the heroic mold. It seemed to him, therefore, that he ought to do the unexpected. Instead of returning to New York, he would try to elude those who were after him, and quietly head off in another direction altogether. Once he had gotten away from his pursuers, he could then return to New York in safety.

"What's more, I knew where he was going. I have several homes over the United States, which is the privilege of one who, like myself, is quite well off. One of my homes is a small and unobtrusive place in North Dakota, where I sometimes go when I feel the need to isolate myself from the too-unbearable insinuations of the world into my private life.

"It made good sense to go there. No one but Cecil and me and some legal representatives knows that the house in question belongs to me. If he got there safely, he could feel secure. He knew that to indicate to me that he was going northwestward would have complete meaning to me, and would mean nothing to anyone who might overhear him. That was clever. He had to hang up quickly because, I presume, he was aware of enemies in the vicinity. He had said, 'I'll see you soon,' by which, it seemed to me, he was begging me to go to my North Dakota home to join him. Clearly, he wanted me to take over the responsibility of defense. As I said, he was not the heroic type.

"He had called me in the morning, and before night fell, I was at my North Dakota house. I remember being grateful that it was early fall. I would have hated to have to go there with two feet of snow on the ground and the temperature forty below."

Rubin, who was listening intently, said, "I suppose that your butler, in weather like that, would have chosen some other place as a hideout. He would have told you he was going southeastward and you would have gone to your home in Florida, if you have one."

"I have a home in Georgia," said Wayne, "but you are correct otherwise. I suppose that is what he would have done. In any case, when I arrived in North Dakota, I found that Cecil was not yet there. I got in touch with the people who care for the place in my absence (and who know me only as a 'Mr. Smith'), and they assured me that nobody, to their knowledge, had arrived. There were no signs of any very recent occupancy, so he could not have arrived and been waylaid in the house. Of course, he might have been interrupted en route.

"I spent the night in the house, a very wakeful night as you can imagine, and an uncomfortable one. In the morning, when he still had not arrived, I called the police. There were no reports of any accidents to planes, trains, buses, or cars that could have possibly applied to Cecil.

"I decided to wait another day or so. It was possible, after all, that he might have taken a circuitous route or paused on the way, 'holed up,' one might say, to mislead his pursuers, and would soon take up the trip again. In short, he might arrive a day late, or even two days late.

"On the third morning, however, I could wait no more. I was

certain, by then, that something was very wrong. I called my New York home, feeling he might have left a message there, and was rather berating myself for not having made the call earlier for that purpose; or, if no message had been received, to have left the number at which I could be reached when the message came.

"At any rate, on the third morning I called, and it was Cecil who answered. I was thunderstruck. He had arrived on the afternoon of the day I had left. I simply said I would be home that night and, of course, I was. So you see my difficulty, gentlemen."

There was a short silence at the rather abrupt ending to the story, and then Rubin said, "I take it that Cecil was perfectly safe and sound."

"Oh, yes, indeed. I asked him about the pursuers, and he smiled faintly and said, 'I believe I eluded them, Mr. Wayne. Or I may even have been entirely mistaken and they did not really exist. At least, I wasn't bothered at all on my way home.' "

"So that he got home safely?"

"Yes, Mr. Rubin."

"And the exhibition curios were intact?"

"Entirely."

"Even the ring, Mr. Wayne?"

"Absolutely."

Rubin threw himself back in the chair with an annoyed expression on his face, "Then, no, I don't see your difficulty."

"But why did he tell me he was going northwestward? He told me that distinctly. There is no question of my having misheard."

Halsted said, "Well, he thought he was being followed, so he told you he was going to the North Dakota place. Then he decided that either he had gotten away from the pursuers, or that they didn't exist, and he thereupon switched his plans, and went straight to New York without having time to call you again and warn you of that."

"Don't you think, in that case," said Wayne, with some heat, "he might have apologized to me? After all, he had misled me, sent me on an unnecessary chase into North Dakota, subjected me to a little over two days of uncertainty during which I not only feared for my collection, but also felt that he might be lying dead or badly injured somewhere. All this was the result of his having told me, falsely, that he was heading northwestward. And then, having arrived in New York, he might have known, since I wasn't home, that I had flown to the North Dakota house to be with him, and he might have had the kindness to call me there and tell me he was safe. He knew the North Dakota number. But he didn't call me, and he didn't apologize to me or excuse himself when I got home."

"Are you sure he knew that you were in North Dakota?" asked Halsted.

"Of course I'm sure he knew. For one thing, I told him. I had to account for the fact that I had been away from home for three days. I said, 'Sorry I wasn't home when you arrived, Cecil. I had to make a quick and unexpected trip to North Dakota.' It would have taken a heart of forged steel not to have winced at that, and not to have begun apologizing, but it didn't seem to bother him at all."

There was another pause at this point, and then Avalon cleared his throat in a deep rumble and said, "Mr. Wayne, you know your butler better than any of us do. How do you account for this behavior?"

"The logical feeling is that it was just callousness," said Wayne, "but I don't know him as a callous man. I have evolved the following thought, though: What if he had been tempted by the ring and the other curios himself? What if it was his plan to dispose of them for his own benefit? He could tell me that he was being pursued, and that would send me off on my foolish mission to North Dakota so that he would have a period of time to put away his ill-gotten gains somewhere and pretend he had been robbed. See?"

Rubin said, "Do you know Cecil to be a dishonest man?

"I wouldn't have said so, but anyone can yield to temptation."

"Granted. But if he did, he resisted. You have everything. He didn't steal anything."

"That's true, but his telling me he was going northwestward and then never explaining why he had changed his mind tells me that he was up to skulduggery. Just because he was too faint-hearted to go through with it this time doesn't excuse him. He might be bolder the next time."

Rubin said, "Have you asked him to explain the northwestward business?"

Wayne hesitated. "I don't like to. Suppose there is some explanation. The fact that I would ask him about it would indicate that I didn't trust him, and that would spoil our relationship. My having waited so long makes it worse. If I ask now, it would mean I have brooded about it all year, and I'm sure he would resign in resentment. On the other hand, I can't think what explanation he might have, and my not asking him leaves me unable to relax in his presence. I find I am always keyed up and waiting for him to try again."

Rubin said, "Then it seems that if you don't ask him, but convince yourself he's guilty, your relationship is ruined. And if you do ask him and he convinces you he's innocent, your relationship is ruined. What if you don't ask him, but convince yourself he is innocent?"

"That would be fine," said Wayne, "but how? I would love to do so. When I think of my long and close association with Alfred Pennyworth, Cecil's uncle, I feel I owe something to the nephew—but I must have an explanation and I don't dare to ask for it."

Drake said, "Since Tom Trumbull knows about all this—what do you say about it, Tom?"

Wayne interposed. "Tom says I should forget all about it."

Trumbull said, "That's right. Cecil might have been so ashamed of his needless panic that he just can't talk about it."

"But he *did* talk about it," said Wayne, heatedly. "He casually admitted that he might have been mistaken about being pursued, and did so as soon as I got home. Why didn't he apologize to me and express regret for the trouble he had put me to?"

"Maybe *that's* what he can't talk about," said Trumbull.

"Ridiculous. What do I do? Wait for a deathbed confession? He's twenty-two years younger than I am, and he'll outlive me."

"Then," said Avalon, "if we're to clear the air between you, we must find some natural explanation that would account for his having told you he was heading northwestward and that would also account for his having failed to express regret over the trouble he put you to."

"Exactly," said Wayne, "but to explain both at once is impossible. I defy you to."

The silence that followed endured for quite a while until Rubin said, "And you won't accept embarrassment as an explanation for his failure to express regret?"

"Of course not."

"And you won't ask him?"

"No, I won't," said Wayne, biting off the remark with decision.

"And you find having him in your employ under present conditions is wearisome and nerve-wracking."

"Yes, I do."

"But you don't want to fire him, either."

"No. For old Alfred's sake, I don't."

"In that case," said Rubin, gloomily, "you have painted yourself into a corner, Mr. Wayne. I don't see how you can get out of it."

"I still say," growled Trumbull, "that you ought to forget about it, Bruce. Pretend it never happened."

"That's more than I can do," said Wayne, frowning.

"Then Manny is right," said Trumbull. "You can't get out of the hole you're in."

Rubin looked about the table. "Tom and I say Wayne can't get out of this impasse. What about the rest of you?"

Avalon said, "What if a third party—"

"No," said Wayne instantly. "I won't have anyone else discussing this with Cecil. This is strictly between him and me."

Avalon shook his head. "Then I'm stuck, too."

"It would appear," said Rubin, looking about the table, "that none of the Black Widowers can help you."

"None of the Black Widowers seated at the table," said Gonzalo, "but we haven't asked Henry yet. He's our waiter, Mr. Wayne, and you'd be surprised at his ability to work things out. Henry!"

"Yes, Mr. Gonzalo," said Henry, from his quiet post at the sideboard.

"You heard everything. What do you think Mr. Wayne ought to do?"

"I agree with Mr. Trumbull, sir. I think that Mr. Wayne should forget the matter."

Wayne rolled his eyes upward and shook his head firmly.

"However," Henry went on, "I have a specific reason for suggesting it, one that perhaps Mr. Wayne will agree with."

"Good," said Gonzalo. "What is it, Henry?"

"I couldn't help but notice, sir, that all of you, in referring to what Mr. Pennyworth said on the phone, mentioned that he said he was going northwestward. That, however, isn't quite so. When Mr. Wayne first mentioned the phone conversation, he quoted Mr. Pennyworth as saying, 'I'm going northwest.' Is that correct?"

Wayne said, "Yes, as a matter of fact, that is what he said, but does it matter? What is the difference between 'northwestward' and 'northwest'?"

"A huge difference, Mr. Wayne. To go 'northwestward' can only mean traveling in a particular direction, but to go 'northwest' need not mean that at all."

"Of course it needs to mean that."

"No, sir. I beg your pardon, Mr. Wayne, but 'to go northwest' could mean one's intention to take a plane belonging to Northwest Airlines, one of our larger plane lines."

The pause that followed was electric. Then Wayne whispered, "Good Lord!"

"Yes, sir. And in that case, everything explains itself. Mr. Pennyworth may have been mistaken about being followed, but, even if he thought he was, he was not sufficiently worried over the situation to follow any circuitous route. He told you he was taking a Northwest airplane, speaking of the matter elliptically, as many people do, and assuming you would understand.

"Despite the name of the plane line, which may have been more accurate at its start, Northwest Airlines serves the United States generally and you can take one of its planes from Minneapolis to New York, traveling eastward. I'm sure that but for the coincidence that you had a home in North Dakota, you might have interpreted Mr. Pennyworth's remark correctly.

"Mr. Pennyworth, under the impression he had told you he was flying to New York, said he would see you soon—meaning, in New York. And he hung up suddenly probably because his flight announced that it was ready for boarding."

"Good Lord!" said Wayne, again.

"Exactly, sir. Then when Mr. Pennyworth got home and found you had been to North Dakota, he could honestly see no connection between that and anything he might have done, so that it never occurred to him to apologize for his actions. He couldn't have asked you why you had gone to North Dakota; as a servant, it wasn't his place to. Had you explained of your own accord, he would have understood the confusion and would undoubtedly have apologized for contributing to it. But you remained silent."

"Good Lord!" said Wayne, a third time. Then, energetically, "I have spent over a year making myself miserable over nothing at all. There's no question about it. Batman has made a terrible mistake."

"Batman," said Henry, "has, as you yourself have pointed out, the great advantage, and the occasional disadvantage, of being only human."

YES, BUT WHY?

James Drake, smoking his cigarette slowly and patiently, sat on the staircase, third step from the bottom, and nodded slightly as Thomas Trumbull strode toward him. Trumbull was almost always the last to arrive at the monthly Black Widowers banquet, but this time he was not quite as late as he often was. Drake stood up and Trumbull, braking suddenly, said, inevitably, "Why are you waiting down here, Jim?"

"To talk to you. You're the only one I haven't been able to reach this last week. Why don't you get an answering service? Or an answering machine?"

"Because," growled Trumbull, "I don't want to be too damned accessible and I don't want too many messages. Those who need to reach me know how."

"Exactly. I needed to."

"All right, now you have me. What's up?" He scowled suddenly. "Bad news?"

"No. Puzzling news. A week ago, Henry called me—"

"What Henry? Our *waiter?*"

"What other Henry would I be referring to on Black Widowers night, Tom? Of course, our waiter. He called me because it's my turn to host the shindig tonight and he asked me if it would be possible for me to refrain from bringing a guest."

Trumbull registered utter surprise. "Why?"

"The point is *he* wants to be the guest."

"*He?* Who'll wait on us?"

"No, no. He'll do the waiting as always. He's not suggesting he sit down and eat with us.—Though he could if he wished; he's a member of the club."

"I know," said Trumbull. "The best one among us. But what's it all about then?"

"He wants to be grilled after the banquet. He's got a problem."

"*He's* got a problem?" Trumbull's voice went up half an octave and several decibels.

Drake put a finger to his lips and looked apprehensively up the stairs to where the four others were having their drinks. "Keep it down. Yes, he does."

"What kind of problem?"

"He didn't say."

"But he's the one who always solves the problems. I don't recall a single time when any of the others of us have managed."

"I know, I know. I told him that," said Drake. "He said he's too close to it, and he wants our help. —Well, listen, I just *couldn't* refuse him."

"No," said Trumbull, "of course not. But it could create problems."

"I know. I've arranged to have Manny Rubin talk about the plot of the mystery novel he's working on now. So don't you stop him this time. We need normal conversation during the dinner or we might embarrass Henry."

"Very well. I'll let him talk, but it surely goes against the grain to hear him pontificate on mystery writing."

The turtle soup and the crab salad had gone the way of all flesh and the roast lamb was being brought on. Emmanuel Rubin drew a breath and continued to speak. "But what you have to be most careful of is the motive. Suppose you have a traditional murder mystery with a closed cast of characters. One of the individuals in the book committed the murder and you know for a fact that no outsider could possibly be involved.

"Well, they might all have access to the means by which the

murder was committed; they might all have had the opportunity; you might arrange for no one to have an alibi. That part is easy. But now comes the question of motive.

"If one of the characters has an overwhelming motive for killing the victim and everyone else stands only to lose heavily by his death, then you make it almost certain that the person with the motive committed the crime.

"There are several ways out of it. You can make the victim so saintly a person that no one would seem to have a motive for killing him. Or you can make the victim so evil a person that everyone would have a motive for killing him. Or—"

Mario Gonzalo interrupted, "You can have a character with a *hidden* motive, can't you?"

Rubin stared at him hotly through the thick lenses of his glasses and his sparse beard seemed to bristle, "I said 'Or,' Mario. Do you mind if I finish?"

"Go ahead," said Geoffrey Avalon, in his impressive baritone. "You know no one can stop you when you're in full flight."

Rubin said, "Or—to finish what I was saying—you can indeed give one person an overwhelming motive, but you can give another character, or several others, motives that are not known at the start and are only gradually revealed."

Roger Halsted said, "It's for that reason I always know for sure that the character with the overwhelming motive is innocent."

"Every once in a while, wise guy," said Rubin, "a clever writer can turn the tables and, having forced attention away from the obvious killer, reveal him as the killer after all."

Rubin went into greater detail, but the conversation began to flag when the coffee and dessert showed up. The evil moment could not be long delayed and when Henry served the brandy—having maintained his imperturbable countenance throughout—Drake, with a sinking sensation, clattered his spoon against his water glass.

"Gentlemen," he said, "as you all know, our esteemed Henry, the man who makes these banquets what they are, wishes to present a problem to us. I have made it quite plain that our record in these matters is an abysmally poor one, but he will have it so, and, of course, we are always at his service figuratively as he is at ours literally. So, Henry, please take a seat at the table."

Henry demurred. "That would not be at all necessary, Dr. Drake."

"Host's decision, Henry. You're a member of the club and from this moment on, you're a partaker of the banquet. Sit down. Mario, drag up a chair."

With a slight nod, Henry seated himself.

Drake said to Halsted, "Roger, you've got the softest voice and are the least opinionated of us. So why don't you do the grilling?"

Halsted took a gentle sip of his Grand Marnier and said, "Henry, I won't ask you to begin by justifying your existence. We know very well how your existence is justified. It is by seeing to it that we have the best banquets in the city, or perhaps in the world. But we want those banquets to continue. Would you object to having us probe into your private life, to have us question what you have to say, to have us try to catch you out in your own statements? In short, will this ruin our relationship?"

Henry said, gently, "I have myself asked for this session, Mr. Halsted. I have heard the manner in which you have grilled dozens of guests, and I am ready to take my turn."

A silence fell over the table and after a full minute, Halsted said, "It's obvious, Henry, that each of us is reluctant to question you, despite your offer to be grilled. May we therefore start with you? Could you tell us, in your own words, what problem is disturbing you, and perhaps, as you speak, questions may occur to us and we may ask them."

"As you wish," said Henry. He paused, as though collecting his thoughts, then said "Gentlemen, we have had a long and happy association—happy on my part, certainly—but it has been, if I may use the expression, a purely professional one. The circumstances of my private life are unknown to you, I believe. You have never questioned me and I have never forced my confidences on you—till now. Gentlemen, as some of you may have taken for granted, I am not married."

Avalon said, softly, "Have you *ever* been married, Henry?"

"No, Mr. Avalon, never. I am an old bachelor and growing older. As you have no doubt heard, old bachelors become accustomed to their own ways and, as the years pass, their singleness becomes ever more precious to them, though there are times, since even old bachelors are human, when they feel lonely. There is a woman—"

"Aha," said Gonzalo, lifting one finger, then falling silent, as though abashed.

"Yes," said Henry, with a small smile, "I have in my lifetime made friends with those of the opposite sex, and have even engaged in some romantic situations—but not so much in recent years. For the last year and a half, though, I have known a woman only slightly younger than myself, who has been a good friend. Her name is Hester Amberley, and that is her real name. I know, better than anyone else, the conditions of confidentiality that exist at these banquets, and so there is no need to conceal anything.

"Hester is as old-fashioned as her name; in fact, as old-fashioned as I am. We have quiet times; we discuss books and the news of the day; we take strolls in the park; we enjoy the newly refurbished Central Park Zoo; we occasionally take in a show. It is a quiet life, but one that is very satisfying. She was married in the past and is a widow, but she has a modest competence as a result. We each have a comfortable apartment, neither of us has financial problems, we are each accustomed to a single life and it really has the potential for an idyllic existence. What we supply each other with is company and a community of interests. Nothing could be more convenient and delightful, until there came a time when—"

"Aha," said Gonzalo again. "A serpent enters the Garden of Eden. Another man Henry?"

"Oh, no," said Henry. "Nor another woman, either. We are each of us beyond the point where we are searching out adventures. Besides, our friendship is sufficiently sensible to continue, I believe, even if third parties had made their appearance. No, the interfering phenomenon is something much more disturbing."

Avalon said, "I would suggest, Henry, that you move on to this interfering phenomenon and tell us what it is."

"In two words, Mr. Avalon, it's anonymous letters."

"Blackmail?" Avalon's eyebrows were raised in surprise.

Henry hesitated. "I can't say blackmail. Simply anonymous letters."

"Suppose you tell us about them," said Halsted, gently.

"They started arriving in the mail a bit over two months ago. They are short letters, printed in straggly fashion on cheap paper, in cheap envelopes. They seem almost illiterate, but the words are spelled correctly and I suppose they were printed with the left hand—or the right hand if the writer was left-handed."

"Have you seen them yourself?" put in Gonzalo, abruptly.

"Yes, I have, Mr. Gonzalo—three of them. Hester destroyed the first few, being very upset and not thinking clearly, I suppose, but when she couldn't stand it anymore she turned to me for help and showed me three letters she had not destroyed. The paper and the envelopes are untraceable, I'm sure, and the postmarks indicate no more than that the letters were mailed here in the city. Hester did not think to handle them with gloves, but the writer was being so careful that I imagine he or she was careful to leave no fingerprints."

Halsted said, "Is it possible to tell us what the letters are about? —Why they upset her so?"

Henry's mouth twitched as though he were meditating a smile and thought better of it. "They accuse her of various crimes, but quite minor ones. Hester is not the woman to have had a past that included murder, theft, or any of the more grandiose criminal activities."

"And she's not accused of them?" said Halsted.

"Not at all. Of the three letters I saw, one accused her of having bought lipstick at the age of sixteen, after her mother had strictly forbidden her to. One, that she had had dinner with a male friend once when her husband was out of town—it mentioned the dinner and it suggested nothing more. The third reminded her that she routinely used company postage for her private mail."

Drake said, thoughtfully, "Those were only the three letters she showed you. Might not some of the letters she didn't show you contain meatier matter?"

"It is possible, but Hester insists that these three are entirely typical, and I believe her. I have never found her dishonest or devious, even when honesty was—inconvenient."

Drake shrugged, as though unconvinced, but he said, "In that case, if we accept your friend's statement, why should these things bother her? If I had a dollar for every teenager who buys and uses lipstick against parental instructions, for every employee who raids the petty-cash box, I'd be a rich man."

"They bother her, Dr. Drake, because she doesn't know who's sending them."

Rubin said, "Let's be logical. Just from the three letters you described, it's someone who knew her well enough to describe her high crimes and misdemeanors as an adolescent as well as a mature woman, so it must be someone who's known her all her life. There can't be many of those."

"Worse than that, Mr. Rubin. There aren't *any* of those. Hester was born in Ames, Iowa, and moved to New York when she had turned twenty-two. Except for two brief visits in the 1950s, she has not been back to Ames. No one she knew there is here in New York—"

"How can she know that?" said Rubin.

"Well, if any are here in New York, Mr. Rubin, they haven't made themselves known to her."

Halsted said, "Some thirty years have passed since her last visit. It's possible an old Ames acquaintance might not want to be known to her. She—or he—may be working at her place of business, and she's never really paid attention to her—or him—and might not recognize the person if she did."

Gonzalo said, "Wait a while. Why does it have to be someone who's known her all her life? These days no one has any privacy. Everything's on computers. If someone tapped into the computers, which hackers seem to be doing all the time, they could find out anything they want."

"No, they can't, Mario," said Avalon, censoriously. "You're just being paranoid about computers. I don't deny that computers are full of details about the financial and medical histories of various people, and I admit this raises the possibility of enormous invasions of privacy, but the computers don't hold *everything*. You don't suppose any time a person takes a stamp from the postage drawer, a relay is tripped and the fact is recorded in a computer under the person's name, address, and Social Security number, do you? Or that every time a teenager explores the boundaries of parental permission, those computers are activated—and some forty years ago, at that, in Mrs. Amberley's case?"

Gonzalo was on the defensive. "They can find out enough. They can find out she was born in Ames, Iowa, and they could go there to gather information about her younger years."

"Why on Earth would they do that?" asked Trumbull, indignantly. "Who would make a round trip of two thousand miles and spend who knows how much time, just to pick up a lipstick misdemeanor?"

Henry said, "That, indeed, is one of the difficulties. The perpetrator is someone who has known Hester all her life, and intimately too, or who can find out, without impossible trouble, the necessary details . . . because apparently all of the sins of which Hester is accused, while minor in the extreme, are real. Anyone who has known her that long and that well she would recognize, and she says there is no one."

"That's not definite enough," insisted Trumbull. "With the best will in the world, she might not recognize something she's not really looking for. Someone who's not courting exposure would deliberately adopt some sort of simple disguise."

"Or else," said Gonzalo in excitement, "it might not be one person at all. It could be two people, one who knows all the wrong things she's doing now, and one who remembers the terrible things she did as a youngster and whom she never even sees, and those two are pooling their efforts."

Avalon said, "I believe we can fairly say if there is a person—or persons—unknown, who is working so hard to make your friend uncomfortable, Henry, it must be someone—or some people—who dislike her intensely. Now it strikes me that it is quite unlikely that person A would hate person B sufficiently to do this sort of thing, without person B being aware of person A's hate. I have a pretty good idea which of the people I am thrown amongst dislike *me* and if one of them disliked me *that* much, I'm sure I'd know which one it was."

Henry said, "There is much in what you say, Mr. Avalon."

"Well, then," said Avalon, "the bit about the stamp-use sounds as though it comes from a fellow employee. Where does Mrs. Amberley work and what does she do?"

"She's a midlevel executive at one of the city's department stores, Mr. Avalon."

"Is she in a position to have fired someone who might be taking revenge? Has she—I don't say she has, and I use it only as an example—snatched up someone's boyfriend or done something else that may have earned her a virulent disregard?"

"No, I'm sure nothing of this sort can be true. It did occur to me, as a matter of fact, that a particular hatred must be at the bottom of this and I questioned her thoroughly on all her co-workers. She denies absolutely that any of them could possibly dislike her enough, or have characters sufficiently psychotic, to do this. It is my experience that people who feel ill-used are quite ready to find other people they know who they feel might be responsible and to blacken their reputations freely. Hester is not likely to do so simply as a matter of course, but she is human enough not to spare someone that she honestly thought would entertain feelings of anger toward her. She says emphatically that no one she knows is likely to choose this course of action—to send her repeated, anonymous letters outlining the shady patches of her life."

"You know," said Halsted, "we're being entirely too rational about this. In the first place, we're assuming people send anonymous letters only out of dreadful hatred, but actually, there can be no logic to it at all. Someone has time hanging heavy on her—or his—hands, and this seems like an interesting game to play, so it's done. No real reason is involved and therefore we can't really expect to work it out by logic. It's just a matter of impulse and a warped notion of fun."

"And how does impulse and fun explain knowing all the intimate details of Mrs. Amberley's life?" asked Avalon, with a touch of sarcasm.

"That's not so hard either," said Halsted. "People are always talking to each other and reminiscing and telling funny stories. Afterward you're not even likely to remember what you said. It's quite possible, for instance, that Hester might have told somebody some story that seemed apropos at the time; a story about the first time she bought lipstick and used it, and put it on all wrong, or forgot to wipe all of it off when she came home and got into trouble, or who knows what. All of these things where you wonder, 'Now how could they possibly know that?' are known because you talk about it to everyone. I know something Manny did at a Bouchercon about eight years ago, for instance, that he probably forgot he told me."

"No, I haven't," said Rubin, hastily, "but I deny it absolutely, Roger, and I'll kill you positively, if you say another word on the subject."

"I have no intention of doing so," said Halsted, haughtily. "I'm merely making a point."

"It's a valid point, Mr. Halsted," said Henry, "but that sort of thing had occurred to me, and I questioned Hester on the matter and she's sure she never talked about these things to her friends at work."

"She can be sure all she wants," said Halsted. "My point is she wouldn't even remember doing so."

"Perhaps you are right," said Henry, "but I have always found Hester to be a reserved individual who talks very little about her private life. In fact, the qualities of reserve and privacy that both she and I exhibit are among the common factors that draw us together and make our friendship a good one."

Gonzalo shook his head. "What's the use of coming to us with this problem, Henry? You've thought of everything we've thought of. You've probably thought of a few things we haven't thought of, and aren't likely to think of."

"It's true that I've expended some time on considering the various possibilities concerning the identity of the writer of these letters, but that is not the thing that really bothers me. Even though I have not come to any conclusion as to the identity of the writer, there's something else that puzzles me more."

"What is that?" asked Rubin.

"By a curious coincidence, Mr. Rubin," said Henry, "you spoke at length, during dinner, concerning the problem of motivation in the stories you write, and it is precisely the problem of motivation that most concerns me in this matter. It has left me so thoroughly at sea that I determined to throw myself on the mercy and minds of the Black Widowers. After all, no matter what any of you might suggest as to the writer of the letters, I would have to answer, 'Yes, but *why*?' Regardless of who is sending these letters, *why* are they being sent?"

The Black Widowers stared at Henry wordlessly.

Henry went on. "You see, it is natural to assume that anonymous letters are sent for a purpose. They may be setting the stage for blackmail or demands for money. They may be aimed at creating a sense of power in the writer and helplessness in the recipient that feeds the sadism of the former. The writer may be trying to make the recipient of the letters feel that, at any moment, the writer will reveal the nature of the accusations to a husband, to a wife, to leaders of the community. The letters would seem to threaten the blasting of the family life of the recipient, the social life, the political or commercial ambitions, or whatever.

"But none of this is true in Hester's case. There is no suggestion of any payoff, and if there were, Hester is not in a position to pay a large sum of money. Whoever writes these letters obviously knows her well enough to know that. Furthermore, there is no one she need fear. She has no husband, no family, no ambitions to smash. And the missteps of which she is accused—they can scarcely be taken seriously. Even if, for instance, it came to be known that she helped herself to the corporate postage, she would get no more than a head-shake as a result."

"But the letters do make her feel rotten just the same, don't they?" said Gonzalo.

"Well, yes, they do," said Henry. "It goes beyond logic, as so many things do. She feels humiliated that someone—anyone—should know so much about her and should take such delight in displaying the knowledge to her. A few of the letters which I did *not* see were apparently intensely embarrassing in revealing some of her more intimate faux pas. She did not tell me what they were and I did not press her, of course. In fact—"

He paused a moment, and Trumbull said, encouragingly, "Yes, Henry?"

"It has bothered her enough to induce what is almost a personality change. Hester has, all the time I have known her, been proud and independent, and now she has become tearful and weak. She almost clings to me. It bothers me that I'm not of more use to her. Especially since I had told her—" He paused again.

Drake cleared his throat and stubbed out his cigarette. "Did you tell her that you solved problems for us, Henry?"

Henry did not meet his eyes. "No, Dr. Drake. Not in so many words, and, of course, never—not at any time—did I mention specifically anything that has gone on within this room. Somehow, though, I did manage to get across the notion that I was rather good at solving problems. I couldn't tell you exactly how I did it, but I see now, looking back upon it, that I have been vain about my abilities, improperly so, and I am justly punished. I don't remember when I fell prey, in this fashion, to my own vainglory; but when, after that, this problem of the anonymous letters arose, she naturally turned to me. I can't blame her for that. Now I have failed, and while that serves me right, I am distressed that she is suffering as a result of my incapacity as well. Somehow her misery has had a powerful effect on me. I want, almost excessively, to help her, and I have become greatly diminished in my own eyes at not being able to."

Halsted said, "Don't put yourself on the rack for this, Henry. I said earlier that people tell more about themselves than they are aware of. Why shouldn't you fall victim to this as well? You're a member of the human race with a considerably larger than average share of the good points it possesses. You can't be blamed if you possess a few of the shortcomings."

Henry shook his head, unsolaced.

Rubin put both his elbows on the table and stared across it at the seated Henry. "Henry," he said, "I'm going to suggest something. I don't want to; actually, I think that the suggestion is unbelievable. However, if there is one thing we have all learned from you, it is to put aside complicated solutions and go for the simplest one. I would like to. Have I your permission?"

"Of course, Mr. Rubin."

"However ridiculous it may sound?"

"Certainly, Mr. Rubin."

"You've known Hester for a year and a half now."

"Nearer to two years, actually."

"And the greatest pleasure you two have had has been your conversations; your discussions that must have ranged wherever they were led and upon which no bars or limits were set."

Henry smiled faintly. "There is always the limit of good taste."

"Which slowly becomes blurred as time goes on. She must have told you a great many things about herself."

"Some things."

"She probably told you more than she told anyone else. — Henry, did *you* write the letters?"

There was an instant stir all around the table; a palpable outcry of indignation.

Rubin raised his arm. "Now hold it. Hold it, all of you. It's a legitimate question." His voice became stentorian, rising above the hubbub. "We have decided it is unlikely that any childhood chum could possibly know what she's doing now, unless she's working at the department store in disguise, which *really* seems unlikely. We are told Hester believes that no one at work dislikes her sufficiently to do this, even if they knew her youthful peccadillos, which seems entirely unlikely, too. And, frankly, I think that there is no chance whatever that two or more people are working together on this. Yet *someone* is writing these letters. Henry knows her best. Henry has the opportunity. I'll bet you anything that Henry thinks it is legitimate and sensible to suspect him."

Henry nodded his head. "It is. I must admit that the possibility would never have occurred to me for I know that I didn't write the letters. You others, however, can't know that and, if so, I must admit I seem a proper, and possible, suspect. The only thing is—"

"Well?" said Rubin.

"We are back to my chief question, 'Yes, but why?' Suppose I had written the letters. You must explain why I should have done so."

Rubin said, "I might as well be hung for a sheep as a lamb. Henry, in all this, we only know what you have told us. You tell us that you have a pleasant relationship with this woman. In fact, from what you say, your relationship has grown warmer since this trouble started. But this is only what you tell us. Suppose you actually dislike this woman so intensely for some reason that you *want* to make her miserable."

There were shouts of anger from the others. Avalon thundered,

"I would like to assure Henry that we accept every word he has told us as complete and unperverted truth."

"All right," shouted Rubin, in return. "I think so too. But we're investigating a problem and any possible solution depends upon whether the initial conditions given us are correct. I don't for a minute doubt Henry's word, but I would like some evidence that does not rest entirely on his word, just as a matter of form."

Henry shook his head. "I cannot supply it. It had never occurred to me that I ought to come here with such proof, and even if I had, what could I have done but brought a letter, which you might have thought I had written myself, or brought Hester herself, whom you might have thought was playing some sort of game in cooperation with me? All I can do is ask once again, 'Yes, but why?' Suppose that, indeed, I hated Hester and wished to make her miserable out of malevolence of spirit. Why, then, should I come to you with a false story. Why?"

Rubin said, "I'm still following this hypothetical thread of argument.—You are doing it to face us with an insoluble problem for the fun of it."

"And, again, why? The pleasure of the warmth of my relationship with the Black Widowers would be at risk if I did such a thing. It is inconceivable to me that I would take such a risk."

"And to us," said Gonzalo, fiercely.

"And to me," said Rubin, "even though I played devil's advocate. Still, it means there is no solution."

Henry said, "On the contrary, Mr. Rubin, I am now quite certain I have the solution—thanks to the Black Widowers."

"What?" roared Rubin. "What solution?"

"As I said at the start, I may have been too close to the problem to see the matter clearly. The questions of the Black Widowers, particularly that of Mr. Rubin, delivered from a greater distance and with a greater detachment, put everything in a new light. I have learned from Mr. Rubin to think the unthinkable. After all, there is someone who knows more about Hester than even I know and who could have written the letters more easily than myself."

"And who would that be?" asked Trumbull.

"Why—Hester herself."

And if over the preceding five minutes the banquet of the Black Widowers had been noisier than ever before, it was now struck with dead silence.

Finally, Halsted said, "To ask you your question, Henry—yes, but why? If finding a motive for you is difficult, then how on Earth can we find a motive for her?"

"Somehow," said Henry, his face a trifle pink, "I think I see why, and it is somewhat embarrassing."

"Tell us," trumpeted Rubin.

"I have told you," said Henry, "that she is a reserved and independent woman; that we have had a cool and entirely intellectual companionship. It may be, perhaps," and here he grew a trifle pinker, "that she found herself dissatisfied with that companionship. She knew that I pride myself on being able to see into a complex situation, and it may be she plotted one in which I would fail."

"Yes, but why?" said Rubin.

"So that she would have a reasonable excuse to be distressed and weak for a considerable length of time. So that she would become dependent on me and cling to me. So that I would be concerned about her, and become more involved with her."

Rubin drew back in indignation. "Do you mean that this woman has been plotting to trap you into some kind of *love affair?*"

"Or marriage. Yes. I rather admire her cleverness in doing this."

"Cleverness?" said Rubin. "Dirty tricks! You just tell her you're not to be snared in that fashion."

"Actually," said Henry, his face now quite red, "it's too late for that. I rather think she has succeeded."

"Henry!" came the universal cry.

"But even if worse comes to worst," said Henry, "I shall not leave my position with the Club. I promise you that."

LOST IN A SPACE WARP

Emmanuel Rubin, as far as it lay within him to do so, looked apprehensive. He fingered his straggly beard and glanced at his watch. It was well after seven in the evening and his guest had not yet arrived.

The other Black Widowers had all assembled for their monthly banquet at the Milano. Even Thomas Trumbull, the cryptologist, had scowled his way to the head of the stairs that led to the Widowers' private dining room and helped himself gratefully to the drink that Henry, that peerless waiter, had kept ready for him.

Geoffrey Avalon, the patent attorney, looked down at Rubin from his lordly six feet two inches (so that they were always the long and short of the Club when they stood together) and said, "I take it, Manny, that you made certain your guest knew where and when we were meeting and that dinner always begins precisely at seven-thirty."

"Absolutely," said Rubin explosively. "He got the usual card giving him the full details."

"I need not tell you," said Avalon, "that our postal service is not always to be relied on."

"Which is why I confirmed everything by phone yesterday," said Rubin. "I should," he added reflectively, "have called for him and brought him here bodily, but he said he had an afternoon date and would arrive on his own."

Mario Gonzalo drifted over, thumbs under his maroon-velvet lapels, and whispered, "Trouble, Manny?"

"As you see, Mario," said Avalon, "Manny's guest is late."

"So he's late. Maybe he's always late. With some people, it's a habit. Look at Tom Trumbull."

"I'd rather not, ordinarily," said Rubin. "And I can't tell you if my guest is always late. I don't know him that well."

"Then why did you invite him?" asked Gonzalo.

"Because he's a promising young writer."

"Oh, Lord," said Trumbull, from some distance away, "another mystery-writing wacko."

"Not mysteries," said Rubin indignantly. "He does science fiction, and does it very well. Or so Asimov says. He recommended him as someone we would enjoy—though I admit I'm dubious about Asimov's taste in these matters."

Gonzalo said, "You mean Isaac Asimov, the well known science-fiction writer."

"I mean Isaac Asimov, the much talked-of science-fiction writer. He does the talking himself, of course."

Avalon smiled. "Why don't you ever bring *him* as a guest, Manny?"

Rubin's eyes opened wide and glared through the thick lenses of his spectacles. "Are you mad? There isn't a person here who could endure him for five minutes. Insufferable, conceited—"

"Talking about yourself again, Manny?" said Roger Halsted, who joined the group.

Rubin swelled visibly, but at that moment there was the sound of footsteps on the stairs and, as a head rose into view, Rubin's expression lightened.

"Ah," he said, "Gary! I'd almost given up on you."

Rubin's guest made his full appearance. He looked young and was rather slight in build, with a prominent chin and a lowering glance. He was carrying an umbrella that looked large, cheap, and insubstantial.

Rubin took him around with delighted relief—"This is Gary Nemerson"—and the young man shook hands one by one as each Black Widower was introduced. "Geoffrey Avalon—Mario

Gonzalo—Thomas Trumbull—James Drake—Roger Halsted. First names all around," Rubin added almost jovially.

Avalon said, "Is it raining, Gary?" He stumbled slightly over the first name, since formality was mother's milk to him.

"No," said Nemerson brusquely. "It's been threatening all day, but it hasn't rained. I should think it would have, after I lost my umbrella—or mislaid it—or something."

Drake cleared his throat. "If you'll look at your fist, Gary, you'll find your umbrella."

Nemerson stared down at the umbrella and shook it aggrievedly. "This isn't it. I just bought it as an emergency measure on my way here." And he placed it in the umbrella stand where several other Black Widower umbrellas of varying vintage were standing.

Henry said, "May I serve you something to drink, sir?"

Nemerson looked at Henry absently. "A little white wine."

He hadn't yet finished it when Henry announced that dinner was being served.

Gonzalo managed to find a seat next to Nemerson. "Do you know Isaac Asimov?" he asked.

"Certainly," said Nemerson. "He's a big name in our field."

"What kind of guy is he? Manny considers him a monster of vanity and arrogance."

Nemerson relaxed into a smile. "He always says things like that. Actually, Rubin and Asimov are good friends. They'd give each other anything they have—except a good word. The trouble with Asimov is he's passe."

"Passe?"

"Absolutely. He still writes the same stuff he wrote forty years ago. He doesn't know any better. It keeps him popular with the younger readers and I suppose that's all he cares about."

Drake said, "I read science fiction now and then, and I consider Asimov a fair writer—though not as good as Clarke, of course. But I'll tell you what I find a bit annoying about science fiction." He coughed at this point, looked at his half-finished cigarette, muttered, "I've got to cut down on these," and stubbed it out. "What I don't like is the antiscientific conventions it makes use of."

Nemerson said coldly, "What anti-scientific conventions are you talking about?"

Drake shrugged, reached for another cigarette, and stopped himself. "Time-travel, faster-than-light velocities, antigravity, telepathy, and so on. Those things are included routinely in four-fifths of the stories that are written, and all are impossible. How many science-fictional characters have slipped through a space warp, for instance, and found themselves in a different universe? Quite impossible."

Nemerson said, "The skill of the science-fiction writer lies in making all these impossibilities seem plausible. He deals, after all, with the consequences of technological change—the *human* consequences, not with the change itself. Who cares if a particular change isn't likely if the consequences are interesting?"

"Besides," put in Halsted, "every form of literature has its conventions. In the mystery field, how likely is it that an amateur sleuth will bump into a mysterious murder wherever he goes? Or that a private eye can consume a gallon of scotch every day and be knocked out by a blow on the head every other day without pickling his liver and scrambling his brain?"

Trumbull added acidly, "And romance writers find all the heroes handsome and all the heroines beautiful and no one ever has a wart or burps at an embarrassing moment."

Avalon said, "Conventions are the behavioral shortcuts of a culture."

Nemerson said, "And what makes a space warp so impossible, anyway? I could swear I've just experienced one."

But Rubin was trumpeting over his shrimp scampi, "What makes all you nonwriter types such experts on literature? Why don't you wait for the grilling and talk to Nemerson instead of to each other? I've given up expecting you to listen to *me*."

• • •

By the time the coffee was served and Henry had placed the brandy bottles on the sideboard, the Black Widowers were in their customary state of benign repletion and even Rubin was almost benevolent as he rattled his spoon against the water glass and said, "Roger, will you do the honors and grill our guest?"

"Wait—I want to ask a question!" said Mario.

"Later," thundered Rubin. "Go ahead, Roger."

"Very well," said Halsted in his quiet voice, as he licked the last of his *coupe aux marrons* off his spoon. "How do you justify your existence, Gary?"

"By being a science-fiction writer," said Nemerson with a snap.

"You consider that important, do you?"

"Yes, I do," said Nemerson, offering no details.

Halsted asked for none. He said, "And how long have you been writing science fiction?"

"I made my first sale five years ago."

"A novel?"

"No, my first novel is now in press, and I've got a contract, for a second one. Till now, my appearances have been in the magazines."

"Do they pay much?"

"No, but I get along."

Again there were no details, and Halsted asked for none. "Are you married, Gary?"

"No." An internal struggle seemed to twist Nemerson's facial expression. Then he said, "I've been contemplating it."

"When?"

"When my novel is published and does reasonably well. Then I can justify the economic risk of marriage—I think."

"You think?"

"Well, it's a serious step."

"How long have you known the young lady?"

"Three years."

"I take it you love her?"

"Why else would I be contemplating marriage?"

"I ask because you seemed uncertain about the matter."

Nemerson nodded. "Right now I *am* uncertain. I'm annoyed with her at the moment."

"Why?"

"I mistrust her sense of humor."

Mario Gonzalo brought his fist down on the table and his expression was dark. "I'm tired of this soap opera that Roger is running. I have a question, and I'm going to ask it. You said you just experienced a space warp, Gary. When and how did you experience it?"

Nemerson looked honestly surprised. "A space warp?"

There was a general stir about the table. Avalon said, "What's this about a space warp, Mario? What are you talking about?"

Gonzalo said, "Gary said it when the rest of you were blatting your heads off, but I'm next to him and I heard him. He said he experienced a space warp, or thought he did. I heard him say that."

Nemerson's face cleared up. "Yes, I did, come to think of it. And that's exactly what I'm talking about right now—about mistrusting Marilyn's sense of humor. —Marilyn is my fiancée."

"What's she got to do with a space warp?" demanded Gonzalo.

Nemerson said, "Space warp was just an expression because Mr. Drake—uh, Jim—brought it up. Actually, I was thinking about my umbrella, the one I lost." He made a wild, outward gesture. "The hell with it. I don't want to talk about my umbrella. Ask me about science fiction."

"No," said Gonzalo, "you don't set the rules on questions, Gary. We do, and you have to answer. That's the condition of the dinner. Manny, you're the host and he's your guest. Tell him."

Rubin pursed his lips, then said, "It goes against the grain to have to agree with Mario, but I'm afraid he's right, Gary. If he wants to hear about the umbrella, you'll have to tell him about it."

"The space warp," said Gonzalo. "That's what I'm after."

"As a matter of fact," said Trumbull, his forehead corrugating, "I'm rather interested in hearing about this combination of umbrella and space warp myself."

Nemerson sighed. "It's something that's of interest only to me, really. I have—or had—an umbrella. It was a folding umbrella that was so small it could fit comfortably in my overcoat pocket, but opened to a considerable spread and could withstand a brisk wind. It was an ideal umbrella. I'd owned it for years, and now I've lost it. I doubt that I'll ever be able to replace it with one as satisfactory and I'm very upset about it."

Avalon said, "I imagine everyone here has lost various umbrellas in his life. You go out with one and take a taxi. By the time you get to where you're going, the sun is coming out from behind the clouds, so you forget you have an umbrella and you leave it behind in the taxi."

"Or," Drake said, "you put it in an umbrella stand, and the rain starts coming down hard and some idiot who didn't bring one of his own calmly appropriates yours."

"That's not how it happened," said Nemerson. "I didn't leave it in a taxi and I didn't have it stolen out of an umbrella stand. Nothing like that. I lost it in Marilyn's apartment."

"Your fiancée's apartment?"

"Yes."

Gonzalo said, in annoyance, "Where's the space warp? I want to hear about that. Tell the whole story, Gary."

Nemerson frowned. "What's to tell? You're making an epic out of a cameo. But all right. Here's the way it goes. Marilyn was having a day off—she works as an administrator at a hospital—and I thought I'd drop over to her apartment in the afternoon and spend some quiet time with her before coming to this appointment. I suppose you don't expect me to give you the details of the conversation or of anything else we did."

"No, no," said Rubin, "it's understood we don't try to break down the walls of decent privacy. Stick to the umbrella."

"Well, as you know, it's been threatening rain all day, so I took my umbrella. Ordinarily I'd put it in the pocket of my overcoat or raincoat and then forget about it till it actually rained. If it didn't rain, it would stay in the pocket safely. However, it's been a steamy, sticky day and wearing a coat of any kind, even a thin raincoat, would be ridiculous, so I carried the umbrella—in my hand."

"Where else would you carry it?" asked Drake mildly.

Nemerson said, "Listen, when I say I carried it in my hand I mean I held it there and never let go. I'm always conscious of the risk of loss—of anything, not just my umbrella. I'm always fanning my pockets to make sure my wallet and keys are in place."

"I do, too," broke in Rubin. "When you live in New York—"

"So I hold onto my umbrella. I don't put it down in a taxi or a bus. Marilyn hates the fuss I make over it. Actually, she hates my being systematic and orderly and says I miss the joy of life by not being more easygoing."

"And does that bother you?" asked Halsted.

"Absolutely. I'm a writer, and I intend to set the world on fire. I'm serious and compulsive about my work and I don't believe you can divide yourself into antagonistic pieces. If I'm going to hard-drive my writing and do it with order and method, I've got to do it in all aspects of my life."

Rubin said, "You won't be as prolific as Asimov whatever you do, and he's an extrovert of the extroverts. You should see him when any female approaches within half a mile of him."

"I don't intend to model myself on Asimov," said Nemerson. "He may be prolific and he's been helpful to me, but I recognize him as a trivial man, and I intend to be an important one. —Anyway, I arrived at Marilyn's place this afternoon holding my umbrella. It was still in its folded state, bone-dry since it hadn't rained. Since I had no pocket to slip it into, I put it on her kitchen table—it's porcelain-topped and would in no way be damaged by the umbrella. What's more, the umbrella was black, so it stood out unmistakably. When I left, I'd pass the table on the way to the door and couldn't miss it.

"Marilyn made her usual dumb cracks about it. She prides herself on having a sense of humor and claims I don't have one, but my writing is well known for its sardonic aspects so I pay no attention to what she says. —In that respect, at least.

"And, as a matter of fact, we had a pleasant afternoon. Making allowance for her penchant for inappropriate remarks of the kind she calls humorous, she's highly intelligent, interesting, and a warm and affectionate person."

Trumbull broke in. "But what does she see in you, then? I mean, you're the kind of intense, driving person she wouldn't be able to endure."

Nemerson eyed him hostilely and said, "I like to think I have some good points that she values. —Anyway, eventually it was time to leave. Manny had made it plain I was expected to be on time, and I intended to be. There was the umbrella on the kitchen table right where I'd put it and I was about to leave, when Marilyn suggested I help myself to a nice cold beer before going out into the steam. I looked at my watch and decided I had time for one beer if I didn't waste time over it. It was a nice thought, but it disrupted my attention to my umbrella.

"After the beer, Marilyn walked me to the elevator, just ten yards down the corridor. We kissed, and I turned away, but even before the elevator arrived I turned back to her and said, 'I forgot my umbrella.'

"I guess I looked perturbed because she said, 'Well, don't throw a fit, no one's stolen it.'

"Back we went to her apartment. I knew quite well I'd left it on the kitchen table. I'd seen it there when I stopped for the beer and I could have sworn I'd picked it up, but I must have been mistaken—I certainly didn't have it with me. But it wasn't on the kitchen table, either.

"That was a terrible blow. I'd seen it there not ten minutes earlier. The breath just went out of me. Marilyn said, 'It must be *somewhere*.'

"I said, 'I put it right here.'

"She said, 'I know, but you must have picked it up and put it somewhere else without thinking.'

"That seemed possible, so we went over her apartment. It isn't a large one. She has a living room, with an alcove serving as a bedroom, plus a bathroom, a small kitchen near the front door, and two sizable closets. It's all simply furnished and there aren't many places where the umbrella wouldn't have stood out easily. And I looked everywhere. I even moved the couch to look behind it and under it, moved all the cushions on the couch and the two chairs, looked on all the shelves of both closets, moving things to make sure it hadn't fallen behind. I went through the bathroom and the kitchen, poked into all the corners. I spent half an hour on it, which made me late here, and I tell you frankly I was in such a rage I almost didn't come at all.

"The point is, it was nowhere, absolutely nowhere, yet I'd seen it on the kitchen table not long before I left.

"Marilyn was no help. She's the one who said, finally, 'I guess it must have dropped through one of those space warps you write about.' She may have thought that was funny, but I didn't think so. Anyway, I bought a cheap umbrella at the corner store, got a taxi, and here I am. And that's the story of my umbrella and the space warp."

There was a short pause after Nemerson had done speaking and then Trumbull said, "I would suggest an easy solution. You left the apartment with the umbrella and dropped it in the corridor on your way to the elevator. You didn't notice, and someone came along, spied a poor orphan umbrella, and adopted it out of the kindness of his heart."

"No," said Nemerson savagely. "In the first place, I didn't drop any umbrella, and if I had it would have made a noise. In the second, I said there was only a ten-yard stretch between Marilyn's apartment door and the elevator bank. It's a straight ten-yard stretch and there was no one else in the corridor when we went to the elevator or when we returned. We would, without fail, have seen anyone who passed.

"And if you think that I would be so lost in a passionate kiss at the elevator that I'd remain unaware of someone's approach, think again. Quite the reverse, I don't intend to be caught in such an interlude and I keep my eyes open. And on the way back to the apartment, I scanned the corridor floor and there was nothing there. A black folding umbrella would have stood out—the corridor's well lit, the carpeting is pale blue, and there are no crannies into which it could have rolled, even if it could roll, which it couldn't."

"You know," said Avalon, attempting to make his baritone voice soothing, "all of us have undoubtedly lost items in our own offices that seem to have dropped through a space warp. I once had a thin pamphlet I used regularly for the reference information it contained. I was using it once on my desk when it disappeared. I ransacked my office as you ransacked your fiancée's apartment before I, too, had to give up. And then one day, two years afterward, I pulled a reference book from the shelf—one that I rarely used. It fell open and there, nestled among its pages, was my long-lost pamphlet. I'd mindlessly used it as a bookmark in the reference book, and when I cleared the reference book off my desk and put it in its place on the shelf I unwittingly carried off the pamphlet with it. If I'd never used the reference book again, I'd never have found the pamphlet, and its disappearance would have remained a mystery to this day."

Nemerson said, "Fine, but my umbrella wasn't a small piece of cardboard that could find its way into all sorts of random places. It was a compact black cylinder ten inches long or so, and about two inches thick. —You know what I think? I think it was something Marilyn arranged."

"How?" asked Gonzalo.

"How do I know how? She gave it to a neighbor to hold for her, or she threw it out the window. What's the difference how? The point is that if she did this as her idea of something funny, then I won't take it. And I won't take *her* if that's her idea of a joke. Life with her would be unbearable if I had to watch out forever for this sort of thing."

Halsted said, "Aren't you being a bit unreasonable, Gary? You say yourself you saw the umbrella on the kitchen table not ten minutes before you left. What could she have done in those last ten minutes? Dashed to the window? Run out the door to a neighbor's? Surely you'd have noticed any such thing if it had happened."

Nemerson was silent.

Drake said, "Roger's making a good point, Gary. Did you notice your fiancée doing *anything* unusual in the ten minutes between your last seeing the umbrella and your leaving the apartment?"

"No," said Nemerson reluctantly, "I didn't. But that doesn't mean she didn't do something. I wasn't watching her lynx-eyed. She might have done something none of us has thought of. She *must* have done something—unless there really *is* such a thing as a space warp."

Henry cleared his throat. "Mr. Nemerson, may I have your permission to ask you a few questions?"

Nemerson's face lifted in clear antagonism and Rubin said hastily, "It's all right, Gary. Henry is a member of the Black Widowers."

"The waiter?" said Nemerson, astonished.

"An esteemed member," said Rubin firmly.

"If that's the case," said Nemerson, "go ahead and ask, waiter."

Henry said, "Thank you, sir. My first question is this. Is your fiancée eating out tonight?"

Nemerson looked confused. "Eating out?"

"Yes, sir."

"I'm not sure. No, of course I'm sure. She was complaining about my going out. You see, I couldn't have brought her with me, as I most certainly would have tried to do ordinarily, because Manny told me this was a strictly stag organization."

There was a general murmur of assent from the Black Widowers.

"Well, that didn't make me exactly popular with Marilyn. She claimed that if I weren't a male chauvinist pig I wouldn't accept an invitation to a stag dinner. Naturally, I didn't see that— Come to think of it, I wonder if that's why she played the trick on me.

Huh, with that kind of desire for petty revenge, the marriage would never work."

Henry said, "I beg your pardon, Mr. Nemerson, but it has by no means been established that your fiancée was responsible for the disappearance of the umbrella."

Nemerson said, "I'm sure she was."

Henry said, "With all due respect, that is a conclusion based on emotion and not on logic. But I am asking if she was going out to dinner."

"Well, she complained that while I was dining out sumptuously, she would have to 'pig out'—her phrase, not mine—on a tunafish salad. I imagine she was just saying that to make me feel guilty."

"Are you saying that she may simply have pretended she would have a tunafish salad in order to play the martyr but that she would actually dine out?"

"No, I don't think so," said Nemerson thoughtfully. "She doesn't like dining out alone. She's not *that* much of a feminist. I'm sure she would be eating at home."

"Then she would be home right now?"

"I'm sure of it."

Henry said, "I have another question. Does she know where you've gone for dinner?"

"Of course. I told you I told her I was dining with the Black Widowers. And I told her what little I knew of the club—what Manny had told me."

"Yes, but did she know to which restaurant you were coming? Did you tell her you were dining at the Milano?"

Nemerson reflected. "No, I didn't mention that. I guess I didn't want her coming to the restaurant, finding an adjoining table, and making faces at us. I didn't know we'd have a private room."

"Then if she wanted to call you right now, there would be no way she could, is that right?"

"I suppose that's right. But why should she want to call me?"

Henry said, "It is my feeling, sir, that after you left, she found the umbrella—and would certainly have called you at once with the news had she known where to call."

Nemerson pressed his lips together, then said unforgivingly, "If she were to say she found it, it would be because she knew all along what she had done with it."

"I don't believe that is the case, sir. I believe I know where the umbrella is and how it got there. I have written down one word on this piece of folded notepaper, which I will ask Mr. Rubin to hold for me. If you will be so kind as to phone your fiancée—and if she tells you she has found it, and if the manner of her finding it matches the word I have written down, then she is quite innocent of your suspicions and the matter explains itself."

Nemerson stared at Henry, then said, "I don't know what this mumbo-jumbo is all about, but I'll call Marilyn."

He rose and went to the wall phone. "I suppose I may use this?"

"Yes, sir," said Henry. "Dial nine first."

With a look of settled dissatisfaction on his face, Nemerson dialed, waited a moment, then said, "Marilyn, this is— *What? You did? Where?* But how—never mind, dear, as soon as I'm through here I'll come over."

He hung up the receiver and turned to Rubin. "Let me see that piece of paper, Manny."

Rubin looked at Henry, who nodded. Rubin handed Nemerson the folded paper. Nemerson opened it, stared at it for a long moment, then fumbled his way to a chair and sat down.

"All right, Henry," he said. "How did you know?"

"You told us yourself, Mr. Nemerson. You said you were on the point of leaving your fiancée's apartment, at which time you said you saw the umbrella on the kitchen table. Your orderly way of handling the umbrella meant, to me, that you must have picked it up and held it in your hand as you were accustomed to doing. In fact, you said yourself that you were under the impression that you *had* picked it up. You said you could have sworn to it.

"Your fiancée then suggested you help yourself to a cold beer and you were willing. On a steamy day like today, the beer could only have been in the refrigerator. You opened the refrigerator door and, I imagine, found the beer cans a trifle awkwardly placed. You therefore put down your umbrella on one of the refrigerator shelves while you reached for the beer.

"Forgetting the umbrella, you closed the refrigerator door and drank your beer. In your later search for the umbrella, you never thought to look inside the refrigerator for it. It is simply not a place one would normally think to look for an umbrella.

"However, when your fiancée set about preparing a tunafish salad for herself, she had to obtain the ingredients from the refrigerator. When she opened the refrigerator door, she must have been astonished to see the umbrella there but she had no way of reaching you."

Nemerson held up the folded piece of paper dreamily. "The word Henry wrote was 'refrigerator.' "

Gonzalo said, "Absolutely great, Henry."

"Thank you, Mr. Gonzalo," said Henry.

Nemerson said, "Now why didn't I think of it?"

Henry said, "As I said, a refrigerator isn't a natural place for an umbrella, sir."

"But you reasoned it out, Henry."

"Yes, sir," said Henry, "but I did it in the cool, unimpassioned aftermath of the event. Had I been caught up in the immediate unexplained loss, I, too, would have been tempted to wonder about the possible existence of a space warp."

POLICE AT THE DOOR

The monthly banquets of the Black Widowers were never models of quiet and serenity, but on this occasion things were unusually noisy. Where, usually, one or another of the members was in a testy mood and made his views known with remarkable vigor, this was one of those rare times when all the Black Widowers were remarkably vehement. It seemed next to impossible for any one of them to complete a sentence or for any listener to determine who was saying what.

"I tell you that when we have a pipsqueak dope-runner like Noriega—"

"Pipsqueak? Why worry about pipsqueaks? What about the situation in South Africa, where we seem remarkably adjusted to—"

"Never mind South Africa. Panama is in our backyard—"

"You make it sound like Pennsylvania. It's a good—"

"I'm talking about the Panama Canal—"

"The less we talk about how we got it in the first place, the better—"

"Look, all of you are missing the point. The drug problem is a matter of demand. The supply—"

"What are the farmers supposed to grow? Coca plants are the only crop—"

"It's good old free enterprise, good capitalist doctrine—"

"Since when have you been such a yodeler on the mountaintops for free enterprise?"

Arnold Kriss, the guest on this occasion, listened gravely, his eyes traveling from one speaker to another. He had a round and chubby face that made him look younger than he was, and curly brown hair that showed no signs of thinning. The well-cared-for fingers of his right hand drummed softly on the tabletop, making way briefly to allow that best of all waiters, Henry, to place the chocolate mousse before him.

Kriss turned to Mario Gonzalo, host for the occasion, who, mindful of his hostly dignity, had contributed very little to the hot discussion. Kriss said, "How long has this club existed, Mario?"

"It was founded during World War Two. Before my time, of course."

Kriss said, in a tone of deep envy, "You fellows must love each other."

Gonzalo turned his attention to Kriss with a look of wonder. "Are you kidding, Arnie?"

"Kidding? Not at all."

"Where do you get this love shtick? We're yelling at each other like crazy."

"But that's what I mean. No one's bothering to be polite. Everyone's saying what he wants to say without regard for anyone's feelings. You can't help but get the idea that there's complete trust among all of you. Everyone knows that nothing he'll say will in any way disrupt a friendship. That's *love.* Come on, Mario, is there anyone here who wouldn't lend you money if you needed it, or put himself out to help if you were in trouble?"

Gonzalo thought about it a moment, his eyes traveling from one squabbler to another. Then he said, "I guess you're right, Arnie. I can count on every one of them, but each one would be so sarcastic at my expense if I came to him with a sob-story that I think I'd try out a handful of strangers first."

"You would not. You'd go to them like a shot." Kriss turned his attention to the chocolate mousse.

As the members were drinking their coffee almost immediately afterward (or, in the case of Kriss, herb tea), Gonzalo rattled his water glass with his spoon.

"Gentlemen of the Black Widowers," he said, "you've all met

my guest, Arnold Kriss, and you all know he's a cellist with the Philharmonic, probably the best cellist it has had in at least thirty years—"

"What is this?" interrupted Thomas Trumbull indignantly, the lines on his tanned forehead turning it into a washboard. "Are you doing the grilling yourself?"

"What I'm doing," said Gonzalo, "is eliminating some of the things there's no point in talking about."

Geoffrey Avalon, hunching his thick eyebrows low, interrupted in his turn to say, "I don't think you should do any eliminating, Mario. I have some questions I'd like to ask about the internal workings of the Philharmonic."

"Maybe we'll get to that," said Gonzalo, "but I'm the host and I'm using host's privilege to turn the discussion in the direction I think proper. Arnie Kriss, as I was about to say, is a celebrity—"

At this, Kriss twisted uncomfortably in his seat and said, "Not really, Mario. I don't have the kind of following the Beatles had, or, in fact, that any third-rate rock star would have."

"Among people like *us* you're a celebrity," said Gonzalo, "and that's all we care about. So we'll take all that as given. Now it's customary for the host to appoint a griller, but I never heard that a host can't appoint himself as griller—"

There was at once a tumult, and Emmanuel Rubin raised an indignant voice, "It's never been done!"

"Just because something's never been done doesn't mean it can't be done, Manny. I'm host tonight and I've got the right to run this banquet as I wish. And I wish to be the griller. I have some questions to ask of Arnie—"

"How can you be an objective griller?" demanded Rubin. "You're a personal friend of the grillee."

"So what? I still want to ask the questions. Host's privilege."

James Drake peered through the smoke of his cigarette and said, "Let's give Mario his way. When he's asked his questions, we can ask sensible ones."

"I second those sentiments," said Roger Halsted in his soft voice. "Go ahead, Mario. Shoot."

"All right, I will." Gonzalo sat back in his chair and straightened his somewhat garish tie. "Arnie," he said, "you're a celebrity among people who have taste. You've been profiled in *The New Yorker* and you've played at a command performance at the White House. You've got it made. So what's the matter? Don't you have any friends?"

Kriss straightened in his chair and looked indignant. "Of course I have friends. What do you think? What kind of question is that?"

"It's a Mario question," muttered Rubin in ax low voice.

"Well, yes," said Gonzalo, "one would think you have friends. I'm a friend of yours—at least I like to think so. But then why do you envy us?"

"Envy you?"

"During dinner, while we were all screaming our heads off, you said to me that we must all love each other, and there was envy in your voice, as though you had no friends who loved you in the same way."

"Love?" Halsted's glance went around the table. "I wouldn't call it love."

"But Arnie did," said Gonzalo. "He said we had the complete freedom to yell at each other and curse each other without fearing anyone would resent it, and that that was love. So I want to know what's behind that, Arnie."

"Nothing," said Kriss, his voice rising in pitch.

"Don't give me that, Arnie. I told you the conditions of the dinner and you agreed to them. We can ask you any questions within the bounds of good taste and human decency and you've got to give a complete and truthful answer. Everything you say will be held completely confidential by us—that includes Henry, who is also a member of the Black Widowers."

Kriss said uneasily, "Well—"

Trumbull growled, "Go ahead, Mr. Kriss. If you have something on your mind, you might as well spill it. You'll probably feel better."

Kriss nodded. "All right. Maybe I will. I'm not sure how to put it, though. I've been in music all my life. Child prodigy and all that. I can't remember anything but concerts and moving that bow back and forth. Don't get me wrong. I love music. It's my life. It's just that every once in a while I get tired. Not of music, but of musicians.—I wouldn't want that repeated, by the way."

"It won't be," said Gonzalo, "I promised you that. Why are you tired of musicians?"

"Almost all the time all I have around me are musicians—that's only natural, even inevitable—but their talk gets monotonous. They've got their special insecurities and jealousies. After a while, none of them has anything to say that I haven't heard a thousand times before. I suppose it's that way in any profession that's deep enough to consume a person.

"Now, you Black Widowers are all what we might call professional men." His eye went from one to another. "Mario's an artist, and if I remember my introductions correctly Mr. Avalon is a patent lawyer, Mr. Trumbull is a code expert, Mr. Halsted is a mathematics teacher, Mr. Drake is a chemist, and Mr. Rubin is a mystery writer. No two alike. And that's good, because if you were all chemists, or all lawyers, or all writers, I have a notion you'd get tired of each other a lot faster."

Halsted said, "You know, Mr. Kriss, you can seek out friends who are not musicians."

"I do," said Kriss energetically. "I do my best to get away from them. It's why I value my friendship with Mario here. And about a year ago, I found something else, too. By sheer circumstance, I met a group of men who play poker regularly and I accepted an invitation to join them. There are five of us now, and we meet every Tuesday night for the game. It circulates among our apartments. Every five weeks or so the game is at mine, and the whole thing is an incredibly welcome relief. Sometimes there's an additional player or two, and sometimes one of us is missing, but there are five regulars—including," he added with satisfaction, "me."

"What kind of people are they?" asked Avalon. "Not musicians, of course."

"Absolutely not. In fact—" Kriss hesitated. "Actually, they're working people. Salt of the earth and all that, but no pretensions to intellectual activity at all. We just play poker and talk about football and drink beer and tell funny stories. In a way, I don't fit in perfectly, and I don't play the best poker in the world—I lose more often than I win—but I can afford the losses and they accept me. They know I'm a musician, but I never talk about it. They may think I blow a pennywhistle. For a few hours each week I'm a man and not a musician. It's wonderful."

"In that case," said Gonzalo fiercely, "why do you envy us?"

"Because something happened."

"Aha," said Gonzalo. "What happened?"

Kriss said, "Something peculiar that just messed up everything."

"That's not informational. You'll have to tell us what it was that messed up everything."

"All right, but it's complicated. I'll have to start by talking about my wife."

"If you wish to do so," said Avalon, "please do. We'll leave it to your good judgment to keep matters within the bounds of good taste."

"There's nothing remotely involving bad taste that's involved," said Kriss. "My wife—Grace—and I married in middle life. I was fifty-three, she was forty-seven. She's my second wife, I'm her first husband. She has no children and mine are grown up. We live together, just the two of us, in perfect harmony. We've stayed in love and we simply do not quarrel."

Trumbull said, "I find that hard to believe, Mr. Kriss. I've never come across any couple that didn't quarrel on occasion, and that certainly includes myself and Mrs. Trumbull."

"It depends on how you define 'quarrel.' Grace and I are both articulate people and we each have strong views. Sometimes those views compete and we have no hesitation in letting each other know that. As you Black Widowers do at your meetings, we yell at each other sometimes. We wouldn't be human, or in love with each other for that matter, if we didn't.

"But when I say we don't quarrel, I mean that our disagreements are always kept within the bounds of decency and fair play. We don't call each other names, we don't throw things, we never use our muscles. And when we do disagree, we make up again before bedtime—as an invariable rule. I'm explaining this so you'll understand how shocking the thing that happened was."

Drake said, "Wait. If your wife didn't marry until she was forty-seven, it's safe to assume that she was living on some inherited competence or on some adequately paying job or profession. Is *she* a musician, by any chance?"

Kriss grinned self-consciously. "Yes, she is, in a manner of speaking. She's a piano teacher—but not a concert pianist, you understand."

"A social difference?" asked Rubin drily.

"Yes, in a way. Still, it makes for marital harmony if we keep each other on an even level. Having lived with her maiden name, after all, for forty-seven years, she has kept on using it with my thorough approval. We put both names on the door when we married—G. Barron and A. Kriss—her name on top because she has students coming to the door all the time."

Rubin said, "Does it bother her that you are much more famous as a musician than she is?"

"I don't think so. She refers to it now and then, perhaps with just a touch of grimness, but you can be sure that *I* know better than to be too aware of it, or to refer to it."

"So what happened?" asked Gonzalo.

"Well, about a month ago we were watching television quietly—and separately. We have two sets in two different rooms and can each watch without being disturbed by the other because we have a sizable apartment and a well built one. She was in her office, with the door closed, watching *Star Trek*, a program she's very fond of. I was in the living room watching a *Kate and Allie* rerun. I was about ten minutes into the program, so it must have been 7:40 P.M. when the doorbell rang. That's always unsettling, because no one is supposed to get up to the apartment without the concierge downstairs ringing us. Of course, it might be a neighbor, or one of the building employees.

"I knew it would be hopeless to expect Grace to answer the door while she was watching *Star Trek*, so I heaved myself out of my chair, went to the door, and, like a true New Yorker, refused to open the door without asking who was there.

"There was no answer, so I opened the peephole and looked out—and, I tell you, I got a grade-A shock, because the hall was full of policemen as far as the eye could see. I opened the door at once and there were five of them—four policemen and a policewoman.

"I looked at them blankly and said, 'What's going on, officers?'

"The policeman in the lead said, in a kind of brusque, official voice, 'We have information that there's a marital fight going on here.'

"Well, I'm sure there are people who are capable of putting on a convincing display of astonishment when they're not, in actual fact, astonished, but I'm not one of them. I was simply astonished at the idea of being involved in a marital fight of a kind that needed police attention, and my astonishment must have impressed the police as genuine.

" 'A marital fight?' I said, stunned. 'Here? In this building?'

" 'In this building,' said the policeman.

" 'Then you have the wrong apartment,' I told him.

" 'No, sir,' he said. 'We were given the apartment number and your name.' And of course my name was right on the door staring at him, so to speak.

"My look of incredulity must have made the policeman feel impelled to justify his intrusion into our life. 'Our information is,' he said, 'that you had a knife at the throat of your wife.'

"Words absolutely failed me at the thought of such a thing

between Grace and myself. No wonder there were five of them. They were expecting a maddened killer, with a knife dripping blood.

"Suddenly I thought of the two television sets that were on. However, we both ran the volume low to avoid troubling the other: my own set was a murmur and I couldn't hear Grace's at all through her closed door. And neither program had been violent. I checked that with Grace later.

"But by then it had dawned on me that I had better produce a wife in one piece. Grace hadn't come out to see what was going on at the door, so I called for her.

" 'Grace!' I shouted. She must have been reluctant to interrupt her watching. I had to call twice more—the second time in considerable agitation, for it seemed to me the police might begin to think I was bluffing and that I had a wife on the other side of a closed door who was either unconscious or dead.

"But finally she came out, clearly in fine shape and good health. 'What's the matter?' she asked, and then she saw the policemen, and asked it again with more urgency.

"I said, 'Someone reported that you and I were having a fight and that I was killing you.'

"It was her turn to be astonished, and the blank surprise on her face was all the policemen needed to see the report was wrong. They turned away and the man in charge said, 'Okay, but we had to investigate the matter, you understand?'

" 'Of course,' I said. 'You had no choice—and I thank you for trying to protect my wife.'

"And they left."

There was a silence, and then Avalon said, "Well, Mr. Kriss, it was an unsettling experience, I'm sure, but there were no later consequences, were there?"

"Not of any definite kind, Mr. Avalon."

Halsted said, "Are you referring to indirect consequences, Mr. Kriss? I imagine it must have created a stir among the apartment staff to have so many police charging up to your apartment. It must have spread among all the neighbors and required embarrassing explanations."

"I certainly offered none," said Kriss stiffly, "and no one said anything directly to me about it. The story may have spread about a marital fight, but there isn't a person in the building who could possibly believe that I had been abusing Grace. We're well known as the Darby and Joan of the apartment house. No, that's not what bothers me."

Gonzalo said, "We're still trying to get to it. What *does* bother you, Arnie?"

Kriss said, "It's the question of who informed the police, of course. Someone called the police emergency number, reported a fight between us with a knife, and gave them the apartment building, the apartment number, and my name. It couldn't be a casual troublemaker. It had to be someone who knew me."

Trumbull said, "Maybe so, but you know a great many people who know your name and address. One of them must have had a few drinks and then got what he thought was the very funny idea of sending the police to your door. There's no way of telling who it might have been."

"You're quite wrong," said Kriss angrily. "As I told you, almost all the people I know are musicians, and none of them would do it. It's not that they're models of virtue, but they don't have that kind of mind, any more than I have. Once they've stopped thinking about music, musicians are a spent force.

"Look, this is the sort of thing a musician thinks is funny: one of them will regale another by saying, 'Isaac Stern was wrapping his violin about one of Paganini's show-off pieces and made certain he hit every note—he left no tone unSterned.' Here's another: Two aspiring violinists had finally achieved their goal and were playing a duet at Carnegie Hall. Naturally, there was a good deal of nervousness, and one of them lost his place in the sheet music. He improvised desperately while trying unsuccessfully to locate the bar he was playing, and finally whispered out of the corner of his mouth to the other, 'Where *are* we?' And the other whispered, 'Carnegie Hall.' *That's* what musicians think is funny—not one of them would ever think that sending the police to my apartment on a false alarm would be funny."

Avalon said gravely, "It's my experience that people can't be categorized that easily. Still, it might be one of your fans—though I should think they wouldn't know your exact address, or that, even if they did, they wouldn't be so disrespectful as to try such a trick."

"I should hope not," said Kriss. "Anyway, I'll tell you who I think it is. I suspect it's one of my poker buddies—maybe all of them." And the lines of his face sank into depression.

"Why do you think that?" asked Gonzalo.

"No real reason, Mario, but they all know exactly where I live. They've been to my apartment often enough. And I told you I don't exactly fit in. For all my trying, they may still feel enough of something different about me to make them pull that trick on me. It makes me feel bad. Very bad. I enjoyed those sessions and now I can't."

"Have you stopped playing poker?"

"Oh, no. We still play, but the pleasure's gone. I keep looking from one to another, wondering which one of them did it. I don't know how much longer I can keep it up. It's spoiled everything."

Drake said, "Have you tried to face them with it? Maybe one or more will confess and you can have a good laugh over it. If you can take the joke like a sport, then they may really accept you. You would have passed a rite of passage, I suppose."

"But it's not my kind of rite of passage," said Kriss impatiently. "And I did face them with it, though not as a group. I thought that if only one of them had done it, he wouldn't like to admit it in front of the others. I took the opportunity of speaking to each one of them separately and mentioning what had happened in as jovial a manner as I could manage. Each one of the four told me it was a dirty trick and didn't show any signs of thinking it was funny. One of them must be lying, I suppose. At least one of them."

"But I take it you get along well with them," said Halsted.

"You've been playing with them for some considerable time and I assume they've never made a move to get you out of the game."

"Never," said Kriss.

"So did anything happen recently that would have made one or more of them annoyed with you? Did you arouse their envy in some way?"

"Not on purpose. Of course, my apartment is somewhat better than theirs are, but not that much so."

Gonzalo said, "You didn't boast about how much you get for a concert appearance or anything like that, did you?"

Kriss looked revolted. "Of course not. You know me better than that."

Avalon said, "Well, let's use our brains. The particular practical joke that was played upon you, Mr. Kriss, put you in the position of being a wife-abuser. Is one of your poker-playing friends a wife-abuser?"

"Not to my knowledge. Of course—"

"Yes?"

"Steve is having trouble with his wife. Not physical, as far as I know. He's been running around, I gather, and his wife caught him at it, so things are antagonistic between them."

"I'm not a psychologist," said Avalon, "but isn't it possible he'd like to beat up his wife and rather than actually do it he worked up a fantasy that you beat up yours."

"Why me?" asked Kriss.

"Perhaps he was annoyed by your calm and pleasant married life. You might have boasted about that, Mr. Kriss."

"I certainly did not—but, of course, when they come to my apartment I can't very well stop Grace from being pleasant and good-humored about the whole thing."

"Well, there you are," said Avalon. "Steve might have some dim idea of getting even. After all, these are not great intellects you're dealing with, Mr. Kriss."

"They're decent men," said Kriss. "I wouldn't like to think Steve would do it for any such silly reason. The suggestion is not proof, you know."

"No, it isn't," admitted Avalon, "but we're not going to get proof unless one of them confesses."

"I wouldn't demand proof," said Kriss. "I'm not going to be reporting anyone to the police. All I want is to be satisfied in my mind who it was, and why."

Rubin said, "Just a thought. Are any of the four actually given to practical jokes? If any of them is given to pulling dumb stunts like this, they'd do it as a way of life. They wouldn't need reasons."

Kriss was thoughtful. "I can't recall that any of them ever told stories about practical jokes he'd played. Joe once palmed all four aces and let us play a game without them. Naturally, each one of us thought one of the others had the aces and when Joe started bidding we thought *he* might have them. He was able to take the pot with a nothing hand. As soon as it was over, he admitted what he'd done, we all gave him what-for, and he never tried anything like that again."

"Maybe not," said Rubin, "but it shows a bent of mind, you know."

Kriss shook his head. "That's not at all convincing."

"Look here," said Drake. "The point is that policemen were involved in this and it strikes me that not many people would try a practical joke that makes policemen as well as some innocent civilian the victims. You, Mr. Kriss, don't see the humor in it, and neither, I'm sure, did the police. If they found out who made the false report, they'd have good motivation for making life miserable for him."

"What are you driving at, Jim?" asked Avalon.

"It just seems to me that whoever did it must be sufficiently familiar with the police to be willing to take a chance. Did one of your poker mates ever have a run-in with the police to your knowledge, Mr. Kriss? Would he be trying to get at the police rather than at you?"

"Nothing like that was ever hinted at," said Kriss. Then, thoughtfully, "Ernie has a cousin, I think, who's a policeman. He mentioned that once or twice, it seems to me."

Trumbull said, "A relative in the police force would make it less likely that a person would play games with the police, if you ask me."

"Unless," said Drake, "Ernie doesn't like his cousin."

"I don't think that's at all meaningful, either," said Kriss.

A silence fell around the table, and then Gonzalo said, "Listen, Arnie, is there anyone at the poker table that you don't particularly like?"

"No," said Kriss. "They're all nice guys. Or I always thought they were till the police appeared at the door."

"Then let me put it another way, Arnie. Even if you like all four, isn't there one you like the least?"

"Well," said Kriss cautiously, "there's Ken. There's nothing wrong with him, really, but he's got a hoarse voice that grates on my ear. My musical sense, I suppose. I just find myself wincing a little sometimes when he talks. What difference could that make?"

"Because I have a theory," said Gonzalo, "that dislike usually works both ways. You don't usually dislike someone who likes you and vice versa. Like and dislike make themselves felt in subtle ways even when you're not aware of it. If you wince at Ken, he's bound to wince at you, and maybe his dislike drove him to the deed."

"I don't believe it," said Kriss.

Avalon offered, "Well, we've managed to show that each one of the four has something about him that makes it possible he's the one who phoned the police. Steve has trouble with his wife and may be jealous of your marital bliss. Joe has a tendency to engage in practical jokes and may have done it to indulge in his caprice. Ernie has a cousin who is a policeman and may have done it either because he is hostile to policemen or unafraid of them. And Ken may have done it out of a vague dislike of you. The trouble is that not one of the four motivations is anywhere near convincing."

Kriss nodded. "That's it. So it ends up where it began. I can't trust anybody at the game and my one nonmusical recreation is probably gone. Is it any wonder I envy you six your stable get-togethers?"

"Not us six," said Gonzalo, "it's us seven. And nobody has asked Henry yet. —Can you make anything of this, Henry?"

Henry, from his post at the sideboard, smiled paternally. "I'm not at all sure I can shed any light on the situation, but I do have some questions to ask, if Mr. Kriss will permit me."

"Go ahead, Henry," said Kriss resignedly. "Everyone else has been at me."

Henry said, "Did the police know who you are, Mr. Kriss?"

"You mean that I'm a well known cellist? I'm sure they didn't. When Mario says I'm a celebrity, he's exaggerating, you know."

"Did they address you by name, or refer to your playing?"

"Not at all."

"Your name on the door must have meant nothing to them, then."

"That's right. I'm sure of that."

Henry said, "And your wife still uses her maiden name on the door?"

"Yes."

"When the police came, they said the incident had been clearly localized by address, apartment number, and name. Did they address you by name? Or did you announce your name?"

"They didn't use my name and I didn't announce it. My name is right there on the door. They saw it."

"But they saw two names, Mr. Kriss, G. Barron on top and A. Kriss on the bottom. Which name had been reported to the police?"

"Why, my name, of—" Kriss stopped cold.

"Exactly, sir. You have *assumed* it was your name that had been reported, but you don't know. No name was actually mentioned, either by the police or by you or, I suppose, by your wife. So it may have been your wife's last name that was reported, not yours. Isn't that right?"

"Oh, my God," said Kriss blankly.

"What difference would it make, Henry?" asked Gonzalo.

Henry said, "There doesn't seem to be any clear candidate for the role of having played this practical joke on Mr. Kriss. Might there be one who would have played it on Mrs. Kriss?"

Kriss groaned. "Of course—there is. There's someone who has been harassing Grace for years, since long before I married her. He phones her frequently, he sends her letters—he won't leave her alone."

"Why?" asked Gonzalo.

Kriss shrugged. "He was a fellow student of hers once. Harmless enough, but somehow he never grew up, I imagine. He seems to have been in love with her back then. I suppose he's never found anyone else and she's his fantasy. He's always been quite harmless, so I didn't think of him in this connection. But, of course, it must be he. He knows Grace is married and resents it and fantasizes her husband might be cruel to her, I suppose.—How is it it never occurred to me it might be *her* name that had been reported?"

"It is my feeling," said Avalon, "that however seriously a male may intellectually accept the concept of his wife's equality, his feeling, viscerally, is that she is merely an appendage."

Kriss seemed too abashed to answer, but Henry said softly, "At least, Mr. Kriss, you can go back to your poker game in full enjoyment."

THE HAUNTED CABIN

Geoffrey Avalon, host of the Black Widower banquet that month, gazed benignly at the five other seated Widowers, and at his guest for the evening, Marcellus DaRienzi. Henry, that unparalleled waiter, would soon be removing the main-course plates, when the last bit of the roast goose, red cabbage, and potato pancakes would be gone.

"I have a rather odd tale that I would like to tell you all before the business end of the meeting begins," Avalon said in his stately baritone.

Emmanuel Rubin looked up at him owlishly through the thick lenses of his glasses with an unaccustomed bonhomie, and patted a stomach full of goose. "Go ahead, Jeff, but don't be tedious."

"I shall try not to be," said Avalon gravely. "It happened two weeks ago. I was on a business trip and had taken a room in a hotel. I needn't mention the name of the hotel, or of the city, to avoid tedium for Manny, and because they have nothing to do with the story. My wife was not with me. That *is* essential.

"I had several hours one afternoon between appointments and I thought I might as well take a nap." He added defensively, "I don't know about the rest of you, but since I am past my first youth I find forty winks after lunch to be most helpful."

"We'll grant you that, Jeff," said Thomas Trumbull, scowling under the crisp, tight waves of his white hair. "I've been known to take such naps myself, and Jim Drake is taking one now."

"Not at all," said Drake indignantly, "I was just resting my eyelids."

"Let me go on," said Avalon. "I fell into a light doze and suddenly felt the poke of a finger on my shoulder, quite a hard poke. Naturally, I woke up at once and, in the confusion of sudden wakefulness, I cried out, "Who? What?" and sat up in bed. The room, as I suppose you can guess, was, except for me, empty. It was afternoon, the sunlight was slanting in—there were no dim corners, all was bright, and the room was empty. The door was securely locked, with an inner chain in place. The windows were locked and they were, in any case, sixteen sheer stories above the street."

"Did you look under the bed?" asked Mario Gonzalo, grinning and smoothing his ascot tie.

"No," said Avalon with a touch of hauteur, "I did *not* look under the bed. There was no room under the bed for a medium-sized dog, let alone a human being. However, I did inspect the bathroom and the closet. Nothing there. And there were no connecting doors to other rooms, by the way. I was alone, absolutely alone."

"So?" said Roger Halsted, pushing away his plate.

"So who poked me?"

"Oh, for God's sake," exploded Trumbull. "It was a *dream*. Haven't you ever dreamed, Jeff?"

"No," said Avalon, hunching his formidable eyebrows low, "it was *not* a dream. I *know* it was not a dream. Someone poked me."

"Listen," began Trumbull, "I've had dreams—"

"Never mind your dreams," said Avalon with unaccustomed abruptness, "this was not a dream."

Trumbull shook his head. "I've never known you to be this stubborn, Jeff, and this stupid."

The guest, DaRienzi, now spoke for the first time since the dinner had begun. He smiled down at his stewed pears and said, "What Jeff is doing here, gentlemen, is posing a locked-room puzzle. Something has happened in a locked room that could not have happened. My friend Jeff is an honest man who is presenting an honest problem and we—or at least you gentlemen of the club—must puzzle out the solution. And saying it was just a dream is not an acceptable solution, is it, Jeff?"

"No," said Avalon, still testy. "*I* know the solution, and so do you, Marcellus, because I told you this earlier in the evening, but I want the Black Widowers to figure it out. I'm telling it to them in orderly fashion, if the idiots would only allow it."

Rubin said, "You're the host, Jeff—you control the evening. Order silence and go on."

Avalon glowered. "Silence! In the empty room, then, I was forced to consider the possibility of a supernatural warning."

The five other Widowers at the table, rationalists all, scrambled to their feet and, the order for silence forgotten, yammered their indignation. DaRienzi kept his seat and smiled.

Avalon raised his hands and thundered, "*Silence!* I don't say I accepted the supernatural as an explanation. I merely say I was forced to consider it. I don't believe in supernatural influences, but even my own firmest beliefs cannot be accepted by myself as unshakeable and invulnerable. Do you mind pursuing rationality that far?"

"As a matter of fact," said Roger Halsted quietly, as he mopped his high pink brow with his handkerchief, "our society is so permeated and drenched with supernatural beliefs of any number of kinds and sorts that even the firmest skeptic may be corrupted, at least momentarily, if the conditions are right."

"Thank you, Roger," said Avalon. "It's exactly what I would have wanted to say. It was two-fifteen when it happened, and if it hadn't been for the fact that I had a wife in New York I would have dismissed the matter. But I couldn't. Some forty-five years of marriage isn't something you can dismiss lightly. I phoned her. She answered at once. I don't know what I would have done if she hadn't answered—if she had been out shopping, for instance. I might well have raced home and made a complete fool of myself. But she *did* answer. I asked how things were and everything was perfectly in order, so I relaxed. And that left only the primary problem. Who had poked me?"

"It was a dream!" said Trumbull stubbornly.

"No," said Avalon. "It *wasn't*. After a while, I gave up the problem and decided to try to sleep again. And I became aware that when I prepare for sleep, at least if I'm alone in bed, I wrap my arms tightly about myself. I also know that in the borderland between sleep and wakefulness, my muscles twitch. I have felt them do so and my wife has commented on it with some amusement.

"And of course, that was the solution. It fully explains the locked-room puzzle without calling upon the supernatural. In the process of falling asleep, my own finger had twitched and jabbed my shoulder." *

Avalon looked about triumphantly and said, "And that is why I have brought my friend, Marcellus DaRienzi, Ph.D., as my guest. He has a natural connection with this sort of thing. And I have managed to finish my story without delaying the grilling too much, so let's proceed. Tom, you skeptic, I appoint you the griller."

Thomas Trumbull studied Avalon's guest. DaRienzi was a cheerful-looking man with tufts of hair down his cheeks and only a tuft on top of his head. He wore old-fashioned round-rimmed glasses and a vest under his suit-jacket, and he had an air of permeating benevolence.

Trumbull said, "Mr. DaRienzi—Marcellus—I will get right to the point without setting you the usual first task of justifying your existence. What is the so-called natural connection Jeff says you have with this mad dream-story he told us?"

Avalon looked offended, but kept silent.

DaRienzi said mildly, 'The connection, I suppose, is that I'm a psychic researcher."

"Oh, Lord," muttered Trumbull, "oh, Lord." Then, more

** The reader may be interested to know that this matter of a poke in an empty room, and a panicky call to a wife, happened to me recently in exactly the manner described here.—I.A.*

loudly, "Does that mean you're trying to prove the existence of telepathy, spoon-bending, ghosts, and fairies at the bottom of the garden? Have you been working on poor Jeff so that he's beginning to be screwed up?"

Avalon looked daggers, but still said nothing.

DaRienzi said, "Why, no, Tom, rather the opposite. I've spent my time investigating and *disproving* reports of the existence of telepathy, spoon-bending, ghosts, and fairies at the bottom of the garden."

"Do you mean," put in Rubin suddenly, "like the Amazing Randi?"

"Something like," agreed DaRienzi, "but not completely. The Amazing Randi is probably the most doughty knight in the fight against hokum and pseudoscience that there is. But he is much in the news and the practitioners of nonsense try to avoid him, so that his task is harder than it might otherwise be.

"I'm not the skilled magician that Randi is, which puts me under a disadvantage. However, I maintain a low profile. I stay out of the limelight so that I am easily accepted as a believer and the fakers don't go to any special efforts to fool me. For that reason, I can usually detect what it is they're really doing. I might say that I have never found any convincing evidence in favor of anything we might call supernaturalism or the paranormal. I'm ready to be convinced that such things exist, but only if the evidence is solid, and it never has been in my experience."

"In that case," said Trumbull, "I presume you don't approve of Avalon's action in calling his wife."

"It did no harm," said DaRienzi. "His momentary weakness in phoning his wife is something any of us might have fallen prey to. As Roger said, the social milieu in which we live makes it almost impossible not to weaken on occasion. And I surely approve of Jeff's final rationalistic solution of this locked-room mystery of his."

Gonzalo interrupted, "Pardon me, Marcellus, I don't want you to take offense, but we have all heard of the Amazing Randi. I have, for one. But I have never heard of you." He looked about. "Has anyone? I mean, besides Jeff?"

"I hope not," said DaRienzi with deep sincerity. "I said I keep a low profile and I mean it. I don't want *anyone* to know me in my capacity as a psychic researcher. That Jeff knows is partly the result of accident, but I am confident of his discretion. And I *hope* that—" He looked about uncertainly.

Jeff said, "As I told you, Marcellus, nothing that is said at a Black Widowers banquet is ever repeated outside these walls. That assurance extends to our waiter, who is, in point of fact, a member of the club."

"Well," said DaRienzi with a remnant of worry in his voice, "I'll accept that."

Halsted cleared his throat and said, "Marcellus, what is your doctorate in?"

"Psychology."

"And do you work as a psychologist? Do you have a university position? Are you in private practice?"

"No to all three questions, Roger. My work consists entirely of the psychic research I've mentioned."

Halsted cleared his throat again and said, "I'm a math teacher at a junior-high school and am therefore very knowledgeable on the subject of inadequate payment. How the devil do you make a living on your psychic research?"

"I don't," said DaRienzi. "At least, I don't have to. My father saw to it that I was left with a secure and entirely adequate income so that I can quite afford to spend my life in doing something I consider very worthwhile and interesting, without regard to payment."

"Lucky fellow," muttered Halsted.

Trumbull reentered the grilling with what was almost a roar. "All right, so you don't need money. But do you mean to tell us that you have no hankering for fame, or at least recognition? Don't you want to have people know of your work?"

DaRienzi reddened slightly. "Why, there, Tom," he said, "you touch a tender point. We live in a social environment whose orientation toward success is as corrupting as its orientation toward supernaturalism. The truth is—and please let me remind you of your assurance of confidentiality—that I *am* writing a book describing my experiences. It will be a startling one and I have many amusing stories to tell that are not at all known to the general public. I don't suppose it will make a great deal of money—debunking books never do. Still, I have a publisher and I'm enjoying the task."

"But you'll blow your cover," said Gonzalo. "I mean, you'll become known and then you'll have the disadvantages of that."

"Scarcely," said DaRienzi with a small laugh. "My picture won't appear in the book and I plan to use a pseudonym. Any success I achieve in the book will redound to the work I've done and not to me personally. Of course, as I approach the end of my life I may reveal my identity if a hankering for any personal fame I can garner in this way overcomes me."

"What progress are you making on your book?" asked Rubin. "Writing isn't an easy job."

"Manny knows," put in Gonzalo at once. "He's a writer and it surely doesn't come easily to him."

"You'll find," said Rubin loftily, "that writers have much to suffer at the hands of ignorant and captious critics. But what progress are you making?"

"As Mario said, writing isn't easy, at least not for me, but I'm almost finished with the first draft. I made major progress late last summer when I was able to use a friend's Vermont home for two weeks. You remember, Jeff, that Harry Weinstein had to spend most of the summer in Europe and he was kind enough to let me have his summer home for the latter part of August. It was very peaceful and quiet, and perfect for what I needed.

"As a matter of fact, he had a special bonus for me. 'You'll like my place, Marcellus,' he said, 'because I've heard a haunted cabin has turned up in the vicinity, and you once said you were interested in such things.'

"And so I had. Such remarks do manage to slip out despite anything I can do, I've often thought it would be an accumulation of such slips that would blow my cover, to use Mario's phrase, and not my book."

Halsted asked, with interest, "Have you investigated haunted houses?"

"Certainly," said DaRienzi. "Half a dozen rather well-known cases, and a number of trivial ones."

"How do you go about it?"

"You examine the place rather meticulously by daylight, but the important test is to spend the night there. A dark and stormy night would be best—" DaRienzi grinned "—but unfortunately the condition of most haunted houses is such that a stormy night would produce as much rain and wind indoors as outdoors."

Halsted said, "And you've actually slept in such houses?"

"Of course." DaRienzi looked about good-humoredly. "Come, you're all rationalists. I heard you jumping all over poor Jeff a while ago. How many of you would prefer *not* to sleep in a supposed haunted house?"

There was a rather sticky silence as the Black Widowers stared furtively at each other.

DaRienzi waited a moment, then said lightly, "I withdraw the question. Everyone has seen enough haunted-house movies in childhood to scar the soul of even the boldest."

"But," said Halsted, "do you actually sleep in these houses?"

"Of course not," said DaRienzi. "You simply spend the night there. After all, you have to stay awake if you're going to be aware of any manifestations. Besides that, the condition of haunted houses is not generally conducive to sleep. The houses are old and full of creaks, the rooms are musty, the beds rickety, and the mattresses beneath contempt. I doubt that anyone, even a posturing daredevil, could actually sleep in one of your typical haunted houses unless he were in the last stages of extreme fatigue."

"I don't suppose you ever came across any manifestations."

"If you mean anything that could be counted as firm evidence of ghostly or paranormal activity, of course not. The true believers always maintain that the manifestations are best received by 'sensitives' and that skeptics are too coarse-fibered to receive the delicate vibrations or whatever. That, however, is only another way of saying that manifestations are received most easily by people who are credulous and suggestible, and we all know that.

"Sometimes, to be sure, manifestations take place that are apparent even to my coarse-fibered, skeptical nature, and then I must nail them firmly to natural causes. I'm usually able to do that, but once I almost failed and I was then in the position Jeff found himself in when he was poked in the hotel room."

"Ah," said Gonzalo with sudden satisfaction. "Now you're talking. Tell us about it."

"I intend to," said DaRienzi, "because it happened last August in the little town in Vermont where I was using my friend's summer home."

"You mean," said Gonzalo, "there *was* a haunted cabin there, as your friend had said."

"Yes, there was, and it gave me quite a turn."

Avalon looked surprised. "You didn't tell me this, Marcellus."

"No, I had no occasion to, but after you told me your locked-room experience this afternoon, and I could see it was your reason for inviting me to the banquet, I thought it would be fitting to tell the story, since it matched yours so well."

"Very well, then. Tell it from the beginning, Marcellus."

"Certainly," said DaRienzi. "I drove there the evening before my formal occupancy was to begin and moved my baggage into the house. I was observed by some of the locals as I drove there, but they showed no curiosity. Harry loaned out his cottage for periods of time nearly every summer, and apparently the locals were used to the succession of 'city fellows' that came there. Besides, the locals kept themselves to themselves, as I found out. They were stolid and quiet, quite like the stereotype of the Vermont backwoodsman. They showed absolutely no interest in me socially, and that, as you can well imagine, was exactly what I wanted.

"I found the cottage in good shape—electricity on, water flowing, a gas range in working order, a comfortably large refrigerator-freezer—but nothing to eat, if you don't count a half empty tin of coffee in the pantry. That was no problem, of course. The next morning, I drove down to the village store about three-quarters of a mile away and stocked up with two weeks of supplies. I did so rather munificently, getting rather more than I needed, because I intended to leave some items in Weinstein's freezer as a sort of rent for the cottage. The storekeeper scared up almost everything I asked for.

"I then spent what I can only describe as a delicious two weeks working on my book, with my papers, notes, and reference materials scattered about me. No one disturbed me, and the weather, except for one dreary day of rain and wind, was fine. When the time came to leave, I was quite regretful."

Gonzalo said, "Don't leave yet. What about the haunted cabin?"

"I'm getting to that. Each evening, except for the rainy one, I'd walk to the village and back, partly for exercise, and partly to buy perishables. I exchanged a few remarks on the weather with any locals I met and they replied noncommittally. They were polite, if not communicative. *Except* in the matter of the haunted cabin. There they unbent as far as a Vermonter could unbend.

"They were willing to point out its location, for instance. I asked them what the haunting consisted of. They didn't know, or wouldn't say. Apparently 'city fellows' had occasionally spent time in the cabin and one old local man said he had heard tell that strange noises and sounds could be heard in the cabin.

"I was suspicious of the whole deal but did my best not to show it. For one thing, the cabin was old but not *very* old. It was not in a dilapidated state. For another, there were no stories to account for the haunting and I considered that very odd. Your haunted house invariably comes with a dark tale of lust, cruelty, murder, or betrayal to account for the haunting, and the deeds almost always date back at least two centuries. Without it, I suspected bald-faced fakery."

Avalon said, "Why? What kind of fakery?"

DaRienzi smiled grimly. "I felt quite firmly that the whole thing was homegrown and of recent vintage. It was invented by the natives themselves as a kind of tourist attraction. I later found out that the village inn had prospered greatly in the last several years, and the Burlington newspapers had run several articles on the haunted cabin. The thing was their Loch Ness monster, if you know what I mean."

Gonzalo snapped his fingers in frustration. "Damn! Then you're saying there was no haunted cabin, after all."

"Of course not," said DaRienzi. "Did you think there would be? Even if the cabin were an old dilapidated wreck and had once been owned by a wicked farmer who abused and killed his innocent wife, do you think it would be haunted? *Really* haunted? — Besides, I haven't finished the story.

"On the last evening there, I intended to inspect the so-called haunted cabin. The storekeeper had the key and he surrendered it to me at my request early in the day, with as near a smile as his habitually dour expression permitted. 'Here you are, sir,' he said. I'm sure he then spread the story and the locals looked forward with anticipation to scaring me and having another story for the Burlington papers, and another infusion of wealth for the village.

"I inspected the house quickly and superficially by day. I didn't want any spying local to get too suspicious about the professionalism of the kind of search I might make. It was very ordinary, with the usual air of quiet and loneliness that long-deserted houses have. I found nothing unusual. After nightfall, I returned. There was no electricity, of course. You can't have that in a haunted house. Ghosts are, in any case, the children of the wavering, flickering shadows of the hearthfire. The steady light of electric bulbs is sure death to ghosts. It was necessary to investigate the house by flashlight, but I had a good one.

"I now gave the house a *real* inspection, foot by foot and inch by inch. I had no trouble discovering the wiring and the microphones. I suppose the local TV repairman had set it up and was under the impression he had done a good job, but he could scarcely expect to fool the trained and practiced eye."

Gonzalo said, "Then it was just as fake as you expected. And an obvious fake, too."

"Why are you surprised?" asked DaRienzi. "All haunted houses are fakes, but very few, I admit, as obviously so as this one."

"I suppose," said Drake, looking thoughtful, "that there was no point in lingering after that."

"On the contrary," said DaRienzi. "I felt it important to stay the night. I was curious as to the sort of manifestations they would manufacture for me. Surely they hadn't wired the place for nothing. And it's a good thing I did, because, as I told you at the beginning, they did startle me. I took off my jacket and shoes and sat in the one chair that looked as though it would bear my weight and be reasonably comfortable. Then I waited."

"Staying up all night is no fun," muttered Trumbull.

"I didn't stay up all night," said DaRienzi. "The manifestations came long before the night was over."

"What were they?" asked Gonzalo eagerly.

"Nothing more than my name," said DaRienzi. "There was an eerie whisper, with just a trace of sound that told me it was coming in over a microphone. 'Marcellus DaRienzi, Marcellus DaRienzi,' then a pause, then again. It was repeated four times altogether and the last repetition of my name was allowed to die away into a third screech that sounded like 'Beware.' It was all very primitive.

"When I decided the show was over at about two A.M., I got up, left, went to Harry's, and slept the rest of the night in comfort. By midmorning I was cleaning up and packing, and by midafternoon I left for New York."

Drake said, "Did anyone ask what had happened the night before?"

"No. They saw me and knew I was alive, but they knew what had happened. And I didn't feel any great need to discuss it."

Gonzalo writhed in his seat and finally said, "I don't want to insult you, but that's a pretty dull ghost story."

DaRienzi didn't seem the least insulted. "Actually," he said, "the ghost story had not yet begun. I was some twenty miles away from the village when it suddenly struck me like an alarm in the night. I had to pull the car over to the side of the road and start thinking."

Avalon frowned. "Thinking about what, Marc?"

"Don't you get it, Jeff? Once you found out your wife was all right, you suddenly realized you had to get to the true point: who had poked you? And once I found out that the house was a patent fake, I suddenly realized I had to get to the true point, too."

"Which was?" said Gonzalo.

"Which was: how did they know my name?"

There was a general look of surprise about the table (and a fleeting smile crossed Henry's face).

Trumbull put the general thought into words, growling, "Why shouldn't they know your name?"

"Because I never gave it to anybody in the village," said DaRienzi, "and not one of them ever asked. I told you I've made a fetish of anonymity in connection with my work all my professional life. I was there to write my book, not to publicize myself. I told no one my name. I regretted allowing anyone to see me, even.

"Do you see the problem this creates? The true believers of psychic phenomena are sometimes forced to admit fakery is involved, but they are then likely to insist that true paranormal effects are produced even in the midst of trickery. Well, then, despite all the wiring, despite the microphonic equipment, did something really paranormal take place? How could anyone have known my name?"

Trumbull said, "I don't think there's much mystery, Marcellus. You must have told someone your name."

"Rely on me," said DaRienzi stiffly, "I didn't tell anyone my name."

"In that case," said Trumbull, "someone must have recognized you."

"I can't believe that. I have very few photos of myself and none at all for distribution."

Halsted said, "They might have seen *you*, not your photograph. After all, you must give talks about your labors, and if you ever gave a talk in Burlington someone from the village may have happened to—"

DaRienzi registered annoyance. "You haven't listened to me. I hold my anonymity sacred. I don't give talks, and I certainly never talked in Burlington."

Rubin said, "Yours is not a common name, so they couldn't have made a lucky guess."

"It's unthinkable that they would."

Rubin said, "Was the name pronounced correctly?"

DaRienzi's face relaxed into a smile. "Good for you. Actually, both names were mispronounced. Marcellus was stressed on the first syllable rather than the second, while DaRienzi was given a long 'i' sound at the close."

"Which means," said Rubin, "that the so-called ghost saw your name but had never heard it pronounced."

"Exactly," said DaRienzi. "I came to the same conclusion."

"Which leads me to think," said Rubin, "that someone broke into your friend's summer house and ransacked your papers and belongings for your name."

"I'm sure that isn't so," said DaRienzi. "They couldn't have ransacked the house without disturbing my papers and I would have noticed that at once. Besides, as it happened, I didn't have my name on anything there."

"Well, then," said Gonzalo, with more than a trace of satisfaction, "you're in Jeff's position. You're forced to consider the paranormal."

"I'm more in Jeff's position than you think, Mario, for, like Jeff, I solved the problem—or at least I found a satisfactory solution that involved nothing beyond the natural."

"And what was that?" asked Avalon.

DaRienzi said cheerfully, "Do none of you see it? It's much simpler than Jeff's solution and doesn't involve personal quirks that no one but the solver would be expected to know."

There was a longish pause, and Drake shook his head. "I'm afraid you've got us. Unless Henry has a suggestion."

"Henry," said Gonzalo abruptly, "what's the answer?"

Henry, from his quiet station at the sideboard, said, "If I may be permitted to say so, gentlemen, the solution was obvious from the start."

"Was it?" said DaRienzi a little captiously.

"I'm afraid so. At the beginning of your stay in Vermont, you bought two weeks' supplies and more at the village store. At today's prices, it may well have come to a sizable bit of money."

"It did," said DaRienzi, beginning to smile.

"And surely, considering our plastic culture, you did not pay in cash."

DaRienzi broke into a roar of laughter. "Got it! You got it! Of course I didn't pay cash. I shoved over my credit card—"

"And your name was on it," said Henry. "And your signature had to be placed on the slip they stamped, and it was so common and ordinary an action that you thought nothing of it, and didn't recall it at once later on. I'm afraid it is much more difficult to be anonymous in our modern society than we imagine."

THE GUEST'S GUEST

The man looked down at his hand and said to the waiter who was standing at the head of the stairs, "The Milano Restaurant, Fifth and Eighteenth, second floor. Right?"

"Perfectly correct, sir," said the waiter smoothly. "And you, I take it, are Mr. Halsted's guest."

"That's right. Roger invited me." He handed his umbrella to the waiter, together with his hat and so on, and carefully removed his coat. "You won't mind checking these for me, Waiter?"

"Not at all. We have a small cloakroom for the special use of the Black Widowers on the occasion of their monthly banquet."

"Good, good—I hope I'm not too late."

"Not at all, sir. The Widowers are all here, but they are still in the cocktail hour. May I bring you something to drink?"

"A dry martini, if you don't mind. —In there?"

"That's right, sir."

The man walked in and Roger Halsted, who was obviously on the lookout, said, "Ah, there you are, David. I was going to give you five more minutes before I started worrying."

"No need," said the guest. "I had absolutely no trouble except for the traffic. It's a little sloshy outside and there's something about even a trace of wet snow that seems to slow everything up."

"So it does," said Halsted. "Here, let me introduce you, David. Fellow Black Widowers, this is my friend, David S. Rose, and you will have to forgive him if, after I introduce all of you, he doesn't remember your names. David is the most absent-minded person I know.

"David, this tall drink of water with the ferocious eyebrows is Geoffrey Avalon, a patent attorney. This short drink of water with a beard he should be ashamed of is Emmanuel Rubin, a mystery writer. This fellow with the grayish-white hair and the scowl is Thomas Trumbull. He works for the government in something he's too ashamed to describe. This one with the little moustache that looks like a smear of dirt is James Drake, a retired chemist. Finally, there's this one who's dressed to kill, and whose color combinations sometimes make us sick. He's Mario Gonzalo, an artist."

"And there's Henry," said Gonzalo.

"Oh, right. Our most important member, Henry, our esteemed waiter, without whom no meeting could possibly be held."

Avalon said, in his startling baritone, "Would Mr. Rose care to repeat our names and thus, perhaps, affix them in his memory?"

Rose laughed. "I'd love to try, but I'd fail. It's all I can do to remember Roger's name. As the evening wears on, I may catch onto the names. Sometimes I do."

"I mean it," said Halsted. "He's got the world's worst memory. Whenever he goes somewhere, his wife has to pin his destination to his shirt so that passersby can help him when he gets lost."

"It's not that bad," said Rose.

David Rose made a rather startling appearance. He was nearly six feet tall, but gave the impression of stockiness. He had bright-red hair, center-parted, and a bright-red beard of moderate length. He had the freckles to go with it, and he wore tortoise-shell glasses that lent him a definitely old-fashioned air. He was clearly an amiable fellow, however, and didn't seem the least put out by Halsted's teasing.

Nor did he seem shy or withdrawn. The conversation returned to where it had been before he had arrived, and it consisted of the nearly inevitable discussion of the Persian Gulf crisis, and of Rubin's loud insistence that Saddam Hussein had to be wiped off the face of the ancient Land of the Two Rivers.*

* Ed. Note: This story was written shortly before the first Gulf War began.

Avalon rumbled, "Who would disagree with you, were it not that we must ask what the consequences would be? Macbeth says, 'If it were done when 'tis done, then 'twere well it were done quickly.' The question is that when it is done, would it indeed be done in the sense that there would be no new problems arising that would be worse than the problem we thought we were solving?"

Rose said, "If we're going to quote Shakespeare, remember that Hamlet says that not knowing what lies ahead 'puzzles the will and makes us rather bear those ills we have than fly to others that we know not of. Thus conscience doth make cowards of us all.' "

Avalon said, "It's not cowardly to consider war only as the last resort, or to pause and think things out very carefully before doing anything that may not prove retrievable."

Rubin said, "It's fight him now as he is, or fight him later when he's worked up nuclear weapons."

The argument grew more heated until Henry's quiet voice said, "Gentlemen, dinner is served."

It wasn't long after Thanksgiving and what the Black Widowers sat down to was the traditional feast. It began with melon and prosciutto, followed by a large bowl of lobster bisque, a salad, and then the inevitable roast turkey, with chestnut stuffing, cranberry sauce, yams, and string beans, and pumpkin pie—or, for those who preferred it, strawberry shortcake. There were also several kinds of breads and rolls, together with generous pats of butter, plus coffee or tea ad libitum.

Roger Halsted, who knew what was coming, used host's privilege to put an end to the Persian Gulf discussion. He said, "We will, one and all of us, get indigestion if we argue out the thing while eating. Let's talk about something else."

And, of course, he had no sooner said that than a deadly silence fell on the table, as no one appeared able to think of a suitable topic.

David Rose grinned, his eyes glinting through his tortoiseshells. "Well, let me start then. This group meets every month, I take it."

"Absolutely. Right here in the Milano," said Avalon, "and we've done so for decades."

"And this is the full number of members? Or are some missing?"

"One or two have died," said Avalon, "or have moved far away from the city, and they have been replaced. We six, however, and Henry are the full number right now and our identity has remained unchanged now for twenty years, though we are one and all of us growing rather precariously old."

"It's delightful," said Rose. "I belong to a group that—"

Gonzalo raised his hand. "You can't talk about yourself during dinner, Mr. Rose. That's for afterward, when we grill you."

"Grill me?" For a moment he looked puzzled. Then he turned toward Halsted. "I remember now, Roger. You warned me about that."

Halsted smiled. "I'm amazed you do remember. But don't worry—it won't hurt."

"I'm not worried," said Rose.

Henry had cleared the table and was serving the concluding brandy when Halsted rattled his spoon against the water glass and said, "Gentlemen, the time has come for grilling our worthy guest. Mario, suppose you take over the task of grill-master."

"Sure," said Gonzalo. He turned to their guest. "We have your name, Mr. Rose, but what we'd like to know is what you do for a living."

Rose said, "I'm a printer. I make a pretty fair living out of it, but what really gives my life meaning is that I'm a book collector. Not an undiscriminating one, of course. No one would have enough room to collect books indiscriminately. What I collect are old books on chemistry, pre-Lavoisier."

Gonzalo looked puzzled at the final word, but said, "Does that mean you're a chemist, Mr. Rose?"

Rose shook his head. "Not at all. I just like those old books and their old woodcuts of chemical instruments, their old ways of describing chemical experiments and so on. I have a number of medieval books on alchemy, too." He felt about his clothing. "I don't think I remembered to bring my cardcase, but you're welcome to visit my establishment and look at the books yourselves if you want to.—Come to think of it, wasn't one of you introduced as a retired chemist?"

Drake coughed through the smoke of his cigarette and said, "That was I. I'd love to look at your collection."

"Yes," said Halsted, "well, don't ask David where his shop is located, he probably doesn't remember. But I do and I'll write it down for you, Jim. It's really an interesting collection he has—you'll enjoy it."

Gonzalo looked impatient. He said, "I'm the grillmaster and I don't want to go any deeper into the collection right now. During the meal, Mr. Rose said he belonged to some group which I think he was going to compare to the Black Widowers."

"Well, yes, I was," said Rose.

"Good. You are now free to do so," said Gonzalo. "Go ahead."

"Thank you," said Rose. "I belong to a group called the Thursday Lunch and, as the name implies, we meet every Thursday for lunch—at the Arts Club, actually. It's a very nice group of slightly superannuated gentlemen—rather like yourselves. In fact, last Thursday I just happened to witness the simultaneous arrival of three of the more important of the Thursday Lunchers, each one with his cane, struggling up the stairs toward the front door. I couldn't help but think that the cane is our mark of distinction."

"How many attend the luncheon?" asked Gonzalo.

"Actually, anywhere from fifty to ninety, depending on the weather and on the nature of the speaker."

"You have speakers, then?"

"Oh, yes. We begin the meeting at noon and there's a half-hour cocktail period. At twelve-thirty sharp, luncheon is served. At one-fifteen P.M., our entertainer is introduced—someone who sings or plays an instrument—and at one-thirty we have our speaker. At two P.M., we break up. The whole thing lasts only two hours, but it's all very congenial and it's the high point of the week for most of us—certainly for me."

"How long have you been a member?" asked Trumbull suddenly.

"Nineteen years. The club was founded in nineteen-oh-five, so it has a longish history as such things go."

"What are the qualifications for entry?" asked Gonzalo.

"To start with, it was a group of newspapermen who met for lunch every Thursday, and for a while it was intended for newspapermen only. However, you know how these clubs tend to expand. We now consider ourselves a group of communicators. Anyone who is engaged in reaching the public with information of some sort or other qualifies. This means the group now includes writers of all sorts—editors, publishers, members of the visual media, artists, and so on. I qualify primarily because I'm a printer, though being a book collector also helps.

"As a matter of fact," Rose went on, "being a printer makes me a particularly useful TL-er, since we put out an annual book in connection with our annual banquet."

"What kind of book?" asked Avalon.

"Nothing elaborate. It lists all the members, with photographs of many of them. It contains some essays—our president is a well-known writer and can be counted on to contribute—and artwork, photographs of all our guests, a list of those members who died in the past year, and so on. I print it without charge and, believe me, the money the club saves in this way is vital."

"But it's money you lose," said Drake.

"Well, money isn't everything, to coin a phrase. The pleasure I get out of the Thursday Lunch restores the balance to my favor and, to be absolutely truthful, the fact that they rather fawn on me for my free printing is also pleasant. But that's just among us, please."

Avalon said gravely, "I hope Roger assured you that anything said at a Black Widowers meeting is considered a privileged communication and never passes beyond these walls."

"So he did," said Rose.

By now, Gonzalo was twitching a little, and scowling. "Listen, Mr. Rose, is there anything about this club of yours that's upsetting you?"

"Upsetting me?" Rose looked surprised. "I can't say there is."

"No little mystery, no little puzzle, nothing that you can't quite explain."

Rose's expression of surprise deepened. "Not at all. Is there supposed to be?"

Avalon said soothingly, "Pay no attention to Mario, Mr. Rose. He's never happy unless there's a puzzle at hand. The rest of us don't require it. —Tell me, what kind of speakers does your club have?"

"It's always been difficult to find speakers. We don't pay, and the audience is less than a hundred and is, by and large, not composed of important and famous people, for all that we're communicators. However, we've had a very good and enthusiastic man in charge of entertainment over the last few years and he gets us some good people—mayors, senators, military men, industrialists, and so on. Actually—and this is something else I wouldn't want repeated—I find the list of speakers a little too much weighted toward the conservative side to suit me, but usually not offensively so. Some years ago, a public figure I found offensively to the right agreed to speak, and that was one of the few meetings I refused to attend."

"Are guests sometimes invited?"

"Oh, yes, that's important. Every guest has to be paid for, so that a good supply of guests not only fleshes out the attendance but the money intake. I once invited Roger to attend one of our luncheons—I'll leave it to him to tell you whether he enjoyed himself."

"I did," said Halsted. "They set a pretty good table."

"And if any of you others," said Rose, "would like to sample the club, it would be easy to arrange."

Trumbull grunted, as though unconvinced of the value of the offer. "Who's talking this coming Thursday?"

"Actually," said Rose, feeling in his suitcoat pocket, "I don't remember. I have the speaker and the entertainment written down because by tomorrow morning I have to have it printed up, if we're going to send out the cards making the announcement in time."

He continued to feel in his pockets. "That's funny."

Gonzalo, who had been slumped in his chair scowling, sat up with sudden interest. "What's funny?"

"I can't find the card. That's troublesome."

"Why?" asked Gonzalo avidly.

"I won't be able to get the cards out if I don't find it." Rose stood up and began emptying his pants pockets.

The others watched until he sat down and said, with a sickly smile, "I don't seem to have it."

Halsted cleared his throat. "Does it matter, Dave?"

"Of course it matters," said Rose petulantly. "Do you think I really like all these jokes about my being absentminded? I don't, you know. Everyone thinks it's funny and I have to go along, but it's not. It's not."

"Actually," said Avalon, "although it may not be funny to those who suffer from the condition, it is associated with intelligence. Some of the brightest people in history were terribly absent-minded. They tell the story of the great mathematician, Norbert Wiener, who was walking along Memorial Drive in Cambridge and stopped to speak to a colleague. When they were done, Wiener said, 'Tell me, when we stopped to speak was I walking away from Mass Avenue or toward it?' His colleague said, 'Away from it.' 'Ah,' said Wiener with satisfaction, 'then I've had my lunch.' I met Wiener once and, I tell you, I believe that story."

Drake put in, "They also tell funny stories about Newton and Einstein and Archimedes, all stressing the absentmindedness factor."

Rose didn't seem consoled by any of this. He said, "Since I don't have the transcendent genius that should go along with absentmindedness, what good are such stories to me?"

Rubin said, "It's not transcendent geniuses only who are involved. Every one of us becomes increasingly absentminded with age. We all speak rapidly and articulately, but every once in a while we get hung up over a word we can't quite call to mind. It's 'at the tip of the tongue,' the saying goes. Well, that happens more and more often as one grows older."

"And how does that help me in my present situation?" demanded Rose.

Trumbull said, "What if you don't send out a card this week? I suppose the membership will know enough to show up Thursday at noon even without it."

"You don't understand, sir. In the first place, the membership wants to know who the speaker is and what he will speak about because on that depends the nature and number of guests they will invite. Without the knowledge, they won't risk it and will arrive without guests. Secondly, the speaker himself wants to be mentioned, and our president is always careful to say something like, 'Well, you certainly drew a good crowd.' Since we don't pay him, it's all the speaker gets. And thirdly, we went through a siege a couple of years ago in which the entertainment and the speakers were often decided on too late and attendance declined and the club nearly died. Since we got in our new man in charge of speakers, that has stopped and the club is flourishing. But any reminder of the bad old days will be much resented, and the blame will be placed squarely on me."

Gonzalo said, "Phone the man in charge of speakers. It might be embarrassing to have to admit you haven't got the information, but he'll give it to you again, won't he?"

"I'm sure he would, but he's away on some business trip and won't be back until next Friday. And I have no way of knowing where to reach him."

"May I make a suggestion?" said Drake. "Why don't we all close our yaps and just sit here quietly? Let's give Mr. Rose a chance. Things are never really forgotten, there's just a problem in recall. If he sits here quietly and relaxes and doesn't try too hard to remember, it may simply come to him. It's there in his mind somewhere."

There was instant silence that persisted for minute after minute while Rose looked back and forth from person to person.

Then he shook his head. "Gentlemen, I'm overwhelmed at your thoughtfulness and sympathy, but it won't do any good. I know there are people who forget and then remember, but I'm not one of them. Believe me, I am not. In my mind, there's a bottomless pit, a black hole. Things that fall in never come out."

Trumbull said, "It must make life very difficult for you."

"It does, but I've learned to adjust. Every little thing that I ought to remember, I write down. My secretary understands that she must remember everything since she can't rely on me to remember anything."

"Well, then," said Gonzalo, "why don't you call her up? She probably knows who the next speaker will be."

"No, that's exactly what she doesn't know," said Rose impatiently. "I got the information late myself, because our speaker-fellow was busy with his forthcoming business trip and managed to send me the information only at the last minute. Now I have to give it to my secretary tomorrow morning so she can get the cards printed up. It means Saturday work and overtime, but that happens once in a while. The trouble is that she won't know the speaker until I tell her and at the present moment it looks as though I won't be able to tell her."

Rubin said, "Will it help if we all try to guess? We can name possible topics for a speaker. There's the Gulf Crisis, for instance. You wouldn't be having some Middle Eastern ambassador talking about Saddam Hussein, would you?"

"We had one last month. It wouldn't be that."

"How about the recent congressional elections?"

Rose shook his head. "I don't think so."

Trumbull said, "Some economist to discuss the forthcoming recession, though I think we're already in one and we're not allowed to say so because it wouldn't be patriotic."

Rose shook his head. He said, "This sounds exactly like the fairy tale about the malevolent dwarf, Rumpelstiltskin. The princess had to guess Rumpelstiltskin's name or lose her baby and she spent a whole year guessing name after name, without result."

"She did get the name in the end," said Rubin.

"Yes, she did, but that's only because she overheard Rumpelstiltskin repeating his own name in triumph, saying that the princess would never guess it. When I was young, I thought that a completely unsatisfactory ending, since I didn't see why the dwarf would be so foolish as to say his own name aloud, and why the princess should be so fortunate as to overhear him. In my case, however, there's no one to give away the name or subject of the speaker, and no one to overhear. My own personal Rumpelstiltskin story can only have an unhappy ending."

Gonzalo looked about suddenly and said, "Where's Henry?"

Avalon said, "You're not going to ask Henry for an answer to *this* problem, are you?"

"Why not? What harm can it do?"

"It can do a great deal of harm, Mario. There simply is no way in which Henry can pull an answer out of a hat and you'll just be embarrassing him. Roger, as host, you can order Mario not to do any such thing. I will not have Henry pained unfairly."

There was a mumble of agreement around the table and Halsted said, "They're right, Mario. Leave Henry alone in this case. That's an order."

Rose was looking puzzled. He said, "What's all this about Henry? He's the waiter, isn't he? Why should he be asked?"

Avalon said, "Because he's brighter than any of us and can usually see farther into a millstone than we can. In this case, though, matters are hopeless and it would be futile to ask him."

"Certainly," agreed Rose.

Henry was suddenly among them, noiselessly as usual. His ordinarily impassive face was distinctly flushed. "My apologies, gentlemen," he said, "I should have been able to help you at a considerably earlier time."

"Help us?" said Rose, with a bit of asperity. "How do you mean, help us?"

"Is it not true that your next speaker will be a William McKechnie, who will discuss the greenhouse effect that now threatens the planet? And will the entertainment not consist of a nightclub singer named Diana Felner?"

Rose's eyes opened wide. "I can't believe it. Of course. That's right. Those are indeed the people."

Gonzalo said, "Aha! And they didn't want me to ask you, Henry."

Avalon said, "In heaven's name, Henry, how on earth could you come up with those names?"

"It was quite simple, Mr. Avalon. I had information the rest of you did not have. When Mr. Rose arrived, he looked down at his hand and read off the name of the restaurant and its address from a piece of pasteboard. I paid little attention to that since I wasn't aware at the time of his inability to remember crucial points.

"He then gave me his coat, his hat, his gloves, his umbrella, and the piece of pasteboard. I deposited everything in the cloakroom and, since one never throws away anything given for the purpose of checking, I placed the pasteboard in his hatband.

"It was far too late in the course of the discussion that I remembered the pasteboard, which none of the rest of you had seen, except for Mr. Rose himself, who had obviously forgotten about it. It occurred to me that since Mr. Rose, as he said, had to write down everything lest he forget, there would always be the problem of finding something on which to make his little notes.

"It struck me that any card has two sides, and if one side is used there is still the other side for further use. I slipped into the cloakroom, obtained the piece of pasteboard with the name of this restaurant on it, and on the other side was other information which I assumed was what Mr. Rose was looking for. In a way, sir, I overheard Rumpelstiltskin."

Henry handed Rose the pasteboard. With a stunned expression on his face, Rose examined each side, and the others flocked about to study it.

Avalon laughed. "As you said, Henry, the matter was very simple, but for a moment or two I really thought you had a special pipeline to all the knowledge in the world."

Henry smiled gently. "I'm afraid that my abilities are only human and quite limited after all, Mr. Avalon. What we must do now, however, is persuade Mr. Rose, somehow, to keep a firm grip on the pasteboard and not allow anything to happen to it. I hesitate to suggest pinning it to his shirt—"

ONE MORE, JUST FOR HARLAN

THE WOMAN IN THE BAR

The hits and outs of baseball did not, as a rule, disturb the equanimity (or lack of it) of a Black Widowers banquet. None of the Black Widowers were sportsmen in the ordinary sense of the word, although Mario Gonzalo was known to bet on the horses on occasion.

Over the rack of lamb, however, Thomas Trumbull brushed at his crisply waved white hair, looked stuffily discontented, and said, "I've lost all interest in baseball. Once they started shifting franchises, they broke up the kind of loyalties you inherited from your father. I was a New York Giants fan when I was a young man, as was my father before me. The San Francisco Giants were strangers to me and as for the Mets, well, they're just not the same."

"There are still the New York Yankees," said Geoffrey Avalon, deftly cutting meat away from bone and bending his dark eyebrows in concentration on the task, "and in my own town, we still have the Phillies, though we lost the Athletics."

"Chicago still has both its teams," said Mario Gonzalo, "and there are still the Cleveland Indians, the Cincinnati Reds, the St. Louis—"

"It's not the same," said Trumbull, violently. "Even if I were to switch to the Yankees, half the teams they play are teams Lou Gehrig and Bill Dickey never heard of. And now you have each league in two divisions, with playoffs before the World Series, which becomes almost anticlimactic, and a batting average of .290 marks a slugger. Hell, I remember when you needed .350 if you were to stand a chance at cleanup position."

Emmanuel Rubin listened with the quiet dignity he considered suitable to his position as host—at least until his guest turned to him and said, "Is Trumbull a baseball buff, Manny?"

At that, Rubin reverted to his natural role and snorted loudly. His sparse beard bristled. "Who, Tom? He may have watched a baseball game on TV, but that's about it. He thinks a double is two jiggers of Scotch."

Gonzalo said, "Come on, Manny, you think a pitcher holds milk."

Rubin stared at him fixedly through his thick-lensed spectacles, and then said, "It so happens I played a season of semi-pro baseball as shortstop in the late 1930s."

"And a shorter stop—" began Gonzalo and then stopped and reddened.

Rubin's guest grinned. Though Rubin was only five inches above the five-foot mark, the guest fell three inches short of that. He said, "I'd be a shorter stop if I played."

Gonzalo, with a visible attempt to regain his poise, said, "You're harder to pitch to when you're less than average height, Mr. Just. There's that."

"You're heavily underestimated in other ways, too, which is convenient at times," agreed Just. "And, as a matter of fact, I'm not much of a baseball buff myself. I doubt if I could tell a baseball from a golf ball in a dim light."

Darius Just looked up sharply at this point. "Waiter," he said, "if you don't mind, I'll have milk rather than coffee."

James Drake, waiting expectantly for his own coffee, said, "Is that just a momentary aberration, Mr. Just, or don't you drink coffee?"

"Don't drink it," said Just. "Or smoke, or drink alcohol. My mother explained it all to me very carefully. If I drank my milk and avoided bad habits, I would grow to be big and strong; so I did—and I didn't. At least, not big. I'm strong enough. It's all very un-American, I suppose, like not liking baseball. At least you can fake liking baseball, though that can get you in trouble, too.—Here's the milk. How did that get there?"

Gonzalo smiled. "That's our Henry. Noiseless and efficient."

Just sipped his milk contentedly. His facial features were small but alive and his eyes seemed restlessly aware of everything in the room. His shoulders were broad, as though they had been made for a taller man, and he carried himself like an athlete.

Drake sat over his coffee, quiet and thoughtful, but when Rubin clattered his water glass with his spoon, the quiet ended. Drake's hand was raised and he said, "Manny, may I do the honors?"

"If you wish." Rubin turned to his guest. "Jim is one of the more reserved Black Widowers, Darius, so you can't expect his grilling to be a searching one. In fact, the only reason he's volunteering is that he's written a book himself and he wants to rub shoulders with other writers."

Just's eyes twinkled with interest. "What kind of a book, Mr. Drake?"

"Pop science," said Drake, "but the questions go the other way.—Henry, since Mr. Just doesn't drink, could you substitute ginger ale for the brandy. I don't want him to be at a disadvantage."

"Certainly, Mr. Drake," murmured Henry, that miracle of waiters, "if Mr. Just would like that. With all due respect, however, it does not seem to me that Mr. Just is easily placed at a disadvantage."

"We'll see," said Drake, darkly. "Mr. Just, how do you justify your existence?"

Just laughed. "It justifies itself to me now and then when it fills me with gladness. As far as justification to the rest of the world is concerned, that can go hang.—With all due respect, as Henry would say."

"Perhaps," said Drake, "the world will go hang even without your permission. For the duration of this evening, however, you must justify your existence to *us* by answering our questions. Now I have been involved with the Black Widowers for more than half of a reasonably lengthy existence and I can smell out remarks that are worth elaboration. You said that you could get in trouble if you faked the liking of baseball. I suspect you did once, and I would like to hear about it."

Just looked surprised, and Rubin said, staring at his brandy, "I warned you, Darius."

"You know the story, do you, Manny?" said Drake.

"I know there is one but I don't know the details," said Rubin. "I warned Darius we'd have it out of him."

Just picked up the caricature Mario Gonzalo had drawn of him. There was a face-splitting grin on it and arms with prodigious biceps were lifting weights.

"I'm not a weight lifter," he said.

"It doesn't matter," said Gonzalo. "That is how I see you."

"Weight lifting," said Just, "slows you. The successful attack depends entirely on speed."

"You're not being speedy answering my request," said Drake, lighting a cigarette.

"There *is* a story," said Just.

"Good," said Drake.

"But it's an unsatisfactory one. I can't supply any rationale, any explanation—"

"Better and better. Please begin."

"Very well," said Just—

"I like to walk. It's an excellent way of keeping in condition and one night I had made my goal the new apartment of a friend I hadn't seen in a while. I was to be there at 9 P.M., and it was a moderately long walk by night, but I don't much fear the hazards of city streets in the dark though I admit I do not seek out particularly dangerous neighborhoods.

"However, I was early and a few blocks from my destination, I stopped at a bar. As I said, I don't drink, but I'm not an absolute fanatic about it and I will, on rare occasions, drink a Bloody Mary.

"There was a baseball game on the TV when I entered, but the sound was turned low, which suited me. There weren't many people present, which also suited me. There were two men at a table against the wall, and a woman on a stool at the bar itself.

"I took the stool next but one to the woman, and glanced at her briefly after I ordered my drink. She was reasonably pretty, reasonably shapely, and entirely interesting. Pretty and shapely is all right—what's not to like—but interesting goes beyond that and it can't be described easily. It's different for each person, and she was interesting in my frame of reference.

"Among my abstentions, women are not included. I even speculated briefly if it were absolutely necessary that I keep my appointment with my friend, who suffered under the disadvantage, under the circumstances, of being male.

"I caught her eye just long enough before looking away. Timing is everything and I am not without experience. Then I looked up at the TV and watched for a while. You don't want to seem too eager.

"She spoke. I was rather surprised. I won't deny I have a way with women, despite my height, but my charm doesn't usually work *that* quickly. She said, 'You seem to understand the game.' It was just make-talk. She couldn't possibly know my relationship with baseball from my glazed-eye stare at the set.

"I turned, smiled, and said, 'Second nature. I live and breathe it.'

"It was a flat lie, but if a woman leads, you go along with the lead.

"She said, rather earnestly, 'You really understand it?' She was looking into my eyes as though she expected to read the answer on my retina.

"I continued to follow and said, 'Dear, there isn't a move in the game I can't read the motivations of. Every toss of the ball, every crack of the bat, every stance of the fielder, is a note in a symphony I can hear in my head.' After all, I'm a writer; I can lay it on.

"She looked puzzled. She looked at me doubtfully; then, briefly, at the men at the table. I glanced in their direction, too. They didn't seem interested—until I noticed their eyes in the wall mirror. They were watching our reflection.

"I looked at her again and it was like a kaleidoscope shifting and suddenly making sense. She wasn't looking for a pickup, she was scared. It was in her breathing rate and in the tension of her hands.

"And she thought I was there to help her. She was expecting someone and she had spoken to me with that in mind. What I answered was close enough—by accident—to make her think I might be the man, but not close enough to make her sure of it.

"I said, 'I'm leaving soon. Do you want to come along?' It sounded like a pickup, but I was offering to protect her if that was what she wanted. What would happen afterward—well, who could tell?

"She looked at me unenthusiastically. I knew the look. It said: 'You're five-foot-two; what can you do for me?'

"It's a chronic underestimate that plays into my hands. Whatever I do do is so much more than they expect that it assumes enormous proportions. I'm the beneficiary of a low baseline.

"I smiled. I looked in the direction of the two men at the table, looked back, let my smile widen and said, 'Don't worry.'

"There were containers of cocktail amenities just behind the bar where she sat. She reached over for the maraschino cherries, took a handful and twisted the stems off; then one by one flicked them broodingly toward me, keeping her eyes fixed on mine.

"I didn't know what her game was. Perhaps she was just considering whether to take a chance on me and this was a nervous habit she always indulged in when at a bar. But I always say: Play along.

"I had caught four and wondered how many she would flick at me, and when the barman would come over to rescue his supply, when my attention shifted.

"One of the men who had been seated was now between the woman and myself, and was smiling at me without humor. I had been unaware of his coming. I was caught like an amateur, and the kaleidoscope suddenly shifted again. That's the trouble with kaleidoscopes. They keep shifting.

"Sure the woman was afraid. She wasn't afraid of the men at the table. She was afraid of *me.* She didn't think I was a possible rescuer; she thought I was a possible spoiler. So she kept my attention riveted while one of her friends got in under my guard—and I had let it happen.

"I shifted my attention to the man now, minutes after I should have done so. He had a moon face, dull eyes, and a heavy hand. That heavy hand, his right one, rested on my hand on the bar, pinning it down immovably.

"He said, 'I think you're annoying the lady, chum.'

"He underestimated me, too; took me for what I was not.

"You see, I've never been any taller than I am now. When I was young I was, in point of fact, smaller and slighter. When I was nineteen, I would have had to gain five pounds to be a ninety-six-pound weakling.

"The result you can guess. The chivalry and sportsmanship of young people is such that I was regularly beaten up to the cheers of the multitude. I did not find it inspiring.

"From nineteen on, therefore, I was subscribing to build-yourself-up courses. I struggled with chest expanders. I took boxing lessons at the Y. Bit by bit, I've studied every one of the martial arts. It didn't make me any taller, not one inch, but I grew wider and thicker and stronger. Unless I run into a brigade, or a gun, I don't get beaten up.

"So the fact that my left arm was pinned did not bother me. I said, 'Friend, I don't like having a man hold my hand, so I think I will have to ask you to remove it.' I had my own right hand at eye level, palm up, something that might have seemed a gesture of supplication.

"He showed his teeth and said, 'Don't ask anything, pal. *I'll* ask.'

"He had his chance. You must understand that I don't fight to kill, but I do fight to maim. I'm not interested in breaking a hold; I want to be sure there won't be another one.

"My hand flashed across between us. Speed is of the essence, gentlemen, and my nails scraped sideways across his throat en route, as the arc of my hand brought its edge down upon his wrist. *Hard!*

"I doubt that I broke his wrist that time, but it would be days, perhaps weeks, before he would be able to use that hand on someone else as he had on me. My hand was free in a moment. The beauty of the stroke, however, was that he could not concentrate on the smashed wrist. His throat had to be burning and he had to be able to feel the stickiness of blood there. It was just a superficial wound, literally a scratch, but it probably frightened him more than the pain in his wrist did.

"He doubled up, his left hand on his throat, his right arm dangling. He was moaning.

"It was all over quickly, but time was running out. The second man was approaching, so was the bartender, and a newcomer was in the doorway. He was large and wide and I was in no doubt that he was a member of the charming group I had run into.

"The risks were piling up and the fun flattening out, so I walked out rapidly—right past the big fellow, who didn't react quickly enough, but stood there, confused and wondering, for the five seconds I needed to push past and out.

"I didn't think they'd report the incident to the police, somehow. Nor did I think I'd be followed, but I waited for a while to see. I was on a street with row houses, each with its flight of steps leading to the main door well above street level. I stepped into one of the yards and into the shadow near the grillwork door at the basement level of a house that had no lights showing.

"No one came out of the barroom. They weren't after me. They weren't sure who I was and they still couldn't believe that anyone as short as I was could be dangerous. It was the providential underestimate that had done well for me countless times.

"So I moved briskly along on my original errand, listening for the sound of footsteps behind me or the shifting of shadows cast by the streetlights.

"I wasn't early any longer and I arrived on the corner where my friend's apartment house was located without any need for further delay. The green light glimmered and I crossed the street, and then found matters were not as straightforward as I had expected.

"The apartment house was not an only child but was a member of a large family of identical siblings. I had never visited the complex before and I wasn't sure in which particular building I was to find my friend. There seemed no directory, no kiosk with a friendly information guide. There seemed the usual assumption underlying everything in New York that if you weren't born with the knowledge of how to locate your destination, you had no business having one.

"The individual buildings each had their number displayed, but discreetly—in a whisper. Nor were they illuminated by the glint of the streetlights, so finding them was an adventure.

"One tends to wander at random at first, trying to get one's bearings. Eventually, I found a small sign with an arrow directing me into an inner courtyard with the promise that the number I wanted was actually to be found there.

"Another moment and I would have plunged in when I remembered that I was, or just conceivably might be, a marked man. I looked back in the direction from which I had come.

"I was spared the confusion of crowds. Even though it was not long after 9 P.M., the street bore the emptiness characteristic of night in any American city of the Universal Automobile Age. There were automobiles, to be sure, in an unending stream, but up the street I had walked, I could see only three people in the glow of the streetlights, two men and a woman.

"I could not see faces, or details of clothing, for though I have 20/20 vision, I see no better than that. However, one of the men was tall and large and his outline was irresistibly reminiscent of the man in the doorway whom I had dodged past in leaving the bar.

"They had been waiting for him, of course, and now they had emerged. They would probably have come out sooner, I thought, but there had been the necessity of taking care of the one I had damaged and, I supposed, they had left him behind.

"Nor, I gathered, were they coming in search of me. Even from a distance I could tell their attention was not on something external to the group, as though they were searching for someone. Attention was entirely internal. The two men were on either side of the woman and were hurrying her along. It seemed to me that she was reluctant to move, that she held back, that she was being urged forward.

"And once again, the kaleidoscope shifted. She was a woman in distress after all. She had thought I was her rescuer and I had left her cold—and still in distress.

"I ran across the avenue against the lights, dodging cars, and racing toward them. Don't get me wrong. I am not averse to defending myself; I rather enjoy it as anyone would enjoy something he does well. Just the same I am not an unreasoning hero. I do not seek out a battle for no reason. I am all for justice, purity, and righteousness, but who's to say which side, if either, in any quarrel represents those virtues?

"A personal angle is something else, and in this case, I had been asked for help and I had quailed.

"Oh, I quailed. I admit I had honestly decided the woman was not on my side and needed no help, but I didn't really stay to find out. It was that large man I was ducking, and I had to wipe out that disgrace.

"At least that's what I decided in hot blood. If I had had time to think, or to let the spasm of outrage wear off, I might have just visited my friend. Maybe I would have called the police from a street phone without leaving my name and *then* visited my friend.

"But it *was* hot blood, and I ran toward trouble, weighing the odds very skimpily.

"They were no longer on the street, but I had seen which gate they had entered, and they had not gone up the steps. I chased into the front yard after them and seized the grillwork door that led to the basement apartment. It came open but there was a wooden door beyond that did not. The window blinds were down but there was a dim light behind them.

"I banged at the wooden door furiously but there was no answer. If I had to break it down, I would be at a disadvantage. Strength, speed, and skill are not as good at breaking down a door as sheer mass is, and mass I do not have.

"I banged again and then kicked at the knob. If it were the wrong apartment, it was breaking and entry, which it also was if it was the right apartment. The door trembled at my kick, but held. I was about to try again, wondering if some neighbor had decided to get sufficiently involved to call the police—when the door opened. It was the large man—which meant it was the right apartment.

"I backed away. He said, 'You seem uncomfortably anxious to get in, sir.' He had a rather delicate tenor voice and the tone of an educated man.

"I said, 'You have a woman here. I want to see her.'

" 'We do not have a woman here. She has us here. This is a woman's apartment and we are here by her invitation.'

" 'I want to see her.'

" 'Very well, then, come in and meet her.' He stepped back.

"I waited, weighing the risks—or I tried to, at any rate, but an unexpected blow from behind sent me staggering forward. The large man seized my arm and the door closed behind me.

"Clearly, the second man had gone one floor upward, come out the main door, down the stairs and behind me. I should have been aware of him, but I wasn't. I fall short of superman standards frequently.

"The large man led me into a living room. It was dimly lit. He said, 'As you see, sir—our hostess.'

"She was there. It was the woman from the bar but this time the kaleidoscope stayed put. The look she gave me was unmistakable. She saw me as a rescuer who was failing her.

" 'Now,' said the large man, 'we have been polite to you although you treated my friend in the bar cruelly. We have merely asked you in when we might have hurt you. In response, will you tell us who you are and what you are doing here?'

"He was right. The smaller man did not have to push me in. He might easily have knocked me out, or done worse. I presume, though, that they were puzzled by me. They didn't know my part in it and they had to find out.

"I looked about quickly. The smaller man remained behind me, moving as I did. The large man, who must have weighed 250 pounds, with little of it actually fat, remained quietly in front of me. Despite what happened in the bar, they still weren't afraid of me. It was, once again, the advantage of small size.

"I said, 'This young woman and I have a date. We'll leave and you two continue to make yourself at home here.'

"He said, 'That is no answer, sir.'

"He nodded and I saw the smaller man move out of the corner of my eye. I lifted my arms to shoulder level as he seized me about the chest. There was no use allowing my arms to be pinned if I could avoid it. The smaller man held tightly, but it would have taken more strength than he had at his disposal to break my ribs. I waited for the correct positioning and I hoped the large man would give it to me.

"He said, 'I do need an answer, sir, and if I do not get one very quickly, I will have to hurt you.'

"He came closer, one hand raised to slap.

"What followed took less time than it will to explain but it went something like this. My arms went up and back, and around the smaller man's head to make sure I had a firm backing, and then my feet went up.

"My left shoe aimed at the groin of the large gentleman and the man doesn't live who won't flinch from that. The large man's hips jerked backward and his head automatically bent downward and encountered the heel of my right shoe moving upward. It's not an easy maneuver, but I've practiced it enough times.

"As soon as my heel made contact, I tightened my arm grip and tossed my head backward. My head and that of the smaller man made hard contact and I didn't enjoy it at all, but the back of my head was not as sensitive as the nose of the man behind me.

"From the woman's point of view, I imagine, there could be no clear vision of what had happened. One moment, I seemed helplessly immobilized and then, after a flash of movement, I was free, while both of my assailants were howling.

"The smaller man was on the floor with one hand over his face. I stamped on one ankle hard to discourage him from attempting to get up. No, it was not Marquis of Queensberry rules, but there were no referees around.

"I then turned to face the larger man. He brought his hands away from his face. I had caught him on the cheekbone and he was bleeding freely. I was hoping he had no fight left in him, but he did. With one eye rapidly puffing shut, he came screaming toward me in a blind rage.

"I was in no danger from his mad rush as long as I could twist away, but once he got a grip on me in his present mood, I would be in serious trouble. I backed away, twisted. I backed away, twisted again. I waited for a chance to hit him again on the same spot.

"Unfortunately, I was in a strange room. I backed away, twisted, and fell heavily over a hassock. He was on me, his knee on my thighs, his hands on my throat, and there was no way I could weaken that grasp in time.

"I could hear the loud thunk even through the blood roaring in my ears and the large man fell heavily on me—but his grip on my throat had loosened. I wiggled out from below with the greatest difficulty though the woman did her best to lift him.

"She said, 'I had to wait for him to stop moving.' There was a candle holder lying near him, a heavy wrought-iron piece.

"I remained on the floor, trying to catch my breath. I gasped out, 'Have you killed him?'

" 'I wouldn't care if I did,' she said, indifferently, 'but he's still breathing.'

"She wasn't exactly your helpless heroine. It was her apartment so she knew where to find the clothesline, and she was tying both of them at the wrists and ankles very efficiently. The smaller man screamed when she tightened the ropes at his ankle, but she didn't turn a hair.

"She said, 'Why the hell did you mess up the response in the bar when I asked you about baseball? And why the hell didn't you bring people with you? I admit you're a pint-sized windmill, but couldn't you have brought *one* backup?'

"Well, I don't really expect gratitude, but—

"I said, 'Lady, I don't know what you're talking about. I don't know about the baseball bit, and I don't go about in squadrons.'

"She looked at me sharply. 'Don't move. I'm making a phone call.'

" 'The police?'

" 'After a fashion.'

"She went into the other room to call. For privacy, I suppose. She trusted me to stay where I was and do nothing. Or thought me stupid enough to do so. I didn't mind. I wasn't through resting.

"When she came back, she said, 'You're not one of us. What *was* that remark about baseball?'

"I said, 'I don't know who us is, but I'm not one of anybody. My remark about baseball was a remark. What else?'

"She said, 'Then how—Well, you had better leave. There's no need for you to be mixed up in this. I'll take care of everything. Get out and walk some distance before you hail a taxi. If a car pulls up at this building while you're within earshot, don't turn around and for God's sake, don't turn back.'

"She was pushing and I was out in the yard when she said, 'But at least you knew what I was telling you in the bar. I am glad you were here and waiting.'

"At last! Gratitude! I said, 'Lady, I don't know what—' but the door was closed behind me.

"I made it over very quickly to my friend's apartment. He said nothing about my being an hour late or being a little the worse for wear and I said nothing about what had happened.

"And what did happen was nothing. I never heard a thing. No

repercussions. And that's why it's an unsatisfactory story. I don't know who the people were, what they were doing, what it was all about. I don't know whether I was helping the good guys or the bad guys, or whether there were any good guys involved. I may have bumped into two competing bands of terrorists playing with each other.

"But that's the story about my faking a knowledge of baseball."

When Just was done, a flat and rather unpleasant silence hung over the room, a silence that seemed to emphasize that for the first time in living memory a guest had told a rather long story without ever having been interrupted.

Finally, Trumbull heaved a weary sigh and said, "I trust you won't be offended, Mr. Just, if I tell you that I think you are pulling our leg. You've invented a very dramatic story for our benefit, and you've entertained us—me, at least—but I can't accept it."

Just shrugged, and didn't seem offended. "I've embroidered it a little, polished it up a bit—I'm a writer, after all—but it's true enough."

Avalon cleared his throat. "Mr. Just, Tom Trumbull is sometimes hasty in coming to conclusions but in this case I am forced to agree with him. As you say, you're a writer. I'm sorry to say I have read none of your works but I imagine you write what are called tough-guy detective stories."

"As a matter of fact, I don't," said Just, with composure. "I have written four novels that are, I hope, realistic, but are not unduly violent."

"It's a fact, Jeff," said Rubin, grinning.

Gonzalo said, "Do *you* believe him, Manny?"

Rubin shrugged. "I've never found Darius to be a liar, and I know *something* happened, but it's hard for a writer to resist the temptation to fictionalize for effect. Forgive me, Darius, but I wouldn't swear to how much of it was true."

Just sighed. "Well, just for the record, is there anyone here who believes I told you what actually happened?"

The Black Widowers sat in an embarrassed silence, and then there was a soft cough from the direction of the sideboard.

"I hesitate to intrude, gentlemen," said Henry, "but despite the over-romantic nature of the story, it seems to me there is a chance that it is true."

"A chance?" said Just, smiling. "Thank you, waiter."

"Don't underestimate the waiter," said Trumbull, stiffly. "If he thinks there is a chance the story is true, I'm prepared to revise my opinion.—What's your reasoning, Henry?"

"If the story were fiction, Mr. Trumbull, it would be neatly tied. This one has an interesting loose end which, if it makes sense, cannot be accidental.—Mr. Just, just at the end of the story, you told us that the woman remarked at her relief that you knew what she was telling you in the bar. What had she told you?"

Just said, "This *is* a loose end, because she didn't tell me a damn thing. I could easily make something up, if I weren't telling the truth."

"Or you could let it remain loose now," said Halsted, "for the sake of verisimilitude."

Henry said, "And yet if your story is accurate, she may indeed have told you, and the fact that you don't understand that is evidence of its truth."

"You speak in riddles, Henry," said Just.

Henry said, "You did not, in your story, mention precise locations; neither the location of the bar, nor of the apartment complex in which your friend lives. There are a number of such apartment complexes in Manhattan."

"I know," interposed Rubin, "I live in one of them."

"Yours, Mr. Rubin," said Henry, "is on West End Avenue. I suspect that the apartment complex of Mr. Just's friend is on First Avenue."

Just looked astonished. "It *is.* Now how did you know that?"

Henry said, "Consider the opening scene of your story. The woman at the bar knew she was in the hands of her enemies and would not be allowed to leave except under escort. The two men in the bar were merely waiting for their large confederate. They would then take her to her apartment for reasons of their own. The woman thought you were one of her group, felt you could do nothing in the bar, but wanted you on the spot, near her apartment, with reinforcements.

"She therefore flicked maraschino cherries at you—an apparently harmless and, possibly, flirtatious gesture, though even that roused the suspicions of the two men in the bar."

Just said, "What of that?"

Henry said, "She had to work with what she could find. The cherries were small spheres—little balls—and she sent you four, one at a time. You had claimed to be a baseball fanatic. She sent you four balls, and, in baseball parlance—as almost anyone knows—four balls, that is, four pitches outside the strike zone, means the batter may advance to first base. More colloquially, he 'walks to first.' That's what she was telling you and you, quite without understanding this, did indeed walk to First Avenue for reasons of your own."

Just looked stupefied. "I never thought of that."

"It's because you didn't and yet incorporated the incident into the account," said Henry, "that I think your story is essentially true."

COMMEMORATION

On the tenth anniversary of Isaac Asimov's death and the thirtieth anniversary of the publication of the first Black Widowers story, Charles Ardai brought the members of the club back together for one last dinner . . .

THE LAST STORY

CHARLES ARDAI

Tom Trumbull was the last to arrive. He flew through the doors of the Milano restaurant, clambered upstairs to the private room where the monthly banquets were held, and deposited his umbrella in the elephant-foot stand just inside the door. He was soaked from the knees down, and he shook each pant leg in turn in a vain attempt to stop them from clinging to his skin. "A scotch and soda—" he began, but a glass was pressed into his hand before he could finish his request.

"Scotch and soda, Mr. Trumbull," said Henry, the Black Widowers' peerless waiter. "For a dying man."

"Come on, Tom," said Emmanuel Rubin, his sparse beard quivering with annoyance. "Sit down. You've kept us all waiting long enough."

"Let him dry off," said Mario Gonzalo, the club's artist member, who was putting the finishing touches on his caricature of the evening's guest. "At his age, catching a cold could be dangerous."

"You're the same age, Mario, and I don't see you worrying about catching a cold," Rubin said.

"That's because I arrived on time, before the rain started," Gonzalo said, "which is more than I can say for you and your guest. Pay no attention to his outbursts, Tom."

"Do I ever?" Trumbull hung his suit jacket over the back of his chair and took a long swallow. To his left, patent attorney Geoffrey Avalon sat stirring the ice in his glass with a long index finger. Avalon took a careful sip, bringing the glass to exactly half full, then set the remainder aside.

Across the table, James Drake and Roger Halsted were embroiled in a heated discussion about science education. It was a topic about which both had strong opinions. As an organic chemist, Drake felt more emphasis on scientific curricula was needed at the precollege level, and as a junior high school math teacher, Roger Halsted passionately agreed. That both men were on the same side of the argument didn't seem to interfere with their ability to carry on about it as though fighting to the death.

To their right and to Manny Rubin's left—which is to say at the head of the table—sat a slight man with a prominent chin and rather less hair than he'd had the first time he'd attended one of the Black Widowers' dinners as a guest. Both of these characteristics were highlighted in the finished caricature Mario Gonzalo now held up for inspection and then pinned to the wall next to his first sketch of Gary Nemerson, completed a dozen years earlier.

"Manny," Trumbull said, his voice rumbling ominously, "I never put it past you to demonstrate ignorance of the rules under which our group operates, but even you must have noticed that not once in thirty years has a guest been invited back for a second dinner."

"That's not a rule, it's just happenstance," Rubin said. "None of your guests has ever merited a second invitation. Gary did."

"Why? Because as one of your fellow writers he's hungrier than our other guests and less well equipped to purchase his own meals?"

"No, because as one of my fellow writers he's got more interesting things to say than any ten of the government types you work with." Rubin turned to his guest. "Tom's just upset because his guest canceled on him the last time he hosted. He's been taking it out on the rest of us ever since."

Nemerson smiled briefly but said nothing. He looked purposeful, even impatient to get on with the evening's grilling. But before it could begin, there was the small matter of the meal.

Henry moved to the far end of the table, opposite Nemerson, and cleared his throat. Looking down, each of the Black Widowers saw that a plate containing an appetizer of ceviche with capers and julienned chilies had, silently and as if by magic, appeared before them.

"Gentlemen," Henry said, "dinner is served."

The main course continued the Latin American theme with grilled strips of pork loin and chorizo on a bed of wilted baby spinach and was followed by a dessert of fresh churros. While everyone else was preoccupied with sampling the dark chocolate and *dulce de leche* dipping sauces, Drake said to Gary Nemerson, "I'm curious—the umbrella you brought tonight, is it the same one that caused you so much trouble the last time you were here?"

Nemerson blushed pinkly, all the way up to his rapidly retreating hairline. "No, as fine an instrument as it was, that umbrella wasn't well enough constructed to outlast a decade of New York winters. I have never found its equal, and the one I brought tonight is nothing special."

"That first umbrella," Drake continued in his hoarse smoker's voice, "the one that almost broke up your engagement until Henry helped you find it, did you ever mislay it again?"

"I protest!" Rubin's beard shook with the force of his exclamation and his eyes, magnified to the size of golf balls behind his thick lenses, strained with indignation. "We haven't finished eating, and he's already starting the grilling!"

"Nonsense," Drake growled. "I'm just making conversation."

"You're in no position to protest, Manny," Trumbull said, "given the breach, if not of rules then at least of tradition, that you've committed tonight."

"Breach?" Manny could barely contain himself. "At least my guest showed up!"

"It's all right, Manny," Nemerson said. "I'm happy to answer the question. No, Mr. Drake, I can't recall another occasion when I mislaid my umbrella, or at least not so completely that I couldn't promptly find it again. I am a careful person, and one of the matters I take particular care about is where I put things, so that I can find them again. I wish other people were half as careful, frankly."

"It's interesting," Roger Halsted said, softly and with a slight stutter, "that people generally take greater care with where they put things when they don't want them found than when they do."

"Oh, I don't think that's true," Avalon said. "It's just that those are the cases you hear about, because they're more interesting. No one would read a Manny Rubin mystery story about someone who carefully puts his valuables in a safe-deposit box and whose heirs find them there, safe and sound, when they go to look. A story about a miser who hides his valuables in an old tree stump, on the other hand . . ."

"Listen to you, 'an old tree stump.' Your concept of mystery plotting stopped with the Hardy Boys," Rubin said. "As it happens, I agree with Roger. People take it for granted that they'll be able to find things when they put them down, and that's how so many things get lost. It's when you want something to be hard for other people to find that you take pains to place it carefully."

Nemerson chose this moment to weigh in, and from the expression on his face it seemed he had more on his mind than idle conversation. "Unfortunately," he said, "my experience is that things can get lost either way, and when you're looking for them it doesn't much matter whether they were hidden on purpose or by accident. I'm dealing with a situation of this sort right now, in fact, and I was actually hoping you might help me with it." Silence greeted this remark from all corners of the room, but Nemerson soldiered on. "Seeing as how you were able to help me so successfully the last time."

"So that's why he merited a second invitation," Trumbull roared. "You brought him because he's mislaid something else—maybe his galoshes this time, or is it his keys? What are we, his personal lost-and-found?"

"Hear him out," Rubin said, with an uncharacteristically conciliatory tone. "I have, and I think you'll find it interesting."

Avalon's luxurious eyebrows crept upward. "I guess the grilling will begin now," he said.

Rubin rattled his teaspoon against the side of his water glass to signal the formal start of the evening's proceedings. "Gary," Rubin said, "as you know, we would normally start by asking how you justify your existence, but you answered the question the last time you ate with us, so I think we can dispense with that bit of tradition this time." He shot a small dirty look in Trumbull's direction, then aimed an index finger across the table at Jim Drake. "Dr. Drake, since you couldn't contain yourself earlier, would you like to do the honors?"

Drake took a pull on the cigarette he'd just lit and balanced it on the edge of his ashtray. "Mr. Nemerson," he said, "would you be so kind as to let us know what you're missing this time?"

"*I'm* not missing anything, exactly," Nemerson said, "or at least not something of mine. Believe me, I wouldn't have come here to waste your time with something petty like galoshes or car keys."

"Or an umbrella," Trumbull said.

"What's happened is this: I've been hired by Singleman & Sons, the publishing company, to finish editing Abraham Beard's last, unpublished anthology of science fiction short stories, *Farthest Frontiers.* You know Beard died recently, I assume?"

"I don't even know who he is," Drake said. "Why don't you start at the beginning?"

Nemerson took a deep breath and a moment to compose his thoughts. "As Manny could tell you, Abraham Beard was a major figure in science fiction publishing. He started as a writer in the pulp magazines back in the forties. He was good, but not great, and, competing with giants like Asimov, Heinlein, and Clarke, he never rose to prominence as a writer. Where he really shone was as an editor, first of a magazine called *Astonishing Science Stories* and then, later, of a line of paperback original novels for Random House. He fell out of sight in the sixties and seventies, when the field became more literary and experimental, but he came back with a vengeance in nineteen seventy-nine when he published an anthology of new stories called *Far Frontiers.*

"*Far Frontiers* was a landmark, and its publication was one of those milestone moments in the field. Later, everyone talked about 'before *Far Frontiers*' and 'after *Far Frontiers.*' Basically, every top science fiction writer of the time had a story in the book, and the quality of the stories was just staggering. As a writer, Beard may have been just average, but as an editor, he was the best in the business, really able to pull amazing work out of his contributors.

"The publishing business being what it is, you won't be surprised to learn that Beard's publisher quickly commissioned a sequel. And in due course the second book came out, under the name *Farther Frontiers,* and it was every bit as good as the first one—but 'due course' in this case was *ten years.* Beard worked on that book so long that no one believed it would ever be finished. It became a joke in the eighties: If someone asked you how you were doing, you'd say, 'The good news is I sold a story, the bad news is I sold it to *Farther Frontiers.*' When the book finally came out in nineteen eighty-nine, it was a huge event, and part of the reason was that everyone had given up on it—and, frankly, on Beard himself. But he showed everyone. On top of everything else, he'd put one of his own stories in the book, and, okay, it wasn't the best story in the book, but it was better than anything he'd written before and it held its own with stories from some really great writers. And privately everyone figured that's why the book had taken so long, because he was waiting till he'd written a story good enough to include. Which was certainly his privilege, God knows."

Nemerson took a sip of water. "So, the second book came out, and it did great business. It even revived interest in the first book, which was reissued, so the publisher had a double hit on its hands. You can probably guess what happened next: They asked him to edit a third volume. And he agreed. He spread the word throughout the science fiction community that this was going to be the final volume, that he was determined to make it the best of the three, and that he wouldn't release it until he was satisfied that it was, even if it meant waiting till the year two thousand.

"Well, the year two thousand came and went, but no book. We knew he'd bought at least some stories—everyone knew of certain writers who had received contracts and checks from Beard, which they talked about with great pride, knowing that they'd be included when *Farthest Frontiers* finally came out. But it didn't come out. And then six months ago, just after his eighty-second birthday, Beard was admitted to the hospital with pneumonia. He fought it for a few weeks and even recovered enough to come home, but a week later he was in the hospital again, and this time he didn't make it.

"The question immediately came up, what was going to happen with *Farthest Frontiers*? It was all people could talk about. Singleman, the publisher, decided it needed someone to go through his papers and see how close to publishable the book was, so they called me."

"Why you?" Halsted asked. "No offense, but you're a young man, in your thirties. I have to assume there are more experienced editors they could have called on for so important a book."

"I've had a bit of success as a novelist over the past ten years," Nemerson said, "but more, to be frank, as an anthologist. My first collection, *Across the Fourth Dimension*, won the World Fantasy Award for best anthology, and two of the stories in my latest are on the final ballot for the Nebula. I've actually become quite well known as an anthologist. In fact, *Locus* magazine once called me 'the next Abe Beard.' "

"So," Drake said, "was the book publishable?"

"Absolutely. I went through his apartment and turned up manuscripts for fourteen stories he had bought, plus a fifteenth he had written himself, and they were all excellent. Even his—in fact, his was probably one of the two or three best in the book. A few of the older ones he'd bought back in the early nineties had some dated references, but it was nothing I couldn't work with the authors to fix. The earlier volumes each had sixteen stories, not fifteen, but one less story this time, that's not a big deal. All in all, I was thrilled with what I'd found."

"So what's the problem?" Drake said.

"It's what I didn't find. There were stories by Ray Bradbury and Arthur C. Clarke, Roger Zelazny, Samuel Delany, Harlan Ellison, Orson Scott Card, Michael A. Burstein, Octavia Butler, even Kurt Vonnegut, but there was no story by Isaac Asimov."

"So? Maybe he didn't write one," Gonzalo said. "When did Asimov die, Manny? Wasn't it around nineteen ninety?"

"Nineteen ninety-two," Manny said.

"And I remember you telling us he was ill for a while before that. Maybe he just wasn't able to write one."

"But he was," Nemerson said. "I know he was."

"How do you know that?" Drake asked.

"Because Abraham Beard told me."

"I think you know that Isaac was something of a mentor to me," Nemerson said. "He helped me get started when I was just a scrawny, teenaged science fiction fan with dreams of one day being a writer. I wrote him letters, and even though he had no reason to, he wrote back and encouraged me. When I moved to New York to go to college, he took me under his wing, introduced me to some of the editors he knew, helped me get started. He even wrote an introduction for *Across the Fourth Dimension*, and I doubt I could have sold the book without it.

"When he died, his family held a memorial service, and one of the people who attended the service was Abraham Beard. I introduced myself to him after the ceremony and offered to take him out to dinner. To my delight, he accepted, and we spent a long night at Sardi's, drinking red wine and telling each other our Isaac Asimov stories. They'd met a few years earlier, apparently, on a science fiction-themed cruise they'd both been booked on as guest lecturers, and I believe Beard may have published him once or twice in his *Astonishing* days as well.

"Toward the end of the evening, we started talking about *Farthest Frontiers.* The book was already three years in the making then, and he told me in confidence that he'd only bought a few stories, maybe three or four. But one of the ones he had bought was by Isaac Asimov.

"He wouldn't tell me anything about the story, he was very secretive that way, even after an evening of drinking had loosened his tongue. But he said it was a really good story, in his opinion one of the best Isaac had ever written. Apparently, he had badgered Isaac to write it while they were on the cruise, and Isaac had hidden himself away in his cabin on the last day and emerged the next morning with a novelette, written out in longhand on a pad of legal paper.

" 'There's your story,' he told Beard, and handed him the pad with a big smile. Isaac took great pride in being almost superhumanly prolific, and he probably saw Beard's request as a challenge.

"Anyway, that's what Beard told me. You should have seen his eyes when he described getting home, unpacking his bags, reading the story, and realizing that far from being the tossed-off quickie he'd expected, it was—in his words—a story good enough to rival 'Nightfall,' or 'Foundation,' or any of the robot stories. I thought about asking if I could see the story, but I figured he'd say no, and anyway I didn't ask.

"And that was the last I heard of it. The one time Beard and I saw each other after that was at a science fiction convention a few years later. I asked him how *Farthest Frontiers* was coming and he just said, 'I never talk about a work in progress, especially not with the competition.' It wasn't even like he was trying to be nasty, it was just a statement of fact, as if he didn't remember our conversation at all. But I figured he was probably getting some heat from his publisher by then, and I didn't want to press the point.

"I didn't think about the story again until I got the call from Singleman. Naturally, the first thing I did when they put me in touch with Beard's estate was to go to his apartment and look for the manuscript. At first, when I didn't find it, I wasn't worried—I knew it had to be somewhere, and in the meantime I had fifteen other amazing stories to read. But eventually I was finished reading them and I went through Beard's files and bookshelves a second time. When that didn't work, I tried to think where else he might have put the manuscript for safekeeping—I looked behind the pictures on the walls, I rolled up the rugs, I flipped through the pages of every book in the apartment, I unpacked the closets, I unfolded the man's undershirts and checked behind the toilet tank—I did everything I could think of. And I found some interesting things—for example, a correspondence between Beard and Heinlein from the forties that might make an interesting book in itself. But what I didn't find is what I was looking for: Isaac's story. And it's driving me crazy. First of all, I know Beard would want the story included in the book, and second of all, a new Isaac Asimov story . . . *I* want to read it."

Nemerson stopped and shook his head. "I don't know whether Beard hid it deliberately, in order to keep it safe, or accidentally, as a result of carelessness, but one way or the other it's now missing, and I don't have much time to find it. Singleman wants to move quickly to get *Farthest Frontiers* into stores, and I have to give them something. The question is, where is the story?"

He sat back in his chair and looked at the men around him. For a moment, no one spoke.

Finally, Rubin said, "I knew Isaac pretty well myself, and the part that doesn't sound right to me is his writing in longhand on a legal pad and not keeping a copy when he finished, especially if the story came out as well as Beard said. All right, he was on a ship, and he had to make do with the materials at hand—but wouldn't he at least have asked Beard to send the story back to him later so he could make a copy for his records? I suppose one possibility is that he did ask for the story back, and then maybe he just never returned it to Beard for some reason, accounting for why the manuscript is now missing."

"No," Nemerson said. "I've been through Isaac's records, even the papers he sent to be archived at Boston University, and there's no manuscript that fits the description. Besides, even if Isaac had asked to get a copy back, Beard wouldn't have sent him the original, he'd have sent a copy. Or if he had sent the original, he'd have kept a copy. Either way, there would still be a copy of some sort for me to find at Beard's apartment."

Avalon made a tent of his fingers and tapped them against his chin. "Tell me something. You said that Singleman put you in touch with Beard's estate. I assume if it had been a relative of Beard's you met with, you would have said they put you in touch with Beard's wife, or his brother, or his daughter, or whomever, but not his 'estate.' So can we conclude that the person you met with was a lawyer?"

"That's right," Nemerson said. "Beard was an only child and never married. His lawyer said he had no living relatives."

Avalon went on in his solemn baritone. "In a case where an author is represented after his death solely by an attorney and there are no clear inheritors, it is not uncommon for intellectual-property assets to be frozen and held in escrow pending a determination as to their value, ownership, and proper disposition. The assignment you undertook for his publisher could be an example of such a determination process. Isn't it possible that the story you're looking for is in the lawyer's possession?"

"I'm afraid not," Nemerson said. "Beard's lawyer gave me access to all materials in his possession. There wasn't much, and the story wasn't there. Just to be sure, I described exactly what I was looking for, and the lawyer said he'd never seen it."

Halsted raised a hand. "When we were talking earlier, Geoff mentioned the idea of storing valuables in a safe-deposit box. Surely Beard would have considered the Asimov manuscript one of his most valuable possessions. Have you checked whether he had a safe-deposit box?"

"He had two," Nemerson said, "and I arranged to have both opened. We found some stock certificates, a few photos of his parents, his passport, and his social security card—but no story."

"How thorough was your search of his apartment?" Gonzalo asked. "You say you went through all his books, for instance, but did you look at the undersides of his shelves? Did you move the bookshelves away from the walls? Did you look under the wallpaper?"

"There's no wallpaper, just paint," Nemerson said, "but yes, I did check under the shelves. And not only the shelves—I checked under his TV set, under his computer, under his mattress. I even unscrewed all the electrical outlets to see if any of them were fakes. I was extremely thorough. I think I've made it clear to you just how important it is to me that I find this story, and I promise I searched every place in the apartment that might possibly be large enough to hold a manuscript."

"Even the lighting fixtures?" Gonzalo said.

"Even the paper towel tube in the kitchen. Even the *flour bin* in the kitchen."

"Even the refrigerator?" Trumbull asked.

"*Especially* the refrigerator."

"Hold on. There's something all of us are overlooking," Trumbull said. "Maybe Asimov wrote the story longhand because a pen and a pad of paper were all he had to work with onboard the ship, but there's no publisher that would accept the story that way when the time came to submit the book. I don't care if you're Isaac Asimov, I don't care if you're Stephen King, you can't turn in a handwritten manuscript. That means that at some point Beard would have had to type the story into his computer in order to print out a copy he could submit. What if he typed it in, but never got around to printing it out?"

"The original manuscript would still have to be somewhere," Rubin said. "It's not like he'd throw it out."

"Probably not, but who knows?" Trumbull said. "Maybe he did. Or maybe he lost it. Or maybe it's still somewhere in his apartment despite all of Gary's efforts to turn it up. But it doesn't matter. Gary doesn't need to find the manuscript, he just needs to find the story. If an electronic copy exists, he's got what he needs."

"I wish it were that simple," Nemerson said. "I checked the computer. The only stories on it were Beard's own work. Other than the one for *Farthest Frontiers*, they were either stories he'd already published or unfinished fragments a page or two long."

"Did you check every file? Even encrypted ones?"

Nemerson nodded. "Beard wasn't exactly what you'd call a power user of the computer. He only had word-processor documents, and not a lot of them. And nothing was encrypted." He looked around the table. "Does anyone else have any ideas?"

"I have one," Avalon said, "but you're not going to like it."

"What?"

"If there is literally no trace of the story and you're sure you've searched everywhere it might be, you've got to consider the possibility that the story never existed in the first place. Think about it—as far as we know, you are the only person who has ever heard of this story, and the only reason you think it exists is because Beard told you about it at the end of a long night of drinking following a memorial service that must have been traumatic for both of you. Maybe he desperately wished he'd gotten a story from Asimov and was shaken by the realization that now it was too late. His subconscious converted his desire into a fantasy that he *had* gotten a story, and maybe because he'd had a few too many drinks that night, he was temporarily unable to distinguish fantasy from reality."

"I don't buy it," Nemerson said. "We'd been drinking, and

maybe that had something to do with why he told me about the story that night and why he didn't remember telling me about it later, but it's not as if we'd reached the point of seeing pink elephants. When he talked about the story, everything he said was very concrete, very specific. All the details about the circumstances of the cruise, for instance—it's true that Isaac was on the cruise, I've checked that. Isaac's wife even remembers him staying in their cabin on the last day to write something, although she didn't remember what it was. No, I'm confident Isaac really did write a story for *Farthest Frontiers* and that there's a copy somewhere in Beard's apartment—I just can't figure out where."

Nemerson glanced around the table, but no one said anything.

"I'm sorry to say we don't seem to be able to help you this time," Trumbull said.

Nemerson sighed. "Well, I appreciate your trying. Maybe I'll do one more search of the apartment, top to bottom, but if that doesn't work—"

"I'm not sure that will be necessary, sir." Henry stepped away from the sideboard, where he had been listening quietly.

"Do you have an idea, Henry?" said Nemerson.

"I do," Henry said. "I am somewhat reluctant to share it with you, because I am not certain it is correct and its implications are rather serious—but the more I hear you gentlemen talk about the situation, the more likely it seems."

"Spit it out, Henry," Rubin said.

"I don't think Mr. Nemerson needs to search any further for the missing story," Henry said, "for the simple reason that I suspect he has already found it."

"I don't understand," Nemerson said.

"You found fifteen stories in Beard's apartment," Henry said, "including one you described as having been written by Beard himself. I believe that is the story you are looking for."

"Impossible!" Nemerson said.

"Consider," Henry said. "The only reason you thought that

story was written by Beard is presumably because his name appeared on the manuscript. But as Mr. Trumbull pointed out earlier, Beard would have had to retype Asimov's story at some point before submitting the anthology to his publisher, and it's a trivial matter to type 'Abraham Beard' on the first page instead of 'Isaac Asimov.' Of course, it is only trivial mechanically—ethically, it's an exceptionally severe offense, perhaps the worst an editor could commit against one of his own authors, particularly one who, posthumously, could no longer defend himself.

"But think about what you have told us. Here is a man who started as a writer side by side with Isaac Asimov, writing for the same publications, but who never achieved more than a fraction of the recognition or success. Such recognition as he did achieve was as an editor, not as a writer, and didn't extend beyond the rather limited world of science fiction publishing. We know he never gave up his desire to achieve success as a writer. It is widely believed that he delayed publication of his second anthology, possibly for years, while he worked on a story of his own to include. We know his third anthology, which given his age and poor health he must have realized would be his last, had already taken even longer to prepare than the second, and from the evidence of the files you found on his computer, it may well have been for the same reason. After all, he had already purchased fifteen stories for the book, if you count the Asimov story and the other fourteen you found—all that was left was for him to complete his own story, and he'd have had the sixteen stories he needed and been done. If he *had* finished a story of his own, especially one as good as the one you described, surely he would have wasted no time in submitting the book to his publisher. The fact that he didn't submit it makes me suspicious that the story with his name on it was not actually his work.

"I imagine that he tried to write a story—he may well have tried for years. But all you found were fragments of a page or two in length, so apparently he wasn't able to do it. When he came out of the hospital for the last time, he may well have known it was the last time. And as he sat at the computer, trying desperately to produce a story good enough to include in his last book, surely he must have been haunted by the memory of Isaac Asimov, one of the most prolific authors in American history, stepping into a cruise ship cabin one morning and emerging the next day with a finished novelette. And not just any novelette—a great novelette, one good enough to appear in *Farthest Frontiers.*"

Henry walked to the foot of the table and fixed Nemerson with a penetrating stare. "You're thirty-two years old, Mr. Nemerson, you're married, you've had some success in your chosen field, and you have practically your whole life ahead of you. But try to imagine what it would be like if you were eighty-two, and dying, and quite possibly a failure in your own eyes, and you saw only one last chance to save your reputation. Maybe the only way you could do so was degrading and despicable—but it was there, it was an available option. And who would ever know? He had the only copy of Asimov's story that existed; he could retype it, destroy the original, and no one would be the wiser. And perhaps he asked himself, who would be hurt? Isaac Asimov, who already had more than four hundred books and countless awards to his name?

"What he did, assuming that he did actually do it, was inexcusable. The act I suspect him of is deeply dishonest, and even if it were true that it hurt no one, which I do not believe, it would still be wrong in every way. But I do not agree that it is impossible."

"No," Nemerson said, "I suppose it's not impossible."

"Gary, you mentioned that Beard didn't appear to be a sophisticated computer user," Trumbull said. "If that's so, he probably didn't know that many word processors automatically save a backup copy each time you modify a document. If he ever typed the story in with Asimov's name on it and only later changed it to his own, you might be able to find an archived backup that shows the original version."

"You can do better than that," Drake said. "I can put you in touch with some researchers at Columbia who have devised statistical techniques to analyze a piece of text and determine how likely it is to be the work of a given writer. You might remember the case, several years back, where this technique was used to unmask the anonymous author of *Primary Colors*, the political *roman à clef.* You can provide plenty of samples of both Asimov's and Beard's work, so it should be a simple matter to run the analysis."

"And it is possible that this analysis will show that I am wrong," Henry said. "If so, I apologize sincerely. But I am afraid this is the explanation that makes the most sense to me."

"Yes, I guess it does to me, too," Nemerson said, "now that you've walked us through it. But I just can't believe he would do it. How could he?"

"It may give you some measure of comfort," Henry said, "to remind yourself that he didn't actually carry the plan out to completion. He never submitted the manuscript in its current form. Perhaps he was just entertaining the idea in a moment of despair, and if he had survived his illness, perhaps he would have changed the name on the story back and spent a few more years working on a story of his own. And perhaps in time he'd have written one, and perhaps it would have been good."

"I don't know," Nemerson said. "Do you really think he deserves the benefit of the doubt?"

"We all do," Henry said.

AFTERWORD: BIRTH OF THE BLACK WIDOWERS

ISAAC ASIMOV

One of the last books Isaac Asimov completed before his death in 1992 was the memoir I. Asimov, *in which he wrote 166 essays concerning the major events and undertakings of his life. Among the topics he discussed was how he came to write mystery short stories in general and the Black Widowers stories in particular.*

I have always wanted to write mystery short stories. At the start I was committed to science fiction, of course, and some of my science fiction short stories were very much like mysteries. This was true of several of my robot stories, for instance.

I also wrote a series of five science fiction stories about a character named Wendell Urth, who solved mysteries without ever leaving home. The first of these, "The Singing Bell," appeared in the January 1955 [issue of *The Magazine of Fantasy & Science Fiction*].

The Wendell Urth stories were fun, but they didn't quite satisfy my desires. I wanted to write a "straight" mystery, with no science fiction angle to it. I did write one in 1955, but *Ellery Queen's Mystery Magazine (EQMM)* rejected it. I finally placed it in *The Saint Mystery Magazine,* where it appeared in the January 1956 issue, under the name "Death of a Honey-Blonde." It was set in a chemistry department, however, so that, while it was not science fiction, I had not entirely freed myself from science.

It was not a very good story and I was disheartened. Nevertheless, the urge to write short mysteries persisted. *EQMM* regularly publishes "first stories," usually short-shorts by writers who had never published before. My chagrin finally bubbled over and I thought, "If these amateurs can do it, why can't I?"

So I wrote a short-short on November 12, 1969, and had it in the mail two hours after I had thought of the idea. *EQMM* took it and ran it under the title "A Problem in Numbers" in the May 1970 issue of the magazine.

But that dealt with a chemistry department, too, as, for that matter, had *The Death Dealers,* my one straight mystery novel up to that time. It irritated me. I wanted to write nonscience mysteries. Why? Science and science fiction had been so good to me. Why should I abandon a faithful wife (so to speak) to lust after some flirtatious stranger?

Well, I had done science fiction. I wanted new worlds to conquer. I had always loved mystery short stories from childhood and I wanted to do mysteries too. Besides, if you want a less idealistic reason, I found mysteries easier to write than science fiction. . . .

My first sale of a story to *EQMM* did not lead to a flood of mystery writing. After all, I never lacked for other things to do. In early 1971, however, Eleanor Sullivan, the beautiful blond managing editor of *EQMM,* wrote me a letter *asking* for a story. Eagerly, I agreed, but now I had to think of a plot.

I got one quickly because two stories above our apartment lived David Ford, a corpulent actor with a resonant baritone voice. (Voices, in my opinion, are much more important than faces to an actor, unless he is the vacuous matinee idol type.) He invited us to his apartment once and we found it crammed to the ceiling with what, in Yiddish, are called *chochkes*—that is, miscellaneous objects which strike the fancy of an omnivorous collector. He told us he once had a repairman in his apartment while he was forced to walk his dog. He was sure that the repairman had taken one or two of his *chochkes,* but he was never able to determine what was missing, or, in fact, whether anything was missing at all.

That was all I needed. I wrote the story quickly and it appeared in the January 1972 *EQMM* under the title "The Acquisitive Chuckle."

I thought of it as simply a story, but when it appeared, [editor] Fred Dannay's blurb announced it as "the first of a NEW SERIES by Isaac Asimov." (The capitalization was Dannay's.) That was the first I heard of *that,* but I was willing to go along with it.

I wrote more and more stories involving the same characters. When I had written twelve and decided to have them collected in a book, Dannay assumed the series was finished and said so in print. He little knew me. I continued the series stubbornly and I have now written no fewer than sixty-five stories. (What's the good of being a prolific writer if you don't proliferate?)

I call the series the Black Widower stories because each one takes place at one of the monthly banquets of a club of that name. The club is modeled unabashedly on a real club of which I am a member, the Trap Door Spiders. . . .

The stories are entirely conversational. The six club members discuss matters in a quarrelsome, idiosyncratic way. There is a guest, who is asked questions after dinner, and whose answers reveal some sort of mystery, which the Black Widowers cannot solve but which, in the end, is solved by the waiter, Henry.

Eventually, the various Black Widower stories were published, twelve at a time, by Doubleday. The books that have appeared, so far, are:

Tales of the Black Widowers 1974
More Tales of the Black Widowers 1976
Casebook of the Black Widowers 1980
Banquets of the Black Widowers 1984
Puzzles of the Black Widowers 1990

I have written five more stories that will be included in a sixth volume someday when the new total reaches twelve....

In the 1970s and 1980s, I wrote something like 120 mystery short stories, far more than the number of science fiction short stories I wrote in that period. I don't think that will change. I enjoy the mysteries more.

Let me explain this. Those 120 mysteries are "old-fashioned." Modern mysteries are more and more exercises in police procedurals, private eye dramatics, and psychopathology, all of them tending to give us heaping handfuls of sex and violence.

The older mysteries, in which there are a closed series of suspects and a brilliant detective (often amateur) weaving his clever chain of inference and deduction, seem to be, for the most part, gone. They are referred to nowadays, with a vague air of contempt, as "cozy mysteries" and their heyday was Great Britain in the 1930s and 1940s. The great cozy writers were people such as Agatha Christie, Dorothy Sayers, Ngaio Marsh, Margery Allingham, Nicholas Blake, and Michael Innes.

Well, that's what I write. I make no secret of the fact that in my mysteries I use Agatha Christie as my model. In my opinion, her mysteries are the best ever written, far better than the Sherlock Holmes stories, and Hercule Poirot is the best detective fiction has seen. Why should I not use as my model what I consider the best?

What's more, every last one of my mysteries is an "armchair detective" story. The story is revealed in conversation, the clues are presented fairly, and the reader has a reasonable chance to beat the fictional detective to the solution. Sometimes readers do exactly that, and I get triumphant letters to that effect. On rare occasions I even get letters pointing out improved solutions.

Old-fashioned? Certainly! But so what? Other people in writing mystery stories have their purposes, which may be to instill a sense of adventure, or a grisly sense of horror, or whatever. It is my purpose in my mysteries (and, in actual fact, in everything I write, fiction and nonfiction) to make people think. My stories are puzzle stories and I see nothing wrong with that. In fact, I find them a challenge, like writing limericks, since the rules for preparing honest puzzle stories are so strict.

This means, incidentally, that the stories do not have to involve pathological acts or violent crime—or, indeed, any crime at all.

One of the mysteries that I had most fun in writing recently was "Lost in a Space Warp," which appeared in the March 1990 *EQMM*. It dealt with a man who mislaid his umbrella in his girlfriend's small apartment and couldn't find it. From the information he gave, Henry deduced where it could be found, without stirring from his position at the sideboard.

What's more, I don't intend to alter the format of these stories. They will stay always the same. The guest of the Black Widowers will always have a mystery to tell, the Black Widowers will always be stumped, and Henry will always come up with the solution. . . .

Why not? The background is an artificial one designed only to present the puzzle. What I intend is to have the reader greet each new story with the comfortable feeling of encountering old friends, meeting the same characters under the same circumstances, and having a fresh mind stretcher over which to try to outguess me.

And in his penultimate Black Widowers collection, Banquets of the Black Widowers, he wrote:

And so I say farewell once again, and very reluctantly. There are few stories I write that I enjoy as much as I enjoy my Black Widowers, and having written forty-eight of them altogether has not in the least diminished my pleasure or worn out their welcome to my typing fingers. I can't guarantee that this is true of my readers, but I certainly hope it is.